LUCIAN: SELECTED WORKS

The Library of Liberal Arts
OSKAR PIEST, FOUNDER

The Library of Liberal Arts

SELECTED WORKS

LUCIAN

Translated, with an Introduction and Notes, by

BRYAN P. REARDON

· ·

The Library of Liberal Arts

published by

THE BOBBS-MERRILL COMPANY, INC.
A Subsidiary of Howard W. Sams & Co., Inc.
Publishers • Indianapolis • New York • Kansas City

CONTENTS

SELECTED WORKS

A True Story

INTRODUCTION

The study of Lucian is a snare for scholars. Extremely little is known of him; and around that little, scholarly inventiveness has built up a number of hypotheses at great variance one with the other. He has been considered, at one extreme, as a third-rate hack with no originality, no sincerity, and not much skill, clumsily pirating the work of a predecessor; and, at the other, as a courageous, sensitive apostle of reason, a major writer who in a barbarous age applied a vivid imagination, rare literary gifts, and a passionate integrity to the arduous search for truth and human dignity. It is not likely that either of these pictures is a true one. Between these extremes, however, lie a number of views that assiduous scholarship can render tenable. Assessment of Lucian depends a good deal upon one's initial attitude; the track of known fact fades almost at the start, and it must be admitted at once that any picture of him must be in some degree speculative.

It is however the belief of the present writer that the reader can trust himself to Lucian; that for all the research that may underlie recent judgments on him, one will not go very far wrong in taking him at his face value. He is very much a child of his time and place; to read him, with an alert mind certainly, is to be at once greatly entertained and instructed. If we know little about him, perhaps we do not need to know a great deal more to make him worthwhile.

Most of the scanty information we have about his life and work comes from his own writings; to it can be added a little external evidence, not very trustworthy. A skeleton chronology can be established from some references in his work to historical events, although very little of this evidence is incontrovertible. On this basis can be reconstructed, with reasonable probability, the main lines of his career; to fill in the details requires ingenuity and optimism, which have not been lacking. The present introduction purports to present a moderate, not too controversial view of Lucian's career; the evidence for it would however require a disproportionate amount of space here.[1]

Lucian was born at Samosata in Syria, probably some few years before A.D. 120.[2] His work *The Dream*—a success story written for his home town, which he revisited when he had made good—informs us that, after leaving school "when approaching manhood," he was apprenticed to his uncle, who was a stonemason; he had already shown artistic inclinations, he says. The apprenticeship was very brief; on his first day he was beaten for breaking a slab of stone, and promptly ran home. That night two figures appeared to him in a dream. One was Sculpture, representing the craft to which he had had so inauspicious an introduction; she promised him a respectable bourgeois trade in the family tradition. The other was Culture, *Paideia;* she held out to him hopes of fame in the art of oratory. In other words, he had ambitions toward a liberal education and a career as a sophist; and in pursuit of these hopes he left Syria and went to Asia Minor, the most flourishing center of Greek culture of his day. There he learned Greek, and learned it astonishingly well. He became as much a master of the language as Conrad became of English, and with the language he acquired a degree of Hellenism that was to make him, in later years, *plus royaliste que le roi*. This, indeed, is the key to the whole understanding of Lucian. His art is one long tribute to and manifestation of the Greek

---

[1] The principal discussions of the subject are to be found in Maurice Croiset, *Essai sur la vie et les œuvres de Lucien* (Paris: Hachette, 1882); Thaddeus Sinko, "De Luciani libellorum ordine et mutua ratione," *Eos,* XIV (1908), 113–58; Rudolf Helm, "Lukianos," in *Real-Encyclopädie der classischen Altertums-wissenschaft,* ed. Pauly-Wissowa, XIII (Stuttgart: J. B. Metzler, 1927), 1725–77.

[2] A brief article on Lucian in the tenth-century lexicon known as "Suidas" appears to suggest that he was born in the reign of Trajan. Although the article is somewhat obscure on the point, and of little value in general, there is no very cogent reason for doubting this. Lucian's birth has, however, been placed as late as 130.

literary tradition, of what he at any rate (like the great majority of his contemporaries) interpreted as the ideal of Hellenic culture.

In Asia Minor he studied hard and acquired what was in fact a fairly formidable "classical education," namely a sound knowledge of the standard Greek authors from Homer to the Alexandrians, thus equipping himself as a "sophist" in the sense of the term current in the second century. The "sophist" of the Second Sophistic, the rhetorical movement of this century, was, as Humpty Dumpty might say, something like a professor, something like a concert pianist, and something like a movie star. What he was not much like was a sophist, if one expects the term to imply, as it did in the fifth century B.C., at least a concern with serious matters. For although many of these later practitioners were very intelligent, and educated up to if not beyond the hilt, they cannot be accused of *gravitas*. The conquests of Alexander and the *pax Romana,* if they settled the political hash of the Greek world, also thereby deprived its art of all sense of civic responsibility. Affairs of state were now in Roman hands, and the fertile Greek, deprived of the ordering his life, turned to its decoration. Such men as Herodes Atticus—"the king of speech," by the testimony of an admiring pupil [3]—were the product of five hundred years of the rhetorical tradition given its credentials by Isocrates, and as such they were indeed the direct descendants of Gorgias and Prodicus. But this is the extent of their affiliation, for Socrates would never have bothered to cross swords with the best of them. Like a professor, a sophist taught and gave lectures; like a concert pianist, he was an itinerant virtuoso of an art; and like a movie star, he could earn adulation and incredible sums of money. He was an entertainer, and his skill was often consummate.

What he spoke on, however, was often extremely trivial. Lucian's own early work is typical of such performances. *Phalaris,* for example, is concerned with a certain Phalaris who had been tyrant of Agrigentum in Sicily in the sixth cen-

---

[3] Adrian of Tyre: Philostratus, *Lives of the Sophists* II. 10.

tury B.C., and who was notorious for his cruelty. This gentleman, we are to suppose, has offered a gift to the oracle at
Delphi; the citizens of Delphi are now debating whether to
accept a gift from such a source; and Lucian presents two
casuistical speeches urging their acceptance of it. The choice
of a situation from "ancient" history, and the propounding of
the less readily defensible case, are characteristic of the rhetorical art of the period. The stock-in-trade of the Second
Sophistic is, precisely, the famous themes and characters of
Greece's greatest period, especially the fifth and fourth centuries B.C.; along with standard heroic mythology and themes
from "classical" literature, this forms a great part of the literary material of the second century. Lucian himself says, in
effect, "if orators were to stop talking about Marathon, they'd
never be able to stay in business"; [4] and the whole considerable
body of his own work proves it. One orator [5] was, in fact, actually nicknamed "Marathon," from the frequency with which
he mentioned in his speeches the heroes who died there in defense of Greece—nearly seven hundred years earlier!

This constant reference to the past is not just a habit; it is a
whole doctrine, and one that is central in the artistic theory
of this latter-day Hellenic renaissance; the doctrine of Mimesis, the continuation by imitation of the centuries-old Greek
tradition. The art of the second century cannot be under-
stood without reference to it. Originality of form and theme
was by no means necessarily praiseworthy; rather, it was suspect. The business of literature was to preserve, not to inno-
vate; what was valuable now was the continuance of the old
tradition rather than the creation of a new one. Nor is it
merely an artistic phenomenon. It is a whole attitude to life
and society, of which literary Mimesis is only one facet. In
literature, critics such as "Longinus" and Dionysius of Halicarnassus had emphasized the achievement of the ancients;
and manuals on rhetoric, such as that of Hermogenes soon
after Lucian's own day, analyzed their works exhaustively and

4 *Zeus Rants* 32.
5 Ptolemy of Naucratis: Philostratus, *Lives* II. 15.

formulated detailed rules for their emulation. Be it said that this worship of the past was not indiscriminate; it was selective, and did not prescribe mere slavish copying. Nonetheless, the hand of the past lay heavy on the present. No charge could be more misplaced than that of plagiarism, for the use of older materials was not an offense, it was virtually an obligation.[6]

Such pieces as *Phalaris* are the staple of the Second Sophistic. Philostratus, in his *Lives of the Sophists,* records example after example: a "Dirge for Chaeronea"; a speech on "Xerxes"; an imaginary lawsuit over the custody of a child born as the result of a rape; a speech advising Darius to bridge the Danube;[7] and many others. And there are other such genres—for instance the *ecphrasis* or descriptive passage, as when Lucian describes a hall he is performing in,[8] or the *encomium* or eulogy, as when he ingeniously praises the ordinary fly;[9] all cleverly handled, and most of them quite trivial in content.

Lucian spent some time in one branch of the sophistic art, namely pleading in law courts; but before long—perhaps soon after 140—he abandoned this for his life's work as a performer. In his new capacity he traveled widely around the Mediterranean, particularly in Greece and Italy (we have glimpses of him in Scythia and on the river Po), and for a number of years held a remunerative post as "public orator" to a town in Gaul—in much the same way as itinerant orchestra conductors are appointed to posts in cities today. We do not know what town it was that so appointed him, but it is of interest that his performances were in Greek; apparently the Greek language and culture were represented strongly enough for such an appointment to be feasible. No detailed picture can be given of his life or work at this period; Lucian says

[6] The doctrine of Mimesis is considered in detail in J. Bompaire, *Lucien écrivain: imitation et création* (Paris: E. de Boccard, 1958).

[7] See Philostratus, *Lives* I. 22, 20; II. 4, 5.

[8] *The Hall.*

[9] *The Fly.*

next to nothing about it, except that he continued in this vein until about the age of forty—that is, until sometime before 160.

After these standard rhetorical works, perhaps about 155, Lucian composed three sets of dialogues that foreshadow what is perhaps his most famous work, the *Dialogues of the Dead*. These are the *Dialogues of the Courtesans, Dialogues of the Gods,* and *Dialogues of the Sea-Gods*. While still display-pieces, they are his first essays in the comedy-dialogue form which he invented. The titles are self-explanatory. The content of the *Dialogues of the Courtesans* is drawn from New Comedy, several of whose characters—young, naïve courtesan and experienced, cynical mother, young lover, slave, *miles gloriosus*—appear in standard situations: boy meets girl, girl loses boy; rivals quarrel; mother instructs daughter in the ways of mercenary love. The pieces might well be excerpts from plays; they are often charming, and in places very frank. The *Dialogues of the Gods* portray well-known scenes from mythology in amusing fashion. They are hardly meant as serious criticism of the Olympian religion, for it had not been taken seriously for some centuries; here again Lucian is a literary artist working with material from the "ancient" world. They do, however, point toward the satirical bent Lucian was to display later. The *Dialogues of the Sea-Gods* are charming restatements of themes from earlier Greek poetry; they have a vivid pictorial quality, and are written with great delicacy of touch.

Lucian began to receive comments from his public on the genre he had invented; the dialogues were praised, he says, for their novelty. In *Zeuxis* and *A Literary Prometheus* he expresses, if not annoyance, at least chagrin at this view.[10]

---

[10] Barbara P. McCarthy, in "Lucian and Menippus," *Yale Classical Studies,* IV (1934), 3–58, argues (p. 5) that *A Literary Prometheus* cannot refer to *Dialogues of the Courtesans* because it describes *Old* Comedy; but in *A Literary Prometheus* (sec. 6) Lucian is emphasizing the *original* distance—ἐξ ἀρχῆς—between the philosophical and comic genres. *Zeuxis* may have been written later, but it is not necessary to the view here put forward.

He would wish his brainchildren to be praised for their beauty, he says, not for their novelty. In this remark is summarized the whole attitude of the doctrine of Mimesis. Lucian expresses the fear that if his innovations are clumsy they may well turn out to be "hippocentaurs," misbegotten hybrids. This is the whole tone of the age in its literary practice, a consideration which must be at the front of one's mind in forming judgment on Lucian. His fears did not, however, prevent him from persevering with his invention, fortunately for posterity. From this point he uses the new form extensively, although not exclusively. This change of habit arises from a change of approach to his sophistic trade.

He now began to take his literary forms and much of his material from philosophy, while borrowing also from Old Comedy. This development in his art has often been represented, not without some encouragement from Lucian himself, as a "conversion" to philosophy. In fact neither now nor at any time did he occupy his mind with anything that could be called serious philosophical thought. He had merely grown tired, as well he might, of the trite themes of fashionable rhetoric, and sought new material and expression for his talents. For them he went once more, as one would expect, to "classical" literature, to a tradition some four or five hundred years old—to the philosophical dialogues of Plato, to the works of Menippus, the third-century Cynic philosopher from Gadara, and to the Old Comedy of Aristophanes.

It is of course true that the philosophical tradition had never died; and hence it arises that in this field Lucian is to some extent a critic of contemporary society. There was enough to criticize and satirize; for if not yet dead, philosophy had been for the last two or three centuries moribund. It was not until a century later that it was to flourish anew with Plotinus. The philosophical scene had not changed very much, indeed, since the last of the great Hellenistic systems had been formulated. The content of Lucian's satire, applicable certainly in some degree to his contemporaries, is nonetheless rooted in tradition as much as are the forms it uses.

A brief examination of *The Sale of Philosophers* will illustrate Lucian's approach. He borrows the idea from Menippus, who is known to have written a *Sale of Diogenes*, but, characteristically, he extends it. Zeus and Hermes are represented as auctioning off specimens from various schools of philosophy. Among these, some clearly represent particular individuals, for instance Heraclitus and Socrates; others, such as the Stoic, represent not an individual but a class. The same examples will show also that Lucian is not necessarily concerned to satirize contemporary philosophy. Stoics in particular did indeed abound in his day, but Socrates had been dead for over five hundred years; and even where Lucian's remarks on these schools do have topical significance, he is always concerned with their traditional rather than their current image. The piece is in fact not so much satire on philosophy as an irreverent comic sketch of some figures and ideas in the history of philosophy, in something like the spirit of that now canonized version of English history, *1066 And All That.*

Here it may be useful to sketch briefly the state of philosophy in Lucian's day. In A.D. 176, Marcus Aurelius endowed four chairs of philosophy at Athens, for exponents of the four "established" doctrines—those of the Academics, Peripatetics, Stoics, and Epicureans. These are the later representatives of the four great systems of the classical and early Hellenistic periods. The Academy had been founded by Plato early in the fourth century B.C.; "Peripatetic" was the name applied to the school founded by Aristotle later in the same century (the name being derived from the habit of discussing philosophical problems while walking about); Stoicism, founded by Zeno about 300 B.C., derived its name from the Stoa Poecile or "Painted Porch" where its earliest adherents met; and at about the same time Epicurus had founded his materialist school upon the "atomist" theory of Democritus. All of these schools, however, had diverged, sometimes considerably, from the paths pointed out by their founders, and their doctrines had become inextricably confused. Academics such as Plutarch could embrace substantial elements of Peripatetic and

Stoic doctrine; Peripatetics could even misunderstand a concept as fundamental to Aristotle's philosophy as that of Form. The Stoic Marcus Aurelius is almost wholly a moralist, but many Stoics of the time concerned themselves with technicalities of logic to the complete exclusion of morals. Epicureanism maintained its rational character firmly, in the face of the growing popularity of superstition and mystery religions; but this very refusal to accommodate other views led to its extinction soon after Lucian's day.

The other doctrines, particularly the Academic and Peripatetic, borrowed very freely; so freely, indeed, that virtually separate schools arose from them. In the second century B.C. the Academic Carneades had borrowed largely from the doctrines of Skepticism, a school founded by Pyrrho in the fourth century B.C. that doubted the possibility of genuine knowledge; and Skeptic beliefs continued to be propounded in Lucian's time. So too did the "eclectic" views imbibed initially by Romans like Cicero who, when they first came into contact with Greek philosophy, tended to synthesize the principal elements of various doctrines; indeed, a "school" of Eclecticism was founded, although it did not last long. Another of the offshoots of Platonism was the Neo-Pythagorean school which arose in Alexandria to preach a doctrine of supernatural intuition of truth, of opposition between mind and matter, and of the existence of divine powers or "daemons"; and which produced, a generation or two before Lucian's day, the "wonder-worker" Apollonius of Tyana. Finally there were the Cynics—with the Stoics, the most influential group of philosophers in the second century. Although they never enjoyed official recognition as a school, they were so notable a feature of life in the early Roman Empire, and figure so frequently (if ambiguously) in the writings of Lucian, that they should be discussed a little more fully.

If several of the schools mentioned above derived their doctrines from Plato's, Cynicism had quite as long a pedigree; for it was founded very early in the fourth century B.C. by another follower of Socrates, named Antisthenes. Antisthenes

admired above all things the independence and will-power
of Socrates and his insistence on the moral function of philosophy; and this remained the inspiration of the school he
founded. Cynic doctrine was simple—indeed, technical or
scientific philosophy was little valued; the end of life was
virtuous action, and virtue was a matter of character, not of
knowledge. Since virtue was the only good, it followed that
material possessions and conventional values were to be disregarded; and hence arose the standard picture, so common in
the pages of Lucian, of the world-renouncing, austere preacher,
simple in his life, rough of tongue, and independent and
frank in his opinions.

The name "Cynic" no doubt arose—as did the names of
other schools—from the meeting place of the founding group,
which was a "gymnasium" or exercise field called *Cynosarges;*
but Antisthenes' successor, Diogenes of Sinope (who spent
most of his life in Athens or Corinth) leaned on the derivation
from *cyn-,* "dog," called himself "the Dog," and held up
animal life as a model for mankind. By his personal example
of a life simple to the point of being uncouth—he was said to
have lived in a large wine jar—and by "fundamentalist"
preaching laced with savage wit, he became the model for
many succeeding generations of these street-corner moralists,
the forerunners of the wandering mendicant friars of the
Middle Ages. Time and again Lucian uses them in his work:
sometimes (as in *Dialogues of the Dead*) in apparent approval
of their unconventional, unsentimental rationalism, sometimes in unrestrained castigation of their coarse tongues, uncouth manners, and exhibitionism; for many of them "wore
the cloth," so to speak, merely the better to pour out their
own venom against society, and for little positive purpose—
the "angry young man" of the twentieth century is not new.

The first century A.D. saw a revival of Cynicism which lasted
some four hundred years, and flourished particularly in Lucian's day. One of its most notable characters is Peregrinus,
whose self-immolation in 165 evoked from Lucian a scathing
denigration of this strange figure. Another is Dio Chrysostom;

Dio, like Lucian, began life as a "sophist" in the sense of the term explained earlier, but when exiled turned to Cynicism; in later life he was used by Rome to help pacify turbulent Eastern mobs aroused by the anarchic harangues of other Cynics.

It was from Cynicism that the Stoic philosophy sprang, a generation after Diogenes' death in 324 B.C. The Stoics, like the Cynics, insisted on the moral function of philosophy; but they sought a scientific basis for moral conduct, declaring virtue and wisdom to be synonymous. Hence arose the development in Stoic philosophy of logic and physics as well as ethics. Particularly under Chrysippus, the third head of the school (*ca.* 280–208 B.C.), all of these branches were developed considerably; and Lucian very frequently points out that many Stoics concentrated upon logic to the exclusion of ethics, thus presenting to the world the unedifying spectacle of the "wise man" conducting himself in the most dissolute of ways. Stoicism, however, found a natural home in the Roman character, and scores of famous figures in Roman history bear witness to the ennobling power of the creed.

In Lucian's day, then, philosophy was a hodgepodge: an assortment of several older doctrines developed from the philosophy of a classical period now five hundred years away, and often altered considerably in the process. Often these "doctrines" were ill comprehended by their own exponents, and amalgamated with little discrimination. Lucian again and again professes himself disgusted, not with philosophy in itself, but with its modern practitioners.

Whether he was ever really interested in philosophy, however, is another matter. In one of his most sustained pieces, *Hermotimus,* he denies all value to the study of philosophy, since one cannot be sure of choosing the right doctrine to study. Granted, the piece is in some degree a rhetorical exercise, as all his works are, but the flow of reason carries too much conviction for us to dismiss it outright as not representing his real thought. Attempts have been made to link Lucian with one or another, or a succession, of the philosophical schools: the Platonist, on the strength of some early dialogues; the Cynic, on grounds that will appear; the Epicurean, largely on the strength of favorable reference to that sect in *Alexander,* a late work. But the relationship is merely that between a writer and his successive literary models; Lucian was no philosopher. Undoubtedly his natural inclination was toward uncommitted rationalism; and if Cynicism figures often in his work, that may be because he himself was "cynical," perhaps, rather than a Cynic. But here too he has his model; and mention must be made here of Menippus, the inspiration of much of his best writing.

Menippus, living in the third century B.C., represents a diluted form of Cynicism. The successors of Diogenes turned to satire—τὸ σπουδογέλοιον, the exposition of serious truths in humorous form—and invented thus the "diatribe," which was to become a standard feature of Cynic and Stoic moralizing technique. Little is known of Menippus apart from what can be deduced from imitations of him by Lucian and the Roman Varro. He is known to have written in various forms, letters to the gods and an account of a journey to the underworld being among the most notable. His message was almost wholly negative: life is not worth serious effort, religion is to be despised, philosophy is futile quibbling. His only "positive" advice was to "take life easy." And Lucian, if he has anything to say, has no more than this.

This, then, is the "philosophy" to which Lucian turned. But in changing his skin he did not change his nature. Indeed, there was no need to. There was in fact not as much difference between rhetoric and philosophy as the names would suggest; witness the career of Dio Chrysostom, and witness the use made of rhetoric by moralizing philosophers. Philostratus includes accounts of the lives of many who "practiced philosophy under the guise of rhetoric" [11]; it is fair to invert the phrase and describe Lucian as practicing rhetoric under the guise of philosophy. His temperament lent itself to handling

11 Philostratus, *Lives,* preface.

Cynic themes particularly, and the combination of this circumstance with his sparkling wit and considerable dramatic talent resulted in the series of works on which Lucian's fame rests, works which show him in his most characteristic vein and at the height of his powers—the satiric dialogues.

Before he embarked on this series, however, Lucian appears to have taken Plato as his model, briefly; it is probably at this period (about 155 to 160) that he composed his "Platonic" dialogues, a few pieces similar in manner to Plato's dialogues and concerned with subjects which can be said to have some philosophical interest. *Anacharsis* discusses physical education, *Toxaris* friendship, *The Parasite* the art of flattery. *Nigrinus,* a work which bristles with difficulties for the scholar, is an account of a philosopher Lucian met in Rome during his early career, and a description of a short-lived access of enthusiasm for philosophy which that personage inspired in him at the time. It contains also a tirade against life in Rome and a eulogy of Athens; about the time when he abandoned traditional rhetoric, Lucian appears to have taken up more or less permanent residence in Athens; and there he stayed for some twenty years or more, though often enough making excursions to various parts of the Greek world—he attended, for instance, all the Olympic festivals from 153 to 165, and the triumphant visit to Samosata mentioned earlier probably took place in 162. It is possibly to this period that *Hermotimus* belongs. Modeled very closely on Plato, the piece is of interest also as being his only attempt at anything like a philosophical *magnum opus*—as well as for its reference to himself as being "about forty" at this time, though this may be only a round figure.

It is with the fifteen satiric dialogues that Lucian's personality comes into full play. These are the works—the works of the "Menippean period"—with which scholarship has most concerned itself. Their content, form, composition, chronology and general interpretation have been subjected to scrutiny often more enthusiastic than rigorous. One of the reddest herrings of twentieth-century scholarship was drawn across the trail of Lucian in 1906 by Helm; [12] and though it was laid to rest in 1934 by McCarthy,[13] its ghost haunts us to this day. By analyzing Lucian's Cynic themes and expressions, and by considering the chronological allusions in these works—allusions which, where they are not contemporary, refer to a period no later than Menippus' own lifetime—Helm comes to the conclusion that

> Lucian was a third-rate hack who found a copy of Menippus' works which were otherwise unknown to the public at this time, and, since they were too long for his purposes, cut them up into shorter bits to which he tried clumsily to give some unity and air of originality. When this raw material began to run out, Lucian was forced to use some of it again, recombining elements which he had already used.[14]

The general modern view is that Lucian was no such slavish copyist or inept adaptor. If he had used Menippus to the extent Helm alleges, he would have been only too ready to proclaim the paternity of his work. Without raising the whole problem in detail, it is safe to say that the evidence is simply too tenuous, and Helm's assumptions too unreliable, to sustain the findings of such *Quellenforschung*, and certainly to warrant Helm's denigration of Lucian. Obviously in some pieces Lucian draws heavily upon what Menippus is known to have written. As obviously, however, his debt to Old Comedy is great in some pieces of the same period. It is far from being proven that his use of this material is not both original and effective, in the very best manner of the doctrine of Mimesis. And one piece is so patently personal in character that it is hard to see how it can be attributed in principle to any source but Lucian.

12 Rudolf Helm, *Lucian und Menipp* (Leipzig and Berlin: Teubner, 1906).

13 Barbara P. McCarthy, "Lucian and Menippus."

14 Fred W. Householder, *Literary Quotation and Allusion in Lucian* (New York: Columbia University Press, 1941), p. 32.

This is the *Double Accusation*—the main source of our knowledge of Lucian's "change of heart." The author is represented as defending himself in Zeus's court against indictments brought by Rhetoric and Dialogue. Rhetoric complains that after being raised from obscurity to fame by her agency, Lucian has deserted her and taken to consorting with Dialogue. Lucian's defense is that Rhetoric behaved like a wanton, and that in any case it was high time for him, at the age of forty, to give up lawsuits and accusations and eulogies and betake himself to the Academy or Lyceum to converse with Dialogue—that is, to turn to philosophic pursuits. Dialogue's charge is that Lucian has abused his dignity in making him treat, not of philosophy, but of comic and Cynic themes, and in "finally disinterring and letting loose on me the prehistoric dog Menippus"; as also in compounding him of prose and verse (a practice borrowed from Menippus, as at the beginning of *Zeus Rants*). To this Lucian replies that he had performed a public service in making Dialogue come down to earth and joining him with Comedy.

A few references provide some foothold in these shifting sands; otherwise we are at the mercy of internal evidence and its manipulators. Here at least, the works of this period must be treated as being of more or less uncertain date from a little before A.D. 160 to about 170. In two dialogues of obviously Menippean inspiration, *Menippus or Necromancy* and *Icaromenippus*, that philosopher is imagined as visiting Hades and Olympus respectively. These works set forth one of Lucian's principal motifs—the Cynic theme of the transitoriness of life and the vanity of human wishes. A like note is sounded in *A Trip to Hades* and *Charon*, which are similar in form to the works just mentioned, and in *Dialogues of the Dead*, the original of the "imaginary conversations" which have continued to appear in European literature to this day. Cynic thoughts, on the theme of poverty, appear also in *Saturnalia*—communications, some in letter form, between Lucian and the father of Zeus—and in *The Cock*.

Scorn for theology furnishes another theme. In *The Refuta-*

tion of Zeus, Zeus Rants, and *The Parliament of the Gods,*
Lucian misses not a trick in facile criticism of the traditional
Olympian religion; and among these pieces *Zeus Rants* has
been thought, with good reason, to be his masterpiece. The remaining satires, *The Sale of Philosophers* and its pendant
The Fisher, the *Symposium* (obviously inspired by Plato's),
and *The Runaways,* display a similar contempt for philosophers, not excluding the Cynics whose tenets Lucian elsewhere finds so congenial (the truth of the matter seems to be
that, if he loved philosophy, "he has dissembled his love, then,
very well" [15]). The *Double Accusation,* already described, also
falls in this period. So too does *Timon,* a not altogether satisfactory sketch on the subject of the famous misanthrope; while
probably of Cynic inspiration, it contains also many reminis-
cences of early comedy, especially of the *Plutus* of Aristophanes.

Brief as this summary of them is, it is these satiric dialogues
that insure Lucian's fame. His subsequent work, however, is
far from being without merit; indeed it includes the best
single piece he ever wrote, in the present writer's opinion—
Hired Companions. This is a work of his last period, however;
before it come a number of others, several of which are in
the form of "pamphlets" or "diatribes." Cynic inspiration is
still evident in some of these, especially the treatises *On Sacrifices* and *On Mourning,* which make no concessions whatever
to popular feeling and normal human sentiments. On the
other hand, *Peregrinus* (written some years after the event it
describes) shows biting scorn for what Lucian regarded as per-
verted Cynicism.

A similar rancor is to be found in a group of vitriolic pieces
probably composed at this time which concern more or less
closely the trade of the rhetorician and *littérateur. The Professor of Rhetoric, The Charlatan, Lexiphanes, The Ignorant
Book-Collector,* and *The Eunuch* are infinitely clever and

---

[15] *The Works of Lucian,* trans. H. W. and F. G. Fowler (Oxford: Clarendon Press, 1905), I, xxx. The introduction to this translation is one of the
best brief accounts of Lucian in any language.

effective; but the reader is likely to find that their most enduring feature is a nasty taste in the mouth. Here Lucian is very much on his own ground; for beyond question his greatest pride was in his complete mastery of a foreign language and the attainment of a style so polished that he is second to none among the writers of his day. And here mention must be made of the literary practice prevailing in Lucian's day.

A principal feature of the Second Sophistic was the "Atticizing" movement. This was a conscious and concerted attempt by writers to arrest the decline into which since the time of Demosthenes and Menander the Greek language, in its vernacular form, had fallen. Here, indeed, is the origin of the linguistic struggle between *katharévousa*, or "purifying"—that is, literary—speech and *demotiké*, or "popular"—that is, spoken —language, which is the most marked feature of the Greek language today. For the Greek language, already at least a thousand years old by Lucian's time, has outlived him by nearly two thousand more and, in its purist form at least, has changed remarkably little during that period. The decline of which Lucian complains began centuries before his own day, with the extension of Greek influence by Alexander. The *koinè diálektos*, or "common tongue," of the New Testament is simpler than Attic, for it was learned by millions as a second language; and by the same token it is less subtle. But pride in the Greek language has always been the most distinctive feature of Hellenism; *bárbaroi* are, strictly, people who do not speak Greek; and there has always been a movement striving for its preservation. After the liberation of Greece in 1827, the tendency to reform asserted itself more strongly, for the *demotiké*, the language of the people, was associated with the emancipation of the people. By now the *demotiké* is itself established as the language of literature, but the *katharévousa* is still important for its use in official contexts, and manuals of modern Greek give both forms of many common words and expressions.

Lucian is thus at the middle of a long linguistic tradition. It cannot be said that he or any of his contemporaries at-

tained pure Attic, but Lucian was not very far from it.[16]
Excessive antiquarianizing he deplored; this was not to honor
and maintain tradition, but to abuse it. That there were
those who were eager to snatch at a word used perhaps only
once or twice in the ancient canon and preen themselves on
its use is shown by *Lexiphanes,* an untranslatable [17] essay in
fustian parody in which Lucian gives an emetic to one such
practitioner of his art. His more general views on the practice of rhetoric are evident in *A Professor of Rhetoric.* This is
an abusive and entertaining tirade against one Julius Pollux,[18]
a contemporary and indeed a rival—for teaching was another
branch of the rhetorician's art; it was, for instance, the basis
of Herodes Atticus' eminence. We do not know that Lucian
taught, but it is probable enough that he did so in Gaul, as
part of his duties; and he may well have continued to teach in
Athens. Lucian's quite genuine concern for literary standards
can be seen in *A Professor of Rhetoric* and elsewhere in his
work; so too can his capacity for taking and giving offense.

Other literary criticism is to be found in *A True Story* and
How To Write History. The latter of these, written about
164, is for most of its length a treatise on how *not* to write
history, abundantly illustrated from contemporary works now
fortunately lost. *A True Story,* an account of an imaginary
voyage written in his last period—that is, after 180—is a satire
on fanciful historians and geographers; it turned out to be
an early Baron Munchausen tale,[19] and as such is yet another
candidate for the title of his masterpiece. The very title is
ironic: "I warn you," says Lucian, "that I am going to tell the
biggest lies you ever heard; and this is the only true statement
in the whole book."

Above all, Lucian had no time whatever for frauds of any

[16] See, e.g., *Lucian: Selected Writings,* ed. Francis G. Allinson (Boston:
Ginn & Company, 1905).

[17] The Fowlers have produced a brilliant paraphrase of it; see *The
Works of Lucian.*

[18] Julius Pollux is the author of an extant word list, *Onomasticon.* The
identification has been questioned, but seems too good not to be true.

[19] *Not* science fiction, as it is often called; there is no "science" in it.

kind—as he himself says; and woe betide a fraud who happened to cross Lucian's own path, for the result is not pretty to contemplate. Perhaps the best illustration of this is a piece called *Alexander, or The False Prophet,* also written after 180. This document, a major source for the study of popular religious practice in the second century, purports to expose a charlatan who operated an oracle in Asia Minor. And, indeed, this it does; but scholarly research [20] has suggested, firstly, that the phenomenon Lucian is attacking may be viewed in a more charitable light; and secondly, that much of the invective in which the piece abounds is nothing more than literary reminiscence, dating back even to Demosthenes' quarrel with Aeschines. The matter goes farther than this, indeed; for Caster has shown also how incomplete is the picture Lucian gives us of the religious atmosphere of his times; in great areas of it he is totally silent. The Christianity then nascent draws from him nothing more than casual patronizing reference; he says nothing on the "new" Eastern cults, such as that of Sarapis, on demonic theology, or on emperor-worship—all of them outstanding features of the spiritual life of his age. *Alexander* is a telltale piece; the very vehemence with which it is written suggests the popularity of the cult it attacks, and what Lucian does say here throws emphasis on what he does not say in general. The fact would appear to be that he is not particularly interested in his own times, unless what happens in them can be illustrated by reference to classical tradition. It is a consideration of paramount importance for the whole study of Lucian; the second century was too recent for him.

But however true this is, one is left, on reading *Alexander* and *Peregrinus* and several of the pieces described above, with an overall impression of a kind of intellectual hysteria; above all, Lucian would seem to say, one must *not be mistaken.* Unless it is entirely wrong to see in Lucian any kind of "mes-

---

[20] Culminating in the work of Caster, *Lucien et la pensée religieuse de son temps* (Paris: Les Belles Lettres, 1937) and *Études sur "Alexandre ou le Faux Prophète" de Lucien* (Paris: Les Belles Lettres, 1938).

sage" at all—and it must be admitted that there may be simply none—this is the dominant note, if not of his thought, at least of his psychology; intelligence is supreme, and irrational conduct is the sin against the Holy Ghost. It is debatable whether his indignation against Alexander outweighs his contempt for Alexander's dupes. The temperament which finds Cynic doctrine congenial, albeit in literary model, betrays itself again where no question of Menippus arises.

The relationship of Lucian to Latin literature is no more satisfactorily settled than the question of his debt to Menippus. He speaks of himself as knowing some Latin; [21] but how much, and how much Latin literature he knew and used, it is hard to tell. He must, one supposes, have been more or less familiar with at least its major figures, although he says nothing about them; like most Greek writers of his day, he appears simply to disregard all things Roman, except to pour discreetly literary scorn on them. *Hired Companions* has much in common with Juvenal's third and fifth Satires. The work is in the form of a letter to a Greek friend, warning him of the dangers that lie in wait for him if he takes service as a tutor with a rich Roman family. It becomes a description of the life at Rome of the *Graeculus esuriens,* the type of the starveling Greek man of letters who tries his fortune in Rome; and it is written with a vivacity which, if it is born of literary reminiscence, speaks volumes for the author's ability to assimilate a tradition; it is in fact hard to believe that he is not describing what he has seen with his own eyes.

It is perhaps convenient here to consider Lucian's relationship with "satire." The word has of course two senses. First, the sense current in English. A favorite term for Lucian in German scholarship is *der Spötter,* "the scoffer." As has been pointed out, to regard him as primarily a critic of contemporary society is seriously to misunderstand his purpose. Nonetheless, not infrequently he does in fact describe aspects of

---

[21] In *Apology for a Slip of the Tongue* 13. See the Appendix, "Lucian's knowledge of Latin," in Henry W. L. Hime, *Lucian the Syrian Satirist* (London: Longmans, Green, and Co., 1900).

contemporary life, even if they were by now some centuries old—*Hired Companions* and *Alexander* are good examples of this—and he was perfectly capable of biting comment on topical themes, as his remarks on literary practice prove. But he was not, it would seem, vitally concerned to reform his times; and hence comes that sense of remoteness from life that one often experiences in reading him, that aura of academicism.

The second sense of "satire" that must be considered here is that expressed in the Latin phrase *satura lanx,* the "mixed dish," and exemplified in the *sermones* or "chatty pieces" of Horace that now go under the name of "Satires" in English. In this interpretation, "satire" is essentially a miscellany on a great variety of subjects, generally but not necessarily with a distinct tendency to moralize. This is the aspect emphasized by Bompaire [22] in his title *Lucien écrivain,* and it is perhaps the more relevant to Lucian. For though the field of satire was, as Quintilian remarks,[23] dominated by Roman writers, the genre has its roots in the Cynic-Stoic diatribes mentioned above, and this is the source of a good deal of Lucian's material. Lucian would appear to derive his inspiration directly from the Greek tradition for the most part, and to take not very much from its Roman inheritors. His work is certainly a miscellany—produced in the atmosphere of the Second Sophistic.

Lucian does appear to have some kind of personal direction, if only in the manner in which he moves from one literary model to another—from pure rhetoric to Plato to Menippus, comedy, and the diatribe; there is in him some fairly consistent element of personality, which will be considered shortly. He falls between the categories of *écrivain* and *Spötter,* although in some degree he is both of these. The term "journalist" has sometimes been used of him; it is accurate in suggesting the variety and limited scope of his work, but to think of him as a sort of ancient "columnist" is wrong; the essence of a columnist's work is topicality, and that is a

[22] J. Bompaire, *Lucien écrivain: imitation et création.*
[23] *Institutio Oratoria* X. 1. 93.

matter of secondary importance for Lucian. Really he is *sui generis:* a literate Hellenist in an age oriented toward the past, adding to a long-standing tradition of literary "satire" the element of his own personality.

Evidently *Hired Companions* rose to reproach its author when, late in life, Lucian took a post of some importance with the Roman administration in Egypt; at any rate, he found it necessary to issue an *Apology* in which he explains—gratuitously, one would have thought—that working for a Civil Service is not the same thing as hiring oneself out as tame intellectual status symbol to a vulgar Roman millionaire. In Egypt he found time, it would seem, to continue his rhetorical performances; and those who play the game of Lucianic chronology are chastened, or should be, by the certain presence in this period of some minor pieces so similar to Lucian's earliest work that, without the references they contain to Lucian as being old, no one would dare place them so late.[24] But it is little enough that we know about these last years. Presumably Lucian died in Egypt; but we do not even know when.

To document Lucian's conscious debt to older literature as thoroughly as Bompaire has done is a valuable service; and Caster has demonstrated how incomplete is Lucian's picture of the second century. These researches are important; they qualify essentially our picture of Lucian as a satirist of his times: though in essence their achievement is to give substance to what the reader may suspect for himself even on first acquaintance with his author, for Lucian is at no pains to conceal his admiration for antiquity. To demonstrate such tendencies in an author, however, though it may and should qualify interpretation of him, is not to deprive him of value, or even to vitiate the pleasure of reading him. Even so thoroughgoing a depreciation as Helm's is beside the essential point, that what he writes is worth writing, and reading, be it "copied" or not; few besides George Bernard Shaw have seen fit to denigrate Shakespeare for his borrowings. As to the

---

[24] Cf. Caster, *Lucien et la pensée religieuse de son temps,* p. 381.

clumsiness Lucian is accused of, we can judge for ourselves from the final product. No one would deny that he is repetitious sometimes to the point of tediousness—although Lucian never intended his works to be tasted otherwise than in sips. But in general it is surely the skill of construction rather than any ineptness that is to be remarked.

What is one to make of Lucian? It would seem that the key to his psychology is his acute intelligence—that, and his Oriental origin and cast of mind.[25] The ability demonstrated abundantly in his early period by the mastery he attained over the Greek language, and by the seemingly casual ease with which he throws off little masterpieces of rhetorical trivia, is equally evident in for instance *Hermotimus,* where Lucian ties up his straw man with even unnecessary adroitness and completeness. The rational process is impeccable; not an argument, not a word, is out of place, as he demonstrates to his own evident satisfaction the foolishness of embarking on any philosophy at all, since none of them can be proved not to be wrong. It is all very logical; indeed, it is logic gone to seed; this merciless rationality never reaches any but negative conclusions. Lucian knows all the answers; and they are all "No." It is this attitude which is at the bottom of his predilection for Cynicism; he is so intelligent that he cannot bear to be fooled. "And then he died" is an unanswerable argument; in face of it, he seems to suggest, we must above all not commit the intellectual error of thinking life meaningful. That men *do* take life seriously is of no interest to Lucian; he cannot hear, and never listens for, the still sad music of humanity.

In this vein, it seems fairly clear, we have Lucian's real "thought," if thought it can be called; for it is rather a psychological predisposition, a function, one supposes, of his biochemical make-up; for all the ideas that he throws off, he can never be credited with cogitation. Certainly to see in his rationalism the voice of an apostle of light wearily but unceasingly battling against the encircling gloom, as some have

[25] On Lucian's Oriental character, see Hime, *Lucian the Syrian Satirist,* pp. 45–47.

done,[26] is to take him altogether too seriously. This is no
ardent champion of truth; and to see him as such is to fall
into the very error of pretentiousness that he would be the
first and most merciless to castigate. He is a writer, not a
thinker. He quite lacks any serious base; his blood is compounded of venom, champagne, and printer's ink. The mere
play of intelligence is all that counts for him, regardless of its
object; he is unanchored, a free-playing brain, an unattached
piece of clockwork. Sustained intellectual effort simply is not
his line. The principal impression that remains after one has
read him *in extenso* is of something lacking, some breadth of
view, some depth. He is a humanist *manqué;* and what is
lacking is humanity.

But as a writer he is of the first order. This same quick
intelligence serves him to perfection in the cut-and-thrust of
dialogue—as in *Zeus Rants,* where he strikes sparks within sec-
onds of putting pen to paper, or as in *The Sale of Philosophers,* where felicities abound from start to finish (the irreverent sketch of the Stoic, for instance, is wickedly funny).
In a hundred places—the *Dialogues of the Sea-Gods* with their
delicate pictures, *Hired Companions* with its sustained Ho-
garthian grim humor, *Alexander* with its crescendo of invective—he plays like a virtuoso on a style of great variety, to
create with apparent ease the effect he wants. He is, simply,
a joy to read.

And this is certainly the criterion he would choose to be
judged by; for his whole ambition was to become an orna-
ment to the Greek literary tradition, and there can hardly be
question that he succeeded. The self-transplanting of this
Syrian from a rather remote provincial town into the highly
sophisticated artistic milieu of metropolitan Greece is one
more manifestation of his adaptability and intelligence; he
learned to have, for the untutored and the non-Hellenic, the
acute distaste that marks the convert. Greece was the natural,
if acquired, habitat of his quick spirit, and the strictness with

26 E.g., Carlo Gallavotti, *Luciano nella sua evoluzione artistica e spirituale* (Lanciano: Carabba, 1932).

which he holds to, and holds others to, the tenets of *Paideia* marks the degree of his enthusiasm for Hellenism. Hence the paucity of his extra-traditional references; hence the purity of his linguistic taste; hence the fastidious pride of his whole bearing as an artist.

In one or two places he speaks of his own aims and attitudes: "I hate frauds, liars and pompous idiots," he says; [27] and elsewhere, "I am an entertainer; I try to amuse; and that is all there is to it." [28] And surely his view of himself is more reliable than the elaborate theories of modern scholars. To be sure, he had his serious side; but, if it is fair to see this in his penchant for Cynicism, it is not very edifying. The born comic who would forsooth play Hamlet seldom makes a good job of it. Better to leave him with Eunapius' epigram in mind: "ἀνὴρ σπουδαῖος" he says, "ἐς τὸ γελασθῆναι": "serious enough—about raising a laugh." [29]

The present selection is intended to exemplify Lucian's treatment of the principal themes outlined above—respectively Cynicism (*Dialogues of the Dead, A Trip to Hades, The Cock*), philosophy (*The Sale of Philosophers, Hermotimus*), religion (*Zeus Rants*), social satire (*Hired Companions*), and literature (*A True Story*). The pieces chosen are generally agreed to be among Lucian's best, but there are many others eminently worth reading. For fuller acquaintance with Lucian, the reader is referred for preference to the translation mentioned above, by the Fowler brothers; a work of loving care for the English language, whose renderings in the more elaborate passages are time and again so felicitous as to leave no further scope for translators. The Fowlers' style is however somewhat formal for dialogue; my intention has been principally to capture the essential vivacity of Lucian. As far as possible I have modernized references, but sometimes I have left them in their Greek form. This is most notable in the case of money, where

---

[27] *The Fisher* 20.
[28] *A Literary Prometheus* 2.
[29] *Lives of the Sophists*, Introduction 454.

any scale of equivalent modern values would be more mis-
leading than useful—partly because Greek drachmas did not
buy the same things as dollars or pounds, and partly because
our money changes its real value so quickly. During the
Peloponnesian War, a drachma a day (equivalent to six obols)
was the normal wage of a soldier or a skilled workman. It is
not clear how far currency had depreciated by Lucian's day;
he speaks (in *The Cock*) of seven obols as what a cobbler
would earn for a pair (presumably) of shoes; but it is never
certain whether he is reflecting contemporary conditions.
Other monetary units were the mina, equivalent to a hundred drachmas, and the talent, equivalent to sixty minas.

I should like to express my thanks to Mr. A. G. Lee, of St.
John's College, Cambridge, and Mr. M. D. MacLeod, of the
University of Southampton, with whom I have had valuable
discussions on Lucian; and to the Canada Council for grants
that have enabled me to consult libraries in Britain. Most of
all I would express my indebtedness to Dr. Ursula Schoen-
heim, of Queens College, New York, who read the whole book
in typescript and whose painstaking labor has saved me from
many errors and many infelicities of expression; for those that
remain, she is not responsible.

                                          B. P. REARDON

SELECTED BIBLIOGRAPHY

ALLINSON, FRANCIS G. *Lucian, Satirist and Artist*. Boston: Marshall Jones Company, 1926.

BOMPAIRE, JACQUES. *Lucien écrivain: imitation et création*. Paris: E. de Boccard, 1958.

CASTER, MARCEL. *Lucien et la pensée religieuse de son temps*. Paris: Les Belles Lettres, 1937.

CROISET, MAURICE. *Essai sur la vie et les œuvres de Lucien*. Paris: Hachette, 1882.

GALLAVOTTI, CARLO. *Luciano nella sua evoluzione artistica e spirituale*. Lanciano: Carabba, 1932.

GAZZA, VITTORINO. "Luciano di Samosata e la polemica sulla filosofia," *Rendiconti del Istituto Lombardo di Scienze e Lettere*, LXXXVIII (1955), 373–414.

HELM, RUDOLF. *Lucian und Menipp*. Leipzig and Berlin: Teubner, 1906.

——— "Lukian und die Philosophenschulen," *Neue Jahrbücher für das klassische Altertum*, IX (1902), 188–213, 263–78, 351–69.

HIME, HENRY W. L. *Lucian the Syrian Satirist*. London: Longmans, Green and Co., 1900.

LATTANZI, GOFFREDO M. "Il 'Luciano' del Gallavotti e gli opuscoli spuri del 'corpus Lucianeum,'" *Il Mondo Classico*, III (1933), 312–17.

——— "Il 'Luciano' del Gallavotti e l'evoluzione spirituale di Luciano," *Il Mondo Classico*, IV (1934), 72–76.

LUCIAN. *The Works of Lucian*. Translated by H. W. and F. G. FOWLER. 4 vols. Oxford: Clarendon Press, 1905.

McCarthy, Barbara P. "Lucian and Menippus," *Yale Classical Studies,* IV (1934), 3–58.

Piot, Henri. *Un personnage de Lucien: Ménippe.* Rennes: Francis Simon, 1914.

—— *Les procédés littéraires de la seconde sophistique chez Lucien: l'Ecphrasis.* Rennes: Francis Simon, 1914.

Putnam, Emily J. "Lucian the Sophist," *Classical Philology,* IV (1909), 162–77.

NOTE ON THE TEXT

I have used the Loeb text throughout. In *Dialogues of the Dead,* however, the traditional order of the dialogues has been retained for convenience in identifying references in critical literature. Loeb VII, x contains a comparative table of the traditional and revised orders of the dialogues.

Lucian abounds in references to classical history, literature, and mythology. I have supplied notes (in the compilation of which I have been much indebted to the Loeb edition) where they seemed necessary to the understanding of the text. For the elucidation of other allusions—to such figures as seemed too well-known, or not important enough in their contexts, to require explanation where they occur—the reader is referred to the Glossary at the end of the volume, and to any standard classical dictionary; the *Oxford Classical Dictionary* (Oxford: Clarendon Press, 1949) and H. J. Rose's *Handbook of Greek Mythology* (6th edn., London: Methuen, 1958) may be particularly recommended.

In the footnotes, *Dialogues of the Dead* has been abbreviated to *D. D., A Trip to Hades* to *Trip, The Sale of Philosophers* to *Sale, Zeus Rants* to *Zeus,* and *A True Story* to *Story.* References to Homer are identified merely as *Odyssey* or *Iliad* with the appropriate book and line numbers.

LUCIAN: SELECTED WORKS

DIALOGUES OF THE DEAD

1
Diogenes and Pollux

DIOGENES. Pollux! I've a job for you as soon as you get up into the world of the living—it's your turn to come to life tomorrow, isn't it? [1] If you see Menippus the Dog [2] anywhere about—you might find him in the Craneum at Corinth or in the Lyceum, laughing at the philosophers quarreling with each other—give him this message: "Menippus, Diogenes says, if you've had a good enough laugh at life on earth, come down here and you'll get a much bigger one. You see, on earth your laughter could never be quite confident; there was so much doubt about what happens after death. But here you'll be on firm ground and you'll never stop laughing—take my word for it—especially when you see rich men and satraps and tyrants reduced to such insignificance and obscurity. Why, the only way you can recognize them is by their groaning and the spineless, ignoble way they carry on when they remember life on earth." You tell him that; and tell him to fill his pouch with plenty of lupines, too, before he comes, and any odd tidbit for Hecate he can find lying about at the crossroads, or a sacrificial egg, or anything like that. [3]

POLLUX. All right, Diogenes, I'll tell him. Tell me what he looks like, so that I'll recognize him.

1 Pollux shared his own immortality with his brother, Castor, when the latter was killed; the two returned to earth on alternate days.

2 This is a play on words; the Greek word κύων, from which "Cynic" is derived, means "dog." See Introduction, p. xvi.

3 Lupines are seeds of the pea family, traditional austere fare for world-renouncing philosophers; Lucian's joke here is that purificatory offerings of food—such as a tidbit or an egg—would often be taken by poor people almost before they reached the altar or the roadside.

DIOGENES. He's an old man, and bald, and his cloak is full of holes; it flutters in the slightest breeze, and the rags hang down in all sorts of shapes. He's always laughing and generally making fun of those charlatans who call themselves philosophers.

POLLUX. He should be easy enough to find from that description.

DIOGENES. Do you mind if I send a message to the philosophers themselves too?

POLLUX. Go ahead; that's no trouble either.

DIOGENES. Tell them to give up their nonsensical babbling altogether—their quibbling about the Whole and making horns grow on each other's head; inventing crocodile puzzles and spurring their wits on to set such unanswerable riddles.[4]

POLLUX. But they'll call me stupid and ignorant if I pull their learning to pieces.

DIOGENES. Tell them from me to go to hell.

POLLUX. All right, Diogenes, I'll tell them that too.

3   DIOGENES. And give the rich this message from me, my dearest Pollux: "Why, oh you vain creatures, do you hoard your gold? Why do you punish yourselves, reckoning your interest and heaping talent upon talent, when you'll have to come here with one obol [5] before long?"

POLLUX. They will receive this message too.

DIOGENES. And tell those who are handsome and strong— Megillus the Corinthian and Damoxenus the wrestler and so on—that there's no such thing as golden hair in Hades, no blue eyes or dark eyes or blushing cheeks, no strong sinews or powerful shoulders; here everything's all mere dust, as they say, and skulls devoid of beauty.

[4] One of Lucian's commonest complaints about philosophers is that they are more concerned with linguistic technicalities than with morality. For other references to Stoic logical puzzles, cf. *Sale* 21–25 and *Hermotimus* 81.

[5] The coin put in a corpse's mouth to pay Charon for ferrying it across the Styx. For the relative value of money, see Introduction, p. xxxii.

POLLUX. I can easily take this message too—to the handsome and strong.

DIOGENES. And tell the poor, my dear Spartan—and there *4* are many of them, weighed down by life and lamenting their poverty—tell them not to weep and wail; tell them we are all equal here, and they will see earth's millionaires no better off than they are. And would you tell your own friends in Sparta they've let themselves go; it won't do.[6]

POLLUX. Not a word about the Spartans, Diogenes; I won't stand for it. But I'll take your messages to the others.

DIOGENES. We'll leave them alone then, if you say so; but carry these messages to the others I mentioned, and say they come from me.

2

The Dead Complain to Pluto About Menippus

CROESUS. Pluto! We won't put up with this dog Menip- *1* pus living with us! Either you move him somewhere else or we'll move somewhere else.

PLUTO. What harm is he doing you? He's a corpse the same as you are.

CROESUS. Every time we groan and lament, remembering what we had on earth—Midas here his gold, and Sardanapalus his unlimited luxury, and I, Croesus, my treasure rooms—he laughs at us and pours abuse on us, he calls us slaves and worthless scum. Sometimes he even disturbs our lamentations with his chanting, and he makes a general nuisance of himself.

PLUTO. What's this they're talking about, Menippus?

MENIPPUS. Oh, it's quite right—I hate them, miserable beggars! They're not satisfied with their bad life, they have to remember it and cling to it even now they're dead. So I delight in annoying them.

[6] Possibly a reference to Sparta's comparative decadence after the Peloponnesian War.

PLUTO. Oh, you shouldn't; they've lost a lot and they're miserable.

MENIPPUS. You approve of their caterwauling? Are you crazy too?

PLUTO. No, it's just that I don't want any trouble among you.

MENIPPUS. Well, you wretched specimens of Lydians and Phrygians and Assyrians, I'm not going to stop—get that into your heads. Wherever you go I'm going to follow you and chant after you and annoy you with my mockery.

CROESUS. This is the limit!

MENIPPUS. Oh no it isn't. The way *you* used to carry on was the limit—making people kowtow to you and lording it over free men and never thinking about death for a minute. That's just why you've got something to moan about now you've lost everything.

CROESUS. O gods! What a lot it was! What a lot I owned!

MIDAS. Oh, what a lot of gold *I* had!

SARDANAPALUS. Oh, what luxury *I* lived in!

MENIPPUS. That's the way! Go on! You keep on moaning, and I'll keep on chanting "Know yourself" [7] at you—it's just the tune to go with your sort of moaning.

3

Menippus, Amphilochus, and Trophonius

MENIPPUS. And yet, though you're both dead, you've had temples built to you for some strange reason! You're considered prophets; silly people have taken you for gods!

AMPHILOCHUS. And is it our fault if they have such foolish ideas about the dead?

MENIPPUS. Well, they wouldn't have if you hadn't gone about posing as miracle men when you were alive, pretending you could foretell the future and prophesy to anybody who asked you to.

---

[7] The motto γνῶθι σεαυτόν, "Know yourself," was inscribed over the entrance to Apollo's oracle at Delphi.

TROPHONIUS. Amphilochus can speak for himself. *I'm* a hero, and I give oracles to anyone who comes to consult me. Evidently you've never been to Lebadea—you wouldn't be so skeptical if you had.

MENIPPUS. Huh! Do I have to go to Lebadea and make a 2 fool of myself, dressing up in linen and crawling on my belly with a cake in my hands through that opening into the cave,[8] to know that you're dead just like the rest of us—and the only difference is that you're a charlatan? Look, tell me—in the name of your prophet's craft—what *is* a hero? I must say I don't know.

TROPHONIUS. A mixture of man and god.

MENIPPUS. So what's neither man nor god—on your own admission—is both together? All right, then, where's your divine half vanished to now?

TROPHONIUS. It's in Boeotia, giving oracles.

MENIPPUS. I can't make any sense out of you. But I can see quite clearly that you're a hundred per cent dead.

4

Hermes and Charon

HERMES. Look, let's add up what you owe me now and 1 have no arguments about it afterward.

CHARON. All right. Better know where we stand—less trouble that way.

HERMES. The anchor you asked me to get you—it was five drachmas.

CHARON. That's pretty steep!

HERMES. Hell, I *paid* five drachmas! And the rowlock strap—that was two obols.

CHARON. Put down five drachmas and two obols.

HERMES. And the needle to mend the sail—it cost me five obols.

CHARON. All right, add it on.

---

8 A ceremony typical of mystery cults, such as the Eleusinian Mysteries.

HERMES. Then the wax to stop up the holes in your boat, and the nails, and the rope you used for the brace—all those came to two drachmas.

CHARON. Well, you got your money's worth.

HERMES. That's the lot, unless there's something we haven't counted. Now, when did you say you'd pay?

CHARON. Oh, I can't just now, Hermes. But if I get a batch of customers in a plague or a war, I'll be able to juggle the fares and make a bit of profit in the rush.

2   HERMES. So for the time being I'm to sit quietly and pray for the worst to happen so that I can get my money back?

CHARON. There's nothing else to do. You can see I've very few customers just now; there's no war on.[9]

HERMES. Better so—even if I do have to wait for my money. But in the old days, Charon—you know what people were like then: men were men, every one of them, most of them covered in blood and wounds. Nowadays they're poisoned by their wives or children, or else they ruin their bellies and limbs with soft living—they're all pasty, miserable specimens, nothing like the old days. Most of them seem to get here through trying to do away with each other for money.

CHARON. Yes, that's what they're after all the time.

HERMES. Well then, you won't blame me if I hound you for mine.

5

Pluto and Hermes

1   PLUTO. You know that old man, the *very* old one, Eucrates the millionaire? He hasn't any children, but there are thousands of people after the money he's going to leave.

HERMES. Eucrates of Sicyon? Yes, I know him. Well?

PLUTO. He's ninety now, but could you let him live an-

---

[9] One of the few references in Lucian that may be contemporary (see Introduction, p. xxi); if so, it dates this work to either 161 or 165 (just before or just after the Parthian War). On the other hand, *D. D.* 27. 2–3 mentions a war as current.

other ninety years—or even more? [10] And grab all those people who are toadying to him—young Charinus, and Damon, and all the rest of them—grab the whole lot, one after another?

HERMES. That would be an odd thing to do.

PLUTO. Oh no; it's just what you should do. Why should they pray for his death and try to get their hands on his money? They've no right to it! The most damnable thing is the shameless way they pay court to him, with black thoughts in their hearts all the time. Everybody knows very well what they really want when he's ill, but still they promise to make offerings if he recovers. There's nothing they won't do, in fact, to get in his good graces. So let him live on and on—and make them die before he does, with their mouths still watering for what they'll never get.

HERMES. That would make fools of them, the rogues.

PLUTO. But he knows very well how to lead them up the garden path, too—he keeps his own hopes high. And though he always looks as if he's "at death's door," [11] in fact he's in much better health than they are, in spite of their youth. They've already split up his money among them; they feed on dreams of luxury. Well, let him slip out of his old age as Iolaus did and become young again—and let them land here right now, just when their hopes are highest, with their dreams of money far behind them. They're a set of rogues— let them die like rogues!

HERMES. Leave it to me. I'll go and get them right now if you like, one after the other. Seven of them, aren't there?

PLUTO. Haul them down here; and make him young again, and he'll see every one of them off.

6

Terpsion and Pluto

TERPSION. Is this right—me dead at thirty, while old Thucritus is past ninety and still alive?

[10] Lucian here deliberately ignores the fact that the human life-span was controlled by Lachesis, one of the three Fates.

[11] A parody of *Odyssey* XI. 608.

PLUTO. Oh yes, very right and proper. He's never in his life wished any of his friends to die, but you spent all your days waiting for him to die and thinking of ways to get his money.

TERPSION. Look, he's an old man. He can't use his money now. He ought to get out of the way and make room for younger men.

PLUTO. That's a new rule, Terpsion—that anybody who can't use his money any more should die to suit you. Fate and nature have decided otherwise, though.

2   TERPSION. Well, I don't agree with their decision. Things ought to go in order of seniority—old men first and younger men after them. It shouldn't be all upside down. These old fogies have no business being alive—only three teeth left, practically blind, can't stand up without a couple of slaves on each side to hold them, nose running, eyes bleary. They get no pleasure out of life in that state—they're living corpses; the younger men all laugh at them. And yet fine strong young men die! "Rivers running backward," [12] that's what that is. At least we might be told when any particular old man really *is* going to die. That would save us wasting our time on some of them. You know what they say about putting the cart before the horse.

3   PLUTO. It's much more sensible than you think, Terpsion. Why do you people grasp after what doesn't belong to you? Why do you thrust yourselves upon these childless old men and make up to them? You look pretty foolish, I can tell you, when you end up in the cemetery before them; everybody thinks it's a great joke. The more you pray for them to die, the more people laugh when you die first. It's a new art you've thought up, falling in love with old men and women—that is, provided they haven't any children; if they have, they don't inspire any affection in you. But you know, a lot of them are well aware that the affection you express for them is pure claptrap. If they do have children, they pretend to hate them,

[12] Part of a famous line of Euripides, *Medea* 410, the import of which is that the order of nature has gone wrong.

so that they can have loving friends too. And then when the will's published, their faithful minions find themselves shut out; the children, the natural kin, get everything—and so they should. Our friends are left to gnash their teeth when they realize they've been had.

TERPSION. You're quite right. When I think of all *I* poured into Thucritus' lap! He always looked as if he was on his last legs. Every time I went to see him I'd find him moaning away, chattering as feebly as a newborn fledgling. I always thought he'd got one foot in the grave already—I used to send him the greater part of what I had to make sure my rivals weren't more generous than I was. Night after night I lay awake worrying, totting everything up and planning every move. In fact, that's what killed me—not getting any sleep and worrying. He swallowed all my bait—and there he stood the other day, roaring with laughter as he watched me being buried. *4*

PLUTO. That's the way! Long live Thucritus! Enjoy your money and make fools of this lot while you're at it! Don't come down here until you've seen the whole lot of them off first! *5*

TERPSION. Well, I must say I'd be only too pleased to see Charoeades die before Thucritus too.

PLUTO. Don't worry, he will. Phidon too, and Melanthus —the whole lot of them—will be here before him, through worrying just as you did.

TERPSION. Good. Long live Thucritus!

7
Zenophantus and Callidemides

ZENOPHANTUS. How did *you* die, Callidemides? I was a parasite of Dinias; I tried to gulp down more than I could manage and choked myself, as you know—you were there when I died. *1*

CALLIDEMIDES. Yes, I was. My death was a bit of a surprise. You know old Ptoeodorus, don't you?

ZENOPHANTUS. No children? Wealthy? I knew you spent a lot of time with him.

CALLIDEMIDES. That's the man. Well, I cultivated him all the time—he'd always assured me I'd be his beneficiary when he died. But things went on like that for ages. The old fellow lived longer than Tithonus, so I thought up a short cut to his money. What I did was, I bought some poison; then I got his wine steward to put it in his glass and keep it ready until the next time he called for a drink—he's a pretty heavy drinker. I promised to reward the wine steward by setting him free.

ZENOPHANTUS. What happened then? Something strange, I bet.

2   CALLIDEMIDES. Well now, we came back from the baths and the lad had the cups ready—the one with the poison in it for Ptoeodorus and the other one for me. But somehow or other he mixed them up; I got the poisoned one and Ptoeodorus the harmless one. He began to drink his, and before he was finished I was flat on my back—I was the corpse instead of him. Do you think that's funny? Look, you shouldn't laugh at your friends!

ZENOPHANTUS. Well, it was a very comic accident! What did the old man do?

CALLIDEMIDES. At first he was very upset—it all happened so suddenly. Then he realized what had happened, I suppose, and he laughed too at what the steward had done.

ZENOPHANTUS. Ah, but you shouldn't have taken that short cut. The main road would have turned out safer for you, even if he was a bit slow coming.

8

Cnemon and Damnippus

1   CNEMON. It's like the proverb; the fawn's caught the lion.

DAMNIPPUS. What's annoying you, Cnemon?

CNEMON. What's annoying me? I've left my money to somebody I didn't want to get it! I've been tricked, miserably tricked! I've passed over the people I most wanted to get what I had!

DAMNIPPUS. How come?

CNEMON. I was cultivating Hermolaus the millionaire, hoping he'd die—he hasn't any children. He was glad enough of my attentions, too. Well, I thought it would be a good idea to make my will entirely in his favor and publish it, hoping he'd follow suit and do the same for me.

DAMNIPPUS. Well? Did he?

CNEMON. I've no idea what *he* said in *his* will; the roof fell in on me and I died on the spot! Now Hermolaus has my money. It's like the pike swallowing hook as well as bait.

DAMNIPPUS. And fisherman too. You've been caught by your own trick.

CNEMON. It looks like it. That's what's making me so miserable.

9
Simylus and Polystratus

SIMYLUS. You've joined us at last, Polystratus! You must be nearly a hundred!   *1*

POLYSTRATUS. Ninety-eight, Simylus.

SIMYLUS. What sort of life have you had this last thirty years? You were nearly seventy when I died.

POLYSTRATUS. Oh, I had a fine time; you'd be surprised!

SIMYLUS. I am! You were old and in poor health, you had no children—how *could* you enjoy life?

POLYSTRATUS. To start with, I could do just as I liked. I   *2* still had plenty of handsome boys and lovely women around me; I still had perfumes and good wine; my table beat any in Sicily.[13]

SIMYLUS. That's a change! You used to be very thrifty, to my knowledge.

POLYSTRATUS. Oh, my dear fellow, it *came* to me in

[13] The luxury of Sicilian tyrants was proverbial.

streams, this luxury—from other people! There were crowds at my doors first thing in the morning; later in the day, all sorts of presents were brought in to me from the ends of the earth—the best things life has to offer.

SIMYLUS. Did you become a tyrant after I died?

POLYSTRATUS. No, but I did have thousands of lovers.

SIMYLUS. Lovers? You? At your age? With four teeth in your head? Don't make me laugh!

POLYSTRATUS. I tell you I had—from the best families in town, too. They were only too glad to cultivate me—old as I was, and bald as you see, and my eyes and nose running. I only had to glance at a man to make him deliriously happy.

SIMYLUS. Why, did heaven answer your prayers and make you young and handsome and desirable again, as Aphrodite did for Phaon when he rowed her over from Chios?

POLYSTRATUS. No. I was just as you see me, but everybody loved me.

SIMYLUS. I don't get it.

3   POLYSTRATUS. Well, it's common enough experience, this passion for old men with plenty of money and no children.

SIMYLUS. Ah, my dear fellow, *now* I get you! Your beauty was a gift of the *golden* Aphrodite!

POLYSTRATUS. Well, Simylus, I did pretty well out of my lovers. They practically prostrated themselves in front of me. Many a time I played hard to get and shut some of them out. They vied with each other, they outdid each other to win my favor!

SIMYLUS. What did you decide to do with your possessions in the end, then?

POLYSTRATUS. For public consumption, so to speak, I told each one of them I'd made him my heir. They all swallowed it; then they really bent over backward to do what I wanted. But in fact I had a genuine will, which I left behind; it told them all to go to hell.

4   SIMYLUS. And who was your heir in that one? A relative?

POLYSTRATUS. Not on your life. A handsome Phrygian boy I'd just bought.

SIMYLUS. How old was he?

POLYSTRATUS. About twenty.

SIMYLUS. Oh yes—I can guess what *his* job was.

POLYSTRATUS. Well, he was much fitter than they were to be my heir. Barbarian and rascal he may be, but by this time all the best people are cultivating him. Anyway, he got my money, and now he's in *Who's Who*. He's got no beard, and his Greek's atrocious, but nobody bothers about that; they call him nobler than Codrus and better-looking than Nireus and cleverer than Odysseus.

SIMYLUS. Doesn't worry me. He can be President of Greece for all I care, so long as that lot don't get the money.

10
Charon and Hermes

CHARON. Listen, I'll tell you how it is. It's only a small boat you're on—you can see that—and it's rotten and full of leaks. If it rolls at all it'll capsize in a minute. And here we are with all you people, and you've all got lots of stuff with you. Well, if you bring it all on board with you, I'm afraid you'll soon regret it—especially any of you who can't swim.

HERMES. What do we do, then, to make it an easy trip?

CHARON. I'll tell you. Strip off your clothes and leave all this excess baggage on the shore; the ferry'll barely take you as it is. Hermes, in the future make sure you don't let anyone on unless he's stripped, as I said, and not loaded down. Stand by the gangplank and keep an eye on them. Take them aside and make them strip before they come on board.

HERMES. O.K., will do. Who's first?

MENIPPUS. Me, Menippus. Here's my knapsack and staff [14] —chuck them in the water. I didn't even bring my cloak—just as well.

HERMES. Ah, Menippus, that's a good fellow. On you go.

[14] The Cynic philosopher's traditional equipment; see Introduction, p. xvi.

You take the front seat, by the helmsman—high up, so that

3   you can watch the rest. Who's this beauty?

CHARMOLEOS. Charmoleos of Megara, Charmoleos the irresistible. My kiss was worth two talents.

HERMES. All right, off with your charms. And your lips—kisses and all. And your long hair. And your rosy cheeks. And your soft skin. That's the way; now you're properly dressed—

4   on you go. Who's this solemn fellow with the purple cloak and the crown?

LAMPICHUS. Lampichus, tyrant of Gela.[15]

HERMES. Lampichus, eh? What have you brought all this stuff for?

LAMPICHUS. What for? Do you expect tyrants to come with nothing on?

HERMES. Tyrants, no; corpses, yes. Off with it.

LAMPICHUS. All right. There you are—there goes my money.

HERMES. And your pride, and your arrogance; they'll overload the ferry if they come on.

LAMPICHUS. Let me keep my crown and cloak, at least.

HERMES. Certainly not. Take them off too.

LAMPICHUS. Oh, all right. Anything else? You can see I've got rid of everything.

HERMES. Your cruelty. Your silly notions. Your insolent behavior. Your temper. Get rid of them too.

LAMPICHUS. There; I've nothing at all now.

5   HERMES. Right; on you go then. You! The fat tubby fellow! Who might you be?

DAMASIAS. Damasias the athlete.

HERMES. Yes, I remember your face. I've seen you many a time at sports grounds.

DAMASIAS. Yes, you have. Let me on; I've stripped.

HERMES. Stripped, my dear fellow? With all that flesh on you? You get it off. You'll sink the ship if you put one foot on. And throw away those wreaths and first prizes.

15 Tyrannies flourished in Sicily; cf. *D. D.* 9. 2 and n. 13.

DAMASIAS. There, I really am stripped—see for yourself. I'm no heavier than the rest of the corpses.

HERMES. You're better off with that weight gone. On you 6 go. Craton! You remove your wealth, and your immorality too —and your luxurious tastes. Don't bring on your funeral paraphernalia, or your family pride. Leave your lineage and reputation behind, and all the honors your city gave you, and those inscriptions to you. Never mind telling us you've got a big tomb—just talking about it weighs the boat down.

CRATON. I'll get rid of them; I don't want to, but what else can I do?

HERMES. Hey! You there in full armor! What's the idea? 7 What's this trophy you're carrying?

GENERAL. Well, I won victories and fought bravely; my country gave me the trophy.

HERMES. Leave it up on earth. We're at peace down here; no need for arms. Who's this fellow? He seems pretty solemn 8 and proud of himself. Look at him frowning and lost in thought, look at that long beard!

MENIPPUS. He's a philosopher—charlatan, more like, a bag of claptrap. Make him strip too; you'll get a big laugh when you see what's under his cloak.

HERMES. Clothes off first, you! Then take the rest off as well! Ye gods! What a load of trickery, ignorance, quarrelsomeness, conceit, unanswerable questions, thorny arguments, complicated ideas! And all that useless bother, drivel, nonsense, and hairsplitting! Heavens above! Look at it! Greed! Self-indulgence! Shamelessness! Temper! Sensuality! Immorality! Don't try to hide them—I can see! Off with your lying and pride and superiority! A cargo ship wouldn't carry you with that load!

PHILOSOPHER. All right—if you say so. There they go.

MENIPPUS. Oh, but look, Hermes, make him get rid of his 9 beard too! Look how heavy and shaggy it is—at least five pounds of hair there!

HERMES. Indeed yes. Take it off as well.

PHILOSOPHER. Who's going to cut it off?

HERMES. Menippus here can get a carpenter's axe and chop it off against the gangplank.

MENIPPUS. Oh no, Hermes, it'd be much more fun if you'd hand me up a saw.

HERMES. The axe'll do. That's the way! You look more like a human being now, without that goat's beard.

MENIPPUS. Shall I take a little off his eyebrows too?

HERMES. By all means. He's got them trained over his forehead as if he were stretching after something. What's this? Crying, you wretch? Afraid of death? Never mind that—you get on board!

MENIPPUS. He's still got one thing under his arm—the heaviest of the lot.

HERMES. What's that?

MENIPPUS. Flattery. It's done him good service in life.

PHILOSOPHER. Look, Menippus, suppose *you* drop your independence and frankness and thick skin and spirit and sense of humor! You're the only one who finds it funny.

HERMES. Don't you do anything of the sort. You keep them. They're light and easy to carry—and they'll come in handy on the crossing. You there—the orator! Throw away your interminable verbosity! And your contrasting clauses and parallel clauses and periods and foreign words and the rest of your weighty language!

ORATOR. All right; there you are.

HERMES. That's the way. Right; now we can cast off. Pull up the gangplank, weigh the anchor, spread the sail. Ferryman, take the wheel. Let's go—and good luck to us! What's all the fuss about? Nitwits! You there, the philosopher—you that just lost your beard! You're the worst of the lot—what's up with you?

PHILOSOPHER. I thought the soul was immortal!

MENIPPUS. Liar! That's not what's bothering him.

HERMES. What is, then?

MENIPPUS. He's thinking he'll never eat expensive dinners

again, or go out brothel-crawling at night with his cloak over his head so that nobody will recognize him, or spend the daytime defrauding young lads of their money for his tuition. That's what's the matter with him.

PHILOSOPHER. Aren't *you* sorry to die, Menippus?

MENIPPUS. Me? I couldn't die soon enough. Nobody had to come to get *me*.[16] Listen! Can you hear people shouting, even as we're speaking? It sounds like people kicking up a row on earth. *12*

HERMES. Yes, I can. It isn't coming from one spot either. There are people crowding into the Assembly, crowing over the death of Lampichus; the women have got hold of his wife, and even his tiny children are being pelted with stones by the other children. There's another lot at Sicyon applauding Diophantus the orator, as he makes his funeral speech for Craton here. Ye gods! There's Damasias' mother wailing away, starting to keen for him with a crowd of women. But there isn't anybody crying for you, Menippus. You're the only one lying in peace.

MENIPPUS. Oh no, not at all. Wait a minute and you'll hear the dogs kicking up a pitiful din over me, and the crows flapping their wings when they gather for my funeral. *13*

HERMES. That's the spirit! Now then, here we are at the other side. You people take that road—straight in front of you —to the last judgment. Charon and I'll go and get another boatload.

MENIPPUS. Have a good trip! Come on, let's go! Well— what are you waiting for now? You've got to stand your trial. They say the penalties are pretty tough—wheels and stones and vultures.[17] Every one of us'll have his life exposed.

---

[16] According to tradition, Menippus hanged himself.

[17] Lucian refers here to the punishments of Ixion, Sisyphus, and Tityus; Ixion was chained to a perpetually spinning wheel, Sisyphus condemned to roll up a hill a stone that slid down again each time he reached the top, and Tityus tortured by having two vultures perpetually devour his liver.

11

Crates and Diogenes

1   CRATES. Did you know Moerichus, the rich man from Corinth—very rich, in fact—the one with all those merchant ships? He had a cousin Aristeas—very rich too—who was always trotting out that tag from Homer: "Either you lift me or I'll lift you." [18]

DIOGENES. Meaning?

CRATES. Well, they used to cultivate each other for the sake of each other's money. They were both the same age, and each published a will in the other's favor: Moerichus named Aristeas as his sole heir if he should die first, and likewise Aristeas named Moerichus. Well, all that had been put down in black and white, and each tried to outdo the other in flattering attentions. All the prophets alike—astrologers and dream-interpreters like the Chaldaeans, and Apollo too, in fact —kept changing their minds about which would come out on top. The scales would dip first one way, then the other.

2   DIOGENES. I'd like to know what happened in the end.

CRATES. They've both died, on the same day! The inheritances have fallen to their relatives Eunomius and Thrasycles, who never dreamed anything like that would happen. The other two were crossing to Cirrha from Sicyon when a northwest wind caught the ship on the beam and capsized it right out at sea.

3   DIOGENES. Serves them right! *We* never had these ideas about each other when *we* were alive. I never prayed for Antisthenes to die just so that I'd fall heir to that stout olive staff he made himself; and I don't think you wanted to inherit my estate when I died—my jar and my knapsack with a couple of quarts of lupines in it! [19]

18 *Iliad* XXIII. 724; Ajax said this to Odysseus during the wrestling match at the games for Patroclus.

19 The "tub" in which Diogenes is usually supposed to have lived was in fact a wine jar. The knapsack and lupines have been mentioned earlier in connection with philosophers; see *D. D.* 10. 2 and n. 14, and *D. D.* 1, n. 3.

CRATES. No—I'd no need, nor had you. We both inherited all that was necessary—you from Antisthenes [20] and I from you—and it was greater and more impressive than the Persian Empire.

DIOGENES. What do you mean?

CRATES. Wisdom, independence, truth, honesty, and freedom.

DIOGENES. Heavens, yes! I remember inheriting that wealth from Antisthenes and leaving even more to you.

CRATES. Everybody else disregarded all that, though; nobody cultivated *us* in the hope of inheriting. It was money they were all after.

DIOGENES. No wonder. They'd nowhere to put our legacies if they got them. They were all falling to pieces like rotten purses, with their soft living. When you put wisdom or honesty or truth into them, it fell through and dropped out. The bag couldn't hold it—it was like the Danaids trying to fill a leaky jar.[21] Gold they held on to, though, tooth and nail, by fair means or foul.

CRATES. Well then, we'll still have our wealth here; they'll bring one obol—and *that's* to pay the ferryman!

12

Alexander, Hannibal, Minos, and Scipio

ALEXANDER. I should get preference over you, my Libyan friend; I'm the better man.

HANNIBAL. No, you aren't—*I* am.

ALEXANDER. Well, let Minos [22] decide.

MINOS. Who are you two?

ALEXANDER. He's Hannibal of Carthage, and I'm Philip's son Alexander.

[20] One of the founders of the Cynic school of philosophy.
[21] This was their punishment in the underworld for murdering their husbands.
[22] One of the judges of the dead in Hades.

MINOS. You're both pretty famous. What's the argument about?

ALEXANDER. About who comes first. He says he was a better general than I.[23] I say it's common knowledge that I knew more about strategy than he did—or practically any of my predecessors either.

MINOS. All right, speak in turn. Hannibal, you first.

2   HANNIBAL. I've gained this much out of being here, Minos—I've mastered Greek now.[24] So he won't even have that advantage over me. I contend that a man merits particular praise who starts from nothing but still achieves greatness, wrapping himself in power and winning authority. Now, I set out for Spain with a few men behind me. At first I was under my brother,[25] but I was judged the best man for the job and given supreme command. I overcame the Celtiberians and conquered western Gaul. I crossed the great mountain range, overran the whole Po Valley, and subdued all those cities. I laid waste the plains of Italy and reached the outskirts of the capital city. In one day I killed so many men that I reckoned their rings in bushels and bridged the rivers with corpses. All this I did without being called the son of Ammon [26] or claiming divinity or relating my mother's dreams; I was content to be a man. The generals matched against me were the most brilliant in the world, the troops I encountered the toughest there were. They were no Medes I fought, or Armenians—they run away before you chase them; they'll give in without a

3   fight to anyone with any nerve. Alexander, on the other hand,

---

23 Elsewhere in our sources Hannibal is reported as acknowledging Alexander's superiority. Perhaps Lucian is simply being inaccurate, but this, unlike the previous dialogues, is merely a rhetorical argument, and he may be taking the less obvious version of the story to give himself a harder task. See Introduction, p. x.

24 Elsewhere Hannibal is said to have written in Greek.

25 Lucian is simply wrong here. There were two Hasdrubals, one Hannibal's brother and the other his brother-in-law; it was the latter who was his commander.

26 Ammon was the Libyan Zeus, and Alexander claimed to be his son as a matter of policy; see D. D. 13. 1 and 14. 1.

took over his kingdom from his father; he extended it considerably, but he had luck behind him. And then, after his victories, when he had beaten that miserable Darius at Issus and Arbela, he abandoned his own traditions and made everybody kowtow to him as to a god. He changed his habits and adopted the Median way of life. He murdered his friends at banquets and had them arrested and executed. When I was commander, my country remained sovereign; when a great enemy fleet landed in Libya and my country sent for me, I answered the summons immediately; I became a private citizen, and when I was convicted I submitted with good heart. This I did though a barbarian; I did not have a Greek education, I could not recite Homer as Alexander could. I was not taught by a scholar like Aristotle. My only asset was my good heart. This is where I claim to be superior to Alexander. He may be a more handsome sight, with his crown on his head—perhaps that impresses Macedonians too—but he cannot therefore claim to be superior to a man of spirit and military skill who relied more on his judgment than on good luck.

MINOS. Not a bad case; better than you'd expect from a Libyan. Well, Alexander? What have you to say to that?

ALEXANDER. Minos, that sort of braggart doesn't deserve *4* a reply. Common report will tell you well enough what sort of king I was and what sort of brigand he was. Still, consider my superiority. I came to power when I was still a youth. I took a firm grip on the land when it was in confusion and caught my father's assassins; then I destroyed Thebes and terrified Greece, and they elected me general. I was not content to rule the Macedonian Empire as my father left it to me; I had designs on the whole earth, and thought shame not to conquer all of it. With a few troops I invaded Asia; at the Granicus I won a great battle; capturing Lydia and Ionia and Phrygia and, in short, beating down everything in my way, I reached Issus, where Darius was waiting for me with a huge army. You know the result of that battle, you know how many *5* corpses I sent down here to you in one day; indeed, the ferryman says his boat was not big enough to hold them all that day, and most of them crossed on homemade rafts. In all these achievements I was at the head of my troops, risking my life and thinking nothing of wounds. Not to mention what happened at Tyre and Arbela, I reached India too; I brought my boundaries to the Ocean, I used their elephants, I conquered Porus. I crossed the Tanais and beat the redoubtable Scythians in a great cavalry battle. I helped my friends, I took revenge on my enemies. If men really did think me a god, the belief was pardonable in view of my achievements. And still another point: when I died I was a king, whereas he was in exile at the court of Prusias of Bithynia—and it serves him right, the savage rogue. I pass over the manner in which he conquered Italy; it was not by force but by craft, bad faith, and deceit—there was nothing respectable or straightforward about it. And in charging me with self-indulgence, I think he has forgotten his own behavior at Capua, when he spent his time with harlots; a splendid general, who put his own pleasure before the crises of war. I scorned the West and turned rather to the East; had I not, it would have been no great trouble to take Italy and Libya without bloodshed, to bring the world under my sway as far as Gades. I did not think them worth fighting; they were already in servile submission to me as their master. I have finished. Minos, decide. I could have said much, but this is enough in itself.

SCIPIO. Listen to what I have to say first.

MINOS. Well, my good man, who are you? Where are you from, that you wish to speak?

SCIPIO. I am Scipio, the Italian general. I am the man who destroyed Carthage [27] and won great victories over the Libyans.

MINOS. Well? What have you to say?

SCIPIO. I agree that Alexander is my superior, but I am Hannibal's: I beat him, pursued him, and put him ignomini-

[27] Again Lucian confuses historical characters. Scipio *Africanus* defeated Hannibal at Zama in 202 B.C.; Scipio *Aemilianus* sacked Carthage in 146 B.C.

ously to flight. Is he not ashamed to contend with Alexander? Not even I, his conqueror, would compare myself with him.

MINOS. Very sensible, Scipio, very sensible. Yes, Alexander must take first place; then you; then, if you agree, Hannibal third—and a creditable third, too.

13
Diogenes and Alexander

DIOGENES. What's this, Alexander? You dead too, just like   *1*
all the rest of us?

ALEXANDER. As you can see. Don't be surprised; I was mortal, and I'm dead.

DIOGENES. Then what Ammon said about you being his son wasn't true? You were Philip's son after all? [28]

ALEXANDER. Evidently. I shouldn't have died if I'd been Ammon's.

DIOGENES. You know, the same kind of tale was told about Olympias too—that a serpent lay with her and was seen in her bed, and that that was how you were born. Philip thought you were his son, but he was wrong.

ALEXANDER. I heard those tales too, just as you did. But I can see now that my mother and Ammon's prophets were making it all up.

DIOGENES. Still, their lies had their uses for you in life. Lots of people were terrified of you because they thought you were a god. Tell me, though—who've you left all that empire   *2*
to?

ALEXANDER. I don't know. I didn't get time to do anything about it—except give Perdiccas [29] my ring as I died. What's the joke?

DIOGENES. I was just remembering the way Greece behaved when you'd just come into power. They flattered you

[28] It is characteristic of Lucian to take a detail from one piece and treat it more extensively in another; see *D. D.* 12. 2 and n. 26, and 14. 1.

[29] One of Alexander's generals.

and elected you their champion and leader against the barbarians; some of them even added you to the twelve deities and built temples to you and sacrificed to you as the son of a

3   serpent. Tell me, where did the Macedonians bury you?

ALEXANDER. I've been lying in Babylon a month now. My Companion Ptolemy has promised to take me to Egypt and bury me there, if he can find the time to spare from his immediate troubles. Then I'll be one of the Egyptian gods.

DIOGENES. Well then, is it any wonder that I laugh? You're obviously still under your illusion and expect to become an Anubis or Osiris even down here! My godlike friend, give up the idea. Nobody can go back to life once he's crossed the lake and passed the entrance. Aeacus sees to that; and

4   Cerberus is no joke either. But I'd be very interested to know how you take it when you think what a sumptuous life you left behind to come down here: bodyguards and Companions and satraps, all that gold, whole nations prostrate before you, Babylon, Bactria, those great elephants; people thought the world of you and heaped honors on you; everybody recognized you when you went out driving in your white headband and purple cloak. Doesn't it hurt to have to forget all that? Silly beggar, why the tears? Didn't your wise Aristotle even teach you not to rely on fortune's favors?

5   ALEXANDER. Aristotle? Wise? The vilest flatterer of the lot! Allow *me* to know about Aristotle. I know how much he asked me for and what advice he gave me. I know what he got out of me by playing on my passion for culture, praising me for my looks one minute—apparently good looks are included in the Good too—and for my deeds and money the next. Money's another Good, too, according to him; that was so that he needn't be ashamed of taking it himself. The fellow was a charlatan, Diogenes—a consummate one. But I did get this much out of his philosophy—I worry about those things you listed a moment ago, and set great store by them.

6   DIOGENES. You know what you should do? I'll tell you how to cure your troubles. Hellebore [30] doesn't grow here,

---

[30] The traditional cure for insanity; cf. *Sale* 23, n. 36 and *Story* II. 18.

so you drink lots of Lethe-water [31]—drink deep, and keep on drinking. That's the way to forget your worries about Aristotle's Goods. Watch out—here are Clitus and Callisthenes [32] and a lot more coming at you to pay you back for what you did to them! They'll tear you apart! You take this other road! And remember what I said—plenty to drink!

14

Philip and Alexander

PHILIP. Try and say you're not my son now, Alexander. You wouldn't have died if you'd been Ammon's.[33]   1

ALEXANDER. Father, I knew perfectly well I was the son of Philip the son of Amyntas, but I thought the oracle would be useful politically—that's why I accepted it.

PHILIP. What? Thought it'd be useful to lay yourself open? You knew those prophets were liars.

ALEXANDER. That's not what I mean. It was the barbarians. They were terrified of me. None of them wanted to go on fighting when they thought I was a god, so they were easier to beat.

PHILIP. *You* never beat anybody worth fighting. They   2 were all cowards that you came up against—with their little bows and bucklers and their wicker shields! Conquering Greeks was a real job—Boeotians and Phocians and Athenians, Arcadian infantry and Thessalian cavalry, Elean javelin men and Mantinean peltasts, Thracians, Illyrians, Paeonians—that really was something. But the Medes and Persians and Chaldaeans—softies covered in gold! Don't you know that a mere ten thousand men beat them before you were born? Ten

---

[31] Lethe was one of the rivers in Hades; its name means "forgetfulness," and the dead drank its waters to obliterate the memory of their former lives. Cf. *Trip* 28–29, where the tyrant is punished by being forbidden to drink Lethe-water, and so must go on remembering his luxurious life on earth.

[32] Two of Alexander's comrades, whom he murdered.

[33] See *D. D.* 12. 2, n. 26.

thousand men under Clearchus marched inland, and the enemy wouldn't even wait to come to grips with them—they ran
away before they were within bowshot.

3   ALEXANDER. Perhaps—but what about the Scythians and
the Indian elephants? They were nothing to laugh at, but I
beat them none the less. And I didn't do it by playing people
off against each other either, or by bribing traitors. Nor did
I ever perjure myself or go back on a promise or break faith
to win.[34] And I suppose you heard how I went after the
Thebans? [35] Though I took the rest of Greece without spilling
a drop of blood.

PHILIP. Yes, I know, I know. Clitus told me—Clitus, the
man you ran through with your spear in the middle of dinner
when he had the nerve to say he thought more of me than of
4   what you'd achieved. And furthermore I hear you threw aside
the Macedonian cloak and began to wear the Persian one, and
assumed the upright tiara,[36] and made free Macedonians kowtow to you. The most ridiculous thing of all is the way you
aped the people you'd beaten, never mind all the other things
you did—locking scholars up with lions, and making all
those marriages, and being altogether too fond of Hephaestion.[37] I heard of one thing only that I approved of—you kept
your hands off Darius' lovely wife and looked after his mother
and daughters. That, I admit, was the way a king should behave.

5   ALEXANDER. But I was always ready to take risks—don't
you approve of that? And I was the first to leap down inside
the wall at Oxydracae; I was badly wounded there.

PHILIP. No, I don't approve, Alexander. It isn't that I
don't think a king should actually be wounded sometimes and

34 Philip did; see the speeches of Demosthenes.
35 Alexander razed Thebes.
36 A symbol of Persian royalty. Alexander was identifying himself with
the people he had just conquered. Cf. D. D. 12. 3.
37 Lucian refers here to the traditional story of Callisthenes' murder,
and to Alexander's political marriage to Roxane of Sogdiana. In his relationship with his lieutenant Hephaestion, Alexander was imitating the
attachment of Achilles, on whom he modeled himself, for Patroclus.

fight at the head of his army, but it wasn't right for you at all. Think: you were supposed to be a god. Every time you were wounded and people saw you carried from the fight on a stretcher, streaming with blood and crying out in pain from your wounds, they only laughed at you. Ammon was shown up too as a fraud, a lying prophet, and his ministers as toadies. Who could have helped laughing to see the son of Zeus fainting and needing medical treatment? Now that you're dead, you must realize that there are a lot of people jeering at your claims when they see the god's body lying stretched out, rotting and swelling as any body does. And then there's this too: you say your divinity was valuable because it made your victories easier; but it took away considerably from the glory of your achievements. Anything you did seemed trivial when it was supposed to be a god who did it.

ALEXANDER. That isn't what men think of me. They compare me with Hercules and Dionysus. And yet neither of *them* could capture Aornos; [38] I was the only one who could subdue it.

PHILIP. There you go! You're talking as the son of Ammon, matching yourself with Hercules and Dionysus. Alexander, you ought to be ashamed of yourself! Drop your conceit! Know yourself! [39] You're dead now—admit it!

15
Achilles and Antilochus

ANTILOCHUS. What an ignoble way to talk about death, Achilles, the way you did to Odysseus the other day! [40] Both your teachers, Chiron and Phoenix, would have been ashamed of you! Oh yes, I was listening; I heard what you said about being ready to be a laborer on earth and work for some land-

[38] The "impregnable" rock in Afghanistan that Alexander stormed.
[39] See *D. D.* 2. 2 and n. 7.
[40] The reference is to *Odyssey* XI, where Odysseus visits Hades (from sec. 3 below, Odysseus is not yet dead). For the following lines, see *Odyssey* XI. 489–91.

less man—"poorly though he may live," you said—rather than be king of all the dead. Now, it may be all right for some miserable coward of a Phrygian to talk like that, to want to hang on to life at any price; but for the son of Peleus, for the bravest warrior of all to have so mean a notion of himself— why, you ought to be thoroughly ashamed of yourself! It contradicts your whole life. You could have reigned ingloriously in Phthia for ages, but you deliberately chose a death that would bring you honor.

2   ACHILLES. Yes, son of Nestor, but then I didn't know what things were like down here. I didn't know which was the better state to be in, and I valued my wretched bit of fame more than life. But now I realize it's no use to me, however men may sing its praises on earth. We're all equal now we're dead; no such things as good looks here, or strength; we're all alike, all here in the same half-light, none of us any different from anybody else. The Trojan dead aren't afraid of me, the Greeks don't treat me as their master. Everybody says just what he likes, and one dead man is as good as another— "the base and noble alike." [41] It distresses me; I'm annoyed not to be alive, even as a servant.

3   ANTILOCHUS. But what can be done about it? This is nature's decree—that we should all die once and for all. It's the way things are; let's accept it and not get annoyed with the way the world is ordered. And anyway, look at your friends—see how many of us there are? Odysseus'll be here too, soon; bound to be. You've got company; it's comforting not to be the only one. There's Hercules and Meleager and other famous people; I don't suppose they'd agree to go back to earth if they were sent up to serve poor men without a livelihood.

4   ACHILLES. You're trying to cheer me up; it's friendly of you, but somehow it distresses me to think of the life I used to lead. You all feel it, too, I'm sure. If you won't admit it, that only proves you're inferior to me, putting up with it in silence.

[41] *Iliad* IX. 319.

ANTILOCHUS. No, Achilles—superior. We can see there's no good in talking about it. We've decided to keep quiet, to put up with it, to endure it—or else we'd look as silly as you do with your daydreams.

16
Diogenes and Hercules

DIOGENES. Well, if it isn't Hercules! Yes, by Hercules, it must be! The bow, the club, the lion's skin, the size of him— nothing missing, it's Hercules! Well, well, well—the son of Zeus is dead! Tell me, my conquering hero, are you a corpse? I used to sacrifice to you on earth—I thought you were a god.[42]

HERCULES. Quite right, too. The real Hercules is with the gods in heaven, "with lovely-ankled Hebe as his wife";[43] I'm his ghost.

DIOGENES. Ghost? A god's ghost? Can one be half god and half dead?

HERCULES. Yes—*he* isn't dead, only me, his image.

DIOGENES. I see. He's handed you over to Pluto as a substitute for himself, so you're dead in his place, then?

HERCULES. That's about it.

DIOGENES. Then how come Aeacus[44] didn't notice you weren't him? He's pretty sharp. You passed yourself off as Hercules right under his nose, and he let you in?

HERCULES. Oh yes; I'm a very good copy.

DIOGENES. Yes indeed, so good that you *are* Hercules. Perhaps it's the other way around—*you're* Hercules, and your ghost's married Hebe in heaven.

HERCULES. You cheeky chatterbox! You'd better stop making fun of me or you'll soon find out whose ghost I am!

DIOGENES. His bow's uncovered—and handy. But why

1

2

3

---

[42] The point of this dialogue is that Hercules had two "fathers," Zeus and the mortal Amphitryon.

[43] *Odyssey* XI. 603.

[44] One of the judges of the dead in Hades.

should I be afraid of you now? I've already died once. Look, tell me, in the name of your Hercules—when he was alive, were you with him? Were you his ghost even then? Or were you one in life but split up when you died, and half went off to heaven while you—the ghost half—naturally came down here?

HERCULES. People who poke fun at others don't deserve any answer; still, I'll tell you that too. The part of Hercules that came from Amphitryon is dead—I'm all that part—and the part that came from Zeus is with the gods in heaven.

DIOGENES. Ah, *now* I get you! Alcmena had *two* Herculeses at once—is that it?—one by Amphitryon and one by Zeus, and people never realized you were twins with the same mother.

HERCULES. No, stupid! We were both one and the same.

DIOGENES. That's a bit hard to follow, two Herculeses joined together. Unless you were some kind of Centaur—man and god joined in one?

HERCULES. Look, don't you think *every*body's made up of two parts, soul and body? Well then, what's to stop the soul—the part that came from Zeus—being in heaven, and the mortal part—me, that is—being among the dead?

DIOGENES. My dear son of Amphitryon, what you say would be all very well if you were a body; but you're not—you're a ghost, and you haven't got a body. It looks as if you're splitting Hercules in three now.

HERCULES. Three? How?

DIOGENES. Like this. If one part's in heaven, and you, the ghost part, are here with us, and the body's become dust on Mount Oeta,[45] that makes *three*. Tell me, whom do you have in mind as father of number three?

HERCULES. Cheeky beggar! You're a smart aleck! And who might *you* be?

DIOGENES. The ghost of Diogenes of Sinope. But Diogenes

---

[45] The body of Hercules was burned in purification on Mount Oeta: see Euripides, *Hercules Furens* and Sophocles, *Trachiniae*, and cf. *Hermotimus* 7.

isn't "among the immortal gods" [46]—heavens, no! He's with all the best corpses, laughing at Homer and all that frigid nonsense.

17
Menippus and Tantalus

MENIPPUS. Why the tears, Tantalus? What are you moaning at, standing there at the edge of the water?   *1*

TANTALUS. I'm dying of thirst!

MENIPPUS. Too lazy to bend down for a drink? Or get some in the hollow of your hand?

TANTALUS. It's no good bending down—the water runs away when it sees me coming! And every time I get any in my hand and bring it to my mouth, I can't even manage to wet my lip; it runs through my fingers somehow and leaves my hand dry again!

MENIPPUS. What a very odd thing to happen. But why do you *want* to drink, tell me? You haven't a body to be hungry or thirsty—it's buried in Lydia somewhere; you're a spirit—how can you still be thirsty or drink?

TANTALUS. That's just what my punishment is—my spirit's thirsty as if it were my body.

MENIPPUS. Well, I'll believe you, if you say thirst's your   *2* punishment. But what are you frightened of then? Afraid you'll die if you don't get a drink? I can't see any other Hades after this. You can't die here and then go somewhere else.

TANTALUS. No, you're quite right. And that's part of the sentence, wanting to drink when I don't have to.

MENIPPUS. Rubbish, Tantalus. You need a drink all right —straight hellebore.[47] People are afraid of water when they're bitten by mad dogs, but you're the opposite—you're afraid of thirst.

TANTALUS. Menippus, I wouldn't say no even to hellebore if I could only get it.

---

[46] *Odyssey* XI. 602.
[47] The traditional cure for insanity.

MENIPPUS. Cheer up, Tantalus. Corpses don't drink, neither you nor anybody else; can't be done. But not everybody's condemned to be thirsty, like you, for water that won't wait for them.

18

Menippus and Hermes

1 MENIPPUS. Where are the handsome men and lovely women, Hermes? Show me around; I'm new here.

HERMES. Haven't time, Menippus. But just look over there to your right; there's Hyacinthus and Narcissus and Nireus and Achilles and Tyro and Helen and Leda—in fact, all the beauties of old.

MENIPPUS. I can only see bones and skulls without any flesh on them. Most of them look alike.

HERMES. Well, those are the people all the poets rave about—those bones you seem so contemptuous of.

MENIPPUS. Still, point Helen out to me; I can't recognize her.

HERMES. This skull is Helen.

2 MENIPPUS. And is this what those thousand ships sailed for from all over Greece? [48] Is this why all those Greeks and barbarians were killed? And all those cities sacked?

HERMES. Ah, but you didn't see the living woman, or else you'd have said the same yourself—that there was nothing reprehensible in "enduring troubles for years for such a woman." [49] If you look at withered flowers when they've lost their color, obviously you won't think them beautiful either. All the same they're very lovely when they're in bloom, when they're still colorful.

MENIPPUS. Well, Hermes, I'm surprised the Achaeans didn't realize it was such an ephemeral thing they were fighting about—and how soon its beauty would fade.

[48] The original of Marlowe's famous line, *Doctor Faustus,* sc. 13.
[49] *Iliad* III. 157.

HERMES. Menippus, I haven't time to moralize with you. You choose a place, anywhere you like, to lie down; I've got to go and fetch the rest of the dead now.

19

Aeacus and Protesilaus

AEACUS. Protesilaus, why attack Helen? Why try to throt-tle her?

PROTESILAUS. Because it's her fault that I died and left my house half-built and my newly married bride a widow.[50]

AEACUS. Well, I think it's Menelaus' fault, for taking you all to attack Troy for a woman like that.

PROTESILAUS. Yes, that's right; it's Menelaus I should blame.

MENELAUS. Not me, my dear fellow; it's much more rea-sonable to blame Paris. He ran off with my wife—and I was his host! It was very wicked. It would serve him right to be throttled by all the Greeks and Trojans too, not just you. Think of all the men he brought to their death!

PROTESILAUS. That's a better idea. You! Paris, you wretch! I'm never going to let you get away!

PARIS. Protesilaus, that would be unjust! And I'm one of your own craft! I'm a lover too, you know; the same god has me in his grip. You know we can't help it; a god drives us wherever he will, and we can't resist him.

PROTESILAUS. Yes, you're right. Well, I wish I could get hold of Eros here and now!

AEACUS. I'll make Eros' plea. He'll admit that perhaps he is to blame for Paris' falling in love; but he says your death, Protesilaus, is entirely your own fault, because when you reached the Troad you forgot all about your newly wed bride and jumped off the ship before anybody else. It was a

1

2

---

[50] A Thessalian, Protesilaus was the first Greek to land at Troy; as had been prophesied, he was killed almost immediately. See *Iliad* II. 701, and cf. *D. D.* 23 for another aspect of the legend.

foolhardy, silly thing to do. You fell in love with fame, and that's why you were the first to die in the landing.

PROTESILAUS. Then I'll make a stronger plea on my behalf, Aeacus. It isn't my fault, it's Fate's; it was my destiny all along.

AEACUS. Quite right. Then why blame present company?

20

Menippus and Aeacus

1   MENIPPUS. In Pluto's name, Aeacus, show me all around Hades.

AEACUS. Can't show you *all* around very easily, Menippus, but I'll give you an idea of the main things. You know this is Cerberus, and this is the ferryman who brought you over; the lake and Pyriphlegethon you've seen already on your way in.

MENIPPUS. Yes, I know all those, and I know you're the gatekeeper, and I've seen the king and the Furies. Show me the men of old—especially the famous ones.

AEACUS. Well, here is Agamemnon, here's Achilles, here's Idomeneus next to him; here's Odysseus; then there's Ajax and Diomede and the bravest of the Greeks.

2   MENIPPUS. So much for you, Homer! All your principal characters lying unknown and unrecognizable on the ground! All so much dust without any meaning! They're "strengthless heads" [51] and no mistake. Who's this, Aeacus?

AEACUS. Cyrus; and this is Croesus; beyond him Sardanapalus; beyond them again is Midas. That's Xerxes over there.

MENIPPUS. Well, well, well! Look at the wretch! Are *you* the man Greece was so scared of? Building bridges across the Hellespont and trying to sail through mountains! [52] And look at Croesus too! And Sardanapalus—Aeacus, let me clout his jaw for him!

[51] A stock phrase in Homer; see *Odyssey* XI. 29, for example.
[52] Xerxes' bridge of boats and canal through Mount Athos; see Herodotus, VII. 22 and 35.

AEACUS. Goodness me, no! You'll fracture his skull, and it's only a ladies' model.

MENIPPUS. Fairy! Well, anyway, I'll spit at him!

AEACUS. Like to see the wise men as well? *3*

MENIPPUS. Heavens, yes!

AEACUS. Here we have Pythagoras, to start with.

MENIPPUS. Hello there, Euphorbus or Apollo or who-ever! [53]

PYTHAGORAS. Drop dead!

MENIPPUS. Thigh not gold now? [54]

PYTHAGORAS. Oh, no. Anything to eat in your bag?

MENIPPUS. Beans, my dear chap. *You* can't eat them.[55]

PYTHAGORAS. Just you give me them. Doctrines are different down here. I've discovered there's no connection here between beans and our parents' heads.

AEACUS. Here's Solon, the son of Execestides, and there's *4* Thales, and there's Pittacus and the rest next to them—seven all told, as you can see.[56]

MENIPPUS. They're the only serene and cheerful ones of the lot. Who's that covered in ash like a loaf baked in embers? He's blistered all over.

AEACUS. Empedocles. He was half-roasted when he got here from Etna.[57]

MENIPPUS. My dear brassfoot, why did you jump in the crater?

EMPEDOCLES. A fit of melancholy.

MENIPPUS. Oh no it wasn't! It was your vanity and pride; it was your boundless folly. That's what got you cooked, you and your slippers. And it serves you right. But your clever

---

[53] A reference to Pythagoras' theory of the transmigration of souls; cf. *Cock* 4.

[54] A tradition concerning Pythagoras; cf. *Cock* 18.

[55] Beans were forbidden by Pythagoras; cf. *Cock* 18.

[56] The "Seven Wise Men." Lists of them vary in ancient sources; here Lucian mentions three of the commonest candidates.

[57] He was said to have died by leaping into the crater of Etna, from which his shoe was later cast up.

dodge didn't work—you were caught dead.[58] And what about Socrates, Aeacus? Where's he?

AEACUS. Oh, him! He's usually talking drivel with Nestor and Palamedes.[59]

MENIPPUS. I'd like to see him, though, if he's about.

AEACUS. See the bald man?

MENIPPUS. They're all bald; you could tell them all that way.

AEACUS. The one with the snub nose, I mean.

MENIPPUS. Just the same; they've all got snub noses.

SOCRATES. Looking for me, Menippus?

MENIPPUS. The very man!

SOCRATES. How are things in Athens?

MENIPPUS. Lots of young lads pretending to be philosophers—very models of philosophers too, the way they dress and walk.[60]

SOCRATES. I've seen any number of them.

MENIPPUS. Yes, and I suppose you saw what Aristippus was like when he joined you, and Plato himself—one stinking with perfume and the other a past master at toadying to Sicilian tyrants.[61]

SOCRATES. What do people think of me?

MENIPPUS. You're a lucky fellow that way, Socrates; anyway, they all think you were a remarkable chap and knew everything—when, if I'm not mistaken, you knew nothing.

SOCRATES. That's what I kept telling them myself, but they thought I was pulling their legs.[62]

---

[58] He wanted to suggest that he had been translated to heaven, but the evidence of his shoe proved that he had committed suicide.

[59] Nestor was talkative, Palamedes clever; cf. *Story* II. 17.

[60] One of Lucian's favorite themes is the contrast between the appearance and the behavior of philosophers; see *Hermotimus* 18 and 80, for example.

[61] This is Lucian's cynical interpretation of Aristippus' doctrine of hedonism and Plato's political experiment in Sicily. See *Sale* for other satirical summaries of philosophical doctrines.

[62] A reference to the famous Socratic "irony"; Socrates criticized others' "knowledge" while protesting, sincerely, that he himself knew nothing, except that he knew nothing. Cf. *Hermotimus* 15, n. 9.

MENIPPUS. Who are these people you've got with you? 6

SOCRATES. Charmides and Phaedrus and Clinias' son.

MENIPPUS. Good old Socrates! Still in practice even here! Still fond of pretty boys! [63]

SOCRATES. Can you think of a better occupation? Look, why don't you lie down and join us?

MENIPPUS. Heavens, no! I'm off to settle by Croesus and Sardanapalus. It should be great fun to listen to them moaning.

AEACUS. Well, I'm off now, too—don't want dead men giving us the slip. You can see the rest some other time, Menippus.

MENIPPUS. Off you go—that's enough for me, thanks.

21

Menippus and Cerberus

MENIPPUS. Cerberus—I'm a dog [64] too, you know, so we're related—tell me, by the Styx, how Socrates behaved when he came to join you.[65] Since you're a god, I expect you can speak like a human being when you want to, as well as bark. 1

CERBERUS. Well, when he was a long way off he didn't seem to be showing any fear on his face as he approached. He didn't look frightened of death at all, and it looked as if he were trying to give that impression to the people standing outside by the entrance. When he ducked down inside the opening, though, and saw how murky it was, he began to hang back. I gave him a nip with the hemlock [66] and dragged him in feet first. Then he began to howl like a little baby—he whimpered about his own children and did all sorts of things.

---

[63] All these young men figure as Socrates' companions in Plato's dialogues. Clinias' son is Alcibiades. Lucian treats Socrates' relationship with them cynically, but cf. Plato, *Symposium* 219.

[64] This is a play on words; see *D. D.* 1. 1, n. 2.

[65] See Plato, *Phaedo* 116–18 for Plato's moving account of the death of Socrates in prison.

[66] "With the hemlock" may be a gloss.

2   MENIPPUS. The beggar was just talking, then—he wasn't really indifferent to death?

CERBERUS. No! When he saw there was no way out, he tried to put a bold face on it; he pretended he was looking forward to what has to happen to everybody, but that was to impress his audience. In fact, I could generalize about all that kind—stout, courageous fellows as far as the entrance, but the real test comes inside.

MENIPPUS. What did you think of the way *I* came?

CERBERUS. A credit to philosophy, Menippus; you're the exception—you and Diogenes before you. No need for any strong-arm methods—you came in readily, without having to be pushed, laughing away, and telling everybody else to go hang.[67]

22

Charon and Menippus

1   CHARON. Come on, damn you—your fare!

MENIPPUS. Shout away if you like, Charon.

CHARON. I've brought you across—give me my fare.

MENIPPUS. Can't. Haven't got it.

CHARON. Anybody's got an obol.[68]

MENIPPUS. Don't know about anybody else—I haven't.

CHARON. Why, damn you, by Pluto. I'll throttle you if you don't pay!

MENIPPUS. And I'll clout you with my stick and crack your skull.

CHARON. You'll have sailed all that way free!

MENIPPUS. Hermes can pay for me; he gave me to you.

2   HERMES. Huh! I'll get rich if I even have to *pay* for the dead!

CHARON. I won't let you off.

---

[67] According to tradition, Menippus hanged himself; cf. *D. D.* 10. 9–13.

[68] The coin put in a corpse's mouth to pay Charon for ferrying it across the Styx; cf. *D. D.* 1. 3.

MENIPPUS. You can dock your ferry and wait, for all I care. How can I give you what I haven't got?

CHARON. Didn't you know you had to bring it?

MENIPPUS. I knew—but I hadn't got it. So? Oughtn't I to have died, then?

CHARON. So you're going to brag about being the only one ever to cross free?

MENIPPUS. Not free, my dear fellow; why, I bailed, and I lent a hand at the oar, and I didn't cry—I was the only passenger who didn't cry.

CHARON. That's nothing to do with me. You've got to pay your obol; it isn't right to get out of it.

MENIPPUS. All right—take me back to life. *3*

CHARON. Oh, a fine idea—then get a thrashing from Aeacus for it?

MENIPPUS. Don't bother me, then.

CHARON. Let's see what's in your bag.

MENIPPUS. Lupines—want some? And a Hecate's supper.[69]

CHARON. Where did you get this dog from, Hermes? The way he went on, too, during the crossing! Laughing and jeering at all the passengers! He was the only one singing; they were all moaning.

HERMES. Don't you know who it is you've brought across? He's independent, no doubt of that—couldn't care less for anybody. That's Menippus.

CHARON. If I ever catch you again——!

MENIPPUS. *If* you catch me. You won't catch me twice.

23

Protesilaus, Pluto, and Persephone

PROTESILAUS. Lord! King! Our Zeus! And Demeter's *1* daughter! Don't say no to a lover!

PLUTO. What do you want from us? Who are you?

---

[69] Austere philosophers' fare and sacrificial offerings; see *D. D.* 1. 1 and n. 3.

PROTESILAUS. Protesilaus, son of Iphiclus, of Phylace. I was in the Greek army—I was the first man to be killed at Troy. What I want is to be released for a bit to go back to life.[70]

PLUTO. Is that what you're in love with? They're all in love down here at that rate, but none of them gets his way.

PROTESILAUS. Oh, but it isn't life *I'm* in love with, lord of Hades; it's my wife.[71] We were newly married; she was still in the bridal bed when I left her to sail off. And then I had the damnable luck to be killed by Hector when we landed. I love her, my lord, and it's torture. Let her see me just for a short time, then I'll come back again.

2   PLUTO. Haven't you drunk your Lethe-water? [72]

PROTESILAUS. Oh yes, sir, I have; but this is too strong for it.

PLUTO. Well, just wait. She'll be here sooner or later—then you won't need to go back.

PROTESILAUS. Pluto, I can't bear to wait! You've been in love yourself before now—you know what it's like! [73]

PLUTO. Look, what good will it do you to go back to life for one day? You'll only be just as miserable again very soon.

PROTESILAUS. I think I can get her to follow me down here; you'll soon have two dead instead of one.

PLUTO. No, can't be done; it isn't right. Never happened before.

3   PROTESILAUS. Let me jog your memory, Pluto. You gave Eurydice back to Orpheus for the very same reason, and you sent my own cousin Alcestis back as a favor to Hercules.

PLUTO. Do you want that pretty wife of yours to see you like that? You're not very lovely—just a bare skull. She won't be able to recognize you—why should she let you in? I'm sure

---

[70] See *D. D.* 19 for another treatment of Protesilaus' case.

[71] Laodamia. She killed herself after Protesilaus' brief return.

[72] Lethe was the river of forgetfulness in Hades; see *D. D.* 13. 6 and n. 31.

[73] Pluto, also called "Hades," had abducted Demeter's daughter, Persephone, to the underworld.

she'll be frightened and run away from you; then you'll have made that long journey up to earth for nothing.

PERSEPHONE. You see to that yourself then, my dear. Tell Hermes to touch Protesilaus with his wand as soon as he reaches the light and make him young and handsome again, as he was when he left the bridal chamber.

PLUTO. Seeing that Persephone supports him, take him away and make him a bridegroom again. But mind—you get one day.

24

Diogenes and Mausolus

DIOGENES. Carian, what are you so high and mighty about? What makes you think you're better than the rest of us?

MAUSOLUS. Well, Sinopean, I was a king to start with— king of all Caria. I ruled part of Lydia; I subdued islands; I crossed and conquered most of Ionia as far as Miletus. Then I was tall and handsome and a mighty warrior. But the greatest thing of all is the enormous monument [74] I'm lying under in Halicarnassus; it's bigger and more beautifully finished than any other dead man's—the finest of stone, and statues of men and horses, absolutely lifelike. You could hardly even find a temple like it. High and mighty? Well, that's why —do you wonder?

DIOGENES. Your royalty and good looks and massive monument?

MAUSOLUS. That's right.

DIOGENES. But my handsome Mausolus, you're not strong and good-looking any more. If we were to pick someone to decide who's better-looking, I see no reason why he should choose your skull rather than mine. They're both bald, and neither has any flesh on it. We're both showing our teeth, we've both lost our eyes, we both have snub noses. I suppose your vault and all that expensive stone might serve for Hali-

[74] His "mausoleum."

carnassus to brag about—they've something to show off to visitors with a building like that—but I can't see what good it does you, my dear chap. Unless you want to say you've a heavier burden to bear than we have, with all that stone to weigh you down.

3   MAUSOLUS. None of it's going to be any good to me, then, all that? Mausolus won't be any better off than Diogenes?

DIOGENES. Any *better* off? My royal friend, he'll be *worse* off! Just think—Mausolus'll start moaning every time he remembers his earthly prosperity, as he called it, Diogenes'll laugh at him. Mausolus'll talk about the vault his wife and sister [75] Artemisia built for him at Halicarnassus, Diogenes doesn't know whether he even has a grave for his body; he didn't give a damn about it, he lived a man's life, and that's *his* life story; and for anybody worth his salt, you servile Carian, it's a loftier monument than yours—and built on firmer ground.

25

Nireus, Thersites, and Menippus

1   NIREUS. Look, Menippus here'll decide which of us is better-looking. Menippus, don't you think I am?

MENIPPUS. I think you'd better tell me who you actually are first.

NIREUS. Nireus and Thersites.

MENIPPUS. Which is which? I can't tell yet.

THERSITES. One point for me right away. I'm just the same as you; you aren't as outstanding as our blind friend Homer claimed—saying you were the handsomest man on earth! My skull's a funny shape, and I was thin on top, but Minos didn't think I looked any worse than you.[76] Come on, Menippus, which of us do *you* think is handsomer?

NIREUS. Me, of course; I'm Aglaea and Charops' son, "the fairest man who came below Troy towers." [77]

---

[75] The wife and sister were one and the same.
[76] Homer represented him as ugly; see *Iliad* II. 217–19.
[77] *Iliad* II. 673.

MENIPPUS. But not the fairest man who came below the
earth as well, as far as I know. Bones are all alike. The only
way of distinguishing your skull from Thersites' is that yours
wouldn't take much cracking; it's fragile—not very masculine.

NIREUS. All right—you ask Homer what I was like when I
was in the Greek army.

MENIPPUS. Daydreams. I'm talking about what I see in
front of me, what you are now. What you were once only your
contemporaries know.

NIREUS. Am I not better-looking here, then, Menippus?

MENIPPUS. Nobody's good-looking, neither you nor anyone else. There aren't any distinctions in Hades; everybody's
equal.

THERSITES. Suits me.

26

Menippus and Chiron

MENIPPUS. Hello, Chiron! I hear you wanted to die, even
though you're a god?

CHIRON. Hello, Menippus. Yes, that's right. I could have
been immortal if I'd wanted, but I've died, as you see.

MENIPPUS. Why this passion for death, then? Most people
aren't too fond of it.

CHIRON. I'll tell you; you'll understand. It wasn't any
pleasure any more, taking advantage of my immortality.

MENIPPUS. No pleasure in being alive and seeing the light
of day?

CHIRON. No, Menippus. *My* idea of pleasure is variety,
not monotony. I kept on living, with the same things there for
me to enjoy all the time—sun, daylight, food, the same seasons,
everything going on in sequence as if one thing were chained
to the next. Well, I got fed up with it. The fun wasn't in
having the same thing all the time; it was in *not* having it
sometimes.

MENIPPUS. That's true. Well, you wanted to come to
Hades; how do you like it now you're here?

2   CHIRON. Not bad, Menippus. Everybody's equal; that's very democratic. And it's all one whether you're in light or darkness. Then again, there's no need to go hungry or thirsty, as people do on earth; we're free of all that.

MENIPPUS. Careful you don't trip yourself up, Chiron. What you say might backfire.

CHIRON. How do you mean?

MENIPPUS. You got fed up with the monotony, the constant similarity of life. Things are the same here too. You might get fed up with them the same way. You'll have to look for a change, and move to some other life—which I don't think you can do.

CHIRON. Well, what can one do then, Menippus?

MENIPPUS. Be sensible and make the best of it, as they say, I suppose; put up with things as they are, and don't get the idea you can't stand it.

27

Diogenes, Antisthenes, and Crates

1   DIOGENES. Well, you two, we've nothing to do; why don't we go for a walk? Let's make for the entrance and have a look at the people coming in—see what they're like and how they all behave.

ANTISTHENES. Let's go; it'll be fun to watch them crying or begging to be set free. Hermes'll have the devil's own job with some of them; even when he's pushing them forward head first they'll dig their heels in and resist with all their might—though they've no call to.

CRATES. I'll tell you what I saw on the way down.

DIOGENES. Go ahead, Crates; some comic sights, I bet.

2   CRATES. Well, there were many more on the journey besides me. Some distinguished people too—Ismenodorus, a rich man from my own town,[78] Arsaces the governor of Media, and Oroetes of Armenia. Well, Ismenodorus had been murdered

---

[78] Thebes.

by brigands at the foot of Mount Cithaeron—on his way to Eleusis, I suppose—and he was groaning away, clutching his wound with both hands and calling out his children's names— they were just tiny when he died. He kept reproaching himself for being so rash; he went over Cithaeron and traveled through the Eleutherae district, which was deserted because of the war, taking only two servants although he had five gold bowls and four cups on him. Arsaces was getting on by now, of course, but he was still an impressive sight, by Jove! He was showing his temper like a real barbarian—got annoyed because he had to walk on his own legs, and kept demanding to have his horse brought to him. His horse had been killed at the same time as he had, you see; in fact they'd both been skewered with the one thrust by a Thracian peltast in the skirmish with the Cappadocians on the Araxes. Well, Arsaces told us how he'd got way ahead of the rest and was charging forward when the Thracian stood his ground, crouched behind his buckler, warded off Arsaces' lance, and drove his own spear through Arsaces and his horse from underneath.

ANTISTHENES. How could he do that with one thrust?

CRATES. Very easily. Arsaces was charging down with a thirty-foot lance. The Thracian pushed it aside with his buckler and the point went past him; then he went down on one knee, received the charge with his spear, and got the horse in the chest. The animal was so spirited and fiery that it speared itself right through, and Arsaces was speared through as well from groin to buttocks. You see what had happened—it wasn't the man who did it, it was the horse. Anyway, Arsaces didn't like being treated the same as everybody else; he demanded to travel down here on horseback. As for Oroetes—well, he was very tender-footed; couldn't even stand up, let alone walk. They're all the same, these Medes, every one of 'em; the minute they're off their horses they can hardly walk—look as if they're tiptoeing on thorns. So, when he threw himself down on the ground and lay there absolutely refusing to get up, our excellent Hermes picked him up and carried him all the way to the ferry. It made me laugh.

6   ANTISTHENES. Me too, when I came down. The others were moaning away, but I didn't mix with them at all. I slipped off and ran ahead to the ferry to get a good seat for the crossing. They were blubbering and being seasick all the way across; it was great fun.

7   DIOGENES. Well, that's the kind of company you two had. I had Blepsias the moneylender from the Piraeus, and Lampis the Acarnanian mercenary, and Damis the Corinthian millionaire with me. Damis had been poisoned by his son, Lampis cut his own throat for love of the courtesan Myrtium, and Blepsias was supposed to have starved to death, poor fellow; he looked it, too—pale as anything and thin as a rake. I asked them how they'd died—I knew very well, of course. Damis blamed his son. I told him it served him right: "There you are," I said, "ninety and living off the fat of the land, millions in the bank, and you give an eighteen-year-old boy a few obols pocket money. What do you expect the lad to do?" The Acarnanian was moaning to himself too and cursing Myrtium. "Why blame love?" I said. "It's yourself you ought to blame; you were never scared of any enemy, you fought like a tiger right in the front line, and yet you're caught by the first tart you come across who can turn on a few tears and sobs. Fine fellow you are!" Blepsias was only too ready to blame himself, though. He called himself an utter idiot for saving his money and letting people who meant nothing to him inherit it—silly beggar, thought he wasn't going to die. It was extraordinarily amusing, though, to listen to them moan-

8   ing. But here we are at the gate! We must watch for them appearing in the distance. Hey! Look at the crowd! All shapes and sizes! And all in tears except the newborn infants! Even the oldest wailing; how come *they* love life so much—are they

9   drugged? Look, I must ask this old chap. Why the tears, dying at your age? My dear fellow, you lived for ages before you came here—what's biting you? Or perhaps you were a king?

BEGGAR. Not by a long shot.

DIOGENES. A governor, then?

BEGGAR. Not a governor either.

DIOGENES. Well, were you rich? Is that what's bothering you about dying—leaving all your luxury behind you?

BEGGAR. No, no, nothing like that. I was nearly ninety, I could barely make a living fishing, I was miserably poor, I hadn't any children, and on top of all that I was a cripple and almost blind.

DIOGENES. And you still wanted to live?

BEGGAR. Yes. Life was sweet and death is frightening. I wish I could escape it!

DIOGENES. You're out of your mind. An old man like you, as old as the ferryman, and you're kicking against the inevitable like a kid! What are we to say about young men now, when people at your age are still in love with life? You'd be better *chasing* death—to cure the troubles of old age. Well, we'd better go now; we'll get some nasty looks if people see us hanging about the entrance—they'll think we're trying to escape!

28
Menippus and Tiresias

MENIPPUS. It's a job to tell now whether you really are   *1*
blind, Tiresias. We're all the same, our eyes are gone—only the sockets left—and without the eyes you can't tell Phineus from Lynceus.[79] But I gather from poetry that you were a prophet, and the only person who was ever both male and female.[80] I'd love to know which is the better life in your experience. Which did you prefer, man's or woman's?

TIRESIAS. Oh, woman's, Menippus, easily. Less trouble. Women boss men about, they don't have to fight or man the battlements, they don't have to argue in parliament, they can't be questioned in court.

MENIPPUS. Yes, but haven't you seen Euripides' *Medea?*   *2*

[79] Phineus was blind; Lynceus ("the lynx") was the farsighted lookout on the Argo.

[80] Tiresias was transformed by Zeus into a woman; see Glossary for details of the legend.

Where Medea tells such a pitiful tale about being a woman—
what a sorry state it is, and what dreadful pain they have to
endure in childbirth? [81] But that Medea scene reminds me—
did you ever give birth when you were a woman? Or were
you barren, did you never have a child in that period?

TIRESIAS. Why do you ask?

MENIPPUS. Oh, it's not a hard question. Tell me, if it's
no bother to you.

TIRESIAS. Well, I wasn't barren, but I didn't actually have
a child.

MENIPPUS. That's fine; I just wanted to know if you were
physically capable of it.

TIRESIAS. Well, yes, obviously.

MENIPPUS. And did your female organs change gradually
and your male characteristics develop? Or did you change into
a man all at once?

TIRESIAS. I don't know why you want to know. I don't
think you believe it did happen.

MENIPPUS. Well, Tiresias, do you expect me to believe
that kind of thing? Do you expect me to accept it blindly, like
an idiot, without wondering whether it's possible or not?

3   TIRESIAS. I don't suppose you believe anything like that,
then? How about the stories of women becoming birds or trees
or beasts, like Aedon and Daphne and Lycaon's daughter? [82]

MENIPPUS. Oh, if I meet any of them, I'll see what *they*
have to say about it. But tell me, my dear fellow, could you
prophesy when you were a woman too, as you could later? Or
did you become a man and a prophet at the same time?

TIRESIAS. You see, you don't know the first thing about
me: you don't know how I settled an argument for the gods
and Hera struck me blind, and Zeus gave me the gift of
prophecy to make up for it.

MENIPPUS. Still clinging to your lies, Tiresias? Well, that's
like all prophets. You never do tell the truth.

[81] Euripides, *Medea* 230–51.
[82] Lycaon's daughter was Callisto.

29

Ajax and Agamemnon

AGAMEMNON. Look, Ajax, why blame Odysseus if you   *1*
went mad and killed yourself—and did your best to kill us too?
The other day you cut him dead when he came to consult the
oracle[83]—your friend, your comrade in arms, and you wouldn't
even speak to him! You strode past with your nose in the air.

AJAX. I should think so, too. He was the one who drove
me mad—the only man to contest my claim to the arms.

AGAMEMNON. Did you think nobody would challenge you?
Did you expect to beat everybody without having to fight for
it?

AJAX. Yes, I did, in a matter like that. The arms were
mine; it was my cousin they belonged to. The rest of you were
much better men than he was, but you didn't enter the contest; you gave way to me. But Laertes' son—why, I saved him
many a time when he looked as if he would be cut to pieces
by the Phrygians—he said he was a better man than I was, and
had a better claim to the arms.

AGAMEMNON. Well, my good Ajax, surely it was Thetis'   *2*
fault? She brought the arms and handed them over to the
Greeks as a body, when she should have let you inherit them,
since you were a relative.

AJAX. No, it's Odysseus' fault. He was the only one who
opposed my claim.

AGAMEMNON. Forgive him, Ajax. He was human; he was
only looking for glory—the sweetest thing there is, the thing
every one of us risked his life for. And he did beat you, after
all—with a Trojan jury at that.

AJAX. I know very well what lady rigged that jury against
me; but one mustn't talk about the gods. As for Odysseus—I
couldn't help hating him even if Athena herself told me not
to.

[83] On his journey to the underworld; see *Odyssey* XI. 541–65.

‹ 30

Minos and Sostratus

1   MINOS. Hermes! Have this pirate Sostratus thrown into
Pyriphlegethon, the temple-robber torn apart by the Chimaera, the tyrant stretched out beside Tityus and his liver
eaten by vultures too. You good ones, off you go, quick as
you can, to the Elysian Fields and live in the Islands of the
Blest; that's your reward for the good deeds you did in life.

SOSTRATUS. Minos! Listen to me and see if my plea isn't
just!

MINOS. What, again, now? Haven't you been convicted,
Sostratus? You're a villain and a wholesale murderer!

SOSTRATUS. Yes, I've been convicted. But is my punishment really just?

MINOS. It certainly is—if it's just to get what you deserve.

SOSTRATUS. Yes, but give me an answer, Minos; it's only
a brief question I want to ask you.

MINOS. All right, but hurry up; there are all the rest waiting to be tried.

2   SOSTRATUS. What I did in life—did I do it of my own free
will, or had it been decreed me by Fate?

MINOS. Decreed by Fate, of course.

SOSTRATUS. So all of us, whether we got a good or bad
name, acted in obedience to Fate?

MINOS. Yes, in obedience to Clotho, who allots his actions
to everyone at birth.

SOSTRATUS. Now then, if a man is compelled by another
to kill somebody, and can't say no because he's under that
man's power—say a public executioner acting under judge's
order, or a bodyguard under a tyrant's—who is responsible for
the killing?

MINOS. The judge or the tyrant, obviously. You can't
blame the sword either; it's just a tool performing this service
for the anger of the man who incurred the responsibility in
the first place.

SOSTRATUS. Thank you for the illustration; it strengthens my case. And if someone brings you gold or silver in person but on the instructions of his superior, to whom are you grateful? Who goes down as your benefactor?

MINOS. The man who sent it. The man who brings it is only an agent.

SOSTRATUS. Then look how unjust it is to punish us! We're instruments of Clotho's decrees. And why reward the others? They're only agents for another's goodness. You certainly can't say any of us had the power to refuse; the instructions were binding.

MINOS. Sostratus, you'll find a lot more inconsistencies if you look close enough. Still, you can have your reward for your questions; you're not just a pirate, you seem to be a bit of an intellectual too. Let him go, Hermes, and cancel his punishment. But don't you go teaching the rest of the dead to ask that sort of question!

A TRIP TO HADES

1   CHARON. Well, Clotho, the boat's been ready for ages.
We're all set to go—bilges empty, mast up, sail on, oars all
fastened; we could weigh anchor and go right now, as far as
I'm concerned. It's Hermes who's keeping us back—he should
have been here long ago. Not one passenger on board—you
can see for yourself; we could have done the trip three times
already today, and now it's getting dark and I haven't taken
a penny. I know what Pluto's going to think; he'll say I've
been slacking, when it isn't *my* fault at all. It's that soul-con-
ductor—he's a fine fellow! He's drunk Lethe-water [1] upstairs,
just like any mortal, and now he's forgotten to come back
here. I bet he's wrestling with the lads or playing his lyre or
spouting speeches to show what drivel he can talk—if he isn't
picking somebody's pocket. Oh yes, he's a fine lad, that's one
of the things he's good at too. He's getting very cheeky to us;
why, he belongs to us, half of him!

2   CLOTHO. Oh, come, Charon, how do you know he isn't
busy? Perhaps Zeus suddenly needed him for some extra job
up top; he's part owner too, you know.

     CHARON. Yes, *part* owner. That doesn't mean he can do as
he likes with him; it isn't fair. We've never kept him down
here when it was time for him to go. No, I know what it
is. All we've got here is asphodel and libations and funeral
cakes and things that people offer to the dead, and besides,
it's so dark and misty and gloomy here, whereas it's bright
sunshine in heaven and there's plenty of ambrosia and as
much nectar as you want. So he prefers to hang about there, I
suppose. Look at the way he darts off when he leaves us; you'd
think he was escaping from prison. But when it comes time
to be back here, he can hardly drag himself along; he comes
on foot, and he takes his time about it too.

3   CLOTHO. Oh, relax, Charon, don't get so worked up. Look,

[1] Lethe was the river of forgetfulness in Hades; cf. *D. D.* 13. 6 and n. 31.

here he comes—speak of the devil! He's brought us a nice crowd—nice herd, more like, the way he's driving them on with that staff of his. Look, though—there's one all tied up, and another one who seems to think it's a great joke! And there's one with a knapsack, and a stick in his hand, keeping them all on the trot—that's a pretty fierce look in his eye! And look, there's Hermes himself! He's soaked in sweat! His feet are all dusty and he's panting fit to burst! What's up, Hermes? What's all the excitement? You do look bothered, I can tell you!

HERMES. What's up? It's this wicked beggar, that's what's up! He ran away—I've had to chase him all over the place. I nearly missed your boat today!

CLOTHO. Who is he? What was he trying to run away for?

HERMES. Oh, that's pretty obvious—he'd rather have stayed alive! He's a king or a tyrant or something—at least, so I gather; he keeps wailing and moaning about the wonderful life he's lost.

CLOTHO. And he tried to run away? Silly beggar! Did he think he could live any longer? His thread was finished!

HERMES. *Tried* to run away? He'd have made it if it hadn't been for my excellent friend here with the stick; he gave me a hand, and we caught him and tied him up. I tell you, he's been resisting from the minute Atropos handed him over to me—pulling me back and digging his heels in. I've had a hell of a job getting him here. And he's been begging me, positively pleading with me, every few minutes, to let him go just for a bit; promised me the earth if I would. Of course, I wouldn't; I could see he was asking the impossible. And then when we were right at the mouth, there I was counting the bodies off to Aeacus as usual, and he was checking them against the counterfoil your sister sent him, when this damned wretch slipped off somehow and I never saw him. So of course we were one short, and Aeacus raised his eyebrows at that. "Now then," he said, "you watch where you try your thieving tricks. You play that game quite enough upstairs. Down here we're very strict; nothing ever gets past us. Look here," he says, "one thousand and four the counterfoil says—it's down in black and white—and you turn up with one missing. Unless you're trying to tell me Atropos has cheated you?" Well, that did make me feel a fool; and then I suddenly remembered all that fuss on the way here. I looked around and *this* one was nowhere to be seen, and I realized he'd slipped off. So I began chasing him as fast as my legs would carry me, along the road back to life, and my excellent friend here volunteered to come with me. We shot off as if it were a race and caught him just as he was getting to Taenarus [2]—you see, he nearly managed it!

5   CLOTHO. And there we were accusing Hermes of neglect!

CHARON. Well then, what are we waiting for now? As if we hadn't had enough delay already!

CLOTHO. That's true—on they go, then. I'll get my notebook and sit by the gangplank as usual and take a note of all their names and where they came from and what they died of as they go on; you take them on board and pack them in. Hermes, put those babies on first. What could they have to say to me?

HERMES. All right. There you are, Charon, three hundred, counting those that were exposed.[3]

CHARON. Lord! What a haul! That's a cargo of green grapes you've brought me.

HERMES. Shall I put the unlamented on next, Clotho?

CLOTHO. The old people? Yes, I'm not going to bother digging up ancient history now.[4] Everybody over sixty, on you go now! What's up with them? Oh, they can't hear me—their

2 One of the traditional entrances to Hades, in the Peloponnesus; now Cape Matapan.

3 Exposure to the elements was a way of getting rid of unwanted babies; Oedipus is an example of such treatment.

4 Literally, "investigating events before Eucleides' time." In 403 B.C., during Eucleides' archonship, the oligarchy of the Thirty, established by *coup d'état* after the Peloponnesian War, was overthrown, and the restored democracy granted amnesty to all those involved in political misdemeanors under the Thirty. Hence τὰ πρὸ Εὐκλείδου, used here and elsewhere by Lucian, means "an old story best forgotten."

ears are stuffed with years. Well, I suppose you'll have to pick them up as well and carry them on.

HERMES. There you are. Next lot, three hundred and ninety-eight, nice and soft and ripe—matured before harvesting!

CHARON. I'll say they're mature—this lot have all turned to raisins.

CLOTHO. Bring on the wounded next, Hermes. Tell me how you died before you go on. Or no, I'll check you off against my papers myself. There should be——eighty-four died in battle yesterday in Media——including Gobares, the son of Oxyartes.

6

HERMES. Here they are.

CLOTHO. Then seven who committed suicide for love—including Theagenes, the philosopher who killed himself for the courtesan from Megara.

HERMES. Right here.

CLOTHO. Where are the men who killed each other fighting over the throne?

HERMES. Right beside you.

CLOTHO. And the man who was murdered by his wife and her lover?

HERMES. Right here.

CLOTHO. Now the victims of justice—those who were beaten to death and crucified. And where are the sixteen who were killed by pirates?

HERMES. Here they are—these wounded men you see here. Shall I put the women on with them?

CLOTHO. Oh yes, and the people who were shipwrecked too—they died the same sort of way. And the fever victims as well, the doctor Agathocles and all. Where's Cyniscus[5] the philosopher? He was due to die from eating a Hecate's supper and sacrificial eggs and a raw squid [6] on top of them.

7

[5] A diminutive, meaning "the little Cynic."
[6] The first two refer to purificatory offerings of food, often taken by the poor; see *D. D.* 1. 1, n. 3. Diogenes was said to have died from eating a squid; cf. *Sale* 10.

CYNISCUS. My dear Clotho, I've been here all the time. What did I do wrong, that you let me stay up there so long? Why, you gave me practically your whole spindle. And yet, you know, I tried often enough to cut the thread and get here, but somehow I just couldn't break it.

CLOTHO. I left you to keep an eye on human frailties and put them right.[7] All right, on you go; good luck to you!

CYNISCUS. Oh no I don't—not till we get this fellow here on, the fellow in chains. I'm afraid his entreaties might soften you up.

8   CLOTHO. Let's have a look at him. Who is he?

CYNISCUS. Megapenthes,[8] son of Lacydes, a tyrant.

CLOTHO. On you go!

MEGAPENTHES. Oh no, please, Clotho; let me go back for a bit—then I'll come myself, you won't have to send for me.

CLOTHO. What do you want to go back for?

MEGAPENTHES. Give me a chance to finish my house first. I left it half built.

CLOTHO. Poppycock! Get in there!

MEGAPENTHES. Lady of Fate, I don't want long—let me stay just this one day, to give me time to tell my wife about my money and let her know where I kept all my treasure buried.

CLOTHO. No, I won't. It's all settled.

MEGAPENTHES. All that gold going to go to waste, then?

CLOTHO. Oh no, it won't go to waste, don't you worry about that. Your cousin Megacles is going to get hold of it.

MEGAPENTHES. That's the limit! My enemy? Why, I'd have put him to death long ago, only I couldn't be bothered!

CLOTHO. That's the man. Well, he's going to survive you forty years, a bit more in fact. And he'll get your concubines and your robes and all your gold.

MEGAPENTHES. That isn't fair, Clotho! Giving my things to my worst enemies!

---

[7] The traditional role of the Cynic "street-corner preacher"; see Introduction, p. xvi, and *Sale* 10–11.

[8] The name means "great grief."

CLOTHO. Why, didn't it all once belong to Cydimachus? Didn't you kill him, my fine friend—and his children, right over his body, when he was still breathing—and take his property for yourself?

MEGAPENTHES. Well, it was mine just now.

CLOTHO. Well then, time's up. It isn't yours any longer.

MEGAPENTHES. Clotho, I want to have a word with you in private—you people stand aside a minute. Clotho, let me run away and I promise you a thousand talents of coined gold, today.

CLOTHO. Still got gold and talents on the brain? Don't make me laugh!

MEGAPENTHES. And I'll throw in those two bowls if you like, that I got when I killed Cleocritus—refined gold, a hundred talents each!

CLOTHO. Haul him on—doesn't look as if he's going to go on of his own free will.

MEGAPENTHES. I call you all to witness, the wall and docks aren't finished yet! I could have finished them if I'd had just five more days.

CLOTHO. Never mind, somebody else will do it.

MEGAPENTHES. Well, anyway, you must admit *this* is a reasonable demand.

CLOTHO. What?

MEGAPENTHES. To live long enough to subdue the Pisidians and impose taxes on the Lydians and build myself a big memorial and inscribe on it all the great military achievements of my life.

CLOTHO. My dear man, it's practically twenty years you're asking for, not just this one day!

MEGAPENTHES. Look, though, I'll give you security for my quick return! I'll even give you my favorite in my place, if you like.

CLOTHO. Aren't you a villain? The times you prayed he'd outlive you!

MEGAPENTHES. That was long ago. I've thought better of it now.

9

10

CLOTHO. He'll be here himself soon enough, don't worry. The new ruler will do away with him.

11 MEGAPENTHES. Well, one more request—don't refuse me this, my lady.

CLOTHO. What is it?

MEGAPENTHES. Tell me how things will turn out now I'm dead.

CLOTHO. All right—it'll hurt you all the more to hear it. Midas, your slave, will have your wife. He's been her lover long enough as it is.

MEGAPENTHES. Well, damn him! I set him free because she asked me to!

CLOTHO. Your daughter will join the ranks of the new ruler's concubines; all the images and statues the city dedicated to you so long ago will be knocked down to give people a good laugh.

MEGAPENTHES. Tell me, won't any of my friends protest?

CLOTHO. Friends? You never had any. What did you do to deserve friends? Get this straight: all those people who groveled before you and said how wonderful you were whenever you said or did anything—they were just scared stiff of you, or else they were out for themselves. It was your power they were so keen on. They just kept their eyes open for the main chance.

MEGAPENTHES. But look here—when they poured their libations at our drinking parties, they used to pray out loud for all kinds of blessings on me; there wasn't one of them who wouldn't have died for me if he could. Why, they—they swore by me!

CLOTHO. Yes, and that's why one of them did you in yesterday when you had dinner with him. It was that last drink he gave you that sent you down here.

MEGAPENTHES. So that was the bitter taste I noticed! But what did he want to do that for?

CLOTHO. You're too inquisitive. It's time you went on board.

12 MEGAPENTHES. Clotho, there is one thing that really

makes me choke—I was desperate to get back to life even for a few minutes and settle it.

CLOTHO. What is it? Sounds pretty formidable.

MEGAPENTHES. As soon as he saw I was dead, my servant Cario came into the room where I lay when it was getting dark; he had the chance, because nobody was even watching over my body. So he brought in my concubine, Glycerium—I suppose they'd been lovers for ages—shut the door, and went to it with her as if there were nobody else in the room. Then, when he'd had what he wanted, he looked at me and said, "You! You little blackguard! Many a thrashing you gave me for nothing!" And with those words he began to tear my hair out and hit me in the face, and he finished by coughing up his phlegm with a great coarse noise and spitting on me. "To hell with you!" he said, and off he went. I was flaming mad, but there wasn't a thing I could do to him; I was already stiff and cold. And that damned girl—she heard somebody coming, so she wet her eyes with spit as if she'd been crying over me, and went off weeping and wailing and crying out my name. If I could only get hold of them ——

CLOTHO. Oh, stop making threats and get on board, or else you'll be late for your trial.

13

MEGAPENTHES. Oh, indeed? And who's going to have the nerve to pass sentence on a tyrant?

CLOTHO. On a tyrant, nobody; but on a dead man, Rhadamanthus. He'll give every one of you a very just and fair sentence, you'll soon see. So don't waste any more time now!

MEGAPENTHES. My lady, make me an ordinary man, make me poor, make me a slave even instead of the king I was once —only do let me go back to life!

CLOTHO. Here, you with the stick, and you too, Hermes —grab hold of his legs and pull him on, since he won't go himself.

HERMES. Come on now, runaway, on you come! Here, Charon, he's all yours; and look—keep an eye on him!

CHARON. Don't you worry—I'll tie him to the mast.

MEGAPENTHES. Why, you ought to give me a first-class seat!

CLOTHO. Oh? Why?

MEGAPENTHES. Why? Heavens above, I was a tyrant! I had any number of guards!

CYNISCUS. Then it serves you right if Cario pulled your hair out, stupid! I'll give you tyranny—I'll give you a taste of my stick!

MEGAPENTHES. Cyniscus daring to shake his stick at me? Why, didn't I nearly have you pegged out the other day for letting your tongue run away with you and telling people off so much?

CYNISCUS. Yes, you did, and for that *you'll* stay pegged out—to the mast.

14   MICYLLUS.[9] Listen, Clotho, isn't anybody going to bother with me? Do I have to go on last because I'm poor?

CLOTHO. And who are you?

MICYLLUS. Micyllus, the cobbler.

CLOTHO. And you're grumbling about being left to the end? Why, look at the tyrant—promising us the earth if we'll let him go for a few minutes! You surprise me, I must say, not being as glad of the delay as he is.

MICYLLUS. Cyclops promised to eat Noman last;[10] but I can tell you, dear lady, that wouldn't cheer me up very much. First or last, the same teeth are waiting for you. Anyway, my case is quite different from the rich man's; our lives are poles apart, as they say. Take the tyrant for example. In life he had every appearance of happiness; everybody feared him, everybody's eyes were on him. When he had to leave behind all that gold and silver, all those clothes and horses and banquets, all those handsome boys and lovely women, naturally he didn't like it; he hated being torn from his possessions. The soul clings like a leech to these things somehow; it's always been attached to them and won't let go lightly. In fact, the bond that ties such people to life is practically unbreakable. Why, even if you drag them away by main force, they set up

9 The principal character in *Cock*, a typical "little man."

10 In the cave of the Cyclops, Odysseus, who had introduced himself as "Noman," was offered the favor of being eaten last; see *Odyssey* IX. 369.

a lament and fall at your feet; they may be brave in every other way, but over this journey to Hades they prove cowards— they turn back, and like rejected lovers they try to look on the world of light even from afar; as that fellow did, though it did him no good—skipping off on the way here, and, when he was here, begging you most piteously to let him go. But *I* had no stake in life—no land, no house, no money or property, no reputation, no statues. So of course I was traveling light, and Atropos had only to give a nod in my direction. I threw away my knife and leather—I was working on a boot—gladly, and jumped up and followed without stopping to put my shoes on or wash the dirt off me. Followed? I led. I faced forwards. There was nothing I left that would make me turn round, nothing to call me back. And, by heaven, already I can see I shall like everything here. What I like more than anything, myself, is that everybody has equal rights and nobody is better than his neighbor. I don't suppose you have to pay debts or taxes—and above all you don't freeze in winter, or fall ill, or get beaten up by the powerful. Everyone's at peace, and the tables are turned—we poor men do the laughing, while the rich are miserable and bemoan their lot. *15*

CLOTHO. Yes, I've noticed you laughing for some time, *16* Micyllus. What was it in particular that amused you?

MICYLLUS. I'll tell you, my dearest goddess. I lived next door to the tyrant on earth, and had a very good view of what went on at his house. Then, I thought him—well, godlike. "Blessed" was my word for him, when I saw the full bloom of his purple robe, his swarm of lackeys, his gold plate, his jeweled goblets, his couches with their silver legs; and the smell of his dinner being cooked drove me out of my mind. I thought him more than mortal man, I thought him triply blessed—I could almost think him better-looking and two feet taller than anyone else; there he was, riding fortune's wave— majestic of movement, haughty of carriage, a figure of awe to everyone he met. And then he died. He looked ludicrous enough in himself, stripped of his finery, but I laughed still more at myself for marveling at such trash—thinking him

happy because his dinner smelled good, congratulating him
on the blood of a shellfish from the Laconian Gulf. And he
wasn't the only one. I saw Gnipho the moneylender as well,
bewailing his lot, cursing himself for not making the most of
his money; he died without ever tasting it, and left all he had
to that unregenerate Rhodochares—who was his nearest relative and had first claim on it legally. I couldn't stop laughing,
especially when I thought how pale and unkempt he always
was, how worry had lined his brow. It was only his fingers that
were rich; they counted in hundreds and thousands as he
amassed money little by little, money that was soon to be
squandered by Rhodochares, lucky beggar! But let's go now.
We'll finish our laugh on the journey, as we see them crying.

CLOTHO. All aboard, so that the ferryman can haul up
the anchor!

CHARON. Here, you! Where do you think you're going?
We're full up. Wait here till tomorrow; we'll take you across
first thing.

MICYLLUS. That's not right, Charon, leaving a corpse
behind! I'm stale as it is! You watch out, I'll have you up in
front of Rhadamanthus for unconstitutional practices!—Well,
what a mess to be in! They're off already, "and I'll be left
behind here, all alone." [11] Wait a minute, though—why not
swim across after them? I don't have to worry about getting
tired and drowning—I'm dead to start with! And in any case
I haven't got an obol, so I couldn't pay my passage.

CLOTHO. Hey, what's he doing? Micyllus, you wait there!
You mustn't cross over like that!

MICYLLUS. Oh, mustn't I? I'll bet I beat you there!

CLOTHO. Oh, look, this won't do! We'd better row across
and pick him up. Hermes, you give us a hand.

CHARON. Where's he going to sit now he's here? We're
full up—you can see we are.

HERMES. Oh—on the tyrant's shoulders?

CLOTHO. Good idea.

11 The Greek sounds like a line from a comic play.

CHARON. Up you go then—get your feet on this criminal's neck. Right—let's go!

CYNISCUS. Charon, I'd better come clean with you right away. I can't give you an obol for the fare. All I've got is my knapsack here and this stick.[12] But I'll bail, if you like, or take an oar; you won't have any fault to find with me if you just give me a strong, well-balanced oar.

CHARON. All right, take an oar. That'll do for your fare.

CYNISCUS. Want a sea chantey as well?

CHARON. Oh, yes, certainly, if you know one.

CYNISCUS. Plenty. But look, we've got competition from these people crying; they'll throw us off the beat.

THE DEAD. Oh, my wealth! Oh, my estates! The house I left! The money my heir will inherit and throw away! My tiny babies! And who will harvest the vines I planted last year?

HERMES. Micyllus, have you nothing to moan about? You mustn't cross without, you know—it isn't right.

MICYLLUS. Oh, go chase yourself. I've nothing to cry about—I'm enjoying the sail.

HERMES. Still, let's have a bit of a moan—just a tiny one. Everybody does, you know.

MICYLLUS. All right then, Hermes, just to oblige you. Oh, my bits of leather! Oh, my old slippers! Alas, my rotten shoes! Oh, what misery! Nevermore to go hungry all day long! Nevermore to wander around in winter with no shoes and hardly any clothes! My teeth will never chatter with cold again! Who'll get my knife and awl?

HERMES. All right, that'll do. We're nearly there now.

CHARON. Come on now, let's have your fares before you go off. You too. There, that's everybody. Come on, Micyllus, you too—one obol.

MICYLLUS. You're joking, Charon. Anyway, if you aren't you might as well write on water, as they say, if you expect

20

21

---

[12] Traditional equipment for the Cynic philosopher; see *D. D.* 10. 2 and Introduction, p. xvi.

to get an obol out of Micyllus. I don't even know whether they're round or square, let alone have one.

CHARON. Huh! A good trip this! *Very* profitable! Still, off you get, all of you. I'll go and get the horses and cattle and dogs and the rest of the animals; they've got to come over now.

CLOTHO. Hermes, you take these people off. I'm crossing back myself to bring over those Chinese, Indopates and Heramithras—they killed each other fighting about boundaries.

HERMES. Right, men, let's go! No, wait—better if you all get into line and follow me.

22   MICYLLUS. Heavens, isn't it dark? Where's our handsome Megillus now? How can you tell whether Simiche's prettier than Phryne [13] in this? Everything looks the same: all the same color, nothing's pretty, not even anything prettier than anything else. Why, even my cloak—I always thought it looked ugly, but now it's just as good as the king's purple one—you can't see much of either of them, they both fade alike into the darkness. Cyniscus? Where on earth are you?

. CYNISCUS. Here, talking to you. Shall we walk together?

MICYLLUS. All right! Give me your hand. I suppose you were initiated at Eleusis? [14] Don't you think it's a bit like that here?

CYNISCUS. Yes, it is—look, there's even a woman coming with a torch! [15] My, doesn't she look frightening? Enough to scare you. I wonder if she's one of the Furies?

MICYLLUS. Probably is, the way she's dressed.

23   HERMES. Here you are, Tisiphone [16]—one thousand and four.

TISIPHONE. Well, I must say Rhadamanthus here has been waiting long enough for you.

RHADAMANTHUS. Put them in the dock, Tisiphone. Her-

---

[13] A courtesan and famous beauty of the fourth century B.C.

[14] The joke is that this would be highly unlikely for a Cynic, since mystic religions were among their pet hates.

[15] The Mysteries were carried on by torchlight.

[16] One of the Furies; the others were Alecto and Megaera.

mes, shout out the names and let's have them.

CYNISCUS. Rhadamanthus, please take me first, in the name of your father, and examine me.

RHADAMANTHUS. Why?

CYNISCUS. I simply *must* prosecute a tyrant; I saw all his dirty work on earth. And I wouldn't expect you to believe me unless you see first what I'm like and what kind of a life I lived.

RHADAMANTHUS. Who are you?

CYNISCUS. Cyniscus, sir, philosopher by bent.

RHADAMANTHUS. Come and stand trial first. Hermes, call the witnesses for the prosecution.

HERMES. Anybody who has anything to say against Cyniscus here, step forward!   24

CYNISCUS. Nobody comes.

RHADAMANTHUS. Oh, but that's not enough, Cyniscus. Take your clothes off, so that I can tell from the marks what you're like.

CYNISCUS. Marks? Where would I get any marks? [17]

RHADAMANTHUS. Every time you do anything wrong in life you get a mark; you can't see it, but you carry it about with you on your soul.

CYNISCUS. Well, there I am naked; have a look for these marks you're talking about.

RHADAMANTHUS. Oh, this one's quite clear—three or four marks, just, but they're very faint; you can hardly see them. Just a minute, though! What's this? Traces and marks of brandings—a lot of them! But they've been rubbed out somehow, or rather beaten out. What's all this, Cyniscus? How come you looked clean at first?

CYNISCUS. I'll tell you. I *was* wicked for a long time, just through ignorance, and piled up quite a few marks that way. Then as soon as I started to be a philosopher I gradually washed all the scars off my soul.

RHADAMANTHUS. Well, that's a very good remedy you

[17] The Greek word στιγματίας, "marked man," has the further meaning "rogue."

used—most effective. Off you go, then, to the Islands of the Blest, to join the virtuous people. But give your evidence against this tyrant of yours before you go. Hermes, let's have some more.

25   MICYLLUS. I'm the same, Rhadamanthus—a trivial case; won't take long to examine. In fact I've been ready stripped some time; go ahead and examine me.

RHADAMANTHUS. Who are you?

MICYLLUS. Micyllus, the cobbler.

RHADAMANTHUS. Good—no marks, quite clear. Off you go with Cyniscus here. Call the tyrant next.

HERMES. Megapenthes, son of Lacydes, step forward! Where are you twisting off to? Come on, get up there—you, the tyrant! It's you I'm calling! Push him to the front, Tisiphone. Give him a shove in the back.

RHADAMANTHUS. Cyniscus, state your charges and let's have your case; here's your man in front of you.

26   CYNISCUS. Well, really there's no need for me to say anything; you'll soon tell by his marks what he's like. Still, I'll uncover him myself for good measure. It'll be a bit clearer if I tell you. Well, this damnable villain—I'll leave out his deeds when he was an ordinary citizen—got a gang of thugs together as a bodyguard and imposed himself on the city as tyrant. He put over ten thousand people to death without a trial and by laying his hands on their property became enormously wealthy. There is no form of excess he has not given himself to. His wretched subjects suffered every variety of cruelty and outrage. He raped girls, he molested boys, he subjected his people to every kind of wanton insult. His contempt for others, his insolence, his arrogance toward anyone who had to do with him, could not possibly meet punishment severe enough. It would have been easier to look the sun straight in the eye than this man. His talent for inventing cruel punishments beggars description. Why, not even his own nearest kin were safe from him! And you can soon prove that this is not just malicious slander; call the people he murdered. No need to; they come unsummoned, as you see; there they are

crowding round him with their hands at his throat. All of these, Rhadamanthus, died at this villain's hands; some of them fell to his plots because they had beautiful wives, some because they protested when he dragged their sons off to outrage them, some because they were rich, and some because they were intelligent, sensible people and never approved his behavior for a minute.

RHADAMANTHUS. What have you got to say to that, you   27
miserable scoundrel?

MEGAPENTHES. I admit the murders he mentions; but all the rest—all that about adultery and outraging boys and raping girls—that's all lies from start to finish.

CYNISCUS. All right, Rhadamanthus, I'll get you witnesses for that too.

RHADAMANTHUS. What witnesses?

CYNISCUS. Hermes, call Megapenthes' lamp and bed. They'll come and tell you what they know very well he's done.

HERMES. Bed and lamp of Megapenthes! Forward! Good, they heard me; here they are.

RHADAMATHUS. Now, tell us what you know about Megapenthes here. You first, Bed.

BED. Cyniscus' charges are all true. But sir, I'm ashamed to talk about it—the things he did on me!

RHADAMANTHUS. All right—that's the best evidence we could have, if you can't bear to talk about it. You next, Lamp.

LAMP. I didn't see what went on in the daytime; I wasn't there. But what he did at night—and what others did to him—I don't like to say. I can tell you this, though: I saw any number of things that are beyond description, monstrous goings-on—outrageous isn't the word. In fact, many a time I deliberately didn't drink the oil, so that I'd go out; but then he actually brought me nearer to him and his behavior. He abused my light in every conceivable way.

RHADAMANTHUS. That's enough witnesses! Take off your   28
purple robe and we'll count your marks. Ye gods! He's livid all over! He's one mass of lines! In fact he's black and blue with marks! Now then, how are we going to punish him?

Throw him into Pyriphlegethon? [18] Or hand him over to Cerberus?

CYNISCUS. No, no! I tell you what—I can think of a novel punishment, just the thing for him. Shall I tell you what it is?

RHADAMANTHUS. Yes, do; I'll be very grateful to you if you will.

CYNISCUS. I understand it is the custom for all shades to drink Lethe-water?

RHADAMANTHUS. It is, yes.

CYNISCUS. Well, make him the only exception; don't let him drink it.

RHADAMANTHUS. What's the idea of that?

CYNISCUS. It'll be an awful punishment for him, remembering his condition and power on earth and constantly recalling the soft life he had.

RHADAMANTHUS. Splendid! That can be his sentence! Take him off and tie him up next to Tantalus to keep his earthly life in mind.[19]

[18] The "river of burning fire" in Hades.
[19] Tantalus was condemned to suffer eternal thirst in Hades; cf. *D. D.* 17.

THE COCK

MICYLLUS.[1] Damn that cock! Blast that screeching cock!   *1*
Won't give a man a minute's peace! Here I am having a
lovely dream—happy as could be, rich for once—and you wake
me up with your piercing, noisy racket! Even in bed I can't
get away from my threadbare life—and it's more damnable
than you are!—But everything's dead quiet! And usually I'm
frozen stiff in the mornings—that's the surest sign day's coming
—but I'm not now. It can't be midnight yet—and here's Wide-
awake squawking the minute it gets dark! You'd think he had
the Golden Fleece to guard. But he won't get away with it. I'll
get my own back, don't you worry, the minute day breaks—
I'll clout you one with my stick! But if I tried it now you'd
only flap about in the dark and cause a lot of bother.

COCK. Micyllus, my master, I thought I'd be doing you a
favor if I raced the night so that you could wake up and get
the best part of your work done nice and early. If you could
get even one boot finished before the sun rises, you'd be that
much farther on toward earning your bread for the day. But
if you'd rather sleep I'll be quiet if you want; I'll make less
noise than any fish. Only watch you don't dream you're rich
and wake up to find the cupboard bare.

MICYLLUS. Zeus of miracles! Hercules save me! What the   *2*
devil's this? A cock talking like a man?

COCK. A miracle, you think, that I speak your language?

MICYLLUS. Miracle? Heaven protect us!

COCK. That sounds very ignorant of you, Micyllus.
Haven't you read your Homer? Where Achilles' horse, Xan-
thus—*horse*, mark you—far from neighing, stands in the thick
of battle talking? Talking verse too, whole lines of it, not
just prose like me. And he was prophesying at that, foretelling
the future. But nobody thought there was anything odd about

---

[1] As in *Trip* 14 ff., Micyllus represents the "little man."

it. Nor did the man who heard him talking call on Hercules to save him, as you did; he didn't think he needed to be "protected" from what he heard. I wonder what you'd have done if the ship Argo had spoken to you? It did speak once. Or if the oak at Dodona had prophesied to you in its own voice? Or if you'd seen hides creeping about, and half-roasted beef bellowing away on the spit? [2] I spend a lot of time with Hermes, the most talkative and eloquent of all the gods; and besides, I live with you and as you do; so it's not surprising I find human speech easy. But if you promise to keep it to yourself, I don't mind telling you how it really comes about that I can speak to you in your own language.

3   MICYLLUS. Is this part of my dream, a cock talking to me like this? Anyway, my dear sir, in Hermes' name tell me what this other reason for your utterance is. I'll keep quiet about it, I won't tell a soul, don't you worry—who would believe anything I said on the authority of a talking cock?

COCK. Well, listen to my story—though I don't suppose you'll find it very credible. I, who am now speaking to you in the guise of a cock, was, not very long ago, a man.

MICYLLUS. Why, yes, of course, I did hear some such tale about cocks—oh, long ago. There was a young man called Alectryon [3] who was a friend of Ares—used to keep him company when he was drinking or went to parties, and gave him a hand in his love affairs; and every time Ares went to see Aphrodite when he was her lover, he took Alectryon along with him and left him at the door to give him the word when the Sun rose—he was terribly worried in case the Sun should catch him at it and tell Hephaestus. And then one day Alectryon dozed off and deserted his post; he didn't mean to do it, but the Sun came on Aphrodite and Ares without any warning—Ares was having a rest, and he wasn't on his guard be-

2 For these phenomena see *Iliad* XIX. 404 ff.; Apollonius Rhodius, *Argonautica* IV. 580 ff. (the Argo's hull contained wood from the talking oak of Dodona, which regularly uttered prophecies); and *Odyssey* XII. 395–6.

3 The Greek word for "cock." He does not figure in the usual version of this legend; see *Odyssey* VIII. 266–366.

cause he was expecting Alectryon to give him the word if anyone came near. And then of course Hephaestus got to know
about it from the Sun and caught them at it—threw the net of
chains around them that he'd had ready for them for a long
time. And when Ares was set free in the circumstances in
which Hephaestus let him go,[4] he was angry with Alectryon
and changed him, armor and all, into this bird, and he ended
up with the crest of his helmet still on his head. And that's
why you cocks let out a shout when you see the Sun rising,
long before it actually appears—you're trying to make it up
to Ares, though it's too late now.

COCK. Yes, there is that story too. But my case is quite
different; it's only very recently that I changed into a cock.

4

MICYLLUS. Oh, how? I'd love to know.

COCK. Have you ever heard of Pythagoras, the son of
Mnesarchus, from Samos?

MICYLLUS. The sophist? The fraud? The man who or-
dained that people shouldn't taste meat or eat beans? Forbid-
ding beans, indeed! Nothing I like better! And trying to make
people believe he was Euphorbus before being Pythagoras?[5]
They say he's a charlatan and a swindler.

COCK. Well, my friend, that's *me*, Pythagoras; so go easy
on the abuse, if you don't mind. You don't know what I was
really like.

MICYLLUS. Wonders on wonders! A philosophizing cock!
But go on, son of Mnesarchus, tell us how it is we see you in
cock shape instead of human. How come you turn up in
Tanagra [6] instead of Samos? It's all very unconvincing; I find
it very hard to believe. Why, I've already spotted two things
about you that aren't like Pythagoras.

COCK. What are they?

---

[4] Hephaestus invited all the gods to come and look at the adulterous
couple in his net.

[5] Lucian refers here to Pythagoras' theory of the transmigration of
souls; cf. *D. D.* 20. 3. "Sophist" here connotes "intellectual charlatan"; see
Introduction, p. ix.

[6] A town in Boeotia famous for game cocks.

MICYLLUS. First, you're talkative, in fact you make a dreadful racket; and Pythagoras, surely, recommended silence for five whole years at a time? And second—and this is completely contrary to your doctrine—when I came home yesterday I'd nothing to give you but some beans, as you'll remember, and you snapped them up without the slightest hesitation. So either you told me a lie and you aren't Pythagoras, or you are and you've broken your own laws. Why, eating those beans is as serious a sin as eating your father's head! [7]

5   COCK. Oh, but you don't understand the reason behind these laws, Micyllus. Different habits are appropriate to different incarnations. I used not to eat beans, because I was a philosopher; but now I may, because they're all right for birds, they're not forbidden for us. Look, though, if you like I'll tell you how I changed from being Pythagoras to this present form, and what lives I've lived, and how I've improved with successive transformations.

MICYLLUS. Go ahead; delighted to hear it. In fact, if I had the choice, I don't know whether I'd rather listen to your marvelous story or have that wonderful dream again that I was having a few minutes ago. They're very much alike, your tale and my heavenly vision, and I like you as much as I like my precious dream.

COCK. Why, are you still gloating over that dream, whatever it was? Still trying to cling to empty visions? You're just mentally chasing the ghost of happiness—"disembodied," [8] as the poet says.

6   MICYLLUS. My dear cock, I'll never forget that vision, I assure you. It dropped honey in my eyes and left me barely able to keep them open—it's closing them in sleep again. It tickled me like a feather in the ear.

COCK. Heavens, that really is some dream! They say dreams have wings but sleep's the limit of their flight. This

[7] A paraphrase of a verse falsely attributed to Pythagoras.

[8] A stock epic epithet, translated elsewhere as "strengthless"; cf. *D. D.* 20. 2 and n. 51.

one's broken the record; [9] it's living in wide-open eyes, you can see it quite plainly. Honey indeed—I'd like to know what it's like, to inspire such passion in you.

MICYLLUS. I'll tell you, gladly. It's a pleasure to recall it and describe it. But what about your transformations, Pythagoras? When are you going to tell me about them?

COCK. When you've finished with your dream and wiped the honey from your eyelids. You go first; I want to know which way your dream came, through the ivory gate or the gate of horn. [10]

MICYLLUS. Neither.

COCK. But those are the only two Homer speaks of.

MICYLLUS. Oh, never mind Homer, he's blathering; he doesn't know anything about dreams. Perhaps that's the way cheap dreams come, the kind he would see—though not very clearly at that, if he was blind himself. Mine was a lovely golden dream, clothed in gold and loaded with gold, and it came through golden gates.

COCK. Enough gold-gathering, Midas! That's certainly where your dream comes from, Midas' wish; you must have been dreaming gold mines.

MICYLLUS. Piles of gold I saw, Pythagoras, piles and piles of it, lovely beyond belief! The gleam that shone from it! What's that bit in Pindar where he praises gold? Can you recall the quotation? I can't remember it; he says water's best and then goes on to rave over gold, and quite right too. It's right at the beginning—best poem he ever wrote.

COCK. I think I know the one you mean:

Water is best; but gold like blazing fire
Gleams in the night excelling lordly wealth. [11]

[9] Literally "jumps beyond the pit dug"; according to tradition one Phayllus, in the course of an athletic contest, jumped farther than the fifty-foot-long pit prepared for the long jump.

[10] See *Odyssey* XIX. 562–67, and cf. *Story* II. 33.

[11] *Olympian Odes* I. 1–2.

MICYLLUS. Yes, that's the one! You'd think he'd had my dream, the way he goes on about gold. And now, my philosophizing cock, I'll tell you all about it. As you know, I didn't eat at home last night. I ran into Eucrates, the rich man, in the market place, and he invited me to come to dinner at the usual time, after my bath.

8   COCK. I'm well aware of that; I was starving all day till you came home very late, and tight; then you brought me those beans you were talking about—five of them; not much of a dinner for a cock who used to be an athlete—I entered the Olympics once, and didn't do badly.

MICYLLUS. Well, when I got back from dinner, I gave you the beans and went straight off to sleep; and then "through the ambrosial night," as Homer says, a really "divine dream" came to me.[12]

COCK. Let's hear about your dinner with Eucrates first, Micyllus. Tell me what the meal was like and how the drinking session went off. No reason why you shouldn't conjure up a daydream of your dinner and have it again. Think about what you had, chew the cud a bit.

9   MICYLLUS. I thought you wouldn't want to be bothered listening to that; but I'll tell you about it since you ask, Pythagoras. I'd never been to dinner with a wealthy man in my life; then yesterday my luck was in and I ran across Eucrates. I said hello to him, called him "Sir" as I always do, and then I started to leave; I didn't want to embarrass him by being seen with him in my old cloak. But he said, "It's my daughter's birthday today, Micyllus, and I'm giving a party; I've invited a lot of friends, but I hear one of them's not feeling well and can't join us at dinner. So you take your bath and come along in his place—that is, provided the man I invited doesn't send word he's coming after all; at the moment I don't know whether he is or not." Well, when I heard that I paid my respects and went off praying to all the gods to afflict him with a fever or pleurisy or gout—the man who was ill, I mean, the man whose place I was taking and whose

12 *Iliad* II. 56–57.

dinner I was to get. I thought the hours would never pass till it was time to get ready; I kept looking at the sundial to see what time it was and when I ought to have my bath. Eventually the time came, and I had a quick wash, dressed myself up smart—put my cloak on inside out, so as to show the clean side—and off I went. At the door I found a whole lot of others waiting, and lo and behold, who was there but the very man I was filling in for, the man who was supposed to be ill! And ill enough he looked, at that: lying on a litter carried by four slaves, and groaning to himself and coughing, a hacking cough deep in his chest, very unpleasant for anybody near him; he was all pale, and his flesh was puffy. He was a man of sixty, about, a philosopher apparently, one of those men who drivel at young lads; and certainly his beard was as long as any goat's.[13] And then, if you please, when Archibius the doctor told him he'd no business coming out in that condition, he said, "A man shouldn't neglect his duties, least of all a philosopher, even if he has a thousand things wrong with him that make life difficult. Eucrates would think me rude." "Oh no he wouldn't!" I said, "he'd be grateful if you'd stay at home to die, if you don't mind, instead of coughing up your last breath with your phlegm at his dinner table." He pretended he hadn't heard my remark—beneath his dignity— and in a minute Eucrates appeared, fresh from his bath. "Professor," he said when he saw Thesmopolis—that's the philosopher—"it was good of you to come in person, but you wouldn't have been any worse off even if you'd stayed away, for I'd have had all the courses sent over to you," [14] and as he spoke he began to lead Thesmopolis in by the hand, while his slaves supported him. So I got ready to leave, but Eucrates turned toward me and hesitated for some time; then, when he saw the disappointed look on my face, he said, "You come in and join us as well, Micyllus; I'll tell my son to go and eat with his mother in the women's quarters to make room

10

11

[13] Lucian is making fun of the solemn appearance of philosophers; cf. *D. D.* 20. 5 and *Hermotimus* 18.

[14] This would be quite normal procedure.

for you." So I went in, though I'd very nearly been licking my chops for nothing, like the wolf; [15] I felt a bit cheap getting Eucrates' boy put out of the dinner, as it would seem. Then it came time to take our places; but first they had to lift Thesmopolis up and set him in his place—and what a job it was too, goodness me! Took five strong lads, as I remember. Then they had to prop him up on every side with cushions so that he'd stay put and be able to last out a few hours. When it came to finding somebody to share his table, nobody fancied being next to him, and I was put there willy-nilly. And then came the meal! Any number of courses, all kinds of things, and all on gold and silver plate! Goblets of gold, handsome boys to wait at table, musicians and comic turns between the courses—oh, it was altogether a wonderful evening! Except that I found Thesmopolis very trying: he made a thorough nuisance of himself, the way he went on about "virtue" or something, and proving that two negatives equal one affirmative, and that if it is day, it isn't night; he even kept on telling me I'd got horns! [16] He went on and on like that, ramming his philosophy down my throat; I didn't want any of it. He quite spoiled my fun—I never got a chance to listen to the lyres and the singing. Well, friend cock, there's the dinner for you!

COCK. It can't have been very pleasant if you had to sit next to that driveling old idiot.

12   MICYLLUS. Well, now I'll tell you about my dream. Eucrates, I dreamed, had no children—I don't know how it came about—and was on his deathbed. He sent for me and made his will with me as sole heir; then, soon afterward, he died. When I came into the money, I found myself ladling out gold and silver, great bucketfuls of it, a never-ending stream of the stuff—the place was overflowing with it; and of course all the rest was mine too, clothing and tables and cups and servants. Then I drove out behind a pair of white horses, with my nose

[15] Who waited all day in vain for a mother to throw her baby to him, as she had threatened to do if it did not stop crying; see Aesop, *Fables* 275 (Teubner edn.).

[16] Typical Stoic fallacies; see *D. D.* 1. 2, *Sale* 21–25, and *Hermotimus* 81.

in the air and everybody staring at me and saying how lucky I was. There were any number of people running in front of me, people on horseback alongside me, more people yet behind; and there was I, wearing Eucrates' clothes and loaded with rings, a couple on each finger. I gave orders to lay on a splendid banquet to receive my friends; they all appeared there and then—that's the way things do happen in dreams. The meal was being served, the wine was being mixed, and in the middle of all this I was drinking everybody's health from golden cups; the cake was coming in, and then you went and crowed—a nice time to pick! You broke up the party, tipped up the tables, and scattered all that money to the four winds. Do you wonder I was annoyed with you? Why, that dream would have done me three nights, easily!

COCK. Gold! Money! Are you so fond of it, then? Is that all you can get excited about, is that your idea of happiness— possessing gold? 13

MICYLLUS. Oh, it isn't only me. You yourself, when you were Euphorbus, used to have your hair in gold and silver clasps when you took the field against the Achaeans—in battle, mark you, where iron gives you better protection; but even then you still chose to run the direst risks with your hair bound with gold. I suppose that's why Homer said your hair was like the Graces', "clasped with gold and silver." [17] No doubt it would look much better, much more charming, laced with gold; they'd offset each other's sheen. Of course, my dear Goldilocks, it's nothing to write home about *you* being fond of gold; you were only Panthous' son. But how about the father of all gods and men, the son of Cronus and Rhea? [18] When he fell in love with that girl in Argos, he couldn't think of anything nicer to change into, or any better way of getting past Acrisius' guards. You know the story, don't you? How he turned into a shower of gold and came through the roof to

[17] *Iliad* XVII. 52.

[18] Panthous was a Trojan priest, and the son of Cronus and Rhea was Zeus; hence the distinction is between a mortal and a god. The following story refers to Zeus's courtship of Danaë.

get to his beloved? Well then, what more need I say? Do I have
to tell you how many purposes gold serves, how it makes everybody who has it handsome and wise and strong, how it brings
honor to people and makes everybody look up to them, how
people that nobody used to know or think anything about
suddenly find themselves stared at in the streets, their names
on everyone's lips—because of their gold? I'll give you an example. You know Simon who lives down the street? He's a
cobbler too; he had dinner here not long ago, that time I
made soup for the Festival of Cronus,[19] with a couple of slices
of sausage in it.

Соск. Yes, I know him—the snub-nosed, stocky fellow.[20]
Pinched our pudding basin—the only one we had—and went
off with it under his arm when he went home; I saw him, with
my own eyes.

MICYLLUS. So it *was* Simon who pinched it! And then he
goes and swears by all the gods that it wasn't! Well, why
didn't you shout out? Why didn't you tell me there and then?
You could see we were being robbed!

Соск. I did crow—it was all I could do at the time. But
what about Simon? You were going to say something about
him.

MICYLLUS. He had a cousin called Drimylus who was
enormously rich, though he never gave Simon a cent when he
was alive—not surprising, because he never touched his money
himself. Well, this Drimylus died not long ago, and Simon
came into everything he had—and you should see him now!
Simon, whose clothes were always scruffy and ragged, Simon
who licked his plate—driving out proud as a peacock in his
carriage, in purple and scarlet robes! He's got servants and
horses and gold cups and tables with ivory feet; everybody
bows and scrapes before him, and he won't even look at me
these days. Why, the other day I ran into him and said "Hello,
Simon!" and he flew into a temper! "Tell that beggar not to

19 The mid-winter festival corresponding to the Roman Saturnalia.

20 This is a pun on the name "Simon"; the Greek word *simos* means
"snub-nosed."

14

abbreviate my name!" he said. "It isn't Simon, it's Simonides!" [21] And the way women go for him now—that's better still! He plays hard to get and looks down his nose at them; some of them he graciously admits to his company, but others he won't have anything to do with—and they go off saying they'll hang themselves! There you are—you see the blessings gold brings! Why, it even makes ugly people good-looking—it's like that girdle the poets speak of.[22] You know what the poets say:

> Gold, fairest gift of all

and

> For it is gold that rules mankind.[23]

What's the joke?

COCK. You're just like everybody else, Micyllus; you don't know what it's like to be wealthy, and you've got quite the wrong idea about it. Believe you me, their life's far more miserable than yours. I can say that, you see; I've been rich as well as poor, many a time, I've tried every kind of life. You'll hear all about it yourself soon.

MICYLLUS. Yes, goodness me, it's your turn now; tell me about your transformations. Tell me what you know about all those lives.

COCK. Well, here goes, then; but I'll tell you this before I start, that I've never seen anyone have a happier life than you.

MICYLLUS. Me! Well, if it's abuse you're looking for, you can have my life—and serve you right! Look, though, start from Euphorbus and tell me how you became Pythagoras and so on right up to the cock. I'll bet you've seen all sorts of things and been through a good bit too in all those different lives!

COCK. How my soul first flew to earth from Apollo's bosom and took on mortal shape, and why this sentence was

15

16

---

[21] A patronymic, suggesting noble lineage; cf. sec. 29 below.

[22] Aphrodite's; see *Iliad* XIV. 214–17.

[23] The first quotation is from the lost *Danaë* by Euripides; the author of the second is unknown. See Nauck, *Tragicorum Graecorum Fragmenta* (Leipzig: B. G. Teubner, 1889), 324 and adesp. 294.

passed upon me, would be a long story; and in any case, it would be sacrilege for me to utter or for you to hear such things. When I became Euphorbus———

MICYLLUS. Hold on a minute. Tell me, my wonderful friend, who was I before I became me? Have I ever been transformed like you?

COCK. Certainly.

MICYLLUS. Oh, do tell me who I was, if you can; I do want to know.

COCK. You? You were an Indian ant—a gold digger.[24]

MICYLLUS. Well, damn me! To think I hadn't the spirit to bring a bit of gold dust from that life to set me up in this one! Anyway, tell me what I'm going to be next as well—I expect you know. I tell you, if it's anything good I'll get up this minute and hang myself from that perch you're sitting on!

17　　　COCK. I couldn't possibly tell you that. Well now, to go back to when I became Euphorbus, I fought at Troy and was killed by Menelaus. Eventually I became Pythagoras—I waited about for a bit without a habitation, until Mnesarchus got one ready for me.

MICYLLUS. Without anything to eat or drink?

COCK. Of course; it's only the body that needs food and drink.

MICYLLUS. Well, tell me about Troy first. Was it as Homer says?

COCK. Homer? What would he know about it? He was a camel in Bactria when all that happened. I can tell you this much, there was nothing particularly remarkable about those days; Ajax wasn't as big as everybody thinks, or Helen as beautiful. I saw Helen; she was fair-complexioned, and very long in the neck—you could tell she was the daughter of a swan. For the rest—well, she was pretty long in the tooth as well, practically as old as Hecuba. After all, it was Theseus who was the first to run off with her—he kept her at Aphidnae—and Theseus was a contemporary of Hercules; and it was in our

[24] Herodotus, III. 102 speaks of ants that hoarded gold.

fathers' day (our fathers' at that period, I mean) that Hercules took Troy the first time—before the Trojan War, that is.[25] It was Panthous who told me all this; he said he'd seen Hercules when he was just a young lad.

MICYLLUS. Well, well. And what about Achilles? Was he such a fine fellow? Better than everybody at everything? Or is that just a tale too?

COCK. Achilles—well, I never came across him. In fact, I couldn't be so sure about the Greeks; after all, I was on the other side. His friend Patroclus didn't give me much trouble, though; I killed him—ran him through with my spear.[26]

MICYLLUS. Yes, and then Menelaus did the same to you, with less trouble still. That's enough of Troy, though; now tell me about when you were Pythagoras.

COCK. To tell you the honest truth, Micyllus, I was a sophist, and that's the top and bottom of it. Mark you, I wasn't without culture. I practiced polite learning, and I traveled to Egypt too, to imbibe wisdom from the priests there; I penetrated their inmost shrines and mastered the sacred books of Horus and Isis; and then I sailed back to Italy and made such a mark among the Greeks in those parts[27] that they thought me a god.

18

MICYLLUS. Yes, so I'm told. You were supposed to have risen from the dead, too, and I gather you showed them your golden thigh from time to time. Tell me though, what possessed you to make that law about not eating meat or beans?

COCK. Oh, don't ask me that, Micyllus.

MICYLLUS. Why not?

---

[25] Cheated by King Laomedon of his promised reward for a service to Troy, Hercules raised an army and captured the city.

[26] Either Lucian's recollection of the story is inaccurate, as in *D. D.* 12, or the cock exaggerates. In any case, the whole story of the *Iliad* is misrepresented. Euphorbus *wounded* Patroclus, and *Hector* killed him, thus incurring Achilles' wrath; this is what provides the motivation for the last three books of the *Iliad*.

[27] The colonies of Magna Graecia, where Pythagoras had a strong following; cf. below and *Sale* 6.

COCK. I'm ashamed to tell you the real reason.

MICYLLUS. Oh, look, don't be shy; we live in the same house, we're friends—I can't call myself your master now.

COCK. There was neither common sense nor philosophical theory behind it. The truth is, I realized that if I held the usual beliefs, like everybody else, people wouldn't take much notice of me; whereas the odder my views were, the more imposing they'd find me. And so I deliberately invented strange tenets while leaving the reasons for them mysterious, so that each person would make a different guess and everybody would be awestruck—as people are by those oracles you can't make head or tail of. There you are, you see! Now it's your turn to laugh at me.

MICYLLUS. Not so much at you as at the people of Croton and Metapontum and Tarentum and the rest, following you without a murmur and worshiping the very ground you trod on. What part did you step into when you'd finished playing Pythagoras?

COCK. Aspasia,[28] the courtesan from Miletus.

MICYLLUS. Fancy that! Then our Pythagoras has been a woman, among other things? Did you once lay eggs, my noble cockerel? Did you lie with Pericles when you were Aspasia— and carry his children? Did you card wool and spin yarn? Did you act the woman as a mistress does?

COCK. I did—and I'm not the only one; there was Tiresias before me, and Caeneus too, Elatus' son—so any wisecracks about me go for them too.

MICYLLUS. Well now, tell me, which did you like best— being a man, or having Pericles on top of you?

COCK. What a question! Tiresias answered it—but it didn't do him much good.

MICYLLUS. Well, even if you don't want to answer, Euripides settled it; he said he'd rather stand with his shield three times than give birth once.[29]

COCK. Well, I'll remind you of that, Micyllus, when

28 The famous "bluestocking" mistress of Pericles.
29 *Medea* 250–51; cf. *D. D.* 28. 2.

you're having labor pains. Won't be long now; you've got a long career ahead of you, and you'll be a woman many times.

MICYLLUS. Oh, drop dead! Think we're all Milesians? Or Samians? I understand you were a pretty boy when you were Pythagoras, and you often played Aspasia to your tyrant——
Well, anyway, what man or woman did you turn up as after Aspasia?   *20*

COCK. Crates, the Cynic.

MICYLLUS. Heavens above! What a difference—a courtesan, then a philosopher!

COCK. Then I was a king; next, a poor man; then a satrap; after that a horse, a jackdaw, a frog, and oh, any number of other things; it'd take far too long to list them all. Latterly I've been a cock quite a number of times. I must say I like the life; I've served in that capacity with lots of people—poor men, rich men, and now you. It never fails to make me laugh, the way you moan and call high heaven to look at the miserable life you have and keep saying how lucky rich people are. You don't know the troubles they see; why, if you knew how worried they are, you'd laugh at yourself for thinking money's such a wonderful blessing.

MICYLLUS. Well now, Pythagoras—look, what *do* you want to be called? I don't want to put you off your story, calling you all these different names.

COCK. Oh, it won't make any difference to me what you call me—Euphorbus, Pythagoras, Aspasia, Crates—I'm all of them, after all. But it might be better to call me Cock, since that's what you see in front of you. You don't want to underestimate the bird; it may not look much, but it's got all those souls inside it.

MICYLLUS. Well then, cock, you've tried pretty well every kind of life; you know it all; so let's have a good clear picture now what these lives are like, one at a time, rich man's and poor man's. I want to see whether it's right, what you said about me being happier than rich men.   *21*

COCK. All right, then, look at it like this. To start with, war doesn't mean much to you. If word comes that the enemy are on the march, you don't have to worry about your land being ravaged in the invasion or your estate laid flat or your vines cut down; all you have to do when you hear the trumpet is look after yourself, if you even bother to do that—find somewhere to hide till the danger's over. But rich men not only have that worry, they have to look on from the walls and watch all their possessions in the country being sacked and plundered, and it's very distressing. If a capital levy has to be made,[30] they're the only ones it affects; if forces have to be put in the field, they get the most dangerous jobs because they're put in command of the infantry or the cavalry. You've only got your wicker shield to carry, you're all ready to run away—and ready to join in the feasting when the general offers sacrifice after a victory.

22   And then again in peacetime you're one of "the people"; you go up to the assembly and lord it over the rich, and they quiver and bow and scrape to you and keep you sweet with handouts. They sweat away to give you baths and plays [31] and everything to your liking, and you keep your eye on them all the time; you're a very harsh critic, practically a slave driver—won't even give them a chance to speak for themselves, sometimes, but pelt them with volleys of stones if you feel like it, or confiscate their property. *You* don't have to live in fear of informers, or fret about burglars climbing in through the roof or digging a hole under your wall and stealing your money; *you* don't have the bother of keeping accounts and chasing debts and wrangling with crooked stewards and constantly turning from one worry to another. No; you finish your boot, you get your seven obols; then, when it gets dark, you knock off and have a bath if you feel like it, then you go and buy a bit of fish or a few sprats or onions and have a fine time, singing all the time pretty well, with poverty for your philosophy—and you couldn't have a better.

---

[30] Throughout this passage Lucian is referring to the fifth century B.C.; see Introduction, pp. x, xxv. Special war taxes were levied according to income.

[31] Individuals bore the cost of training choruses for plays.

And the result is that you're in the best of health, you're   *23*
tough, cold weather doesn't bother you; working hard puts
a keen edge on you, gives you a formidable resistance to diseases that other people give in to. Why, you never have anything seriously wrong with you. Oh, you may have a touch of
fever now and again; but give it its head for a day or two,
and you shake it off in a minute and go about your business
—your fever takes fright and vanishes without more ado when
he sees the way you knock back cold water and send the doctor packing when he calls. But the rich—poor beggars, they've
no self-discipline; they get all the diseases under the sun—
gout, T.B., pneumonia, dropsy; that's what comes of their
expensive dinners. I tell you, they're like Icarus, some of them;
they soar high in the air and fly near the sun, not realizing
that it's wax their wings are stuck on with; and then, sooner
or later, they fall headlong into the sea—and what a splash
they make! The ones who generally stay in the air and end up
without a mishap are those who follow Daedalus' example
and don't let their thoughts get too lofty or exalted, who fly
so low, indeed, that they're liable to get their wax wet with
spray from the sea.

MICYLLUS. Very reasonable and sensible.

COCK. Oh, yes, but you'll find some nasty shipwrecks
among the others: Croesus with his wings clipped, climbing
the pyre to amuse the Persians; or Dionysius discovered as a
schoolmaster at Corinth when his tyranny capsized—the empire he used to rule, and then to end up teaching children to
read!

MICYLLUS. Tell me, cock, how did you find life as a king?   *24*
You say you were one once. Just heaven, I bet—life's biggest
prize in your hands!

COCK. Oh, don't remind me of it! It was a dog's life! Everybody else thought it was heaven, as you say, but I had endless private worries.

MICYLLUS. Worries? What worries? That's very surprising;
I can't really believe that.

COCK. Well, the country I ruled was quite big; it was

fertile and populous, and attracted as much regard for its beautiful cities as any land you care to name. It had navigable rivers, and fine harbors around the coasts. I had considerable military resources—well-trained cavalry, a large bodyguard, warships—and so much wealth that I couldn't count it all, great quantities of gold plate, all the trappings of power proliferating around me, far more than I could ever need. Whenever I went out, the people prostrated themselves before me. They thought it was some kind of god they gazed on; they came running in crowds to behold me, pressing in on each other—some of them even climbed on to housetops in their passion to get a good clear view of my horses and robes and crown and the procession that escorted me. Oh, I didn't blame them—they didn't know any better—but I knew the worries and torments that surrounded me, and I could only feel sorry for myself. I was like those great statues by Phidias or Myron or Praxiteles; take any of them, and it's all very splendid from the outside—why, there's Poseidon or Zeus or whoever it is, standing there with his thunder or lightning or his trident in his hand, gold or ivory throughout—but take a look at what's inside! Bars and bolts and nails here, there, and everywhere, planks, wedges, pitch, clay, a veritable nest of ugliness—never mind a nest of mice and vermin of all shapes and sizes too, as often as not. And being a king is just the same.

25   MICYLLUS. You haven't told me yet where the clay and bars and bolts are in being a king. What *is* it that's as ugly as you say it is? I can see where your statue simile *does* fit very well, because it must really make you feel like a god to drive out among gaping crowds and rule so many people and have everybody bowing to you as if you were divine. But what about the inside of *that?*

COCK. Where do you want me to start? Fears, apprehensions, suspicions: your courtiers hate you and plot against you, and you can't get any sleep for them, and when you do it isn't sound. Your waking hours are filled with complicated schemes and constant disappointments. You dream of uproar.

You haven't a minute to yourself, what with seeing to finan-
cial affairs and dispensing justice and leading your armies,
with giving orders and signing agreements and making calculations. You can't even dream of snatching a bit of pleasure;
you have to take everybody's well-being on your own shoulders, and the worry's endless—

Sweet sleep
Came not to Agamemnon, Atreus' son,
Who pondered many a problem in his heart [32]

—while the Achaeans were all snoring! Croesus is worried because his son's dumb, Artaxerxes because Clearchus is hiring
mercenaries for Cyrus, Dionysius because Dion murmurs in
Syracusan ears; Alexander worries when Parmenio wins good
opinions, Perdiccas when it's Ptolemy, and Ptolemy when it's
Seleucus.[33] And these aren't the only worries—your favorite's
embraces are reluctant, your concubine loves someone else,
you hear rumors of a rebellion afoot, a handful of your guards
whisper among themselves. Worst of all, it's your nearest and
dearest you must watch out for most carefully; from them you
must constantly look out for trouble. Why, I was poisoned
by my son and he by his favorite—who in turn, no doubt, met
some similar fate.

MICYLLUS. Oh, the hell with that! It sounds dreadful! I
can see I'm far better off bending over my last than drinking
people's health from golden cups—in hemlock or aconite! The
only risk I run is, my knife might slip and miss its cut, and
then I cut my fingers and draw a drop of blood. But according to you, *they're* liable to be poisoned every time they sit
down to one of their fine meals—on top of the endless worries they live with! And then, when they do fall, they look
like nothing more than actors in tragedies; you'll often see a
man play Cecrops or Sisyphus or Telephus, complete with
crown and ivory-handled sword and long hair and gold-

26

[32] *Iliad* X. 3–4.
[33] These quarrels among Alexander's generals led to the division of his
empire.

spangled cloak, and then miss his footing and fall down right in the middle of the stage—it happens every day, and what a laugh the audience get out of it! His mask's smashed, and his crown, and the actor himself gets a bloody coxcomb; a great length of bare leg shows, his splendid clothing turns out to be dirty rags underneath, and you can see his ugly buskins, far too big for his feet. There you are, you see? You've got me talking in similes now, my fine cock! Well, that's what it looks like to me, being a tyrant. But what about when you were a horse or a dog or a fish or a frog? How did you like life then?

27   COCK. That would be a long story to start on; we haven't time now. Really, though, the long and short of it is that every one of those creatures has a more peaceful life of it than men have, to my mind; they live to suit their physical needs and desires, and that's all. You'll never come across a horse who collects taxes, or a frog who impeaches his fellows, or a jackdaw who sets himself up as a teacher, or a gnat who cooks, or a cock who's a lecher, or any of the tricks you men get up to.

28   MICYLLUS. That may be; but I don't mind admitting how I feel about it, and that is that I still can't shake off this longing to be rich—I've felt like this since I was a boy. In fact my dream's still in my mind's eye, thrusting the gold at me. And it really does make me choke to see that damned Simon rolling in luxury the way he is.

COCK. Oh, I'll cure you of that. Come on then, get up and come with me; it's still dark. I'll take you to see this Simon you're talking about, and to a few other wealthy houses; then you'll see what kind of a life they have.

MICYLLUS. How? The doors are locked—unless you're going to make me break in?

COCK. No, no, I'm not. I'm sacred to Hermes, you see, and he's given me a special privilege. My longest tail-feather—the soft, curly one—see it?

MICYLLUS. You've got two like that.

COCK. Yes; well, it's the one on the right. Anyone I allow

to pull it out and hold it in his hand can open any door for as long as I want him to, and see everything without being seen himself.

MICYLLUS. I didn't realize *you* were a wizard. Well, the minute you give me a chance like that, you'll very soon see everything Simon's got shifting over to my house here—I'll go in and shift it! And he'll be back where he was, tugging away with his teeth at shoe-soles! [34]

COCK. No, that would be wrong. I have my instructions from Hermes that if anybody who gets the feather does anything like that, I must crow and have him caught red-handed.

MICYLLUS. Don't pull my leg! Hermes is a thief himself— fancy him not wanting others to act as he does! Anyway, though, let's go. All right, I'll keep my hands off the gold—if I can.

COCK. Pluck my feather out first, Micyllus. What's all this? You've plucked them both out!

MICYLLUS. Make it a bit safer. And besides, think how odd you'd look with only half a tail; you don't want to be unbalanced.

COCK. Oh well, all right. Do you want to go to Simon's first or go and see some other wealthy man?

29

MICYLLUS. Oh no, let's go and see Simon—of course, his name's twice as long now that he's rich, if you please! Well, here we are at the door—what next?

COCK. Touch the lock with the feather.

MICYLLUS. Right. Ye gods, it's opened it! It's like a key!

COCK. Lead on. Do you see him, sitting up counting his money?

MICYLLUS. I see him. Goodness, what a dim light! That lamp's thirsty. And look how pale he is! Whatever's come over him? He's all shrunken and withered up! Worry, I suppose; I haven't heard there's anything else the matter with him.

COCK. Listen! He's talking to himself; you'll find out what's the matter with him.

[34] To stretch the leather.

SIMON. Well now, that seventy talents I've buried under the bed—that's absolutely safe, nobody else knows about that. But I think my stable boy, Sosylus, saw me bury that other sixteen in the manger; anyway he's spending all his time about the stable, and he doesn't usually waste much energy on his job—he's not overfond of work. And I'll bet there's been a lot more than that stolen too—or else how could Tibius afford that whopping great fish I hear he bought yesterday? Or that earring for his wife—*five drachmas!* I'm damned if it isn't *my* money they're chucking about! And then there are all those cups hidden away—they aren't safe either; I'm scared somebody's going to dig a hole under the wall and pinch them. There are plenty of people jealous of me and just looking for their chance—especially Micyllus along the street.

MICYLLUS. Ye gods, how right you are! I'm like you—I go off with people's pudding basins under my arm!

COCK. Ssh! He'll catch us!

SIMON. I suppose I'd better stay up and keep my eye on it all. I'll get up and do my rounds. —Who's that? I see you, burglar! Oh, thank heavens, you're only a pillar—that's all right. I'll dig my gold up and count it again; perhaps I miscounted just now. —Look out—they're at it again! Somebody made a noise! They're coming to get me! I knew it! Enemies wherever I turn! They're all after me! Where's my dagger? If I catch them———I'd better bury the gold again.

30   COCK. Well, there you are, Micyllus: that's Simon for you. Let's go and see somebody else while it's still dark.

MICYLLUS. What a miserable life! I hope my enemies get rich if that's what it means! Just let me clip his ear for him and I'll be with you.

SIMON. Who hit me? Help! Help! I'm being robbed!

MICYLLUS. That's right, you shout for help! Sit up till you turn yellow like your gold—you're practically stuck to it as it is! —Let's go and see Gnipho the moneylender, shall we? [35] He lives quite near here. —There we are—this door opens too!

31   COCK. See, he's not in bed either; too much on his mind—

[35] Cf. *Trip* 17.

all his interest to work out. He's worn his fingers to the bone with it. Well, he'll have to say goodbye to all this soon and become a beetle or a gnat or a nasty little fly.

MICYLLUS. Yes, I see him—poor devil! What a stupid way to live! Why, he isn't much better off than a beetle or a gnat as it is! He's worn himself to a shadow with his calculations, like Simon. Let's go and see somebody else.

COCK. What about your friend Eucrates, then? —There we 32 are, that's *that* door open too! In we go.

MICYLLUS. All this was mine a few hours ago!

COCK. Still dreaming of money? Well, take a look at Eucrates—look what his slave's doing to him! At his age!

MICYLLUS. Ye gods! The filthy beggar! The lecherous old ——it's—it's downright depravity! It isn't natural! And there's his wife at it too in another room—with the cook!

COCK. Well now, Micyllus, would you like to come into 33 this too? Would you like to have *everything* Eucrates has?

MICYLLUS. I should say not! I'd starve first! He can keep his gold and his dinners; I'd rather be satisfied with a couple of obols than let my servants dig into me like that!

COCK. Well now, it's getting day—see, there's the dawn. We'll have to go home; you'll see the rest some other time.

THE SALE OF PHILOSOPHERS [1]

1   ZEUS. You there, set the seats out and get the place ready for people to come in! You—bring the specimens in and stand them in a row! But clean them up a bit first; make them worth looking at, so that they'll attract lots of attention. Hermes—you make the proclamation.

HERMES. Buyers! Into the sale room now, and good luck to you! Philosophers for sale! All shapes and sizes! Assorted doctrines! Cash down or twelve months' credit on security!

ZEUS. Plenty of customers. Don't waste time—can't keep them waiting. Let's go.

2   HERMES. Which do you want to put up first?

ZEUS. This long-haired fellow, the Ionian. He looks pretty formidable.

HERMES. Pythagoras! Step down off the platform and let the customers have a look at you.

ZEUS. Well, tell them about him.

HERMES. One philosopher going—no superior, very impressive. Who's for him? Who wants to be Superman? Who wants to understand the cosmic harmony? Or live another life?

[1] The Greek title literally means "The Sale of Lives"; βίος, "life," can also mean "biography," as in Plutarch's *Lives*. Here the predominant notion is of specimen characters of philosophers; the word is variously translated. Lucian protests in *The Fisher* (a sequel to this piece, which seems to have aroused hostility) that he was not criticizing individuals, but in fact several of the figures he uses are readily recognizable, and are here represented by their own names and not by the names of the schools associated with them (e.g., Socrates, not Socratic). The reader is referred to any standard history of Greek philosophy for a full account of the doctrines mentioned; brief entries are included in the Glossary and notes. Lucian's superficial accounts are of course intended only to amuse; they are, however, more or less self-explanatory. For the prices that the specimens fetch, see Introduction, p. xxxii.

BUYER. Looks all right—what does he specialize in?

HERMES. Arithmetic, astronomy, magic, geometry, music, sorcery. First-class fortuneteller you're looking at.

BUYER. Can I ask him questions?

HERMES. Go ahead, and good luck to you.

BUYER. Where are you from?

PYTHAGORAS. Samos.[2]

BUYER. Education?

PYTHAGORAS. Egypt: local sages.

BUYER. Tell me, what will you teach me if I buy you?

PYTHAGORAS. I shan't *teach* you anything; I'll remind you.[3]

BUYER. How will you remind me?

PYTHAGORAS. I'll purify your soul first, and wash the dirt off it.

BUYER. All right, say I'm purified. How do you go about this reminding?

PYTHAGORAS. The first thing is a long silence. Not a word for five years: not a sound.

BUYER. My dear man, you'd be a good teacher for Croesus' son.[4] I'm a chatterbox, I don't want to be a statue. Never mind—what comes after the five years' silence?

PYTHAGORAS. You'll learn music and geometry.

BUYER. A delicious road to wisdom—learn to play the lyre!

PYTHAGORAS. Then counting next.

BUYER. But I *can* count.

PYTHAGORAS. How do you count?

BUYER. One, two, three, four——

PYTHAGORAS. See? What you call four is ten, a perfect triangle—what we swear by.[5]

2 Pythagoras here, and later Heraclitus and Democritus, are represented as speaking in the Ionic dialect.

3 The theory of *anamnesis;* see Plato, *Meno.*

4 Who was dumb; see Herodotus, I. 34 and 85.

5 $1 + 2 + 3 + 4 = 10$; the triangle is

BUYER. Well, by your almighty Four, I never heard anything more divine or sacred!

PYTHAGORAS. Then, my friend, you'll learn about earth and air and fire and water—their courses, shapes, and motions.

BUYER. Shapes? Fire and air and water?

PHYTHAGORAS. Very distinct shapes. Nothing can move without shape and form. Besides that, you'll learn that God is Number and Mind and Harmony.

BUYER. Would you believe it!

5   PYTHAGORAS. And on top of what I've said, you'll learn that though you think you're a unity, in fact you're one thing in appearance and another in reality.

BUYER. What? I'm somebody else? Not the man who's speaking to you?

PYTHAGORAS. You are now. But once you appeared in another body, with another name; and you'll change again hereafter.[6]

6   BUYER. You mean I'm going to take lots of shapes and never die? But that's enough of that. What are your views on food?

PYTHAGORAS. I eat nothing living, but anything else. Except beans.[7]

BUYER. Why not beans? Don't you like them?

PYTHAGORAS. It isn't that. They're sacred; their nature's a mystery. In the first place, they're pure seed. If you peel one while it's still green, you can see it's built like a man's privates. And if you boil one and expose it in the moonlight for a determined number of nights, you get blood. More important still, the Athenians always use them to choose their officials with.[8]

BUYER. Excellent arguments: very reverent. Now strip; I want to see you naked too. Ye gods, he's got a golden thigh!

---

[6] The theory of transmigration of the soul.

[7] Cf. *Cock* 4–5 and 18. Lucian embroiders Pythagoras' doctrine slightly in the present passage.

[8] Beans were used as lots in Athenian elections.

He must be a god, not a mortal! Oh, I must have him. What do you want for him?

HERMES. Ten minas.

BUYER. I'll take him at that.

ZEUS. Take the customer's name and address.

HERMES. He's from Italy, I should think—round about Croton or Tarentum or one of those Greek towns.[9] But he hasn't bought him for himself; he's acting for a syndicate—must be three hundred of them.

ZEUS. They can take him away! Next lot!

HERMES. You want this scruffy one from the Black Sea?

ZEUS. Yes, all right.

HERMES. Hey, you! You with the knapsack and the sleeveless cloak! [10] Come on down and walk round the room! Next lot, one manly specimen! Spirited, independent—splendid fellow! What am I bid?

BUYER. Independent? Are you selling a free man? [11]

HERMES. That's right.

BUYER. Aren't you afraid he might have you up for kidnapping? He might even take you to the Areopagus.[12]

HERMES. Oh, he doesn't mind being sold. He feels completely free.

BUYER. But what use would he be? Look at the dreadful state he's in—he's filthy! He'd do for digging or for fetching water, I suppose.

HERMES. Not only that—put him to guard your house and he'll be much more reliable than any dog. In fact Dog's actually his name.[13]

BUYER. Where's he from? What does he claim to do?

HERMES. Better ask him that.

7

9 Magna Graecia; see *Cock* 18 and n. 27 there.

10 A garment typical of the Cynic philosopher; cf. various *D. D.*

11 There is a play on $\grave{\epsilon}\lambda\epsilon\acute{v}\theta\epsilon\rho os$, which means both "free" and "independent" in the sense of "aggressively self-reliant."

12 Roughly equivalent to "Supreme Court."

13 This is a play on words; the Greek $\kappa\acute{v}\omega\nu$, from which "Cynic" is derived, means "dog."

BUYER. I'm scared of him; he looks sullen and moody. He might bark at me if I go near him—or even bite me. See how he's got his stick up? Look at the way he scowls—and that nasty threatening look in his eyes!

HERMES. Oh, don't be frightened—he's tame.

8   BUYER. Well—to start with, where are you from, my good man?

DIOGENES. Everywhere.

BUYER. What do you mean?

DIOGENES. You see before you a citizen of the world.

BUYER. Who's your ideal?

DIOGENES. Hercules.

BUYER. Well, you've got a club like him. Why not wear a lionskin too?

DIOGENES. My cloak's my lionskin. I'm a soldier as he was —pleasure's what I'm fighting. I'm a volunteer, not a conscript. My purpose is to purify people's lives.

BUYER. That's a splendid purpose! But what's your line, particularly? What's your method?

DIOGENES. I liberate mankind by treating their passions. Briefly, I aim to be a spokesman for Truth and Candor.

9   BUYER. All right, spokesman; if I buy you, how will you handle me?

DIOGENES. The first thing I'll do if I take you in hand will be to strip your easy life off you. I'll shut you up with Want and give you a coarse cloak to wear. Then I'll make you work till you drop. You'll sleep on the ground and drink water and fill your belly with what you can get. If you have any money you'll go and throw it in the sea under my regime. You won't bother about marriage or children or homeland; all that will be stuff and nonsense to you. You'll leave your own home and live in a funeral vault or an abandoned tower or even a jar.[14] Your knapsack will be full of lupines [15] and books packed to the covers with writing. You live like that

[14] Diogenes lived in a jar, not a tub, as is usually supposed; cf. *D. D.* 11. 3.

[15] Seeds of the pea family, traditional philosophers' fare; cf. *D. D.* 1. 1.

and you'll say you're happier than the King of Persia. Whipping and torture won't bother you a bit.

BUYER. Won't bother me? Won't feel any pain if I'm whipped? What do you think I am—a tortoise? A crab?

DIOGENES. You'll put that line of Euripides into practice—with a slight adjustment.

BUYER. What line?

DIOGENES. "Your mind will hurt, the tongue will feel no pain."[16] These are the essentials: go ahead boldly and be abusive to everybody alike, king or commoner. Don't be timid about it; it'll make them take notice of you, they'll think you tough. Use rough language and a harsh tone; snarl like a veritable dog. Scowl, and let your gait suit your scowl. Behave like a savage beast, in fact, all the time. Have no shame, and don't bother about decency and moderation. Wipe the blush right off your face. Make for places where the crowds are thickest, and when you find them, fix your mind on a solitary existence. Have nothing to do with anybody; don't let anybody near you, friend or stranger—that would destroy your authority. And what people don't do even in privacy, you do boldly where everybody can see you—go for the laughs in your love life. And finally, if you feel like it, swallow a raw squid or cuttlefish and die.[17] That's the kind of happiness we'll fix you up with.

BUYER. Well, I don't want it. Ugh! What a nasty unnatural life!

DIOGENES. But look you, it's so simple; anybody can live it, it's there for the taking. You don't need education or any rubbishy theories; this is a short cut to fame. Even if you're an ignoramus—a tanner or fishmonger or joiner or moneychanger—there's nothing to stop you from becoming famous. All you need is a thick skin and a brass neck and a good sound course in how to be abusive.

BUYER. Well, I don't want you for that kind of thing. You

---

[16] *Hippolytus* 612, "My tongue has sworn, my mind remains unsworn."
[17] As Diogenes was said to have done; cf. *Trip* 7, n. 6.

might make a sailor, though, in a pinch, or a gardener, but only if he'll let you go cheap—two obols at most.

HERMES. He's yours. Take him. We'll be glad to be rid of him. He's just a general nuisance, the way he shouts and insults everybody alike with his foul tongue.

12 ZEUS. Call another one. The Cyrenaic—that one with the purple robe and the wreath on his head.

HERMES. Attention please, gentlemen! This lot's expensive—cost you real money. A sweet specimen going! An ecstatic specimen! Who's eager for a soft life? Any bids for a hedonist? [18]

BUYER. Here, you, come and tell me what you can do. I'll buy you if you're any use.

HERMES. Don't bother him with questions, sir; he's drunk. He can't answer anyway—his tongue's lost its foothold, as you can see.

BUYER. Who in his right senses would buy such a moral wreck? What a wanton wretch! What a smell of scent off him, too! Can't walk without staggering and falling over! Hermes, you tell me what he's like. What's his specialty?

HERMES. Well, briefly, he's good company, he can put away his share of liquor, he's very good for a spree with a flute girl—just the thing for a dissolute, lascivious master. And then he's a connoisseur of cakes and a highly experienced cook; a real expert in easy living. He was educated at Athens and also served tyrants in Sicily; they thought the world of him. His doctrine, in a nutshell, is to despise everything, make use of everything, and draw pleasure from everywhere.

BUYER. You'd better look for somebody else—somebody with plenty of money. I'm not up to buying a gay character.

HERMES. Looks as if we've got this one on our hands, Zeus. Can't sell him.

13 ZEUS. Put him on one side and bring on another. No—

[18] According to the Cyrenaics, pleasure was the highest good. Details are contributed to the following sketch by Aristippus, the founder of the Cyrenaic school.

these two, better—the laughing one from Abdera and the weeping one from Ephesus.[19] I'll sell them as a pair.

HERMES. Come on, you two, down here! An excellent pair going! What am I bid for the cleverest pair you'll find?

BUYER. Heavens, aren't they different? One of them can't stop laughing, and the other's crying his heart out—looks as if he's in mourning! You there! What's up? What's the joke?

DEMOCRITUS. What's the joke? You make me laugh, you and all your goings on; that's the joke.

BUYER. What's that you say? You're laughing at us all? You think our life's nothing?

DEMOCRITUS. That's right. It's empty and meaningless, just atoms moving in the infinite.

BUYER. Oh no it isn't. It's you that's infinitely empty— that's the truth of it. Damn your insolence, wipe that grin off your face! —And you, my dear sir—I'd be much better talking to you, I think. Why are you crying?

14

HERACLITUS. I am considering the human situation, my friend. It calls for tears and lamentation; we are doomed from the start. Wherefore I pity man and mourn for him. Of the present I take no great account, but what will be hereafter is grief unmitigated; I mean conflagration and universal disaster. For this I sorrow, and because nothing abides; all things are stirred together as into porridge. Pleasure is one with pain, knowledge with ignorance, great with small; up and down they go, around and about, changing places, the sport of time.

BUYER. What then is time?

HERACLITUS. A child at play, quarreling, agreeing at the checkerboard.

BUYER. And what are men?

HERACLITUS. Mortal gods.

BUYER. And gods?

[19] Democritus of Abdera founded the "atomist" theory of matter; Heraclitus of Ephesus held that fire was the primary substance of the universe and that everything was in a state of flux, and was nicknamed "the obscure" for his enigmatic assertions.

HERACLITUS. Immortal men.

BUYER. Talking in riddles, eh? Composing puzzles? You're as bad as Apollo's oracle—quite incomprehensible.[20]

HERACLITUS. I am not interested in you.

BUYER. Then nobody in his right mind's going to buy you.

HERACLITUS. Young or old, buy me or buy me not, the hell with the lot of you.

BUYER. This poor devil's not far from the nuthouse. I'm not buying either of them.

HERMES. They stay unsold too.

ZEUS. Put another one up.

15   HERMES. That Athenian? The chatterbox?

ZEUS. Yes, all right.

HERMES. You there! Come here! Going, one virtuous, intelligent specimen. Any bids for his holiness?

BUYER. Tell me, what do you specialize in?

SOCRATES. I'm a lover of youth. I know all about love.[21]

BUYER. Expect me to buy you? It's a tutor for my boy I want—and he's a handsome lad!

SOCRATES. What better companion than me could you find for a handsome lad? I'm not a lover of the body; it's the soul I find beautiful. Nothing to worry about; even if they lie under the same cloak with me, you won't hear them complain about the way I treat them.

BUYER. I don't believe you. A lover of youth, and you don't mess around with anything but the soul? Despite the opportunities when you're under the same cloak?

16   SOCRATES. Why, I swear by the dog and the plane tree, that's the truth of it!

BUYER. Ye gods! What a funny oath!

SOCRATES. What's funny about it? Don't you think the dog's a god? Look at the fuss they make of Anubis in Egypt!

---

[20] Cf. *Zeus* 31.

[21] Socrates expounds his views on love in Plato's *Symposium;* see 219 there for his relations with young men.

And what about the Dog Star in the heavens, and Cerberus in the underworld?

BUYER. All right, I was wrong. Well, what's your way of life?

17

SOCRATES. I live in a state I fashioned for myself, under an original constitution and my own laws.[22]

BUYER. Tell me one of your decrees.

SOCRATES. All right, I'll tell you my decree about women; it's the principal one. No woman belongs to one man: they're available to anyone who wants them.

BUYER. What's that? The laws of adultery are swept away?

SOCRATES. Heavens, yes, and all the pusillanimous arguments on that subject, in a word.

BUYER. What's your doctrine about handsome boys, then?

SOCRATES. Their kisses will be the prize for excellence, for splendid, spirited deeds.

BUYER. Very generous, aren't you? What's the principal thing in your philosophy?

18

SOCRATES. Forms of reality, patterns. Everything you see —earth, what's on it, sky, sea—all of these have invisible images outside the universe.

BUYER. Where?

SOCRATES. Nowhere. If they were anywhere they wouldn't exist.

BUYER. I can't see these patterns you talk about.

SOCRATES. Of course you can't; you're spiritually blind. *I* can see the patterns of everything—an invisible you, another me—two of everything, in fact.

BUYER. What good eyes you've got! You're a clever fellow —I must have you. Look, what do you want for him?

HERMES. Give me two talents.

BUYER. I'll buy him at that. But I'll pay you later.

HERMES. What's your name?

19

22 I.e., "Plato's" Republic (cf. *Story* II. 17), the inspiration for which came to some degree from Socrates. In the figure of Socrates, Lucian is also sketching Plato and the Academics, his descendants.

BUYER. Dion of Syracuse.[23]

HERMES. There you are—take him, and good luck to you. You, the Epicurean—you're up next! Any bids for this one? He's a pupil of the two that were up for sale a minute ago, the laughing one and the drunken one.[24] But he has one more feature—he's more impious. Otherwise he's a sweet specimen: quite a gourmet.

BUYER. How much does he cost?

HERMES. Two minas.

BUYER. There you are. But hold on a minute—what does he like to eat?

HERMES. Sweet things—anything with honey in it. Dried figs best of all.

BUYER. That's easy enough. I'll buy him some Carian fruitcakes.

20   ZEUS. Call another. That one there—that close-cropped, sullen one, the Stoic.

HERMES. Good idea. It looks as if there's quite a mob of city men waiting for him to come up.[25] Pure virtue for sale! The perfect way of life for sale! Who wants to be the only know-it-all?

BUYER. Don't follow you.

HERMES. This chap's the only wise man, the only handsome man, the only just man, brave man, king, orator, rich man, lawgiver, et cetera, et cetera.[26]

BUYER. Is he the only cook, then? And the only tanner and carpenter and so on?

HERMES. I suppose so.

[23] A disciple of Plato and a minister of Dionysius; after the latter's overthrow as tyrant of Syracuse in 345 B.C., Dion in fact tried to found a state built on Platonic lines.

[24] Epicurean atomism is derived from Democritus, and Epicurean hedonism from the Cyrenaics.

[25] Stoicism was very popular among men of affairs; it proved particularly congenial to the Roman temperament. The Stoics are Lucian's favorite target; with this sketch, cf. *Hermotimus*.

[26] I.e., by Stoic definitions of wisdom, justice, etc., the possession of these virtues necessitated a Stoic attitude.

BUYER. Here, you, sir, come here; I think I'll buy you.   *21*
Tell me what you're like. Don't you mind being sold as a
slave?

STOIC. No. That's beyond human control, and what's
beyond human control is indifferent.

BUYER. I don't understand you.

STOIC. Don't you? Don't you understand that in such
matters some are preferred and some, on the other hand, are
not-preferred? [27]

BUYER. I still don't understand.

STOIC. I don't suppose you do. You're not used to our
technical terms, and you're incapable of conceptual repre-
sentation. The real philosopher, the man who's learned logic
properly, knows not only this but the nature of complete and
incomplete predicates too, and the degree of difference between them.

BUYER. In philosophy's name, don't be mean—at least tell
me what they are, complete and incomplete predicates. They
sound very impressive somehow, the way they roll off the
tongue.

STOIC. Of course I'll tell you. Suppose a lame man suddenly hurts his lame foot on a rock; then the lameness—which
he had to start with, you see—is a complete predicate; now he's
got an incomplete predicate, namely his wound, as well.

BUYER. How very subtle! What else do you specialize in?   *22*

STOIC. Verbal snares. I trap people who talk to me and
stop their mouths and make them shut up—I muzzle them, in
fact. This is called the power of renowned syllogism.

BUYER. Heavens! That sounds powerful! I'll bet you always win.

STOIC. Well, take an example. Have you a child?

BUYER. Suppose I have?

STOIC. If your child wanders near a river, and a crocodile

[27] As they helped or hindered the virtuous life. Lucian's satire here and
in the following passage is directed against the Stoic concern with technical logic rather than morality; cf. sec. 22 below, "verbal snares," and
Hermotimus 81–82.

sees him and catches him, and then promises to give him back to you if you can tell him correctly what he has decided to do, give the child back or not—what would you say he'd decided to do?

BUYER. That's a tricky question. I don't know what I'd say to get the child back. For heaven's sake, *you* answer and save my child—quick, before the crocodile swallows him!

STOIC. Don't worry! I'll teach you stranger things than that.

BUYER. Such as?

STOIC. The Reaper, the Master,[28] and above all Electra and the Hooded Man.

BUYER. Hooded Man? Electra?

STOIC. *The* Electra—Agamemnon's daughter. She knew and didn't know the same thing. Orestes was standing beside her before she recognized him; she knew that Orestes was her brother, but didn't know that this was Orestes. But the Hooded Man—that really is a wonderful argument for you. Tell me, do you know your own father?

BUYER. Yes.

STOIC. Well, if I put a hooded man beside you and asked you if you knew him, what would you say?

BUYER. No, of course.

23   STOIC. But this hooded man *is* your father all the time. So if you don't know this man, clearly you don't know your father.

BUYER. Oh, no. I'd take his hood off and find out who he was. But never mind—tell me, what's the purpose of philosophy? What will you do when you've reached the peak of virtue?

STOIC. Then I'll apply myself to the chief natural goods, wealth, health, and so on. But there's a lot of hard work to do first, sharpening the sight on closely written books, collecting scholarly comments, and filling myself up with wrong usages and strange words. And the main thing is, you can't

---

[28] Fallacies, the details of which are unknown.

be a philosopher unless you go out of your mind and take the cure three times running.[29]

BUYER. A very noble, manly program. But how about your Stoic habit of moneylending, like Gnipho? Does that show you've been cured and are perfectly virtuous?

STOIC. Yes. At least, only the philosopher is fit to be a moneylender. For since he specializes in drawing conclusions, and lending money and drawing interest on it are obviously not very different from drawing conclusions,[30] what applies to the one applies to the other—only the real philosopher can do it. And draw not just simple interest like other people, but interest on interest; you know that there's first interest and second interest, a sort of second generation of the first?[31] And of course you follow the reasoning of the syllogism, "If he gets the first interest, he will get the second; but he *will* get the first, therefore he *will* get the second."

BUYER. Are we to say the same, then, of the fees that you get from young men for teaching them philosophy? Clearly only the real philosopher can get money for his virtue.

STOIC. That's right. I take money not for myself, you see, but for the giver's own sake. For some men are outgiving and others are intaking. I'm training myself to be intaking and my students to be outgiving.

BUYER. No! The other way around! The student should be intaking. You're the only rich man, so you should be outgiving.

STOIC. You're joking, sir. Take care I don't shoot you down with my indemonstrable syllogism.

BUYER. What's dangerous about that?

STOIC. It'll put you out and strike you dumb and dislocate your intellect. But best of all, I can turn you into a stone right now if I like.

24

25

[29] As Chrysippus, Cleanthes' successor as the head of the Stoic school in the third century B.C., was said to have done; cf. *Story* II. 18.

[30] In the Greek, the verb used for "to draw conclusions" is a compound of the simple verb λογίζεσθαι, "to draw interest."

[31] τόκος, "interest," means literally "offspring."

BUYER. A stone? My dear chap, you aren't Perseus.

STOIC. Just you listen. Is a stone a substance?

BUYER. Yes.

STOIC. Isn't an animate being a substance?

BUYER. Yes.

STOIC. And you're an animate being?

BUYER. I suppose so.

STOIC. Then you're a substance, so you're a stone.

BUYER. Stop it! Analyze me properly, for heaven's sake, and make me a man again!

STOIC. Easy. Be a man again. Tell me, is every substance an animate being?

BUYER. No.

STOIC. Is a stone an animate being?

BUYER. No.

STOIC. Are you a substance?

BUYER. Yes.

STOIC. You're a substance, but still an animate being?

BUYER. Yes.

STOIC. Then if you're an animate being, you're not a stone.

BUYER. Thanks very much. I felt like Niobe—my legs were getting cold and stiff already. I'll buy you. How much is he?

HERMES. Twelve minas.

BUYER. There you are.

HERMES. Are you sole buyer?

BUYER. Heavens, no! There are all these men here.

HERMES. Well, there are plenty of them, broad-shouldered fellows—just right for the Reaper.

26   ZEUS. Don't waste time. Call another—the Peripatetic.[32]

HERMES. You there—that fine fellow, that rich fellow! Now, gentlemen, buy my wise man! Knows simply everything!

BUYER. What's he like?

[32] The following sketch touches on some Aristotelian logical doctrine and scientific experiments.

HERMES. Restrained, decent, agreeable company. Best of all, there are two of him.

BUYER. Two? How come?

HERMES. One aspect outside, another inside. So remember, if you buy him, one of him's called Exoteric and the other Esoteric.[33]

BUYER. What's his particular intellectual line?

HERMES. That there are three kinds of good—spiritual, physical, and external.

BUYER. That's a doctrine one can grasp. How much is he?

HERMES. Twenty minas.

BUYER. That's a lot.

HERMES. Oh no, my dear fellow. He seems to have a bit of money himself, you see. You buy him while there's time. He'll teach you lots more things right away—how long a gnat lives, how far down sunlight goes in the sea, and what an oyster's soul's like.

BUYER. Heavens, what a scholarly mind!

HERMES. Ah, but if you heard some of his other ideas! Much more penetrating than these. All about generation and birth and the formation of the embryo in the womb, and how man is a creature that laughs, whereas an ass is a creature that doesn't laugh or build houses or sail ships either.

BUYER. Very impressive, all that knowledge. Very useful too. Twenty, you say? All right, I'll have him.

HERMES. Right.

ZEUS. Who's left?

27

HERMES. This Skeptic here. Hey, Coppernob![34] Come here and be auctioned! Hurry up! Not many to sell you to; most of them are drifting off now. Still—any bids for this one?

---

[33] A reference to the traditional division of Aristotle's works into "popular" ("exoteric") and "for the initiated" ("esoteric"). Aristotle himself uses the former to mean "common" or "standard," of philosophical arguments, and does not use the latter at all.

[34] Pyrrhias ("Coppernob") is named after Pyrrho, the founder of the Skeptic philosophy here sketched; its principal tenet was the impossibility of knowledge.

BUYER. Yes, me. But tell me first, what do you know?

PYRRHIAS. Nothing.

BUYER. How do you mean, nothing?

PYRRHIAS. I don't think there *is* anything at all.

BUYER. Aren't *we* something?

PYRRHIAS. I'm not even sure of that.

BUYER. Nor even that you're somebody?

PYRRHIAS. I'm much more doubtful still about that.

BUYER. What a state to be in! Well, what's the idea of these scales?

PYRRHIAS. I weigh arguments in them. I balance them till they're equal, and when I see they're exactly alike and exactly the same weight, then—ah, then!—I don't know which is the sounder!

BUYER. What are you good at apart from that?

PYRRHIAS. Everything except catching a runaway slave.

BUYER. And why can't you do that?

PYRRHIAS. My good man, I can't apprehend anything.[35]

BUYER. I don't suppose you can. You seem slow and stupid. Well, what's the end of your knowledge?

PYRRHIAS. Ignorance, deafness, and blindness.

BUYER. You'll be unable to see or hear, you say?

PYRRHIAS. And unable to judge or feel either. No better than a worm, in fact.

BUYER. I must buy you for that. How much shall we say for him?

HERMES. One Attic mina.

BUYER. There you are. Well now, you—I've bought you, eh?

PYRRHIAS. I'm not sure.

BUYER. Nonsense! I *have* bought you, and I've paid my money.

PYRRHIAS. I defer judgment; I'm considering the matter.

BUYER. Look, you come with me—you're my slave.

PYRRHIAS. Who can tell whether what you say is true?

[35] This is a pun on the Greek καταλαμβάνω, meaning both "seize" and "conceive."

BUYER. The auctioneer can. My mina can. These people here can.

PYRRHIAS. Is there anybody here?

BUYER. I'm going to put you on the treadmill, then. I'll show you I'm boss—the hard way!

PYRRHIAS. Suspend decision on it.

BUYER. Oh ye gods! Look, I've already told you my decision.

HERMES. Stop dillydallying, you, and go with him—he's bought you. Gentlemen, we invite you to come tomorrow; we'll be putting up ordinary people, workmen and tradesmen.

HERMOTIMUS

1   LYCINUS. To judge by your book, Hermotimus, and the speed at which you're walking, I should say you're in a hurry to get to your tutor. You were meditating about something as you walked; your lips were going and you were muttering away to yourself, waving your hand all over the place as if you were mentally composing a speech—cogitating one of your barbed questions,[1] no doubt, or pondering some scholarly problem. Trust you not to waste your time even while you're en route somewhere. You're always at it, you've always got some weighty thing on hand that'll help you in your studies.

    HERMOTIMUS. Yes, Lycinus, that's about it. I was going over yesterday's lecture in my mind, recalling everything he told us. One mustn't let any opportunity slip, to my mind; you know how true the Coan doctor's[2] remark was, "Life is short, but art is long." And it was only the art of medicine he was talking about, and that's easier to comprehend; philosophy you won't reach however long you take unless you keep your eyes wide open and fixed intently, without blinking, on your goal. And there's so much at stake—whether you're to waste away miserably with the great rabble of ordinary people, or become a philosopher and attain happiness.

2   LYCINUS. What a wonderful picture you draw of the rewards. But you're not far away from them now, I imagine, to judge from the time you've been studying philosophy, and the considerable effort, too, that you seem to have been putting into it this long time past. Why, if my memory serves me correctly, for nearly twenty years now I've never seen you engaged in anything other than going to lectures—and gen-

[1] Hermotimus is a Stoic, and although Lycinus—that is, Lucian—says that his objections to the study of philosophy would apply to any creed, in fact there are particular references to Stoicism throughout.

[2] Hippocrates.

112

erally bent over your book and writing up your lecture notes, always pale with meditation and physically worn out. Why, you're so immersed in it I don't suppose you relax even in your dreams. Well, when I consider all this, I imagine it won't be long now before you seize hold of happiness—unless, indeed, you've made its acquaintance long since and never said a word to us about it.

HERMOTIMUS. How could I have? I'm only now beginning to get a glimpse of the road. Virtue dwells a long, long way off, according to Hesiod,[3] and the path to where she dwells is long and steep and rough; those who travel it must spend a great deal of sweat.

LYCINUS. And haven't you sweated and traveled enough, then?

HERMOTIMUS. No, indeed; if I'd reached the top, there'd be nothing standing between me and supreme felicity. As it is, I'm still beginning, Lycinus.

LYCINUS. Well, anyway, the same Hesiod says that beginning is half the battle,[4] so surely it wouldn't be too much to say you were halfway there now?

HERMOTIMUS. Not even that far, yet; it would be an achievement if I were.

LYCINUS. Well, where *shall* we say you've reached?

HERMOTIMUS. Lycinus, I'm still in the foothills, just making an effort to start out; but it's slippery and rough, and I need a helping hand to pull me up.

LYCINUS. Surely your master is capable of doing that for you? He can let down a golden rope to you from up on top at the summit, like Zeus in Homer [5]—namely, his own teachings—and draw you up thus, you see, haul you up to himself and virtue, since he reached the top himself long ago.

HERMOTIMUS. You've hit on the very thing he is doing, Lycinus. Why, I'd have been drawn up and joined the people

3

3 *Works and Days* 289.

4 *Works and Days* 40.

5 This is one of Lucian's favorite references, from *Iliad* VIII. 23–27; cf. *Zeus* 14 and 45.

at the summit long ago as far as he's concerned; but my own part is still wanting.

4   LYCINUS. Well, you must be of good heart and keep your spirits up; look to the end of the road and the happiness that dwells on high—especially with him helping you in your quest. Tell me, though, what hope does he hold out? When does he think you'll reach the top? Does he expect you to get there by next year—after the other Mysteries, say, or the Panathenaea?

HERMOTIMUS. Too soon, Lycinus.

LYCINUS. By the next Olympiad, then?

HERMOTIMUS. That's a short time, too, for a training in virtue and the attainment of happiness.

LYCINUS. Well, then, surely after two Olympiads? Or else you could surely be accused of being bone-idle, if you can't make it in all that time; you'd have time to go from the Pillars of Hercules [6] all the way to India and back again three times, easily, even if you wandered among the intervening tribes instead of going straight ahead all the time. Tell me, just how much higher and more slippery is the rock on which your Virtue dwells than the Rock of Aornos that Alexander took by storm in a few days?

5   HERMOTIMUS. The case is not the same. Virtue is not, as you suppose it is, something that can be overcome and stormed in a moment, not though ten thousand Alexanders should assault it; otherwise there would have been any number scaling the heights. As it is, quite a few people do start out in high confidence, and make some progress—some of them very little, others more—but when they reach halfway they encounter all sorts of difficulties and discomforts, and lose patience; they turn back, panting and sweating, unable to stand the strain. But those who persist in their efforts do reach the summit; and thereafter they live in complete felicity, looking down on the rest of mankind from their vantage point as on ants.

LYCINUS. My goodness, Hermotimus, what little creatures

6 The Straits of Gibraltar.

you make us out to be! Not even pygmies—we really are
groveling on earth's very surface! Well, no wonder; you're
already aloft in your thoughts, above us. Well, *we*—the common crowd, we who crawl about the earth—we'll pray to you
along with the gods. You're above the clouds; you've attained
what you've been striving after for so long.

HERMOTIMUS. Oh, if only one *could* attain it, Lycinus!
But there's a great deal to come yet.

LYCINUS. Yes, but you haven't said how much, in actual 6
figures.

HERMOTIMUS. No—I don't know myself, with any accur-
acy. I imagine it won't be more than twenty years, though.
Surely I'll have reached the summit by then.

LYCINUS. Heavens! What a long time!

HERMOTIMUS. Oh, yes; it's a considerable prize I'm striving for.

LYCINUS. Well, perhaps so. But about this twenty years—
how do you know you'll live that long? Has your teacher
promised that you will? Is he a prophet or a soothsayer as well
as a philosopher? Is he versed in Chaldaean lore? They claim
to know all about these things. Surely you wouldn't go on
making all this effort if you weren't sure whether you would
live to attain virtue? Surely you wouldn't exhaust yourself
night and day if you didn't know that Fate was not going to
catch up with you and take hold of you by the foot just as you
were getting near the top, and haul you off with your hopes
unfulfilled?

HERMOTIMUS. Now that's enough of that, Lycinus! Those
are words of ill omen. I only hope I live long enough to attain wisdom and enjoy even one day of felicity.

LYCINUS. One day? Will that be enough for you—after
the way you've sweated?

HERMOTIMUS. Even the tiniest fraction of a day would be
enough.

LYCINUS. But how can you know that felicity *is* up there? 7
And that it is worth all you put up with for it? You've never
been there yourself.

HERMOTIMUS. No, but my teacher has told me, and I trust his word; he knows very well, since he is already at the top himself.

LYCINUS. In heaven's name, what sort of thing did he say was there? What kind of happiness? Wealth, I suppose, and fame, and the very last word in pleasure?

HERMOTIMUS. My dear friend, you mustn't talk like that! These things have nothing to do with the virtuous life.

LYCINUS. Well then, if it isn't these, what kind of advantage *does* he say you'll win if you continue with your training to the end?

HERMOTIMUS. Wisdom and courage, the essence of beauty and justice, firm knowledge and conviction about the nature of everything. As for wealth and fame and pleasure and all bodily things, all these you strip off and cast aside at the bottom before you begin the climb. Just like Hercules, who burned on Oeta before his deification; you know the story—how he cast aside all the mortal part of him, that he had from his mother, and flew up to heaven pure and undefiled with his divine part, sifted by the fire.[7] Well, my exemplars are stripped by philosophy, as by fire, of all that seems wonderful to the misguided generality; and when they reach the top, to live in felicity, they have no thought, even, of wealth and fame and pleasure any more—rather they laugh at people who think these things are real.

8   LYCINUS. By Hercules on Oeta, they're stout fellows, and lucky ones too, by your account. But tell me—do they ever come down from their heights, if they should want to, to enjoy what they've left behind them? Or must they stay up on top once they've got there, and live with Virtue, and laugh at wealth and fame and pleasure?

HERMOTIMUS. That isn't all, Lycinus; whoever attains the perfection of virtue will not be a slave to anger or fear or desire or grief or any such affection.

LYCINUS. And yet—if I am to tell the truth unhesitatingly

[7] The legend forms the subject of Euripides, *Hercules Furens* and Sophocles, *Trachiniae;* cf. *D. D.* 16.

—but no, I really shouldn't; it's irreverent to poke one's nose into wise men's business.

HERMOTIMUS. Oh, don't be like that! You speak your mind.

LYCINUS. Oh, but look here, my dear friend—I really can't.

HERMOTIMUS. Now don't be shy, my dear fellow; tell me. There's no one else here.

LYCINUS. Well then, I followed most of your explanation and I quite believed what you were saying about them grow-ing wise and brave and just and so on—I found it quite be-guiling, in fact. But when you came to the bit about them despising wealth and fame and pleasure and not being subject to anger or grief, well, at that point—since we're alone—I stopped short. I thought of the way I saw somebody behaving yesterday—shall I tell you who it was, or can we do without the name? *9*

HERMOTIMUS. No, no, you tell me who it was, too.

LYCINUS. In fact it was your own teacher—a venerable man in every other way, and a very old man now.

HERMOTIMUS. Well? What was it he was doing, then?

LYCINUS. You know that foreigner from Heraclea that he's been teaching philosophy to for years now? That fair-haired, argumentative fellow?

HERMOTIMUS. I know the man you mean—Dion?

LYCINUS. That's the man. Well, I suppose he was overdue with his fees; anyway, the other day the old man hauled him into court by the scruff of the neck, shouting and storming at him; and if it hadn't been for the intervention of some of his friends, who got the youth out of his hands, I'm sure he'd have held on to him and bitten his nose off. He was furious!

HERMOTIMUS. Oh, he's a rogue, that one; he's always the same—quite immoral about paying debts. I assure you my teacher never yet treated any of his other debtors that way; and there are plenty of them—but they pay him his interest regularly. *10*

LYCINUS. But my dear sir, what does it matter to him if

they *don't* pay? He's been purified now by philosophy; he has no further need of what he left behind on Oeta.

HERMOTIMUS. You don't suppose it's for himself that he's made a fuss about a thing like that? No, no; the truth is he has young children, and that's what he's so concerned about—he doesn't want to leave them destitute.

LYCINUS. He should bring *them* up in the pursuit of virtue too; then they can share his felicity and look down their noses at money.

11   HERMOTIMUS. Lycinus, I haven't time to argue with you about it now; I'm in a hurry to get to his lecture, or I'll find myself left completely behind.

LYCINUS. Don't worry, my friend; truce is proclaimed today. I can save you the rest of your walk.

HERMOTIMUS. How do you mean?

LYCINUS. You won't find him just now, if the notice is right: there was a board hanging on his door, saying in large writing, "No class today." Apparently he was invited to dinner by the famous Eucrates last night—it was a birthday party for Eucrates' daughter. There was a good deal of philosophical discussion while they were all drinking, and your man got a bit annoyed with Euthydemus the Peripatetic during an argument he had with him about the usual Peripatetic criticisms of Stoicism. Well, the party went on till midnight, it seems, and what with all the shouting, he got a headache and a temperature; I imagine he'd had a bit too much to drink as well— I suppose they were all drinking each other's health—and too much to eat, too, for an old man. Anyway, he was very sick, apparently, when he got home. He managed to count and lock up carefully the slices of meat he'd handed to his servant, who was standing behind him at table; then he gave instructions not to admit any callers, and since then he's been asleep. I heard his servant, Midas, explaining all this to some of his students; then they turned and went away too—there were quite a lot of them.

12   HERMOTIMUS. Which of them won the argument, though

—my teacher or Euthydemus? Did Midas say anything about that?

LYCINUS. Well, at first it was pretty even, apparently; but in the end your side won—the old man proved much the superior. In fact Euthydemus didn't come out of it unscathed, so they say; he got a great crack on the skull. The presumptuous fellow kept on arguing and wouldn't admit he was in the wrong. Well, they happened to be sitting next to each other, and when Euthydemus refused to give in, your excellent teacher clouted him with a goblet he was holding, as big as Nestor's. And that's how he won.

HERMOTIMUS. Splendid! That's the way to deal with people who won't give in to their betters!

LYCINUS. Very reasonable. Euthydemus ought to have known better than to irritate an old man who was above anger and knew how to control his temper, when he had such a heavy goblet in his hand. But look, we haven't anything else to do; won't you tell me how you began the study of philosophy? I'm your friend; and perhaps I could start learning now and go the rest of the way with you, if it isn't too late for me; you're my friends, and I don't suppose you'll shut me out.

13

HERMOTIMUS. Oh, I only wish you would, Lycinus. You'll very soon see how superior you'll be to everybody else. I assure you, your mind will operate so far above the common plane that you'll think everybody else children compared to yourself.

LYCINUS. I'll be content if after twenty years I've reached your present state.

HERMOTIMUS. Don't worry. I was your age when I became interested in philosophy. I was about forty—I imagine that's what you are now.[8]

LYCINUS. That's right. So you take me and lead me by the same road; that's only fair. But tell me, first, do you let pupils

---

[8] "About forty" is the age at which, in the *Double Accusation*, Lucian represents himself as "deserting rhetoric for philosophy"; see Introduction, p. xxi.

argue about anything they don't agree with, or aren't novices allowed to do that?

HERMOTIMUS. Indeed they aren't. But *you* may ask questions if you like as you're learning: argue away, you'll learn more easily.

LYCINUS. Excellent idea, Hermotimus, by Hermes himself, whose name you bear. Now tell me, is there one road only to philosophy—the Stoic road? Or is it right what I hear about there being many other schools of philosophy?

HERMOTIMUS. Oh, there are a great many—Peripatetics, Epicureans, some who take Plato as their patron; and then there are Diogenes' school, and Antisthenes', and Pythagoras', and more yet.

LYCINUS. Right, then: there are a lot of them. Now tell me, do they teach the same doctrines or different ones?

HERMOTIMUS. Oh, different, totally different.

LYCINUS. And the truth, presumably, must lie with one of these doctrines—not with all of them, if they're all different?

HERMOTIMUS. That's right.

LYCINUS. Come then, my dear friend, tell me—when you first began to study philosophy and there were many gates open to you, on what authority did you pass by the others and turn to Stoicism and think that *that* was the way to enter in to virtue, the only true creed, which showed you the direct road, while the rest were blind alleys that would lead you nowhere? What was the criterion you used in coming, at the time, to this conclusion? Now please don't think of yourself as you are at present—that is, halfway to wisdom, if not already there, and far more capable of distinguishing the better from the worse than we ordinary people are. I want you to answer in the character you then had as an untrained layman, such as I am now.

HERMOTIMUS. I don't see what you're getting at.

LYCINUS. Well, it's really a perfectly straightforward question. Put it this way: there are any number of philosophers—Plato, for instance, and Aristotle, and Antisthenes, and your predecessors Chrysippus and Zeno, and all the rest. On what authority was it that you set the rest aside and chose, from the whole lot of them, the doctrine you did choose, the one you saw fit to study? Did the Pythian announce to you that the Stoics were the best of men, and send you off to their doctrine as he directed Chaerephon? [9] He has a habit of turning people into different philosophical channels—he knows what would suit each individual, I suppose.

HERMOTIMUS. Oh no, nothing like that, Lycinus; I certainly didn't ask for divine guidance.

LYCINUS. Was that because you didn't think it was all that important, or because you thought you were capable of choosing the best path to take all by yourself, without divine help?

HERMOTIMUS. I thought I could do it myself.

LYCINUS. Well, do teach me this first of all, how to choose at the outset, right at the beginning, which is the best, the true philosophy, the one to choose, putting aside the rest.

16

HERMOTIMUS. I'll tell you: I noticed that it was the one most people made for, and deduced that it was the best.

LYCINUS. How many more chose Stoicism than chose the Epicurean or Platonic or Peripatetic creeds? You must have counted them, obviously, as one would in an election.

HERMOTIMUS. Oh no, I didn't count them; I just guessed.

LYCINUS. Oh, come now, you're not trying to instruct me at all; you're just pulling my leg—saying you made such important decisions by guessing at numbers! You're trying to hide the truth from me.

HERMOTIMUS. Oh, that wasn't the only test. Common report said that the Epicureans were self-indulgent hedonists, the Peripatetics grasping and quarrelsome, and the Platonics arrogant and vain; but the general opinion of the Stoics was that they were courageous and their understanding compre-

[9] Chaerephon, when he asked Apollo's oracle who was the wisest man on earth, was told "Socrates"—to the great astonishment of Socrates, who searched for the god's meaning and concluded that he was wise because he "knew that he knew nothing." Cf. *D. D.* 20. 5, n. 62.

hensive, and that whoever took their path was the only king, the only rich man, the only wise man, and everything rolled into one.

17   LYCINUS. Of course it was other people who told you all this about them? Obviously you wouldn't have paid much attention to this eulogy if it had come from the Stoics themselves.

HERMOTIMUS. Certainly I shouldn't. No, it was other people who said that.

LYCINUS. Not their philosophical opponents, I suppose?

HERMOTIMUS. Oh, no.

LYCINUS. The man in the street, then?

HERMOTIMUS. Exactly.

LYCINUS. Now look here, you're pulling my leg again! You're not telling the truth. You must think it's Margites [10] or somebody you're talking to, expecting me to believe that when it came to making a choice of what was best in philosophy and philosophers, an intelligent man like Hermotimus with forty years of life behind him was quite satisfied to take the word of the man in the street! No, I really can't believe that.

18   HERMOTIMUS. Oh, I assure you, Lycinus, it wasn't only the word of others I went by: I used my own common sense. For instance, I could see that they walked in a dignified manner and were decently dressed; that they always had a contemplative air and a manly countenance, and their hair was generally cut close; there was nothing effeminate about them, nor on the other hand anything unduly negligent, as with those Cynic scarecrows; [11] they behaved in a moderate manner, and anybody will tell you that's the best way to behave.

LYCINUS. And did you also see them acting the way I just said I myself had seen your own teacher acting—lending money and screaming for payment, quarreling furiously in

---

10 *Margites*, a mock-epic sometimes attributed to one Pigres, who may have lived *ca.* 500 B.C., relates the adventures of the foolish Margites, a figure of fun of a type common in folklore.

11 Cf. Diogenes in *Sale* 7–11.

company, and generally showing off? Or doesn't that worry you, so long as they're decently dressed and have long beards and short haircuts? According to Hermotimus, then, our strict rule for the future, our straight edge to judge these matters by, is to be this—we are to discern men of worth by their dress and the way they walk and the way they wear their hair; and anyone who doesn't meet these requirements and doesn't go about with a frown on his brow and a cogitative expression on his face is to be rejected and discarded. Come, come, Hermotimus, you're *still* trying to make fun of me: you want to see if I'll realize I'm having my leg pulled.

HERMOTIMUS. What makes you say that?

LYCINUS. Why, my dear man, this test you're talking about, this judging by appearance, is a test for statues! And they're much more handsome to look at, much better dressed, because your Phidias and Alcamenes and Myron were aiming at good looks when they made them. But even supposing you're right, supposing that *is* the proper criterion to apply, what happens if a blind man wants to study philosophy? How is he to tell who professes the best creed if he can't see how they dress or carry themselves?

HERMOTIMUS. Lycinus, I'm not talking about blind men; I'm not interested in blind men.

LYCINUS. Ah, but my good sir, we ought to have some universally applicable way of deciding matters of such weight and such general interest. Still, if you like we'll exclude the blind from the study of philosophy, since they cannot see— although they're the very people who have most need of philosophy, to comfort them in their misfortune. Still, what about people who can see, now? However sharp-sighted they may be, what insight can they get into spiritual attainments from this outer cover? What I mean is, was it not love of the intellectual qualities of the Stoics that made you attach yourself to them, in the expectation of intellectual improvement for yourself?

HERMOTIMUS. Certainly it was.

LYCINUS. Well now, how could you distinguish between true and false philosophers by the characteristics *you* mention? The qualities we're looking for aren't as obvious as that;

19

20

they're secret and hidden, they only gradually reveal themselves after long association, in what a man says and in the
way he suits his actions to his words. I suppose you've heard
Momus' criticism of Hephaestus? If you haven't, I'll tell you
now. The story is that Athena and Poseidon and Hephaestus
fell to arguing over who was the best craftsman. Well, Poseidon made the bull, Athena invented the house, and Hephaestus, you see, made a man. Then they went to Momus and
asked him to give his decision. Momus examined each of the
products. We won't bother with what he said about the others,
but his criticism of the man was as follows: his creator, he
complained, hadn't thought to make a window in his chest, so
that it could be opened and everybody could see his thoughts
and intentions and whether he was telling the truth or not.
Well, Momus' views on man must be attributed to bad eyesight; *you* evidently can see better than Lynceus,[12] you can see
what's going on in a man's heart. It's all an open book to
you, you not only know every man's desires and opinions, you
can even tell the good from the bad.

21   HERMOTIMUS. Now you're joking, Lycinus. I made my
choice in all reverence and do not regret it, and that is good
enough for me.

LYCINUS. And yet, my friend, you won't tell me too? You'll
see me perish with the mob and do nothing to help?

HERMOTIMUS. Why, you won't accept anything I say!

LYCINUS. Quite the opposite, my dear fellow—you won't
say anything I can accept. Well, since you're deliberately keeping me in the dark and begrudge me the chance of rising to
your heights in philosophy, I'll try, as best I can, to discover
for myself what the true criterion should be in these matters,
and what is the safest way of making one's choice. Will you
listen, please?

HERMOTIMUS. Indeed I will, Lycinus; you may well come
up with a bright idea.

LYCINUS. Well then, pay attention and don't laugh at me
if I conduct my inquiry in a very amateurish way; that's the

12 The farsighted lookout on the Argo; his name means "the lynx."

way it has to be, since you who know better refuse to give me any clearer information. Let us imagine Virtue, then, as a kind of city whose inhabitants live in felicity, as your own teacher would put it, and he is one of those inhabitants; they are perfect in wisdom, courageous every one of them, just, temperate —in fact, virtually gods. You will never, so I understand, find any of them attempting any of the shocking practices of our everyday life, such as theft or assault or profiteering; life there is peaceful and harmonious. And well it might be, since they never come up against any of the things which to my mind are the occasion of discord and dispute and treacherous machinations in other cities; since they do not consider money and pleasure and fame any cause for quarreling, and indeed have long since expelled them from the city as not being necessary to society. The result is, they live a life of peace and utter felicity, in equity, equality, liberty, and all the other desirable conditions.

HERMOTIMUS. Well now, Lycinus, surely all men should strive passionately to be citizens of such a city? And neither reckon the effort of getting there nor be disheartened by the time it takes, so long as they *are going* to get there and be registered themselves on the citizen roll and enjoy the privileges of that status?

LYCINUS. Heavens above, we should expend all our energies on this above all things and put other things aside. If our country in this world lays claim to us, we should not pay great heed to that, nor if we have children and parents should we weaken when they cry and would hold us back. By all means let us exhort them to take the same road; but if they will not or cannot, we should shake them off and head straight for that city of bliss; and in our eager speed cast off our very coat, if they lay hold of it to detain us, for we need not fear exclusion, not though we arrive naked. You see, I've heard life there described before now, by an old man who once urged me to follow him to that city. He was to lead the way himself, and said he would register me when I got there, enroll me in the tribe and introduce me to his own clan, so that

I could share in the universal felicity. "But I harkened not," [13] in my youthful folly—that was some fifteen years ago; if I had, I might now be in the very outskirts, even by the gates.

Anyway, among the numerous things he said about the city, if I remember rightly, was this: that all its inhabitants are newcomers, strangers to it, and not a single one is indigenous to it; that among them are to be found a great many non-Greeks, slaves, cripples, dwarfs, and poor men—in fact anyone can become a citizen, since the requirements for registration make no mention of wealth or dress or height or beauty or family or illustrious lineage. All this has no place at all in their society. All anyone needs to become a citizen is good sense, a passion for the good, energy, perseverance, and the ability to stand up without weakening to all the difficulties he will meet on the way; and anyone who displays these qualities, and continues his journey to the city till he reaches his goal, automatically becomes a citizen, whoever he is, and has the same rights as anyone else. As for being better or worse, or noble or common, or slave or free man, no such ideas —in fact no such words—even exist in the state.

25   HERMOTIMUS. Well, you can see that all my exertions, in striving so eagerly to become myself a member of that beautiful and happy city, are not for nothing; it is no mean aim.

LYCINUS. Why, Hermotimus, I am myself passionate in the very same quest. There's nothing I would rather have happen to me, and if the city were close at hand and visible to everyone, I assure you I'd have gone there myself long ago without any hesitation, I'd have joined the ranks of its inhabitants long since. But since, according to you and your poet Hesiod, it is situated very far off, one must find a road that will lead to it and a guide, the best we can find—don't you agree?

HERMOTIMUS. How else could one get there?

LYCINUS. Well now, as far as promising goes, and claim-

[13] The source of this quotation is not known. This passage has been interpreted as referring to Lucian's meeting with the philosopher Nigrinus, described in his *Nigrinus;* cf. Introduction, p. xix.

ing to know all about it, there are plenty of people who will undertake to guide you, plenty of them, standing about ready to go, and every one of them claims to be native to it. But there doesn't seem to be one single road; there are any number of them, all going different ways and none the same as any other. They go West and East and North and South, it seems, one through fields and trees and moist, shady places, a pleasant road with nothing to oppose your progress or make the going difficult; another stony and rough, with promises of parching heat, and thirst, and sweat. And yet they're all supposed to lead to the selfsame city, though they end up at the opposite ends of the earth.

And that's just where my whole difficulty lies. No matter *26* which one I approach, there's a man standing at the end of every road, just at the entrance to it, looking eminently reliable and holding out his hand to me, urging me to take *his* way. Every one of them says that he's the only one who knows the direct route, and that the rest are off course and have never been there themselves or followed in the train of anyone who could show them the way. I go to his neighbor; he makes exactly the same promises about *his* road, and *he* abuses all the others; and his neighbor likewise, and so on with the lot of them. Believe you me, the multiplicity and variety of roads disturbs me not a little; I don't know where I am; and worst of all is the way the guides try to outdo each other in lauding their own wares, every one of them. I tell you, I don't know where to turn; I don't know which one to follow to reach the city.

HERMOTIMUS. Oh, I can solve your problem; take the *27* word of those who have traveled the road before you and you can't go wrong.

LYCINUS. Yes, but who are they? Those who have traveled *which* road? Followed *which* guide? It's the same problem coming up in another form, you see—we've merely changed the terms from things to people.

HERMOTIMUS. How do you mean?

LYCINUS. Well, if one took Plato's road and traveled with

him, that is obviously the road one would recommend; if Epicurus', *that* is; and so on; *you* would recommend *yours*. Surely that's what happens, Hermotimus?

HERMOTIMUS. Naturally.

LYCINUS. Well then, you haven't solved my problem at all. I'm as much in the dark as ever as to which traveler to believe. I see that each one of them, and his guide himself, has tried only one and now recommends it as the only one leading to the city. But I can't know whether he's telling the truth. I'll grant, perhaps, that he has reached *an* end and seen *a* city. But I still don't know, surely, whether it was the right one, the one you and I are so eager to live in, or whether, when Corinth was his destination, he ended up in Babylon and thought he'd seen Corinth; surely not everyone who has seen a city has seen Corinth, Corinth not being the only city there is? But the most difficult thing about the problem is the knowledge that there *can* only be one true road. There is only one Corinth, and the other roads lead anywhere but to Corinth—unless one be so far demented as to think that the Hyperborean route [14] and the Indian route both lead to Corinth.

HERMOTIMUS. Oh, how could they? They all lead different ways.

28   LYCINUS. Well then, my dear Hermotimus, the choice of road and guide needs more than casual attention; we mustn't just let our feet take us where they will, as the phrase goes, or before we know it we'll be off on the road to Babylon or Bactria instead of Corinth. It isn't a good idea to leave it to luck, either, and hope to hit on the right road by setting off any old way without even making any inquiries. We *could* be lucky, of course; quite possibly it has turned out right now and then through the centuries; but surely we have no business taking reckless chances in such serious matters, or confining our hopes within such slender possibilities—trying to sail the Aegean or the Ionian sea on a wickerwork mat, as the proverb has it. We can't blame fortune if her slings and arrows don't quite hit the target of truth; there are so many

14 I.e., the route to the north.

kinds of falsehood that it's a million-to-one chance. Even the archer in Homer, Teucer I think, couldn't manage it; he aimed at the dove but cut through the string.[15] No, it's much more reasonable to expect your arrow to hit one of any number of other marks rather than just that one of all the lot.

And just how dangerous it can be to land up on one of the wrong roads instead of the direct one, by trusting to luck, in our ignorance, to make our choice for us better than we could, I will illustrate by the example of a man who casts off from his moorings and commits himself to the winds; that is to say, it isn't easy for him to turn back and make harbor again; he simply has to let himself be driven about the high seas. He'll be seasick as like as not, and scared stiff, and the swell will give him a splitting headache; and the truth is, he should never have set sail in the first place without first climbing up a cliff to see if the wind was right for him to sail to Corinth, or without selecting the best navigator he could find and a stout ship strong enough to stand up to the high seas.

HERMOTIMUS. Yes, that's much the better way. I know very well, though, that you can make the rounds of the whole lot and you won't find better guides or more skilled navigators than the Stoics. If you really do want to reach Corinth eventually, you'll follow them, in Chrysippus' and Zeno's footsteps. That's the only way.

LYCINUS. Ah yes, but that's what they all say, Plato's fellow traveler and Epicurus' follower and all the rest: every one of them will say I won't reach Corinth unless I go with *him*. So I must either believe them all, which is absurd, or disbelieve them all alike; and the latter course is far the safer, until we discover the truth.

Look, suppose that I, in my present state of ignorance about which among all of them is telling the truth, were to choose your doctrine on your authority; you are a friend of mine but still you know only the Stoic doctrine, that is the only way you have traveled. And suppose some god were to bring Plato and Pythagoras and Aristotle and the rest of them

29

30

15 *Iliad* XXIII. 865–67.

back to life, and they crowded around me and questioned me —or indeed took me to court and severally brought suits against me for maltreatment. If they said to me, "Dear Lycinus, on what grounds, on what authority, did you give precedence over us to Chrysippus and Zeno? We are much their seniors; they are creatures of yesterday; yet you gave us no chance to state our case, you made no trial of our doctrine at all"—well now, if they said that, what answer could I give them? Would it do to say "My friend Hermotimus told me to"? No; I know what they'd say. "Lycinus," they would say, "we don't know this Hermotimus, whoever he is, nor does he know us. You had no right to condemn us, to give judgment in default against all of us, on the authority of a man who has acquaintance with only one of the roads of philosophy, and perhaps not a very close acquaintance at that. Legislators enjoin different procedure on juries, Lycinus. They may not listen to one side and then refuse the other permission to put the arguments it thinks to its advantage. They must attend to both alike, for by comparative examination of the arguments they can more easily discover what is true and what is false. And if they do not attend to both alike, the law allows appeal to another court."

31   That's the kind of thing they'd probably say. Or one of them might even proceed to interrogate me further, as follows: "Lycinus, imagine an Ethiopian who had never seen any other kind of man, such as us—he's never been out of his country in his life; suppose he were to insist, in some Ethiopian assembly, that there were no such beings as white or yellow men, or anything but black men, anywhere on earth— would they give him credence? Or would some Ethiopian elder say to him, 'How do *you* know, you presumptuous fellow? You've never been out of our country at all; you haven't the slightest idea what things are like elsewhere.'" I should say the old man's question was justified. What do you suggest, Hermotimus?

HERMOTIMUS. Say what you said. The old man's rebuke seems very proper to me.

LYCINUS. To me too. But I'm not sure if what follows will seem equally proper to you too, though it certainly does to me.

HERMOTIMUS. What is that?

LYCINUS. Obviously my interlocutor would go on from   *32*
there and say: "Well now, Lycinus, let us draw an analogy, in the man who only knows about the Stoic doctrine, like this friend of yours, Hermotimus. He's never been abroad, to visit Plato's country or Epicurus or in fact anyone else at all. So then, if he says there is no such beauty or truth in the majority of doctrines as there is in Stoicism, wouldn't you naturally consider him presumptuous in proclaiming his opinions on them all when he only knows about one—when he's never so much as set foot outside Ethiopia?" What am I to answer?

HERMOTIMUS. Tell him the perfect truth, of course: that while it is Stoic doctrine we study intensively, since that is the philosophy to which we are committed, we are not ignorant about what the others teach, also. Our teacher actually goes through their doctrines with us too, in passing, and of course adds his own comments and demolishes them.

LYCINUS. Do you really think the disciples of Plato and   *33*
Pythagoras and Epicurus and the rest will let that pass without comment? Don't you think they'll laugh out loud and say to me: "Look at the way your friend Hermotimus goes on, Lycinus! He accepts without qualm what our opponents say about us; he thinks our doctrines are as they are described by people who either know nothing about them or else misrepresent them deliberately. If he saw an athlete limbering up before a contest, kicking into the air or letting fly with his fists at nothing as if he were really hitting his opponent, would he, if he were the umpire, rush to proclaim him invincible? Or would he think that these displays of youthful energy were easily put on and quite safe, since there was no opponent present, and that the victory could only be awarded when he overcame and mastered his opponent and the opponent admitted defeat, and was not to be awarded otherwise? Well then, tell Hermotimus not to suppose that his teachers

are victorious, or our doctrines easily overthrown, from the evidence of this shadowboxing; *we* are not there. That would be like the houses children build; they make them fragile and can knock them down at the first blow. Or like people practicing archery: they tie up a bundle of twigs, stick it on a pole a few yards away, take aim, and let fly at it; when they hit and pierce the twigs, they at once shout out as if they'd achieved something difficult by getting their arrow through the bundle. That isn't what the Persians or Scythian archers do; to start with, they're generally on horseback and in motion when they shoot; and then they want their targets to be moving too, not standing waiting for the arrow to strike, but moving past at the highest speed they can muster. And you know, they can generally bring wild animals down; some of them can hit birds. If they ever want really to test the impact of their missiles on a target, they set up a piece of hard wood or a rawhide shield and pierce it, assuming that then their arrows would pierce armor too. So tell Hermotimus from us that what his teachers are bringing down is straw targets of their own devising—and they claim to have mastered armed men: they draw pictures of us and box with them, and then when they win, as of course they do, they think it's us they've beaten. No—we apply to them, every one of us, Achilles' remark about Hector—'they do not see the face of my helmet.' " [16]

34   That's what they'd say, every one of them, one after another. And Plato, I imagine, would tell one of his fund of Sicilian stories: the story of Gelo of Syracuse, who had bad breath but did not know it for a long time, because no one could nerve himself to bring such an accusation against a tyrant, until finally a foreign woman came into contact with him and actually did tell him about it. Gelo went to his wife and was angry with her for not telling him, when she of all people knew he had bad breath. She begged his forgiveness, saying that since she had had no experience of, or close contact with, any other man, she had thought that all men had

[16] *Iliad* XVI. 70.

similar breath. Well, Hermotimus' only association has been
with the Stoics, Plato would say; no wonder he doesn't know
what other men's mouths are like. And Chrysippus too would
say the same, if not more vehemently, if I were to leave him
aside without a trial and head for Platonism on the advice of
someone whose only association had been with Plato. In a
word, my position is that so long as there is any doubt about
which is the right philosophical doctrine to embrace, one
should not embrace any; to do so would be to offend against
the rest.

HERMOTIMUS. For heaven's sake, Lycinus, let's leave Plato   *35*
and Aristotle and Epicurus and the rest of them in peace. I'm
not up to arguing with them. Let's hold our own inquiry, you
and I, as to whether the business of philosophy is what I say
it is. As for Ethiopians, and Gelo's wife—why go bringing her
into the argument from Syracuse?

LYCINUS. All right, they must clear out of the way, if you
think they are superfluous to the argument. You go ahead,
then; I'm sure your words will be worth listening to.

HERMOTIMUS. It seems to me perfectly possible to arrive
at knowledge of the truth by a thorough study of Stoic doctrine alone, without going through all the other doctrines and
becoming expert in every one of them. Look at it this way. If
someone tells you merely that two and two are four, must you
go around to all the other mathematicians you can find in
case one of them makes it five or seven? Or would you know at
once that he's telling the truth?

LYCINUS. I'd know at once.

HERMOTIMUS. Then why on earth do you consider it impossible for a man to come into contact with the Stoics alone,
discover that they tell the truth, put his trust in them, and see
no need for the others—since he knows that four can never
be five, even if ten thousand Platos and Pythagorases say it is?

LYCINUS. That's irrelevant to our argument. You're com-   *36*
paring things everybody agrees on with matters of debate,
which are a very different proposition. Tell me, have you ever
met anyone who said that two and two make seven or eleven?

HERMOTIMUS. Of course not. It would be crazy to say that.

LYCINUS. Now then, have you ever—and please try to be honest—have you ever met a Stoic and an Epicurean who did *not* disagree about premises and ends?

HERMOTIMUS. No, I have not indeed.

LYCINUS. Well now, my fine fellow, take care you don't manage to pull the wool over my eyes—and me your friend! We're trying to find out which doctrine expounds the truth, and you beg the question; you hand the victory to the Stoics by assuming they're the people who make two and two four, when it isn't evident at all. The Epicureans and Platonists would say that *they* make it four, and you say it's five or seven. Isn't that what it amounts to when you hold that beauty is the only good and the Epicureans hold that pleasure is? When you say everything is material, and Plato maintains that there is an immaterial element in being as well? You're going much too far, as I said; you're laying hold of the point at issue and handing it to the Stoics as if it were indisputably their private property, despite the others who also lay claim to it as *their* own. Surely that's just the very thing we have to decide? Now, if it is proved that the Stoics alone make two and two four, it is time for the rest to keep quiet; but so long as they dispute this very point, we must give ear to all alike, or we can expect to be thought biased in our decision.

37   HERMOTIMUS. I don't think you understand my meaning, Lycinus.

LYCINUS. You'll have to make it clearer, then, if that isn't it.

HERMOTIMUS. You'll soon see what I mean. Suppose two men go into the temple of Asclepius or of Dionysus, and then one of the sacred bowls is discovered to be missing. Of course they'll both have to be searched, to see which of them has it hidden in his clothing.

LYCINUS. Certainly.

HERMOTIMUS. One of them is bound to have it.

LYCINUS. Bound to, if it's missing.

HERMOTIMUS. Well now, if you find it on the first man

you search, you won't then make the other man take his clothes off—he obviously hasn't got it.

LYCINUS. No, obviously.

HERMOTIMUS. And if we *don't* find the bowl in the first man's clothing, the second man must have it, and there's no need to search him in that case either.

LYCINUS. No. He's got it.

HERMOTIMUS. And so it is with us: if we find the bowl already in the Stoics' hands, we won't bother to continue the search with the others; we've got what we've been looking for all the time. Why go to any more trouble?

LYCINUS. No reason why—if you *do* find it, and if you can be sure it *is* the missing bowl when you've found it, and if in fact you have any means of recognizing the temple property. But in our case, my friend, to start with, it isn't two men who have entered the temple, so that one of the two of them is bound to have the stolen goods; it's a great many people. Then again, we don't know what the missing article really is; it may be a bowl or a cup or a garland—every one of the priests gives a different description of it. They don't even agree on what it's made of—some say bronze, some silver, others gold, others tin. So you'll have to make all the visitors strip, if you want to find the missing article; and in fact even if you find a golden bowl on the first man, you'll still have to make the others strip.

HERMOTIMUS. Why?

LYCINUS. Because it isn't certain that it's a bowl that was missing. But even if everybody should agree on that, they don't all agree that it's gold. And even if it's common knowledge that it's a gold bowl that's missing, and you find a gold bowl on the first man, you still can't stop there; you'll have to search the rest, because it isn't clear that this is the sacred bowl—you'll agree that there are any number of gold bowls?

HERMOTIMUS. Of course.

LYCINUS. Well then, you'll have to go around to all of them and search them all; you'll have to put everything you find on everybody in a pile in the middle and guess what in

38

39   the pile is most probably a sacred object. You see, what's caus-
ing all the trouble is the fact that everyone you're going to
make undress is bound to have something, a cup or a bowl or
a garland, and it may be bronze or gold or silver; but whether
what he has is a sacred object is as yet uncertain. Inevitably
you don't know which man to accuse of robbing the temple,
since even if they all had similar objects, it would still be uncertain which had committed the theft of the sacred property;
people do have private property too, you know. And our
perplexity is due purely to the fact that the missing bowl (let's
say it's a bowl) has no inscription. You see, if it had had the
god's name on it, or the name of the person who dedicated it,
it would have given us far less trouble: as soon as we found
the one with the name on it, we'd have stopped and not put
the rest to the trouble of taking their clothes off. I suppose
you've often been to watch athletic contests?

HERMOTIMUS. Oh yes, you're quite right—many a time,
and in many a place.

LYCINUS. And have you ever sat near the judges themselves?

HERMOTIMUS. Goodness, yes; last year at the Olympic
Games, Evandridas of Elis booked a seat for me in the Elean
enclosure, just to the left of the international judges. I was
very curious to get a good look at their whole procedure.

LYCINUS. Then you know too how they match the competitors in the wrestling and the pancratium?

HERMOTIMUS. Oh, yes.

LYCINUS. Well, you can describe it better than I can, since
you've seen it with your own eyes.

40   HERMOTIMUS. Well, in the old days, when Hercules was
judge of the games, laurel leaves——

LYCINUS. Oh, never mind the old days, Hermotimus. You
tell me what you saw with your own eyes.

HERMOTIMUS. A silver urn, from the temple property, is
set out, and into it are put little lots, about the size of beans;
these have letters marked on them in pairs, alpha on the first
two, beta on the second two, gamma on the third, and so on
according to the number of entries in the event: there are

always two lots with the same letter on them. Well, next each competitor comes up, asks Zeus's blessing, puts his hand in the urn, and draws one of the lots; after him comes another; and to each one is allotted a policeman, who holds his hand down so that he cannot read the letter on his lot. Then when they all have their lots they form a circle, and the officer in charge, I think it is, or it may be one of the judges—I forget the details—goes around examining the lots; and so, you see, he pairs off one with an alpha with the man who has the other, for a bout of wrestling or the pancratium; and the betas likewise, and all the other pairs of letters in the same way. That's if there's an even number of competitors, eight or four or twelve; if there's an odd number, five or seven or nine, an odd letter is written on one lot and put in with the rest, without any corresponding lot. The man who draws this one gets a bye into the next round, since he has no opposite number; it's quite a stroke of luck for an athlete, since it means he'll be fresh and matched against a tired opponent.

LYCINUS. Hold on—that's just what I wanted. Now suppose there are nine of them, and they've all drawn their lots and have them in their hands. Well now, you go around—I'll make you judge and not just a spectator—you go around inspecting the letters; you can't discover who has the bye, presumably, without going around them all and pairing them off.

HERMOTIMUS. How do you mean?

LYCINUS. You can't find the letter that indicates the bye right away; at least, you may find it, but you won't know that that is it. There's been no indication that it's kappa or mu or iota that decides who gets the bye. When you come across alpha, you look for the man with the other alpha, and when you have them both, they constitute a pair. Similarly, when you come across beta you find out where the other beta is, corresponding to the one you've found; and so on with the lot, until the only man left is the one with the single letter that has no partner.

HERMOTIMUS. But suppose you come upon him first or second—what will you do then?

LYCINUS. No, no—you're the judge; I want to know what

41

42

you will do. Will you say there and then that this is the bye? Or will you have to go around the whole circle to see if there isn't perhaps a twin to it? You can't tell which is the bye, you know, without seeing everybody's lot.

HERMOTIMUS. Oh yes I can, Lycinus; it's easy. If there are nine competitors and I come upon the letter epsilon first or second, I know that it's the man who's got *it* who gets the bye.

LYCINUS. How?

HERMOTIMUS. Like this: two of them have alphas, two betas, and of the remaining four one pair are bound to have gammas and one pair deltas. On these eight competitors, four letters have been used up; so obviously the only letter that can be the odd one is the next letter in the alphabet, epsilon; so whoever has it has the bye.

LYCINUS. Shall I congratulate you on your acumen, or should I oppose your views with mine, for what they may be worth?

HERMOTIMUS. Heavens, yes, do, though I simply cannot see what reasonable view you could urge that would be opposed to mine.

43   LYCINUS. Well now, what you say is based on the assumption that the letters must be an alphabetical sequence, with alpha first, for instance, beta second, and so on, until at some one letter the number of competitors runs out; and I grant you this is what happens at the Olympics. But suppose we pick out five letters in no particular order, from the whole alphabet—say, chi and sigma and zeta and kappa and theta. We put four of these, in duplicate, on eight competitors' lots, and zeta only on the ninth—with the intention, you see, that that shall indicate the bye. Now, what are you going to do if you find the zeta first? How are you going to know that it's the man with zeta who gets the bye, other than by going around to everybody and discovering there isn't another zeta to correspond with it? You can't deduce it from the alphabetical order, as you can in your theory.

HERMOTIMUS. That's a very difficult question.

LYCINUS. Look, let's look at the same thing another way. **44**
What about using for our lots not letters but signs and characters such as the Egyptians use instead of letters? They have any number of them—men with dogs' heads, men with lions' heads, and so on. Or no, we won't use those, they're grotesque; let's use straightforward, simple forms. Let's draw men on two lots, as best we can, horses on two others, two cocks, two dogs, and make the drawing on the ninth a lion. Well now, if you come upon this lot with the lion on it right at the beginning, how will you be able to tell that that's the one that indicates the bye, except by going around examining all the rest to see whether anyone else has a lion?

HERMOTIMUS. I can't answer that, Lycinus.

LYCINUS. No wonder; there isn't any very convincing an- **45**
swer. So, if we want to find either the man with the sacred bowl or the man with the bye or the man who will best guide us to the city we're looking for, our Corinth, we must necessarily go to all the candidates and examine them all; we must give them a thorough search; we must make them strip and compare them. Even so it won't be easy to discover the real truth. The only kind of person whose advice I'd take on philosophy, and which doctrine to adhere to, would be someone who knew what all of them said; no one else would be qualified; I should not take anyone's advice while he remained ignorant of even one doctrine, for that could be the best one. Look—if someone produced a handsome man and said he was the handsomest man on earth, we should not take his word for it unless we knew that he had seen every man on earth. He might indeed be handsome, but our informant could not know that he was the handsomest man on earth, not without seeing all the men on earth. And *we* aren't simply trying to find beauty; we're trying to find the highest beauty; and if we don't find that, we shall not consider that we have achieved anything. We aren't going to be content with whatever degree of beauty we come upon; it's pure beauty we're looking for, and pure beauty must necessarily be one.

HERMOTIMUS. That's true. **46**

LYCINUS. Well then, can you name anyone who has tried every philosophical road, who knows the doctrines of Pythagoras and Plato and Aristotle and Chrysippus and Epicurus and the rest, and has ended up by choosing one out of all of them because he has proved it genuine, because he has found by experience that it alone leads straight to felicity? If we could find such a man, we'd give up worrying about the matter.

HERMOTIMUS. It isn't easy to find such a man.

47   LYCINUS. What are we going to do, then? We mustn't give up, surely, just because we haven't got such a guide at the moment. The best and safest thing to do is for each of us to tackle the subject himself and go through every doctrine, examining carefully what each of them says. Don't you agree?

HERMOTIMUS. Well, it looks like it, from what we've said. But doesn't your previous objection apply? Once you launch out and spread sail, it isn't easy to turn and head for home again. How can you take all the roads if, as you say, you can't get off the first?

LYCINUS. I know—we'll do what Theseus does in plays. Ariadne will give us a ball of thread as we go into each labyrinth, and then we'll have no difficulty getting out—we'll simply take up the thread again.

HERMOTIMUS. Who's going to be our Ariadne, then? Where do we get the thread?

LYCINUS. Don't worry, my friend. I think I've hit on something we can hold on to to help us find our way out.

HERMOTIMUS. What?

LYCINUS. It isn't my own idea; it's the advice of one of the wise men—"Be sober, and remember to disbelieve." If we don't just believe everything we hear, but do as a jury does and let the other side state its case too, perhaps we'll get out of the labyrinths without any difficulty.

HERMOTIMUS. Good idea; let's do that.

48   LYCINUS. Well now, which shall we start with? Perhaps it won't matter. Start with any one—Pythagoras, say, if that's how it turns out. How long do we suppose it will take to be-

come thoroughly acquainted with Pythagoreanism? You mustn't forget to include the five years of silence, remember.[17] With those five years, then, thirty years will do, I should say—or if not that, at the very least twenty.

HERMOTIMUS. Let's say twenty.

LYCINUS. Then after that clearly we have to give Plato as much again, and Aristotle no less on top of that.

HERMOTIMUS. Oh, no, no less.

LYCINUS. As for Chrysippus, I shan't ask you; I've already heard you say that forty's hardly enough.

HERMOTIMUS. That's right.

LYCINUS. And so on for the others, Epicurus and the rest. And I'm not exaggerating these figures, as you'll realize if you think how many Stoics and Epicureans and Platonists there are who are in their eighties but still admit that they don't know all about their respective doctrines, not so as to be masters of them. And if they don't admit it, Chrysippus and Aristotle and Plato would certainly say it. Socrates would above all, and he's just as good as they are; he used to din it into everybody's ears not just that he didn't know everything but that he didn't know anything at all—except that he was ignorant.[18] Let's go back to the beginning now and reckon up. Twenty we said for Pythagoras, as many again for Plato, and so on for the rest of them. What does it come to, then, all told, if we assume only ten philosophical creeds?

HERMOTIMUS. Over two hundred.

LYCINUS. Shall we cut it down by a quarter, and say a hundred and fifty years will do? Or cut it in half, even?

HERMOTIMUS. You're a better judge of that than I am. 49 Even if you do, I can see that very few are going to manage to go right through with it, even if they start the minute they're born.

LYCINUS. Well then, if that's the case, how do we stand? Are we going to go back on what we agreed earlier, namely that the only way to choose the best of many creeds is to try

[17] Cf. *Sale* 3.
[18] The famous Socratic "irony"; cf. *D. D.* 20. 5 and sec. 15, n. 9 above.

them all? We did say, didn't we, that anyone who chose without trial was conducting his search for truth more by guesswork than by good judgment?

HERMOTIMUS. We did.

LYCINUS. Well, we'll simply have to live that long; no other way for it, if we want to make sure our choice is correct by trying them all, and then when we've chosen, study our philosophy, and when we've studied it, attain felicity. But anything less than that is dancing in the dark, as they say; we'd just knock up against anything at all, and assume that whatever came to hand first was what we were looking for, because we didn't know the truth. And even if we *did* accidentally stumble on the truth, we'd have no way of being certain that that was what we were looking for; there are many similar objects, every one of them claiming to be the real truth.

50   HERMOTIMUS. Lycinus, I suppose your arguments are logical enough; but to be honest with you, you really do annoy me, the way you insist on being so precise. You carry it too far; there's no need for it. It looks as if I was in for trouble when I came out of the house today, running into you like that. There was I near the fulfillment of my hopes, and you come along and cast me into despair—trying to prove it's impossible to find truth since it takes so long.

LYCINUS. Surely, my friend, it would be much more appropriate to blame your father, Menecrates, and your mother, whatever her name was—I don't know—or indeed go even farther back and blame the human condition—for not making you as long-lived and durable as Tithonus, but instead circumscribing your longevity as other men's, and limiting you to a century at most. All *I've* done is help you examine the case and deduce the logical consequences.

51   HERMOTIMUS. No, that isn't it. The truth is, you like acting the bully. For some reason or other you can't stand philosophy and you're just poking fun at those who practice it.

LYCINUS. Hermotimus, the nature of truth is a subject

that wise men like you and your teacher are much better qualified to discuss than I am. But I do know this much about it—it isn't very pleasant to listen to. People would far rather listen to lies; they're more attractive, and therefore more acceptable. Truth admits no counterfeit coin to her presence; she speaks frankly to men, and offends them thereby. Why, look at this present case: I've offended you by helping you discover the truth of it, by showing you how difficult it is to attain what we are both passionate to pursue. It's as if you were in love with a statue and hoped to gain your goal, under the delusion that it was human, and I realized that it was only stone or bronze and told you as an act of friendship that your desires were impossible to achieve, and then you thought I was ill-disposed to you because I would not let you deceive yourself with your grotesque and unattainable hopes.

HERMOTIMUS. We shouldn't study philosophy, then? We 52 should give ourselves up to idleness and live the life of the ordinary man? Is that what you're saying?

LYCINUS. Now when did you hear me say that? No, what I'm saying is not that we shouldn't study philosophy; but that since we should and since there are many roads to philosophy, and every one of them claims to entail the acquisition of virtue as well, and since it is far from certain which is the right road, we should be very careful in making our choice. Now, it proved impossible to choose the best course, of the many open to us, without testing all of them; and then it became apparent that the process of trial was rather long. Well, to repeat my question, what do you think? Will you join the train and philosophic company of the first man you come across and let him count you as a windfall for him?

HERMOTIMUS. Well, look, just what kind of answer *do* 53 you want? You maintain that no one is competent to judge on his own account unless he lives as long as a phoenix and spends his life going around to one school after another, trying them all out; but you refuse to accept previous experience or the general verdict and testimony!

LYCINUS. *General* verdict! Whose *general* verdict? Who

can speak from experience of *all* the doctrines? If there be any such, one man is quite enough for me; no need for general agreement. But if it's general *ignorance* you're talking about, I'm not impressed by mere numbers—not while their utterances depend on knowledge of none or one of all the doctrines.

HERMOTIMUS. You're the only man who ever beheld truth. All the others are fools, if they study philosophy.

LYCINUS. Hermotimus, it's misrepresentation to say that I in any way put myself above other people, or consider myself among the knowledgeable to start with. You're forgetting what I said: I don't know the truth, I don't lay claim to superiority; I agree that I am as ignorant of the truth as anyone else.

54 HERMOTIMUS. Well, Lycinus, perhaps it's logical to say you have to turn to every doctrine and test what it says, and that's the only way to choose the best. But to give so many years to each separate investigation is ridiculous. As if you can't judge them in their entirety from specimens! I should think it was in fact very simple, and wouldn't take much time at all. Why, you know the story about one of the sculptors—Phidias, I think: just by seeing a lion's claw he worked out the size of the whole lion if it were modeled in proportion to the claw. And you yourself, if you were shown a man's hand and nothing more, and the rest of the body were concealed from you, surely you'd know right away that it was a man that was concealed, even without seeing the whole body. Well then, it would be easy to grasp the principal tenets of all the doctrines in just a few hours. This excessive care, that entails so extended an examination, is quite unnecessary for choosing the best; one can make one's judgment from a summary knowledge.

55 LYCINUS. Dear, dear! How you do insist that you can know the whole from the parts! And yet I remember hearing the opposite—that if you know the whole you will know the part, but if you only know the part you won't thereby know the whole. I'll show you what I mean: tell me, would Phidias,

when he saw the lion's claw, ever have known that it was a lion's if he had never seen a whole lion? If you saw a man's hand, could you have said it was a man's without first having known or seen a man? No answer? Shall I answer for you? The only possible answer is No, you couldn't have. It looks as if Phidias has ended up not getting anywhere; he's sculpted his lion to no purpose, for evidently his contribution to the argument is "nothing to do with Dionysus."[19] Where is the similarity between the cases? The only thing that enabled you and Phidias to recognize the parts was your knowledge of the whole—that is, the man and the lion; whereas in philosophy, in Stoicism for example, how *can* you imagine the rest from part of it? How can you say it's beautiful? You don't know the whole from which the parts come.

As to your statement that it is easy to inform yourself on the principal beliefs of all the philosophies in a small part of one day—their principles and ends, their views of the gods and the soul, which of them maintain that all is matter and which hold that immaterial factors exist too, and that some hold goodness and happiness to consist in pleasure and some in beauty, and so on—well, if this is what you mean by "informing oneself," it *is* easy to pronounce an opinion; it's no trouble at all in fact. But to know which one teaches the truth is not, I am afraid, a matter for a part of a day, but requires many days; otherwise, why ever have each sect written hundreds and thousands of books on these very points? I imagine it's to convince people of the truth of these brief summaries that you think so readily digestible.

No, as far as I can make out, your method is still going to require a seer to help you choose the best course, if you won't tolerate spending time on making a careful choice by personal examination of the whole and of every individual item. Indeed, that would be a short cut; it would avoid complications and delays if you sent for a seer, listened to all

56

19 I.e., irrelevant; the phrase comes from an early criticism of Greek tragedy, which although it was performed at the festival of Dionysus soon began to use themes that were "nothing to do with Dionysus."

the summaries, and sacrificed a victim over each one. The god will save you endless bother by showing you what to choose by the victim's liver. Or if you like I can suggest another way, even simpler, which doesn't involve sacrificing these victims to any god or calling in any of these expensive priests. You put into an urn a number of tablets, each marked with the name of a philosopher, and get a young boy, whose parents are both living,[20] to go to the urn and pick out the first tablet that comes to his hand; then for the rest of your life you pursue the philosophy of whatever man wins the draw.

HERMOTIMUS. Lycinus, I'm surprised at you, acting the fool like this. Tell me, have you ever bought wine yourself?

LYCINUS. Yes, often.

HERMOTIMUS. Well now, did you go around to all the wine shops in town, tasting and examining the wines and comparing them?

LYCINUS. Certainly not.

HERMOTIMUS. No, what you do is order the first sound wine you come across that's worth buying.

LYCINUS. Heavens, yes.

HERMOTIMUS. And could you tell from that little sip what all the wine is like?

LYCINUS. Yes, I could.

HERMOTIMUS. Now then, suppose you were to approach the wine merchants and say, "My good men, I want to buy a half-pint of wine. Each of you must let me drink the whole of his jar; then I can discover by going through it all who keeps the best wine and whom to buy from." If you said that, wouldn't you expect them to laugh at you? And if you went on bothering them, probably to souse you in water?

LYCINUS. Indeed yes, and it would serve me right.

HERMOTIMUS. Well then, it's exactly the same with philosophy. Why do you have to swallow the whole jarful, when you can tell from a little sip what the whole is like?

LYCINUS. You're a slippery customer, Hermotimus; you

20 A sly reference to magic formulae.

run through one's fingers. Only you've helped my case; you thought you'd escaped, but you've fallen into the same net.

HERMOTIMUS. How do you mean?

LYCINUS. You're taking something whose nature is self-evident and known to everyone—wine—and comparing it with things that are fundamentally different, things that are obscure and that nobody can agree on. I can't imagine how you can think philosophy and wine are similar—except in this one respect, that philosophers sell their learning as shopkeepers their wares; and most of them dilute it, too, and defraud their customers with short measure. But let's consider what you're really saying: thus, you say that all the wine in the jar is consistent in quality—and perfectly right you are, goodness knows; and then that if you draw off and taste a tiny sip of it, you'll know at once what the whole jar is like—and that is equally correct, and I should never have disagreed. But now, what follows? Do philosophy and philosophers, such as your teacher, tell you the same things every day and stick to the same subjects? Or do they say different things at different times? Obviously they have a great deal to say, my friend; or you would never have stayed with him for twenty years, wandering and roaming around like Odysseus, if he'd kept on repeating himself; one hearing would have been enough.

HERMOTIMUS. Obviously.

60

LYCINUS. Then how could you have known the whole from the first taste? For it was not all uniform, like wine; it was one new point after another, all the time. So, my friend, unless you imbibe the whole jar, you're going about in your drunken state to no purpose, since, as far as I can see, the god has hidden philosophic Good right at the bottom of the cup, under the very dregs; so you'll have to drain it all down, right to the last drop, or else you'll never find that nectar for which I think you've been thirsting many a day. To your mind, its nature is such that you will become all-wise on the spot by tasting and swallowing even the tiniest drop—just as the prophetess at Delphi is supposed to be inspired as soon as she drinks from the holy spring, and so to give oracles to those who consult her. But it appears that isn't the case; at any rate, you've drunk over half the jar, and yet you said you were still at the beginning.

61   No: consider whether this is not a better illustration of philosophy. We'll keep your jar and your shopkeeper, but the contents of the jar will be not wine but a collection of seeds—wheat on top, then beans, then barley; below that, lentils, then peas, and all sorts besides. Well now, you want to buy seed, and you go to the shop; the shopkeeper takes a sample of the wheat from its layer and puts it into your hand for you to look at. Now, could you tell by looking at it whether the peas were good too, the lentils soft, and the beans not empty?

HERMOTIMUS. Certainly not.

LYCINUS. Well then, nor can you tell what the whole of a philosophical doctrine is like from one statement made at the beginning. It isn't consistent in quality, like the wine to which you compare it, maintaining that it will be like the drop you tasted; it is evidently of a different nature, and requires more than a casual examination; because whereas buying bad wine involves only the loss of a few pennies, losing oneself in the common crowd (as you yourself put it at the beginning of our discussion) is not a trivial risk. Furthermore, the man who demands that he be allowed to finish the jar in order to buy a half-pint involves the merchant in loss with his skepticism and his experiments; whereas philosophy will not suffer in the same way—however deep you drink of it, the jar grows no emptier and the merchant suffers no loss. The deeper it is drained the more it fills up, as the proverb says; quite the opposite of the jar of the Danaids, for it would not hold what was poured into it, but let it straight through; but the more you take from philosophy, the more remains.

62   And there is something else, in similar vein, that I should like to say about the sampling of philosophy. Do not think that I defame philosophy if I say that it is like a deadly poison, hemlock or aconite or something of that kind. For they too, though they can kill, will not do so if you scrape off with the edge of your nail a tiny little sample to taste; unless they are taken in the proper quantity and manner and form, the taker will not die. Now you wanted to claim that the tiniest quantity was sufficient to give a complete knowledge of the whole.

HERMOTIMUS. Oh, have it your own way, Lycinus. Well 63 then, do we have to live a hundred years, and go to all this bother? Is this the only way to become philosophers?

LYCINUS. The only way; and no wonder, if what you said to start with is true—that life is short, but art is long. But look, I don't know what's come over you; you're annoyed because you can't turn into a Chrysippus or Plato or Pythagoras before sunset, if you please!

HERMOTIMUS. You're trying to get the better of me: you're driving me into a corner. I've never done you any harm. You're envious, that's obviously what it is, because I've got somewhere in my studies while you've wasted yourself, and you a grown man.

LYCINUS. Well, do you know what you should do? Treat me as a lunatic and pay no attention to me; let me rave away, and you go forward on your way as you are and carry out your original intentions in these matters.

HERMOTIMUS. Why, you're so overbearing you won't let me make my choice until I've tested them all.

LYCINUS. Indeed I certainly shan't ever change my views; better be clear about that. You call me overbearing; but that's putting the blame where no blame lies, as the poet has it,[21] as long as you can't bring up any logical argument in your support, to release me from logic's grip. Why, look you now, logic is going to be much more overbearing yet with you—but perhaps you'll acquit logic and blame me?

HERMOTIMUS. More overbearing yet? And how, pray? I'm astonished logic has anything left to say.

LYCINUS. It says that seeing all the philosophies and going 64 through them all is still not enough to enable you to choose the best, that the most important thing is still missing.

21 *Iliad* XI. 654.

HERMOTIMUS. And what is that?

LYCINUS. Critical and analytical equipment, a sharp intellect, an accurate mind, integrity—such as befit him who is to pass judgment on matters of such import. Without these, a complete inspection is useless. So, logic says, even a man so equipped must be given plenty of time to bring all the philosophies together, take his time, linger over the problem, and only make his choice after considering it many many times. He will not be influenced by any candidate's years or appearance or reputation in philosophy; he will act as do the Areopagites,[22] who conduct their trials in the darkness of night, so as to consider not the pleaders but the pleas. Only then will you be able to make your choice, and so pursue philosophy, on solid grounds.

HERMOTIMUS. Yes—in the afterlife. From what you say no human life would be long enough: approach all doctrines, examine each one closely, after examination make your judgment, after judgment choose, and after choosing pursue philosophy—that's the only way, you say, to find out the truth, and there is no other.

LYCINUS. Why, Hermotimus—I hesitate to tell you, but even this is not enough yet. We seem to be taking it for granted that we have made some solid discovery, when in fact we haven't. We're like fishermen who cast their nets and, when they feel a heavy pull, haul them in expecting a great catch of fish; but instead, after dragging them up with much sweat, often find a stone or a pot full of sand. I'm afraid our catch is of that kind.

HERMOTIMUS. I don't know what these nets you talk about are supposed to be. I know this—you've got me all tied up in them.

LYCINUS. Well now, try to slip through the meshes; you can swim as well as anybody, thank goodness. What I mean is this: even if we extend our examination to every sect, and even if we manage to get through it sometime, to my mind the fundamental point will still be unproven as to whether

22 Members of the Areopagus, or Supreme Court.

any of them possesses what we are looking for, or whether they are all equally ignorant.

HERMOTIMUS. What? Not one of them necessarily possesses the truth?

LYCINUS. I cannot be certain. Do you think it impossible that they are all in error, and truth is something else, which none of them has yet discovered?

HERMOTIMUS. How can that be?

66

LYCINUS. Like this. Suppose the number we want is twenty. Suppose, for example, a man takes twenty beans in his hand, closes his fist, and asks ten people how many beans he has in his hand. They make various guesses—seven, five, thirty, ten, fifteen—various different numbers, in short. Now, it is possible, is it not, that one of them may actually hit upon the right number?

HERMOTIMUS. Yes.

LYCINUS. But, now, nor is it impossible for all of them to say various different numbers, wrong numbers, not the right one, and for none of them to say that the man has twenty beans. Is that not so?

HERMOTIMUS. It isn't impossible.

LYCINUS. Well now, in the same way all the philosophers are trying to find out the nature of happiness; they give various accounts of it—some say it is pleasure, some beauty, and some the other things people say about it. Now, it is likely that one of these actually is happiness; but it is not unlikely that in fact it is something different from all of them. It would appear that we've been working the wrong way around; we've been rushing to get to the end before we've found the beginning; we ought to have waited till it was established that the truth has been discovered, and that some philosopher unquestionably knows it, and then conduct our inquiry as to whom we should listen to after that.

HERMOTIMUS. So what you're saying is, we're not bound to be able to discover the truth even if we go right through the whole of philosophy?

LYCINUS. My dear friend, don't ask me; ask logic itself

again. Perhaps logic will reply that it is still not guaranteed, not so long as it remains uncertain whether it is one of the things our friends the philosophers say it is.

67   HERMOTIMUS. According to you, then, we'll never find the truth; we'll never become philosophers; we'll have to give up the idea altogether and live like the man in the street. Anyway, that follows from what you're saying, that philosophy is impossible and unattainable for a mere mortal. You maintain that if a man proposes to be a philosopher, he must first choose the best philosophy; and the only way to choose correctly, you say, is to go through the whole of philosophy and choose the truest doctrine. Then when you reckoned up the number of years each one would call for, you went beyond all bounds and drew it out to several generations. Truth will arrive too late for any man's lifetime. And after all that, you even say that the crucial point is a matter of doubt, whether philosophers in all time past have ever arrived at the truth or not.

LYCINUS. Well, Hermotimus, how can *you* swear to it that they ever have?

HERMOTIMUS. I can't swear to it.

LYCINUS. And yet, how much else I've consciously overlooked! Although it too calls for long examination.

68   HERMOTIMUS. Such as?

LYCINUS. Does it not come to your ears that there are Stoics and Epicureans and Platonists who allege that some of their number know their respective doctrines but others do not—though in every other respect they are very reliable?

HERMOTIMUS. That is true.

LYCINUS. Well now, don't you think it's going to be a great deal of trouble to tell who are the ones who do know their doctrine, and separate them from those who don't although they profess it?

HERMOTIMUS. A great deal.

LYCINUS. Then, if you're going to know who is the best of the Stoics, you'll have to approach at least most of them, if indeed not all, and try them out, and appoint the best of them your teacher. But first you must train your critical faculty in such matters, or you may inadvertently choose the worst. Now, look how much time this too is going to need. I deliberately left it out of the discussion before—I was afraid you would be angry. Yet surely this is the most important and most necessary equipment of all in such matters—matters of doubt, debatable matters, that is? Your only reliable, firm hope in the search to discover the truth is to possess the ability to distinguish and separate the true from the false, to tell, as silver-assayers do, the honest, true coin from the counterfeit. If you were approaching the examination of doctrines with this ability, this equipment, well and good; but without it, be assured there is nothing to prevent one after another of them from leading you by the nose. You will follow the proffered shoot like a sheep; or rather, you will be like water on a table top, directed this way and that by the trailing of a finger tip; or, indeed, a reed growing on a riverbank, bending to every breeze, though it be but the lightest breath of air that makes it quiver.

Now, if you could find a teacher of some attainments in the art of demonstration and logical method, and get him to teach you, obviously you'd have no more difficulty. The best would be apparent to you at once: truth would be induced to appear by your art of demonstration, falsehood would be refuted, and you would have firm ground for assessing and choosing and entering upon the pursuit of philosophy; you would enter into the possession of felicity, so passionately desired, to live with her and enjoy, in short, every good thing there is.

69

HERMOTIMUS. Splendid, Lycinus! Why, this is a much better idea! It gives us a reasonable hope to cling to. That's obviously what to do—find a man who can train our powers of analysis and judgment and, particularly, demonstration. Why, the rest will be easy after that! It won't give us any bother and it won't take up much time. Well, I must say I'm grateful to you now for finding us this short cut, this royal road.

LYCINUS. And yet you've no reason to be grateful to me

yet. I haven't found anything or shown you anything that will bring you any nearer the realization of your hopes. In fact, we're much farther off than we were before; we're "still no better off for all our sweat," as they say.

HERMOTIMUS. What do you mean? Some pretty miserable, pessimistic notion, from the sound of it.

70 LYCINUS. I mean that even if we do find someone who claims he is skilled in demonstration and can teach the art to others, presumably we aren't going to take his word for it there and then? We're going to find someone else who is competent to decide whether or not his claim is valid; and even if there is someone at hand, we still aren't going to be sure that this arbiter knows the difference between a good and a bad judge—we need another arbiter to set over *this* man himself, surely? After all, how could *we* tell who is best fitted to pass judgment? You can see how far this goes: it's endless; it's impossible to call a halt and stop the process. You'll notice that all the demonstrations one could think up are themselves of dubious validity and have no sound basis. Most of them in fact, in struggling to convince us that it is genuine knowledge they convey, use means of doing so that are themselves open to question. Others try to draw analogies between the obscurest of questions and the most obvious truths, which have nothing in common with them, but which they claim demonstrate the validity of their arguments. It's as if you were to claim that one could demonstrate the existence of the gods from the fact that there obviously are altars to the gods.[23] So we're going around in circles; we're back to the problem we started with.

71 HERMOTIMUS. What a way to treat me, Lycinus—making my treasure out to be ashes! I've just been wasting all that time and labor, then?

LYCINUS. Well, Hermotimus, it will greatly temper your distress to realize that you're not the only one to be disappointed of the splendid hopes you cherished. Everyone who pursues philosophy is fighting over the donkey's shadow, so to speak. Why, who *could* go through all the process I've out-

23 Cf. *Zeus* 51.

lined? It's impossible; you yourself admit that. At the moment you're acting, so it seems to me, like the man who cries and rails against fortune because he can't rise into the sky, or plunge into the depths of the sea and swim underwater from Sicily to Cyprus, or take wing and fly from Greece to India in a day. And what is responsible for his distress, I imagine, is that he had had hopes: he had had dreams in which all this happened, or he imagined it all in his own mind—without first asking himself whether his visions were attainable, and such as befitted humanity.

You too, my friend: you've been dreaming, many and marvelous dreams; and logic has dug you in the ribs and startled you out of your sleep, and you are annoyed at her for it—your eyes are scarce yet opened, and you do not find it easy to shake off your sleep, so pleasant have been the visions you've been seeing in it. It's what happens to people who daydream of happiness: just as they're well launched into their dreams, rolling in money, digging up buried treasure, ruling nations, as happy as can be in all sorts of ways—and these fancies the goddess Daydream bestows with light and lavish hand, for she is a bounteous lady and says no to nothing, even though you would grow wings, or rival the Colossus in size, or discover whole mountains of gold: well then, when they are occupied with these fancies and their slave comes in on some mundane errand—he wants to know where the money's to come from to buy bread, or what he is to say to the man who's come for the rent (and he's been kept waiting so long)—they get annoyed, as if by bothering them with these questions the slave had snatched all their happy dreams from them; they practically bite the nose off him.

But don't *you* let yourself be thus affected toward me, my dear friend. There were you, digging up your treasures, flying aloft, entertaining various extravagant fancies and unattainable hopes; and there was I, your friend, unwilling to look on idly while you spent your whole life in a dream—a pleasant one, maybe, but still a dream. I call on you to wake up and turn to some ordinary business, such as will take you

72

through the rest of your life while you fill your mind with the thoughts of common humanity. For your present business, your present thoughts, are no better than Centaurs and Chimaeras and Gorgons and the other creatures of dreams, the creations of poets and painters with their ranging imaginations, creatures that never were nor ever could be: and yet the common throng believe in them, fascinated by the very sight and sound of such grotesque novelties. And you're as bad; you've been listening to some storyteller telling you that there lives a woman of surpassing beauty, more than the Graces themselves or Aphrodite; and then, without waiting to find out whether he was telling the truth and this female did exist somewhere on earth, you fell in love with her there and then, just as they say Medea fell in love with Jason in a dream.

73

Now, what induced that emotion in you and all the rest who are in love with the same vision was principally, to my mind, the fact that your storyteller, having once obtained credence, was consistent in his elaboration of the idea. That was the only thing you considered; by that means he was able to lead you by the nose when once you had given him his initial hold on you; that's how he led you to the object of your emotions, by what he called the direct road. After that it was easy, I imagine. None of you turned back to the entrance to ask whether it was the right one, and whether you had not slipped inside the wrong door. You all followed in the footsteps of the men who had been there before you, like sheep following their leader, when you should have considered right at the beginning, at the threshold, whether you should go in.

74

You'll follow my meaning more easily by considering the analogy of one of your bold poets telling of the existence, once upon a time, of a man with three heads and six hands. If you accept that in the first place without making difficulties about it or asking whether it is possible, if you take his word for it, he'll at once elaborate the fiction in a consistent manner: our friend will have six eyes and six ears and three voices; he'll speak, or eat, with three mouths at once; he'll have thirty fingers instead of ten all told like us; and should he have to fight, three of his hands will have each some kind of shield and the other three will be wielding a battle-axe and a spear and a sword. And who could refuse to believe all this now? It's consistent with the beginning—*that's* where you ought to have considered whether to believe him, whether you could grant the possibility, before he got any farther. But once grant that and the rest follows naturally; there's no way of stopping it. It's difficult to disbelieve the details now, because they're consistent with the beginning, they suit it—and you granted the beginning.

It's just the same with people like you. In your emotion, your passion, you fail to ask yourselves what you think of the case at each entrance; then consistency drags you onward, and it never enters your head that a thing can be self-consistent but still false. If you're told, for instance, that two fives are seven, and accept that without doing the sum for yourself, your informant is naturally going to go on to say four fives are fourteen, and so on as far as he likes. That's the way they go on in geometry too—that wonderful pursuit! They demand of their catechumens that they grant a set of monstrous, untenable postulates—points without magnitude, if you please, lines without breadth, and that kind of thing—and on these rotten foundations they build rotten structures; and when they come to the *Q.E.D.* they insist they're right, although their premises are false.

And it's exactly the same with you people; you grant the premises of any given doctrine and accept what follows from them, assuming that the consistency of the argument proves its truth, when in fact it is a false consistency. And some of you die in hope, before you see the light and condemn your deceivers; some do realize that they've been duped, but too late—they're old men by that time, and can't face recanting. They're ashamed to have to admit at their age that they've merely been playing childish games and didn't realize it; so they cling to their ways for very shame, vociferously accept their situation, and proselytize busily, so as not to be the only

75

ones deceived, but to have the comfort of seeing many another in like case with themselves. They see too that if they let the truth be known they will forfeit the respect and eminence and honor they now enjoy. So they say nothing, if they can avoid it; they know how far they have to fall to the level of everyone else. You won't come across very many with the courage to face up to it, say that they've been deceived, and try to turn away others who are on the same path. But if you do come upon such a man, call him an honest man, a good and righteous man—a philosopher, if you like, for he is the only man to whom I do not begrudge the name. The rest, though, either have no knowledge of truth, though they think they have, or do know the truth but conceal it in their cowardice and shame, in their desire for men's good opinions.

76 But come now, for goodness' sake let's disregard everything I've said; we'll treat it as ancient history,[24] drop it here and now, forget it. We'll assume your philosophy, the Stoic philosophy, is the true one and the only true one; now let's see whether the Stoic philosophy is attainable and practicable, or whether all its adherents are wasting their efforts. You see, I hear tell of the wonderful promises it makes, of how happy its practitioners are to be, once they reach its heights; they alone, it is said, will possess and enjoy every true good. And about this point I now make, you will perhaps be better informed than I am. Have you ever met an eminent Stoic who fits that description? One who never gives way to sorrow or anger or degrades himself with pleasures? Who is above envy, who looks down on money? Who is in fact happy, as the model and norm of the virtuous life should be? Anyone who falls short in even the smallest degree is imperfect, you see; he may be pre-eminent in every way, but if he is not perfect, he cannot yet be called happy.

77 HERMOTIMUS. I never saw any such.

LYCINUS. Good—no deliberate untruth. But what are you expecting from your pursuit of philosophy, then? You can see that neither your teacher nor his nor his again, nor any of them

[24] The Greek contains a reference to Eucleides; cf. *Trip* 5, n. 4.

to the tenth generation back, has ever become truly wise and hence happy. Nor can you truthfully say it's enough to come near to happiness, because it isn't any good at all; if you stand just outside the door, you're just as much in the street and the open air as if you were a long way out—with this difference, that in the first case it'll worry you more to see at close quarters what you've missed.

So that's why you're wearing yourself out with all this hard work—to come *near* to happiness (I'll grant you that you do get that far): that's why you've let so much of your life slip by, while you nod over your studies all night and end up numb with exhaustion. And you're going to go on laboring away, you say, for at least another twenty years—so that when you're eighty, if you have any guarantee you'll live that long, you can be numbered, for all your efforts, among those who are not yet happy! Unless you think you'll be the one person who does succeed, and your pursuit will lead you to attain a state that a great many good men before you, far swifter in their search, have not attained? Well, attain it then, if you will; seize it and have it whole. But I tell you: in the first place, I cannot see what this good can be, to be commensurate with labors like yours; and in the second, how long will you have left to enjoy it? You'll be an old man by the time you attain it, with one foot in the grave, as they say; you'll be past all pleasure. Unless you're practicing for the next life, my heroic friend? So that, once you know how to live, you'll live it better when you reach it? That's like spending so much time and attention on preparing a better dinner that you starve to death in the meantime. *78*

But there's another thing I think you haven't ever noticed. Virtue is a matter of action—just, wise, courageous action; but you people (when I say "you people," I mean the leading philosophers) disregard that and give your attention to searching out and making up miserable sentences and syllogisms and logical problems.[25] You spend the greater part of your lives on them, and it's the man who's best at that sort of *79*

[25] For examples of these, cf. *Sale* 20–25.

thing who is accounted winner among you. That, I imagine, is what leads you to admire this teacher of yours, this old man; he lands people who cross swords with him into difficulties and he knows how to snare people, how to ask questions, how to twist arguments—all the tricks, in fact. You entirely ignore the fruit—the criterion of action, that is—to fuss over the skins and cover each other with the leaves in your arguments. Isn't that all you're doing, Hermotimus, all of you, from morning to night?

HERMOTIMUS. That's all it is.

LYCINUS. Wouldn't one be right, then, in saying that you're hunting the shadow and letting the body go, looking for the snake's skin and neglecting the reptile? Better still, you're behaving like a man who fills a vessel with water and then pounds it with an iron pestle. He may think what he's doing is necessary and useful; what he doesn't see is that he can wear his arms out with pounding, as they say, and the water will be just the same as it ever was.

80   Let me, at this point, ask you whether you'd like to be like your teacher in other respects, apart from what he talks about? Would you want to be so hot-tempered, so pusillanimous, so quarrelsome—or indeed so self-indulgent, even though he isn't generally thought to be? No answer? Shall I tell you what I heard the other day? A man was defending philosophy—a very old man, whose company is in great demand among young men on account of his philosophical standing. Well, he was demanding payment from one of his students and growing very angry about it; it was overdue, he said, long past time for payment— it had been due a fortnight ago, on the first of the month, by

81   the terms of their agreement. There he was, fuming away; and the lad's uncle happened to be there, a countryman, quite unsophisticated in comparison with your crowd. "My dear man," he said, "stop going on about the dreadful way you've been treated! We've bought words from you and haven't yet settled the account, that's all; what you sold us you still have yourself—your learning hasn't diminished at all. But the boy's not a whit better for your attentions in what I most wanted

when I sent him to you in the first place. He's seduced my neighbor Echecrates' innocent daughter—raped her, in fact; he was very nearly prosecuted for criminal assault, only I bought him off for a talent—Echecrates is a poor man. And the other day he hit his mother when she caught him smuggling the wine jar out under his cloak—a contribution to a party, I suppose. While in temper and willfulness and impudence and cheek and mendaciousness he was far better last year than he is now; though that's just where I'd have liked him to get some good of you, instead of learning the stuff he reels off to us at table every day—we don't need it: all about a crocodile who caught a child and promised to give him back if the father answered—I don't know what; and how when it's day it can't be night.[26] Why, sometimes his lordship even twists arguments somehow or other to prove we've got horns on our heads.[27] We just laugh at him when he goes on like that, and particularly when he stuffs up his ears and repeats 'conditions' or something to himself, and 'states' and 'conceptions' and 'presentations,' and a whole list of words like that. We hear him actually saying God isn't in heaven but permeates everything, sticks and stones and animals, right down to the meanest things; and when his mother asks him what all that nonsense is for, he just laughs at her and says, 'Well, if I can once get this "nonsense" down pat, there'll be nothing to stop me from being the only rich man and the only king and considering everybody else as slaves and rubbish compared to me.' "

That was what he said. Now listen to the reply the philosopher made, and how fitting it was for a man of his years. "And don't you think your boy would have behaved far worse," he said, "if he'd never come to me? Heavens, he might have ended up in the hands of the public executioner. As it is, philosophy and his respect for philosophy have put a curb on him. Because of this, you find him comparatively moderate,

[26] The criticisms of Stoicism contained in the following passage are a favorite theme of Lucian; cf., for example, Sale 20–25.

[27] By asking "Have you lost your horns?"

you can still put up with him; he's ashamed to appear unworthy of the dress and name of philosophy, for they go with him everywhere and keep control of him. So I'd be justified in taking my fees from you even for what out of respect for philosophy he *hasn't* done, never mind any improvement I've brought about in him. Why, nannies will tell you children ought to go to school; even if they're still too young to learn anything useful, at least they're out of mischief there. So I think in general I've done my duty by him. You bring anyone you like here tomorrow, anyone who's familiar with the subject, and you'll see how the boy can ask questions and answer them, how much he's learned, how many books he's read now about axioms, syllogisms, conceptions, properties, and other difficult subjects. What has it to do with me if he hits his mother or seduces innocent girls? I wasn't asked to be his keeper."

83   A man of his years, and that's what he had to say for philosophy! *You* tell me, Hermotimus, do *you* think that's a sufficient reason for pursuing philosophy—that it keeps us from worse things? Or had we other expectations from it when we chose to enter on it to start with, other, that is, than that we'd go about behaving better than Tom, Dick, or Harry? Still no answer?

HERMOTIMUS. What do you expect? I'm practically in tears! The truth of what you say comes home to me; I can only weep for all the time I've wasted—aye, and all the money I've paid out too. And what have I got for it? Toil and sweat. Oh, I feel such a miserable wretch! It's like sobering up after a drunken party; I can see now what it was I was so enamored of and I can see what it's done to me.

84   LYCINUS. My dear fellow, there's no need to cry about it. Aesop's story has a very sensible point to it, to my mind—the story where he tells how a man sat down on the shore at the water's edge to count the waves, but lost count. He was very annoyed with himself and upset, until the fox came along and said, "Why get upset over what's past? What you ought to do is forget it and start counting again from now." Well, *you* would be better off—since you've made your decision—con-

tenting yourself with an ordinary life and living in harmony with the generality of men. Put aside your fantastic, conceited hopes; don't be ashamed, if you've any sense, to unlearn all you've learned, old as you are; change your course for a better one. And don't think, my dear friend, that I've said all I have said because I'm set against Stoicism or have some special grudge against its adherents. My arguments apply to all doctrines; I'd have said the same to you if it had been Plato or Aristotle you'd taken to, dismissing the rest without hearing their cases. It happens to be Stoicism you chose, so my argument appeared to be directed at that doctrine; but it has no special application to it.

85

HERMOTIMUS. You're right. Well, I'm going, and I'm going to do just that. I'm going to change completely, even in appearance. Before very long you'll see me without this long shaggy beard and unnaturally restrained manner; I'm going to relax completely and let myself go. Perhaps I'll even put on a purple cloak, to let everybody know I'm finished with the old nonsense. I only wish I could bring up all the rubbish they taught me. I can tell you this, I wouldn't think twice about drinking hellebore, not for Chrysippus' reason [28] but the opposite—to clear my head completely of their teachings. Well, I'm very grateful to you, Lycinus. There was I being swept along in a turbid, savage torrent, drifting with the stream and making no effort to do otherwise, and you appeared on the bank and fished me out—just like the *deus ex machina* in plays. I should think I've good reason actually to shave my head like people who escape unharmed from shipwrecks,[29] to celebrate today the escape I've had in dispersing that thick fog from before my eyes. And if I ever meet a philosopher after this, even accidentally, when I'm walking down the street, I'll turn aside and avoid him as I should a mad dog.

86

---

[28] I.e., to enable him to pursue philosophy. Hellebore was the traditional cure for insanity, and Chrysippus was said to have taken it three times; cf. *Sale* 23 and *Story* II. 18.
[29] Cf. *Companions* 1.

ZEUS RANTS

1   HERMES.
  Zeus, why so thoughtful, muttering to thyself,
  Pacing about, and pale as any sage?
  Thy counsels and thy troubles share with me;
  Do not despise a servant's foolish words.[1]

ATHENA.
  Yes, mighty potentate, our father Zeus,
  Bright-eyed divine Tritogeneia begs thee
  Speak, do not hide thy thoughts from us; reveal
  What gnawing worry frets thy heart and soul.
  Why sighest thou deeply? Why so pale thy cheek?

ZEUS.
  There is no dreadful sorrow, you might say,
  No fell disaster, fit for any play,
  To which I could not add a dozen lines!

ATHENA.
  Apollo! What a way to start a speech!

ZEUS.
  Men! Spawned by earth to fearful devilment!
  And you, Prometheus—what you have done to me!

ATHENA. What's wrong? Speak out—you're with the family!

ZEUS.
  O rushing, crashing lightning bolt, what will you do?

HERA. Give it a rest, Zeus! Calm down! *They* may be

---

[1] The opening speeches of this piece provide one of the best examples in Lucian of that mixing of verse with prose which the author borrowed from Menippus; see Introduction, p. xxi. The device is not really much used. Here Lucian parodies various passages of Homer and Euripides: *Iliad* I. 363, VIII. 31, III. 35; *Orestes* 1–3; *Hercules Furens* 538; *Phoenissae* 117.

good at acting the buffoon and reeling off speeches, but *we're*
not; we can't play up to you, we haven't swallowed Euripides
whole. Do you think we don't know what's bothering you?   *2*

ZEUS.

Thou know'st not, else would'st thou lament aloud!

HERA. I know what's the matter with you: you're in love,
and that's the long and short of it. Well, don't expect me to
"lament." I've seen it all before. It isn't the first time you've
treated me like this—not by a long way. I suppose you're suffering the torments of love for some new Danaë or Semele or
Europa you've found, so you're wondering whether to change
into a bull or a satyr or a golden shower and come through
the roof into your lady's bosom. That's what these symptoms
mean, this groaning and weeping and pallor—you're in love.

ZEUS. Simple creature, thinking love's what's bothering
me, love and all that nonsense!

HERA. You're Zeus. What else can it be?

ZEUS. Hera, the divine situation is very precarious; we're   *3*
on the razor's edge, as they say, between retaining our respect
and honors on earth and being totally disregarded, losing all
our prestige.

HERA. Don't tell me the earth's brought forth giants
again? Or have the Titans broken their bonds and overpowered their guards and taken up arms against us again?

ZEUS.

Fear not, for Hell does not endanger Heaven.

HERA. Well then, what else can it be that's bothering you?
I don't understand this sudden transformation from Zeus to
Polus or Aristodemus [2] unless it's something like that.

ZEUS. Yesterday, my dear, Timocles the Stoic and Damis   *4*
the Epicurean got into an argument about providence. I don't
know how it began, but a whole crowd of reputable people
were listening—that's the most annoying part of it. Damis
maintained that the gods don't exist, let alone supervise or

2 Famous actors of the fourth century B.C.

control the course of things, while Timocles—he's a fine fellow, he is—tried to uphold our cause; and then a whole mob gathered around. They didn't settle their argument; they broke it up, and arranged to finish the discussion some other time. Now everybody's agog to see which of them's going to present the better argument and win the debate. You see the danger? Our fate's hanging by a hair; it all depends on one man! There are only two ways it can turn out: either they decide we're just names and set us aside, or Timocles wins the argument and we retain our honor.

5   HERA. This really is serious. No wonder you were spouting tragedy over it!

ZEUS. And you thought I was thinking of Danaë or Antiope or somebody, with everything falling to pieces! Well now, Hermes, Hera, Athena, what are we going to do? You've got to do your share of the thinking too.

HERMES. Well, I think you should put the problem before the whole body. Call an assembly.

HERA. I agree with him.

ATHENA. I don't. You can't set the whole of heaven worrying and let it be seen that you're disturbed. No, settle it privately. See to it that Timocles wins the debate and Damis is laughed out of the whole thing.

HERMES. You can't keep it quiet, Zeus. The debate'll be public. You'll be called an autocrat if you don't let everybody in on it—it's important to them all.

6   ZEUS. Yes, you're right. All right, make a proclamation. Everybody to come here.

HERMES. Right you are. —All the gods to come to assembly! Hurry up, come on, all of you—important meeting!

ZEUS. What a bare, uninspired, prosaic way of making a proclamation! Is that the way you convene an important meeting?

HERMES. How do you want me to do it?

ZEUS. How do I want you to do it? Dress it up a bit. Make your proclamation in verse, say—make it sound fancy and poetic. You'll get them here all the better.

HERMES. Maybe—but that's a poet's job, that is, or a bard's. I'm no good at verses. I'll ruin the proclamation. I'll put too many feet in—or not enough. It'll be such bad verse they'll laugh at me. I've seen them laugh at Apollo for some of his oracles, you know, and people don't have time to scan them generally, they're busy enough trying to make sense out of them.

ZEUS. Well, put plenty of Homer into your proclamation —the verses he used to summon us together with. I suppose you remember them?

HERMES. Not that well by any means, not offhand. Still, I'll give it a try:

> Come every god and goddess,[3]
> And every river save for Ocean's stream,
> Come every nymph to council now with Zeus,
> All ye that feast on glorious hecatombs
> And sit at smoking altars, deities
> High-grade, low-grade, or quite anonymous.

ZEUS. Splendid, Hermes! Well done! And look, here they come now. You take over. Seat each one according to his value —his material and workmanship: gold in the front row, silver behind them, then ivory, then bronze, then stone. When you get to the stone ones, give the best seats to Phidias' work and Alcamenes' and Myron's and Euphranor's—real artists like them. Shove the rubbishy, inartistic stuff right out of the way somewhere and keep them quiet. They'll always fill out the meeting.

7

HERMES. Right. They'll sit in order of precedence. But how about a statue that's made of gold, and heavy, but sloppily made and very ordinary and ill-proportioned? Is he to sit in front of a bronze statue by Myron or Polyclitus, or a stone one by Phidias or Alcamenes? Or should I give preference to good art? I'd better know.

---

[3] This line is a syllable short in the Greek. In view of Hermes' remarks in his previous speech, this deficiency may well be intentional.

ZEUS. Well, you should really. All the same, you'll have to give the golden one the best seat.

HERMES. I see. Seat them according to cost—by wealth, not merit. All right—come on, you golden fellows, front row! It looks as if the barbarians are going to monopolize the best seats, Zeus.[4] You see what the Greeks are like—attractive, handsome, made by craftsmen, but stone or bronze all the same, every one of them; ivory at best, the costliest of them, just a gleam of gold in them, enough to give them a touch of brightness—but even they are wooden underneath, and they've got great droves of mice sheltering in them like naturalized citizens. But Bendis and Anubis there and Attis next to him and Mithras and Men—they're solid gold and heavy; they're really valuable.

POSEIDON. Hermes! Here's this dog-faced Egyptian[5] in front of me, Poseidon! I ask you, is it right?

HERMES. I know, earth-shaker, but you're poor. Lysippus used bronze for you because the Corinthians hadn't any gold at the time. This fellow's a mint richer than you are. You'll have to put up with a back seat and not lose your temper when a fellow with a gold snout as big as his gets precedence.

APHRODITE. Well, then, give me a front seat somewhere, Hermes. I'm gold.

HERMES. Not as far as I can see, Aphrodite. Unless my eyes deceive me, you're white marble—Pentelic, I'll bet. Then Praxiteles decided to turn you into Aphrodite, and you landed up in Cnidos.

APHRODITE. Why, don't you believe Homer? He calls me "golden Aphrodite" dozens of times in his poems.

HERMES. Yes, and the same man called Apollo "rich in gold" and "wealthy." But you'll see him too sitting with the hoi polloi somewhere. He's lost his laurel wreath—the pirates

---

4 For centuries before Lucian's time, opulently worshiped eastern ("barbarian") cults had been spreading in popularity, e.g., those of the deities mentioned below (see Glossary; also Introduction, p. xxv).

5 Anubis.

got it—and he's had his lyre pegs pinched. You consider yourself lucky you're not right at the back of the meeting.

COLOSSUS. But who'd have the nerve to argue with me?   *11*
I'm Helius—look at the size of me! Why, if the Rhodians
hadn't seen fit to make me such an outsized monster they
could have had sixteen golden gods made for the price. So I
ought to be valued accordingly. And besides, I'm artistic and
well-made for all my size.

HERMES. What do we do here, Zeus? I'm in a quandary.
If you go by what he's made of, well, he's bronze; but work out
what he cost to make, it would be a fortune.

ZEUS. What did he have to come for, to sneer at the others
because they're small, and mess up the seating plan! Look, my
dear fellow, we can't put you in the front row however much
you deserve precedence over the gold ones. Everybody else
would have to stand up to make room just for you to sit
down. One cheek would take up the whole of the Pnyx.[6] You'd
ter stand up for the meeting and bend down to the assembly.

HERMES. Look, here's another tricky one, Dionysus and   *12*
Hercules here. They're both bronze and both made by the
same sculptor, Lysippus. Worst of all, they're of equally good
family—they're both your sons. So which of them goes first?
They're arguing like fury, you can see.

ZEUS. We're wasting time, Hermes. We should have got
on with the meeting long ago. Tell them to sit down anyhow
for the time being, anywhere they like. We'll have another
meeting sometime to settle all this, and I'll work out an order
of precedence for them then.

HERMES. Ye gods! What a row! They're shouting for their   *13*
shares as usual. "Where's the nectar?"—it's the same every day.
"The ambrosia's finished!" "Give us the hecatombs!" "Don't
hog the sacrifices!"

ZEUS. Tell them to stop that nonsense and be quiet,
Hermes, so that they can hear what they've been called together for.

[6] The Athenian assembly place. Lucian assumes that heaven is just like
home.

HERMES. They don't all understand Greek, Zeus, and I'm not a polyglot—I can't announce in Scythian and Persian and Thracian and Celtic. I think I'd better motion them to be quiet with my hand.

ZEUS. Yes, do that.

14   HERMES. Good—there they are, making less noise than the sophists. Time for your speech now. —Come on now—they've been gaping at you for ages to see what you'd have to say.

ZEUS. Well—look, Hermes, you're my own son, I needn't feel shy about telling you what's happened to me. You know how confident I've always been with meetings—how I could always talk big?

HERMES. Oh yes—I used to be terrified of you when you made a speech, especially when you threatened to let that golden cord of yours down and draw land and sea up from their foundations, gods and all.

ZEUS. Well, my child—I don't know what it is; perhaps it's because of this dreadful crisis, perhaps it's the size of the audience—the hall's packed with gods, just look at them—anyway, today my mind's all confused and I'm trembling and tongue-tied. And the oddest thing of all is, I can't remember the introduction I prepared for myself, to create a good impression with them right at the beginning.

HERMES. Zeus, you've ruined everything. They're wondering what's up, with you not saying anything; they're quite expecting some dreadful calamity to be announced, the way you're putting it off.

ZEUS. All right then—shall I trot out that introductory line Homer uses?

HERMES. Which one?

ZEUS. "Harken me, all ye gods and goddesses." [7]

HERMES. No, no, no! *We've* had quite enough of your imitations already. Forget that tenth-rate versifying. What you *can* do is reel off one of Demosthenes' *Philippics*—doesn't matter which; make a few slight alterations. That's the way everybody makes speeches these days.

[7] *Iliad* VIII. 5.

ZEUS. That's it! That's a nice, easy short cut to eloquence
—just the thing when you're in a spot!

HERMES. Hurry up and begin, then.   15

ZEUS. Men of Heaven! You would give much, I presume,
to know just what it is that has occasioned this present assembly; and this being so, you may be expected to attend to my
words with eagerness. Now, gods, the crisis in which we find
ourselves as good as raises up its voice and cries to us to take
firm grasp of the situation; and we, to my mind, are just dismissing it. And now—oh, I can't keep up this Demosthenes [8]—
now I want to make clear to you what it is that disturbs me
and has led me to call this meeting. You know that yesterday
Mnesitheus the merchant skipper made his thanks offerings
for coming out alive when his ship was nearly wrecked off
Caphereus. Well, those of us that he invited went off to the
banquet in Piraeus; and in due course, after the libations, the
rest of you went your various ways, and I went up to town,
since it wasn't very late, for a stroll around Ceramicus [9] in the
evening. As I was walking about, I was thinking to myself how
stingy Mnesitheus was. Sixteen gods to dinner, and all he
offers is a cock, and a wheezy old one at that; one cock, and
four grains of incense, so mouldy that they fizzled out the
minute they touched the hot coals—didn't even make enough
smoke to tickle your nostrils. And all this despite his promises:
whole hecatombs, it was, when the ship was inside the reef
and actually heading for the rocks.

Well, there I was, pondering all this, when I came to the   16
Painted Porch.[10] There I saw a big crowd gathered, some of
them in the Porch itself, a lot of them outside, and some sitting on the benches shouting at each other for all they were
worth. Well, I guessed what it was—philosophers of the argumentative type you find—and I was right, so I decided to stop
and hear what they had to say. Under cover of the thick mist

---

[8] See Demosthenes, *Olynthiacs* 1. 1–2.

[9] The Potters' Street in Athens.

[10] The Stoa Poecile, the home of Stoic philosophy in Athens; see sec. 32
and n. 21 below.

that surrounded me, I assumed their garb and lengthened my beard, so that I looked just like a philosopher. Then I elbowed my way in through the mob—nobody recognized me—and there I found Damis the Epicurean, the scoundrel, and Timocles the Stoic, bless him, arguing very vehemently. Timocles was sweating, in fact, and his voice had already cracked with all the shouting, while Damis was goading him still more with his sarcastic wisecracks.

17   Well now, it turned out to be us that all this argument was about. Damis, the rogue, maintained that we took no thought for mankind and paid no attention to what went on on earth; he practically denied our very existence—that was what his argument obviously came to. And he had some support. The other man, Timocles, was on our side. He fought for us till he was quite hot under the collar; he did his very best to put our case. He said we *were* concerned for mankind, he showed how we conduct life harmoniously and arrange everything in appropriate manner. And, as a matter of fact, he did have some support on his side too. But he was tired out by now, he had difficulty in getting the words out; and most of the audience seemed to favor Damis. I realized what was at stake, and told Night to cover the meeting and break it up; then they went off, but they agreed to follow the argument to its conclusion the next day. I mixed with the crowd as they went home, to find out what their views were. They agreed with Damis and already took his side strongly, though there were also some who would not prejudge his rival's case, but wanted to wait and see what Timocles would say the next day.

18   And that's why I've called this meeting. It isn't a thing to be treated lightly, gentlemen, when you realize that our position, our prestige, our income depend entirely on mankind. Why, if they were to get it into their heads that we don't exist at all, or that even if we do we're quite indifferent to them, there's an end to all the sacrifices and honors and marks of respect we get from earth. We'll find ourselves sitting around uselessly up here starving; no more feasts—and you know

what they mean to us—no more assemblies or games or sacrifices or all-night vigils or processions. So you see, it's pretty bad; and we'd all better try and think of some way out of the mess we're in—some way of making sure that Timocles convinces them and wins his case, and that Damis is laughed out of court. I must say I'm not at all convinced that Timocles can manage it by himself without help from us. All right, then—Hermes, make the formal proclamation, then they can get up and say what they have to say.

HERMES. Now hear this! Silence in heaven! The meeting will come to order! Are there any contributions from full-fledged divinities in good standing? What's all this? Nobody got anything to say? All struck dumb? What's the matter—is it too much for you, what you've just heard?

MOMUS. "Spiritless, spineless creatures every one" [11]—but *I'd* have plenty to say if I could let myself go.

ZEUS. You go right ahead, Momus. It's obviously going to be for the general good if you speak freely.

MOMUS. Well listen then, gentlemen. I'll speak from the heart, as the saying goes. I tell you, I've been quite expecting this. It doesn't surprise me to find ourselves in such a mess, or to see all these sophists springing up. It's we ourselves who give them grounds for being so free with their tongues; by all that's just, we've no call to get annoyed with Epicurus and company and their successors for getting these ideas about us into their heads. What on earth do you expect them to think when they see life in such confusion around them—the good neglected, wasting away in poverty and sickness and slavery, and the most arrant scoundrels preferred in favor, rolling in money, and ordering their betters about? People robbing temples and getting away with it, while sometimes others who've done no harm in the world find themselves crucified and flogged? I ask you, do you wonder they think we don't even

19

20

11 *Iliad* VII. 99; literally "May you all become water and earth," Menelaus' reproach to the Greeks when they shrink from accepting Hector's challenge.

exist when they see what goes on? Particularly when they hear oracles say that so-and-so [12] has only to cross the Halys to "destroy a mighty empire," without saying whether it's his own or his enemy's, or that

Divine Salamis will bring death to mothers' sons [13]

—the Greeks were mothers' sons as well as the Persians, surely? Why, they hear poets describing our love affairs and quarrels, and how we hurt each other and end up in prison or in slavery, and all the endless trouble we have—and we're supposed to be supremely happy and indestructible! Of course they laugh at us! Of course they dismiss us! And we're annoyed when a few of them who aren't quite addlepated pull the whole thing to pieces and conclude we've no control over providence? We ought to be only too pleased that anybody goes on sacrificing to us at all, the way we misrule.

21   And while we're on this, tell me, Zeus—we're all by ourselves, there aren't any human beings in this gathering except Hercules and Dionysus and Ganymede and Asclepius, and they're naturalized—honestly now, did you ever bother about life on earth enough to find out who the bad were and who the good? No, you didn't. If Theseus hadn't killed the malefactors, Sciron and Pityocamptes and Cercyon and the rest, just incidentally on his journey from Troezen to Athens, for all you and your providence did there'd have been nothing to stop them from going on running riot and living off murdered travelers. The same with Eurystheus: if he hadn't been a righteous and humane and thoughtful man and gone to the trouble of finding out how the various regions were getting on and sent that energetic, lively servant [14] of his off on his labors, why, *you*, Zeus, you wouldn't have given a minute's thought to the Hydra or the Stymphalian birds or the Thracian horses or the Centaurs' drunken behavior.

[12] Croesus; see Herodotus, I. 91.

[13] Herodotus, VII. 141; the famous oracle that told Athens to seek its safety in "wooden walls." See n. 19 below.

[14] Hercules.

No, the truth of the matter is that we sit here with one   22
thought in mind: are the sacrifices coming up? Are the altars
reeking? Everything else is let drift on its own course. Well, it
just serves us right, and we'll go on being treated like that
when men begin to look about them and realize it doesn't do
them any good to sacrifice and organize processions in our
honor. Before we know where we are, we'll find the Epicuruses
and Metrodoruses and Damises openly laughing at us and
easily getting the upper hand over our advocates; they'll have
them where they want them. Well, it's up to you to find a
remedy and put a stop to it all; you brought it on yourselves.
It doesn't bother *me* if nobody pays me any attention; nobody
ever did, in the days when you were still on the top of the
wave and reveling in your sacrifices.[15]

ZEUS. Pay no attention to his nonsense. He always was   23
awkward—a bit too ready to find fault. The excellent Demosthenes points out how easy it is to criticize and make charges
and accusations; anybody can do that. It takes a real statesman, and an intelligent one, to suggest improvements—and
I'm quite sure the rest of you will do that without any comments from him.

POSEIDON. Well, in general I'm an underwater man, as   24
you know; I mind my own business in the depths, doing my
best to save sailors and help ships on their way, and calming
the winds down. Still, I am interested in these questions too,
and my view is that this Damis you told us about had better be
put out of the way before he ever gets to the debate—a thunderbolt or something would do it. Otherwise he might win
the argument—you say he has a convincing manner, Zeus.
And it would show mankind, too, that we're on the track of
people who retail arguments like that about us.

ZEUS. Are you pulling my leg, Poseidon? Or have you   25
completely forgotten that we've no hand in these decisions?
It's the Fates who spin each man's destiny for him—thunderbolt or sword or fever or consumption. Why, if it were up

[15] Momus is convenient to Lucian's purpose but seldom figures in Olympian mythology; hence this remark.

to me, do you think I'd have let those temple-robbers get away at Olympia the other day without a thunderbolt in their backs? Two of my curls they lopped off and made away with—six pounds apiece. Or you yourself—would you have let that fisherman from Oreus pinch your trident at Geraestus? In any case, people will say we're losing our tempers because this debate's got under our skin and we're afraid of Damis' arguments, and that's why we're doing away with him before he can be set against Timocles; they'll think we're just giving ourselves a walkover.

POSEIDON. And I thought I'd hit on a nice, easy short cut to victory!

ZEUS. No, no, Poseidon, your idea's too fishy. It's very stupid to get rid of your opponent before the fight starts; he dies undefeated and leaves his argument behind him, and it's still debatable and undecided.

POSEIDON. Oh well then, you think up something better, if "fishy" is the best you can say of my idea.

26   APOLLO. If we young fellows without gray beards had been entitled to speak too, perhaps I could have made some useful contribution to the discussion.

MOMUS. Apollo, this is too important a debate to apply age limits. Anybody's free to speak up. Why, it would be a fine thing if we quibbled over legal qualifications with our very existence at stake! And anyway, you're fully entitled to speak by now. You came of age ages ago; you're on the voting list of the Twelve Olympians, and you were practically a member of the Council in Cronus' day.[16] Don't play the young lad with us; you go right ahead and say what you think. No need to feel embarrassed about your smooth cheeks—look at the long, shaggy beard your son Asclepius has! In any case, now's the time to prove how clever you are. Show us you aren't wasting your time sitting at the Muses' feet up on Helicon, discussing philosophy.

16 Apollo—the type of masculine beauty—is always represented as beardless, but here Lucian emphasizes the antiquity and importance of his cult, in terms of Athenian constitutional procedure.

APOLLO. Momus, it's not your job to give me permission to speak; it's Zeus's. If he gives the word, I should hope I could make some intelligent contribution that wouldn't disgrace my education on Helicon.

ZEUS. Go ahead, my boy, speak. Permission granted.

APOLLO. Well now, our friend Timocles is a good, pious   27
man, thoroughly versed in Stoic doctrine. He is, in fact, familiar as a philosopher to many young men, and makes a good income out of them in that line. In private conversation with pupils he's very convincing, but when he has to speak in public he loses all his confidence; he isn't a very good speaker and he has a foreign accent. The result is, he's laughed at in company. He isn't fluent; indeed, he stumbles and gets confused easily, particularly when with all these shortcomings he tries to show off with fancy language. He's an extremely acute and subtle scholar, according to people who know more about Stoicism than I do, but when he attempts oral exposition he just can't do it; he makes a mess of it. He gets confused and doesn't make himself clear, his explanations are obscure—indeed his answers to questions are far more unintelligible than the questions themselves—and people laugh at him because they can't follow him. I do think clarity's important; above all, you must take great care to make sure people follow you.

MOMUS. You're quite right to say people should make   28
their meaning clear—though you can hardly claim to be much of an expert at it yourself, with your oblique, mysterious oracles; you usually sit on the fence, and people need another Apollo to tell them what you mean. However, what do you think we should do in this case? What treatment do you advise for Timocles' ineffectiveness as a speaker?

APOLLO. See if we can't find him somebody to do his   29
talking for him—one of these clever fellows you come across, someone who'll take his ideas and give them proper expression.

MOMUS. Now you really are talking like a juvenile. You ought to be back at school. Somebody to do his talking for

him, indeed! A group of philosophers, and Timocles has to
have somebody with him to explain his views to the company
—while Damis speaks in his own person and with his own
tongue! Timocles engaging his own private actor and feeding
his notions into his ears, and the actor making pretty speeches
—probably without any comprehension of what he's told to
say! Why, the crowd would roar their heads off—bound to.
No, we'll have to think up something better than that. Look,
my dear fellow, you say you're a prophet—you've made a fair
bit of money at it, you even got gold bricks once.[17] Why not
show off your skill? Now's the very time for it. If you're a
prophet you must know what's going to happen in this debate; tell us which of them's going to win.

APOLLO. How can I? I haven't got my tripod with me,
or my incense; and I'd need a prophetic spring like the one
at Castalia.

MOMUS. There you are! The minute things get difficult
you try to get out of it!

ZEUS. Never mind, my boy—you have a go at it. Don't
give that slanderer the chance to abuse you. He'll say your art
depends on your tripod and water and incense, and make fun
of you for not being able to do without them.

APOLLO. Well, father, it'd be better to do this sort of
thing at Delphi or Colophon; I'd have all the tools there that
I generally use. However, I'll have a go—although as I say I
haven't any equipment or anything. I'll try and forecast the
winner. You'll have to bear with me if the scansion's a bit out.

MOMUS. Go ahead then—but remember, Apollo, *be clear*.
Don't give us an answer that needs a lawyer or an interpreter
to expound it itself. We don't want any of your "lamb's flesh
and tortoise boiling in Lydia"[18] this time; you know what
we're trying to find out.

ZEUS. What on earth are you going to come out with,
my boy? Why, it's enough to frighten anybody the way you go
on even before you prophesy. He's changed color, his eyes are
rolling, his hair's standing on end, he's making frantic ges-

---

[17] From Croesus; see Herodotus, I. 50.
[18] Herodotus, I. 47.

tures—he's possessed! He's off in a trance! Enough to make you shudder!

APOLLO. 31
 List ye to this oracle of prophetic Apollo
 On the chilling strife begun by loud-shouting men
 Armed with dense words. In the ambiguous hiss
 Of battle, each side will strike many a blow
 At the tough ploughshare's frame. But when the
  vulture
 Catches the grasshopper with his curved talons,
 Then for the last time will the rain-bringing crows
  caw,
 Mules win, and the donkey will butt his swift foals.

ZEUS. Well, what's the big joke, Momus? It's nothing to laugh at, what we've got on our hands. Stop it, you idiot! You'll choke if you laugh like that!

MOMUS. Can't help myself, Zeus, the oracle's so clear—transparent, it is!

ZEUS. Oh? Well, perhaps you'd be good enough to explain to us what on earth it's getting at?

MOMUS. Why it's perfectly obvious; no need for a Themistocles.[19] What the oracle says, quite expressly, is that he's a charlatan and you're donkeys and mules to listen, and you've no more sense than grasshoppers.

HERCULES. Father, I know I'm not a full member, but 32 I'm not going to let that stop me from saying my piece. What you ought to do is let them meet and carry on with their argument, and then, if Timocles is getting the best of it, we'll let the discussion about us continue; but if anything goes wrong, why, what about me giving the whole Porch a shake and pulling it down on top of Damis? That'll teach him to talk like that about us—damned insolence!

ZEUS. By Hercules, Hercules, what a crude suggestion! Just like a Boeotian![20] Kill all those honest men for one

---

[19] Themistocles interpreted the oracle referred to in sec. 20 and n. 13 above as meaning that Athens should build a fleet.

[20] Boeotians were considered stupid by Athenians, and Thebes, the capital city of Boeotia, claimed to be the birthplace of Hercules.

scoundrel? And destroy the Porch? With those pictures of Marathon and Miltiades and Cynegirus? Why, if they came down how do you think the orators could go on orating? They'd lose their prize theme! [21] In any case, perhaps you could have done something of the sort when you were a man, but now that you're a god surely you realize it's only the Fates who can do that sort of thing? We've no jurisdiction at all.

HERCULES. So when—I killed the lion and the Hydra it was really the Fates working through me?

ZEUS. Of course it was!

HERCULES. And now if anybody assaults me—robs my temple, say, or knocks my statue over—I mustn't make mincemeat of him unless the Fates decided it long ago?

ZEUS. You certainly mustn't.

HERCULES. Well just you listen, Zeus, while I give you a piece of my mind—you know that line in the play,

I'm a blunt man; I call a spade a spade.[22]

If that's the state we're in, you know what you can do with your divine honors and your smoking fat and victims' blood— I'm going to hell. At least I'll scare the daylights out of the ghosts of the monsters I slew, when they see me with my bow ready.

ZEUS. Oh, just the right thing to say! You should have given it to Damis to use—that *would* have got us out of the mess! Talk about inside information! Here—who's this in such a hurry? Bronze, nice clean lines, old-fashioned hair-do— why it's your brother, Hermes, from the market place near the Porch.[23] Look, he's covered in pitch—that's these sculptors,

33

21 Much of the matter and illustration used in contemporary rhetoric was chosen from the fifth and fourth centuries B.C.; see Introduction, p. x. The pictures mentioned here justify the name "Poecile," or "painted"; see sec. 16, n. 10 above.

22 The source of this quotation is unknown.

23 A statue of Hermes in the public square, or *agora*, was called *Hermes agoraios,* which Lucian turns into Hermagoras, the name of a famous second-century B.C. writer on rhetoric.

taking casts of him every day. —Well, my boy! What's all the hurry? News from earth?

HERMAGORAS. Big news! Very serious indeed!

ZEUS. Let's have it, then. Is there something else coming up that we haven't noticed?

HERMAGORAS.
　　　Serving as model, half an hour ago,
　　　With sculptors tarring me from back to front
　　　And taking off impressions of my chest—
　　　I know I must have looked a funny sight
　　　Wearing that dummy breastplate—such a crowd
　　　Appears, and with them come a couple of types
　　　With sickly faces, shouting each other down,
　　　Sparring with logic. Damis was one of them——[24]

ZEUS. Oh, for goodness' sake cut out the blank verse! I know the men you mean. Well, tell me, have they been at it long?

HERMAGORAS. No, they were still skirmishing when I left —hurling abuse at each other at long range.

ZEUS. Well then, gentlemen, there's nothing to do but bend down and listen to them. Hours! Draw the bolt, open heaven's gates, and pull the clouds aside. Ye gods, what an enormous audience they've collected! I can't say I like the looks of Timocles. He's trembling, he's all confused—he's going to ruin everything today, he is. He's obviously not going to stand up to Damis. Well, what we can do is pray for him

　　　Silently to ourselves, lest Damis hear.[25]

TIMOCLES. What's that, you sacrilegious scoundrel? The gods don't exist? Don't give a thought to mankind?[26]

34

35

---

[24] A parody on Euripides; cf. *Orestes* 866, 880.

[25] Cf. *Iliad* VII. 195.

[26] Beginning with this speech, Lucian rapidly switches the scene back and forth between Olympus and Athens, a device that he uses elsewhere in his writings. The argument about providence that follows is his version of the standard Stoic and Epicurean positions.

DAMIS. Oh no, you answer my question first. What makes you think they do exist?

TIMOCLES. Oh no, you blackguard, you answer!

DAMIS. No, no—*you!*

ZEUS. Ah, our man's much the better of the two at this— much better voice for a slang-match. Come on, Timocles! Abuse him, cover him in it! That's your strong point. Don't try anything else or he'll muzzle you—he'll have you as speechless as a fish!

TIMOCLES. Look here, I swear by Athena I'm not going to answer first.

DAMIS. All right, you win—you and your oath! Fire away, question me—but no abuse, please.

36   TIMOCLES. Good. Well then—damn you!—don't you think the gods exercise providence?

DAMIS. Of course they don't.

TIMOCLES. Don't they? All our lives are without providence, then?

DAMIS. That's right.

TIMOCLES. The care of the universe isn't in any god's control, then?

DAMIS. It isn't.

TIMOCLES. And everything moves at random?

DAMIS. It does.

TIMOCLES. You hear what he says? It's intolerable! Stone him! Stone the blasphemer!

DAMIS. Why stir people up against me? Who do you think you are, getting all worked up on the gods' behalf? Why, they don't get worked up themselves! Look, they haven't done anything to me, and they've been listening to me for ages— if they *are* listening.

TIMOCLES. Oh yes, Damis, they are, they're listening all right—and they'll get you some day.

37   DAMIS. And when are they ever going to get the time to bother about me, if they've all that on their hands and all the endless business of the universe to manage, as you say they have? They've been too busy to punish you for your continual

perjuries and all the rest of—well, I don't want to be forced to break the agreement and resort to abuse, as you did. But for the life of me I can't think of any better way they could have proved their concern than by crushing you as you deserve. No, obviously they're not at home just now—they're the other side of Ocean, perhaps, "among the blameless Ethiopians." [27] They're constantly running off there, looking for a dinner—invite themselves, sometimes.

TIMOCLES. I shall treat the remark with the contempt   *38* it deserves.

DAMIS. No, you tell me what I've been trying to get you to tell me all this time—what gave you the idea that the gods exercise providence?

TIMOCLES. I'll tell you what gave me the idea. The order of nature, to start with: the sun never strays from his course, or the moon either; the seasons revolve, plants grow, living creatures are born—and they're designed so effectively for eating and moving and thinking and walking and building and cobbling [28] and so forth. Well, to my mind this is all providence's doing.

DAMIS. You're begging the question. You haven't proved yet that it *is* by providence that all this comes about. I quite agree that this is the nature of things, but that doesn't commit me to accepting any kind of design in it. It's possible that things which sprang up at random now come together in the same way regularly. What you're doing is giving the name of "order" to inevitability. And you get angry when people don't follow you all the way; all very well when you're enumerating the marvels of nature and going into raptures over them, but you then maintain that they prove that everything's ordered by providence. "This doesn't ring true," as the quotation goes; "bring me other proof." [29]

TIMOCLES. I don't think any other proof is called for,   *39*

----

27 *Iliad* I. 423.

28 A sly reference to Socrates' habit of illustrating philosophical argument by reference to mundane occupations such as cobbling.

29 The source of this quotation is unknown.

besides what I've said. I'll give you some, all the same. Do you consider Homer an excellent poet?

DAMIS. Oh, indeed yes.

TIMOCLES. Well, *he* illustrates divine providence, and that was enough for me.

DAMIS. My dear man, anybody will agree with you that Homer is a good poet, but not that he or any other poet is a reliable authority in these matters.[30] They're concerned with bewitching their audience, not with truth, surely? And that's why they enchant you with meter and feed you stories, employ all their tricks, in fact, to induce pleasure. Tell me, though, what particular passages of Homer induced you to think as you do? Was it where he tells about the conspiracy to tie Zeus up, by his daughter and brother and wife? If Thetis hadn't called in Briareus, the excellent Zeus would have been captured and put in chains.[31] And then in gratitude to Thetis he deceived Agamemnon by sending him a lying dream, to bring about the deaths of a lot of the Achaeans.[32] You realize what he was up to? He couldn't throw a thunderbolt at Agamemnon himself and burn him to cinders, because that would have shown what a double-crosser he was. Or perhaps it was the story of Diomede that convinced you? Diomede, who wounded first Aphrodite and then Ares himself, on Athena's instructions;[33] and very soon the gods were at each other's throats and challenging each other, males and females alike, without discrimination;[34] and Athena beat Ares—I suppose he was tired out with the wound Diomede gave him[35]—and

Hermes the stout luck-bringer rose against Leto.[36]

[30] The attitudes of Timocles and Damis illustrate well the traditional reliance upon Homer as a comprehensive authority, and the reaction of some philosophers against this attitude. Cf. Plato's views in the *Republic* II. 377 ff.

[31] *Iliad* I. 396 ff.
[32] *Iliad* II. 5 ff.
[33] *Iliad* V. 330 ff. and 846 ff.
[34] *Iliad* XX. 54 ff.
[35] *Iliad* XXI. 403 ff.
[36] *Iliad* XX. 72.

Or was it the story of Artemis that won you over? How Artemis was always grumbling at something, and felt insulted because Oeneus didn't ask her to dinner, so she sent an enormous great boar—far too powerful for anybody to stand up against—to ravage his land?" [37] Perhaps that's how Homer convinced you, with stories like those?

ZEUS. Oh, heavens—listen to the noise the crowd's making! They're all on Damis' side. Our man's in a spot; he's sweating, he's trembling—looks as if he's going to throw in the towel. Now he's looking about for some way to slip off and run away.

41

TIMOCLES. I suppose you'll say there's nothing in Euripides either, then? He brings the gods themselves on stage, and represents them as protecting noble heroes but crushing wicked and impious rogues like you.

DAMIS. My dearest Timocles, my noblest philosopher, if you're convinced by playwrights putting gods into their plays, then you must logically consider the divinity to reside in one of two places—either in Polus and Aristodemus and Satyrus,[38] for the time being, or in the actual masks, buskins, long gowns, cloaks, gloves, false bellies, padding, and what-have-you, the properties they use to deck out their plays. And surely that's absurd, because look how freethinking Euripides is when he says what he really thinks, in his own person, when there aren't any dramatic exigencies to consider:

> Do you behold the ether, there on high,
> Boundless, encircling earth in soft embrace?
> *That* you must think your Zeus, *that* call your god.

Here's another example:

> Zeus—whoe'er Zeus may be, for I know not,
> Save by what people say [39]

—and so on.

[37] *Iliad* IX. 533 ff.

[38] Actors; see sec. 3 and n. 2 above.

[39] Both of these quotations are from lost plays; according to Plutarch, *Moralia* 756C, Euripides changed the second in deference to criticism.

42   TIMOCLES. Well, all mankind, all nations, believe in the gods and hold festivals to them. Are they all suffering from delusions?

DAMIS. Thanks for reminding me. National beliefs are an excellent proof of what a shaky business theology is. Why, there are as many beliefs as there are nations; the confusion's unending. The Scythians sacrifice to the scimitar, the Thracians to Zamolxis, a slave who ran away from Samos and went to Thrace. The Phrygians worship Men, the Ethiopians Day, the Cyllenians Phales, the Assyrians a dove, the Persians fire, the Egyptians water—at least, that's the general object of worship in Egypt, but they have local gods as well—at Memphis it's the ox, at Pelusium it's the onion; elsewhere it's the ibis or crocodile or baboon or cat or monkey. They've even got village gods—the right shoulder in one village, and across the river it's the left; or half a skull, or a pot bowl, or a plate. Now my dear Timocles, you must admit this is ridiculous.

MOMUS. There you are; told you so. It was all bound to be brought out and looked at very closely.

ZEUS. Yes, you did tell us, Momus. And it's quite justified criticism. I tell you, I'm going to try and straighten all this out if we get out of this mess safely.

43   TIMOCLES. Why, you—you heretic! Who do you think's responsible for oracles and prophecies if it isn't the gods and their providence?

DAMIS. I'd keep quiet about oracles if I were you. You're liable to be asked to pick your favorite. How about the one Apollo gave to the Lydian? That was completely ambiguous; it was two-faced, like some of those Hermae you see with a double face—whichever side you look at them from, they look alike.[40] I ask you, if Croesus "crosses the Halys," what is there to show it'll be his own and not Cyrus' empire he'll destroy? Yet the Sardian paid a pretty hefty price, poor devil, for that double-edged line.[41]

40 These were small busts, not necessarily of Hermes himself, surmounting four-cornered posts; such figures were found in public places and in front of private houses.
41 Cf. sec. 20 and n. 12 above.

MOMUS. Listen to him! Just what I was afraid he'd say! Where's our handsome harpist now? You go down and defend yourself against him!

ZEUS. It's no time for recriminations, Momus. You'll be the death of us.

TIMOCLES. Watch what you're doing with your blas- *44* phemy, Damis! Why, you're—you're overthrowing the gods' very sanctuaries and altars! That's what it amounts to, what you're saying.

DAMIS. Oh no, not all the altars. If they only reek of incense and perfume they aren't really doing any harm. But Artemis' altar among the Taurians—the altar she used for her hideous festivities [42]—I'd be only too glad to see it turned upside down from top to bottom.

ZEUS. Where the devil did he get all this from? There's no way of stopping him! Won't let any of us off! Street-corner demagogue! He's too free with his tongue.

> He lays his hand upon the guilty man
> And then upon the innocent alike.[43]

MOMUS. Oh, you won't find many innocent among us, Zeus. I shouldn't be surprised if he lays into one of the most prominent of us before he's through.

TIMOCLES. Atheist! You'll be telling me you can't hear *45* Zeus thundering next!

DAMIS. How can I avoid hearing thunder? But whether it's Zeus who causes it you may know better than I do—perhaps you come from somewhere where the gods live? Yet, you know, ask anybody who comes from Crete and he'll tell you another story: he'll tell you that one of the local sights is a tomb with an inscription on a pillar above it, saying that Zeus won't thunder anymore—he's been dead for ages.

MOMUS. I knew he was going to say that—saw it coming a mile off. What's up, Zeus? Pale? Well, well! Teeth chatter-

---

[42] See Euripides, *Iphigenia in Tauris;* Lucian is referring to the practice of human sacrifice.

[43] *Iliad* XV. 137.

ing? Come on now, buck up—you should treat these manikins with contempt!

ZEUS. Contempt? But look at the crowd that's listening! See, they've made up their minds—they're against us. Damis has got them by the ears; they're with him all the way.

MOMUS. Well, just let down your golden cord, any time you feel like it, and

Haul them all up, and land and sea as well.[44]

46   TIMOCLES. Tell me, you rogue, have you ever been to sea?

DAMIS. Oh yes, often.

TIMOCLES. Well then, what actually made you move was the wind striking the sheet and filling the sails, or else the oarsmen. But wasn't there a man in charge, a captain, and wasn't he the one who kept the ship on a safe course?

DAMIS. Certainly.

TIMOCLES. Well now, the ship wouldn't have sailed without a captain to steer it. And do you think this whole universe moves without a captain and helmsman?

ZEUS. Very clever, Timocles: a very forceful analogy.

47   DAMIS. My pious Timocles, you'd have found that your real captain always made his plans and his preparations and issued his instructions to the crew beforehand; you wouldn't find anything useless or purposeless on board ship, anything not wholly useful or indispensable to the voyage. Whereas this captain of yours, the one you say is in command of this great vessel, he and his crew show no sense whatever of what's appropriate in their arrangements. Why, the forestay might well be fastened to the stern, or both sheets to the bows; the anchor might be made of gold and the figurehead of lead; the ship might be decorated below the waterline and left plain *48*   above it. As for the crew, you'll find a lazy, incompetent wretch, with no spirit for the work, on double or triple pay, while another man, who's fearless as a diver and good at

44 Cf. *Iliad* VIII. 23–27. Lucian repeats this illustration often; cf. sec. 14 above.

swarming the rigging, who's uniquely skilled in all the arts of the sailor, is set to bail the ship.

And it's the same with the passengers: a blackguard sits on the bridge beside the captain, with everybody bowing and scraping before him; others like him, rakes, parricides, blasphemers, are treated with respect and given the best seats in the ship, while any number of decent people are packed in the hold and trodden underfoot by people who are really their inferiors. Why, consider the conditions Socrates and Aristides and Phocion sailed in; they didn't even have their daily bread, they crouched on bare boards beside the bilges, unable even to stretch their legs; and think what luxury Callias and Midias and Sardanapalus reveled in and how contemptuously they treated their subordinates. That's what goes on on board 49 your ship, my clever friend, and that's why so many ships are wrecked. If there really were someone in charge, if there were a captain on duty directing the ship, in the first place he'd have made it his business to know which of the passengers were worthwhile and which weren't, and in the second he'd have given them all their due according to their worth. The best of them would have got the best places, on deck at his own side, the others would have gone below; some of the best he'd have invited to his table, to ask their opinions about things. And among the crew, the keen man would have been made lookout or mate, or anyway something superior to the rest, and the idler and lead-swinger would have got a clout on the head with the rope's end half a dozen times a day. No, my dear man, it looks as if your metaphorical ship hasn't struck it lucky with its captain; it's liable to capsize.

MOMUS. Damis really has got the tide with him now; his 50 sails are full and he's sweeping on to victory.

ZEUS. Looks like it. Timocles never gets hold of a forceful idea; he just ladles out commonplaces and platitudes one after another, and they're all so vulnerable.

TIMOCLES. Well then, since my ship analogy doesn't strike 51 you as very convincing, here's my last hope, my sheet-anchor as they call it; it will certainly be too strong for you.

ZEUS. Whatever can he be coming up with?

TIMOCLES. Here's a syllogism; is it logical, can you upset it? If there are altars, there must be gods; now, there *are* altars; so there *are* gods.[45] What have you to say to this?

DAMIS. Let me laugh my head off first, then I'll tell you.

TIMOCLES. It looks as if you're never going to stop. At least tell me what you find so funny about my syllogism.

DAMIS. You don't realize what a slender thread your anchor's hanging by—your sheet-anchor, too. Why, you're making the existence of the gods dependent on the existence of altars; that's how you hope to secure your anchorage! Well, you say that's the strongest sheet-anchor you've got, so we can go home now.

52   TIMOCLES. Ah! You're off first—you admit you're beaten, then?

DAMIS. Why, yes, Timocles. You've slipped out of my hands; you've taken refuge at your altars, like a persecuted man, and—I swear it by your sheet-anchor—I'm ready to make a truce with you on your own altars, now it's come to that, and not quarrel about it any more.

TIMOCLES. You're pulling my leg! You—body snatcher! You damned, detestable villain, you miserable slave! Do you think we don't know who your father was? Do you think we don't know your mother was a harlot, and you strangled your brother, and you go around fornicating and molesting young boys? You shameless rake! Here, don't run away! I'll give you a thrashing to take with you! Why, I'll cut your throat with this broken pot—you filthy villain!

53   ZEUS. Well, gentlemen, Damis is off, and roaring with laughter, and there's Timocles chasing him and shouting names at him. He doesn't like Damis laughing at him. He'll hit him on the head with that pot, by the look of it. Well, what are *we* going to do now?

HERMES. Looks to me as if the man in that play was right:

---

45 Cf. the syllogism in *Sale* 25, and see *Hermotimus* 79 for a disparaging view of Stoic philosophical technique.

Brazen it out and no great harm is done.[46]

After all, what great harm *is* done if a few people go off with these notions? There are many more who think the opposite: the great mass of the Greeks, and the barbarians without exception.

ZEUS. Ah yes, Hermes, but there's a lot in Darius' remark about Zopyrus, and I feel the same; I'd rather have one Damis on my side than have ten thousand Babylons to draw on.[47]

[46] Menander, *Epitrepontes* (Teubner edn., ed. Koerte, Vol. I [Leipzig, 1957], p. 44, fr. 9).

[47] See Herodotus, III. 153 ff.; especially 160.

HIRED COMPANIONS [1]

1   My dear friend,

I propose to describe to you what is entailed in being a hired companion: what one must put up with, how one has to behave when subjected to the test of a great man's friendship, if friendship is a fit name for such slavery.

But where shall I begin, where shall I leave off, as they say? [2] I am familiar, you see, with many if not most of the tribulations involved. Not from personal experience—heavens, no! I never had any necessity to gain such experience, and I hope to goodness I never shall. But many men who have fallen into this kind of life have told me their tales—some still in that calamitous condition, by way of bewailing the extent and nature of their troubles, and some who like escaped prisoners took a certain pleasure in recalling what they had been through, indeed went into joyous detail about what they were now rid of.

These latter were the more credible as witnesses in that they had been through the whole ceremony, so to speak; they were initiates, and had seen it all, from start to finish. I therefore gave more than desultory and casual attention to their stories of metaphorical shipwreck and unexpected delivery. They were like a crowd of men gathered near a temple,[3] with their hair cut short,[4] all talking about the heavy seas and storms and headlands, how they jettisoned their cargo, how the mast snapped, how the rudder broke off; and invariably

---

[1] Cf. Juvenal's third Satire in general for this piece and its sequel, the *Apology for "Hired Companions"*; see Introduction, p. xxvi.

[2] Odysseus' remark to the Phaeacians (in *Odyssey* IX. 14).

[3] I.e., having made their thanksgiving offerings, and now telling their tale to win charity.

[4] Cf. *Hermotimus* 86.

the Dioscuri [5] appear—they are stock characters in that sort of sad story—or some other *deus ex machina* takes his seat at the masthead or stands by the helm and guides the ship to some quiet beach; and once it has reached there the ship itself can break up quietly in its own good time, while the crew land safely by the grace and favor of the deity.

Of course, they make a long dramatic story out of it; they overdo it, for their need is urgent and they think that more people are likely to help them if they represent themselves as being in favor with the gods as well as victims of misfortune. The others, though, with their tales of domestic storms and heavy seas—heavy? goodness, enormous, mountainous (if one can speak of mountainous seas)—tales of how calm the sea was when they first set sail, and the hardships they suffered all through the voyage from thirst and seasickness and salt seas breaking over them, and how finally their ill-starred vessel broke up on some hidden rock or wild headland while they swam ashore in wretched plight, poor creatures, naked and devoid of the first necessities—well, in their case I suspected that they had suppressed the worst of it in their descriptions, had deliberately forgotten it, out of shame.

I intend otherwise. I shall not hesitate to describe to you in detail, my dear Timocles, these dangers and whatever others I may by inference discover to be involved in such association; for if I am not mistaken, you have been interested in this kind of life for a long time. The first time I noticed it was one day when the conversation turned to this sort of situation, and somebody in the company said he thought it was a good way to earn a living, and they were very lucky to have the chance—on friendly terms with the best people in Rome, eating expensively and never paying anything toward it, living in fine houses, traveling in perfect ease and comfort, perhaps even lording it snootily behind a pair of creams—and then, on top of that, they're actually paid quite a good salary for enjoying this friendship and these benefits: people like that, he said, don't have to sow or plough at all, they find everything

2

3

5 Castor and Pollux, the guardian spirits of sailors. See Glossary, "Pollux."

they want growing on trees—well then, when you heard that, and other remarks like it, I could see you gape at the thought; your mouth opened at the bait, as wide as it would go.

Now, I want to discharge my responsibility in the matter once and for all. I do not want to leave it open to you in future to say that I watched you swallow this bait, and the great hook along with it, without laying a restraining hand upon you; that I did not snatch it away before it disappeared down your gullet, that I failed to expose it to you before you rose to it. I do not want it ever to be said that I looked on while you were hooked and well and truly caught, that I watched you nibbling and being landed by brute force, that I stood by shedding tears when it was no use—a charge which if made could not be dismissed lightly, for I could not evade it by saying there was nothing positively wrong in not giving you due warning. So pay attention from the start. Have a look at the actual net and see how fine the mesh is—but not from inside it! Do it now, from outside, while you can take your time; don't wait until you're caught. Take the prongs of the spear into your hands; examine the hook carefully and notice how the barb acts in the opposite direction from the point; test it properly against your inflated cheek. If you think it is not very sharp, that you could get away from it, that even if it did pull strongly and held you firmly when you resisted, the wounds it would inflict would not be very painful, then write me down as a coward who goes hungry *because* he is a coward; and for yourself, summon your courage and fall upon your prey, if you will, like a cormorant swallowing the bait whole.

4   This whole account is, I admit, inspired principally by your case, but it is addressed to others besides philosophers like yourself and people who are committed to a serious course in life; it applies also to grammarians, rhetoricians, musicians, in fact to all those who see fit to become paid companions on the basis of their cultural attainments. And they are all treated pretty much alike; there is no question of the philosopher's being accorded greater privileges; indeed, he suffers rather greater indignity, inasmuch as he is thought no worthier than his fellows, and is treated by his employer with

no more respect. In any event, the responsibility for whatever I may reveal as my story proceeds lies primarily with the perpetrators of such conduct, but also, though in lesser degree, with those who acquiesce in it; I am blameless, unless it is reprehensible to speak truth and speak it plain. As for the other rabble—physical training instructors and toadies, limited creatures, mean of intelligence and appropriately menial in station—in the first place it would serve no purpose to dissuade them from such associations, for they would not listen, nor indeed is it fair to reproach them for not leaving their masters no matter how arrogantly they are treated by them; they are in their element, they are suited in this sort of occupation. Besides, they would have nothing else to turn to for support, to keep themselves in employment—take this from them, and at once they lose their trade, they are idle, they are superfluous. They are not, then, ill-treated, nor, any more, is their masters' behavior outrageous; in the words of the proverb, what would one do with a chamberpot but make water in it? No, they expect such contemptuous treatment when first they enter a house; it is their trade to endure and put up with what comes to them. But the case of men of culture, such as I mentioned a moment ago, very properly elicits our indignation. We should spare no effort to turn them aside and snatch them away to retain their freedom.

I think it would be well first to examine the reasons that   5 lead men to adopt this kind of life, and to demonstrate that they are by no means compelling or coercive; for thus we can cut the ground from under their feet, forestall their arguments, remove the first premise that underlies their voluntary slavery. Most of them advance poverty as their motive. The need to support life is, they think, sufficient cover for their desertion to such employment; they consider it apology enough to say that they can be forgiven for seeking to escape poverty, the worst of life's tribulations. Theognis is ready at hand to support their case:

Every man subdued by poverty [6]

6 Cf. Theognis, 173.

is much on their lips, and all the other bogies our more
ignoble poets have raised on that subject.

Now if I could see that such engagements actually did bring
them release from poverty, I should not insist on too stringent
a definition of liberty in my attitude to them. But in fact their
sustenance is sick men's fare, to quote the famous orator.[7]
How then can one avoid the conclusion that this is but another point on which their estimations are awry, when the
basic condition of their existence remains unaltered? They are
still poor, that is; they still need their wages, they cannot save
anything, there is nothing to spare for a rainy day. Their
salary—even if they *are* paid, and paid in full—vanishes to the
last penny, and still they are short of essentials. It were better
not to devise such devices; they only safeguard poverty, they
aid and abet her. Better to find means to destroy her altogether, and in pursuit of that end perhaps even, if need be,
"plunge into ocean's depths"—eh, Theognis?—"from beetling
crags," as you say.[8] But when a chronic pauper, a destitute
who works for hire, imagines that by working for hire he has
evaded poverty, the only conclusion one can draw is that he
is deceiving himself.

6   There are others who protest that poverty would not in
itself have frightened them into submission had they been
capable of working for their daily bread like others; but that
they are physically exhausted with age or sickness, and have
turned to this as being the easiest way of earning a living.
Well now, let us look at this. Is the case as they say? Or does
not this "easiest way" in fact involve them in considerable
labor—more than other people—before they lay hands on their
wage? It would be a wish come true, surely, to have money on
tap without toil or labor. The truth of the matter beggars
adequate description: so much toil and labor does their employment involve that health is more than ever necessary in
its prosecution. It is the very occupation that demands it in
highest degree; there are innumerable claims on one's strength

7 Demosthenes, *Olynthiacs* 3. 33.
8 Theognis, 176.

every day in life, which reduce the victim to utter exhaustion. But that I shall speak of in due course, when I describe the whole range of hardships the life involves; for the present, suffice it to suggest that this is not any more convincing a reason to offer for selling oneself than was the other.

We are left with the true reason, one they would never confess: self-indulgence. They are overcome by the thought of all that gold and silver, they gloat over the meals in prospect, over the luxurious surroundings; hope crowds in on every side, and they rush into houses expecting there and then positively to gulp down gold with mouths wide open and no one to check them. That is the inducement that makes slaves of free men: not the need for essentials, as they pretend, but the desire for luxuries, an unholy passion for all that wealth and plenty. And of course they have no luck. They are like hapless lovers: the objects of their desire, skilled and experienced in such relations, take them under control and treat them with disdain, ensuring the continuance of their attention and affection. No taste do they give them of enjoyment of their love, not even the lightest kiss; conquest, they know, would mean disenchantment, which to prevent they stand most jealously on guard. For the rest, though, they keep their lover always in hope; despair, they fear, may distract him from his passion, he may fall out of love with them. Whence they will smile at him and give him promises; always they are going to do something for him, extend him some favor, some costly attention—some day. And then, before they know it, age creeps upon them both, and they are past their prime: the one past loving, the other past according favors. All they have achieved in life is hope.

Now, a man is not, perhaps, altogether to be reproached for putting up with anything in the pursuit of pleasure. He can be forgiven for enjoying it and devoting all his efforts to its attainment. —And yet surely there is shame and degradation in selling oneself for it? Is there not a far greater pleasure in liberty? —Still, suppose it forgivable—if pleasure is forthcoming. But to put up with much that is unpleasant merely in the

7

8

hope of pleasure is to my mind ridiculous and foolish; especially when one can see that the hardships are manifest, apparent, and inevitable, while the object of these vague aspirations, the pleasure, has never yet materialized in all this time and what is more is never likely to, in any honest judgment. Odysseus' crew at least ate the lotus[9] and found it sweet when they set aside all else; if they made light of honor, it was for present pleasure. It was not unnatural to forget honor when their hearts were thus engaged. But to submit to imprisonment; to stand and watch another man sate himself with the lotus in the mere hope that he may some day give you a taste of it, although he never does; to forget honor and decency in the process; and with all this *still* to go hungry— ye gods, it is absurd. That really does deserve a Homeric thrashing.[10]

9 Well now, that, I think, is a fairly accurate statement of the motives that entice men into this sort of association and make them of their own volition hand themselves over to the wealthy to do with as they will. Or perhaps it is worthwhile mentioning also those who are actually elated by the mere thought that they are known to associate with the noble and the eminent; for there *are* people who consider even this a conspicuous mark of distinction. Personally I would not have and be seen to have the company of the Great King[11] himself if that company were to be of no advantage to me.

10 We have seen what they hope will happen. Let us now look, between ourselves, at what does happen: at the trials of the aspirant, the tribulations of the incumbent, and, to crown it all, the dénouement of his life's drama. For, I assure you, it is not even as if one could say that such a post, however uncomfortable, is at least there for the taking, without much trouble; that one has merely to make the decision and the whole business is easily effected. Oh no: you'll have to chase about here, there, and everywhere; to dance attendance con-

9 *Odyssey* IX. 82–104.
10 Cf. *Iliad* II. 265, where Odysseus thrashes Thersites.
11 The King of Persia.

stantly at your patron's door; to get up at the crack of dawn and hang about waiting for him to appear. You'll be jostled about; you'll find the door shut in your face; you'll be cursed often enough—"Of all the brass neck!" they'll say, "damned nuisance!" Your life will be ruled by a Syrian doorkeeper who murders the Greek language and a Libyan nomenclator who won't remember your name unless you make it worth his while. And more yet: there are your clothes to think about. They must be such as accord with your patron's dignity, and that will stretch your resources past the breaking point; and see you choose his favorite colors, or you'll be out of harmony, you'll clash with your surroundings. You'll sweat in his train—or rather in his van, for there you'll be thrust by his household, to swell his private procession. And for days on end he won't even look at you.

But one day your luck is in. He notices you; he calls you *11* to him; he asks you some random question. Then, then, the sweat runs down you! Your head spins madly, you tremble—a fine time to tremble! The company are vastly amused by your confusion; and as like as not, if asked who was the king of the Achaeans, you'll answer, "They had a thousand ships." The good-natured will put this down to shyness, but the forward to cowardice, and the spiteful to ignorance. Having found his first friendly gesture so difficult to negotiate, you go away condemning yourself to deep despair. Whereupon

> Many a sleepless night you pass,
> And many a bloody day [12]

do you go through—not, heaven knows, for Helen or for Priam's Troy, but for the pittance that informs your hopes.

But as in a play, some god turns up to arrange things for you; and then follows the examination, to see whether you know your stuff. Your plutocrat sits and listens to your praise and compliments; quite a pleasant interlude for him, but for you it has the aspect of a struggle for existence, your whole life depends on it. For the thought inevitably enters your

[12] *Iliad* IX. 325–26.

mind that in all probability you will never get a job with
anyone else if you strike this first employer as spurious coin
and he rejects you. A thousand and one thoughts distract you:
you are jealous of your competitors (we shall assume that
others are interested in the same post) ; you are dissatisfied
with all your answers; you are pessimistic, you are optimistic.
Your eyes are riveted on his face: if he turns up his nose at
some remark you make, you are done for; if he listens to you
12   with a smile, you rejoice, your confidence soars. You come under fire from your opponents, who are no doubt numerous;
each of them is pushing some rival's claim, and lying in ambush for you. Just think of it! A man with a long beard and
gray hair under examination to see if he is any use; and some
think yes, and some think no!

Half-time is called in this long encounter; then all your
past life is busily rummaged. It only takes a word, elicited
from some compatriot who has a grudge against you, a neighbor who has crossed swords with you on some trivial matter—
the suggestion of "adulterer" or "pederast"—and that's it! his
word is gospel. But if they all approve of you one after another they are suspect, their evidence is dubious, they are
corrupt. No, you need a great deal of luck and no opposition
at all; that is the only way you will succeed.

Well then, suppose you *are* lucky in everything, beyond
your wildest dreams. The great man has approved your answers; the friends whose judgment he most respects, who guide
him in these matters, have not influenced him against you;
what is more, his wife agrees, and neither his steward nor the
comptroller of his household has anything to say against you.
No one has found any fault with your character. All is propi-
tious, on all sides the auguries bode well.

13   So you have succeeded! Happy, happy man! You have won
your Olympic wreath—or rather you have taken Babylon,
have stormed the heights of Sardis! The horn of Amalthea[13]
will be yours, you will drink the milk of birds! Now, the rewards will have to be considerable, proportionate to the trou-

13 The Horn of Plenty.

ble you have had, if your crown is to be more than just leaves. The salary determined for you must be generous, and available without fuss when you need it. Your position in general must be one of privilege. No need to tire yourself out any more, running about in the mud all day and lying awake all night: you can do what you've always dreamed of doing, put your feet up and sleep; all you have to do is what you were engaged to do in the first place, what you're paid to do.

That's how it ought to be, Timocles, and there would be no great objection to bowing the neck to a yoke like that; it's light, it's easy to bear; above all, it's gilded. But that is far from being the way of it—in fact it's nothing like it. Once you have actually entered into this relationship, a thousand and one things happen that no free man should tolerate. Let me detail them, and judge for yourself whether anyone of any education at all could stand it.

Shall I begin with the first dinner? For you may expect an invitation to dinner as a foretaste of the association then commencing. Well, forthwith somebody will come up to you, deputed to transmit the invitation: a servant, a sociable fellow. You must secure his good graces; and you don't want to appear gauche; so you slip something into his hand, five drachmas at least. He goes all coy: "Oh, no, sir, I couldn't!" he begins, "goodness me, you mustn't!" But he lets himself be persuaded in the end and goes off with a broad grin on his face at your expense. You get out clean clothes; you have a bath, make yourself as presentable as you can, and duly turn up. You're afraid you may get there before everyone else, and that would be unsophisticated, just as it would be vulgar to be the last to arrive. So you are careful to enter at just the right moment. You are received with deference, and shown to your place a little above your patron, just next to a couple of his old friends, say.

It's like entering the courts of heaven: everything's new and strange to you, you gaze all around you in wonder, excited at everything that's going on. The servants are looking at you, all the company watch to see how you'll behave. Your pa-

14

15

tron's interested in you too; he's instructed some of his servants to keep an eye on you to see if you keep looking at his children or his wife when you think nobody will notice. The other guests' attendants notice how put out you are by the unfamiliar situation; they crack jokes among themselves at your expense. You've brought a brand-new napkin;[14] this is taken to prove that nobody ever asked you to dinner before. No wonder you're in a sweat; you're lost. You're thirsty, but you daren't ask for something to drink—that might suggest you were a drinker. All sorts of dishes appear beside you; they're in some sort of order, but you don't know what to take first or second; you'll have to watch your neighbor out of the corner of your eye, do as he does, and find out what comes where.

16   What with one thing and another, you don't know what you feel; your mind is thoroughly confused, you're scared out of your wits at every single thing that happens. One moment you're thinking what a lucky man your patron is, with his gold and his ivory and all the luxury he lives in, and the next minute you're feeling sorry for yourself—you're nobody, do you call yourself alive? And then every so often the thought comes into your head that you're going to have an enviable time of it, reveling in all that luxury, enjoying it as an equal. An exquisite picture of your future existence you sketch: nothing but Dionysian feasts, and handsome youths, as an added touch, ministering to you and smiling sweetly. You keep quoting that line of Homer:

Who can blame Trojans and well-greaved Achaeans [15]

for all their labors and sufferings, if such bliss was their goal?

Next come the toasts. He calls for a great beaker and drinks your health—"To the Professor!" or whatever it is he calls you. You take the bowl, but in your ignorance you don't know that you're expected to make some kind of reply, and you earn the name of a boor.

17   In any case, with that toast you've made enemies of many

14 Guests brought their own napkins.
15 *Iliad* III. 156, Helen being what they fought for.

of his old friends. Some of them were annoyed before that, when you were shown to your place at table—arrived that day, and given a place above men who have been drinking the dregs of slavery this many a year! Immediately they start talking about you: "This is the last straw! Playing second fiddle to people barely in the house a minute! Rome is open to none but these Greeks! What have they got that we haven't? Do they think they're doing us a big favor with their wretched chatter?" Somebody else will chime in: "Did you see how he drank? Did you see how he grabbed at his food and stuffed it down him? Rude beggar—you'd think he was starving! Never even dreamed of eating white bread before! Or capon or pheasant either—he's barely left us the bones!" And then another: "Don't be silly—he'll be joining us before five days are past, you'll see, moaning just like the rest of us! He's like a pair of new shoes just now, treated well and taken care of; but when he's been worn a few times and loses his shape in the mud he'll be thrown under the bed to rot like us, for the bugs to live in." Well, there are plenty of variations on that theme from *them,* and in all probability some of them are already getting ready to blacken your name.

The whole dinner, of course, is in your honor, and the con- 18 versation is mostly about you. But the wine is deceptive and potent; you're not used to it, and you drink too much. Your belly makes its needs felt, and you're in a bad way; it would be bad manners to leave the table before the rest, but it isn't safe to stay there. The drinking is protracted, conversation is interminable, and entertainments multiply, for he wants to show off everything he has to you. You take great punishment: you can't see what's going on, you can't hear when some favorite lad of his sings or plays the lyre. You force yourself to utter some compliment, but inwardly you're wishing an earthquake would cave the whole house in or that a fire would be reported and the party would break up at last. And that, my 19 friend, is your first dinner—and it's your best. It's not to my taste; I'd rather eat thyme with salt, if I could choose when I ate, and how much.

Well then, passing over the dyspepsia and nocturnal vomiting consequent upon all this, the next day you'll have to come to an agreement about salary—how much you're to be paid a year, and when you're to get it. He'll have two or three of his friends with him when he calls you in. "Have a seat," he says. Then he starts. "Well," he says, "you've seen how we live by now—nothing pretentious or highfalutin, just an ordinary, simple household. You must consider yourself one of the family. It would be silly to entrust you with the most important thing I have, my own soul, or indeed my children's"—if he has children to be tutored—"and then not give you an equally free hand in every other way. But we must make some definite arrangement. I can see of course that you're not a man who wants a lot, you're quite content in yourself; and I realize that it's not the money that's brought you here, but other things—the regard we'll hold you in, and the respect everyone will have for you. But still, we'd better settle something definite. Well, you say what you want. Don't forget, my dear fellow, what we may be expected to give in the way of presents on various holidays throughout the year— we shan't forget things like that, too, even if we don't include them in this arrangement. And, you know, there are quite a number of occasions in a year when you'll make a bit that way, so obviously when you bear that in mind you won't charge us too much in actual salary—especially as you educated people would naturally be above money considerations." That'll be his line. He's had you agog with hope, and you're eating out of his hand. You for your part have been dreaming of a supertax income, of owning great estates and rows of houses. Gradually it dawns on you that *he* has no such intentions; still, your eyes light up when he says you're to be "one of the family," and you take that at its face value— never thinking that in a matter like that "there's many a slip 'twixt the cup and the lip." [16]

At last you're so embarrassed that you say "I'll leave it to

16 The Greek is a quotation from Homer, *Iliad* XXII. 495, "wets the lips but not the palate," quite close to our proverb.

you." "No, no," he says, "I'm not going to decide"; and he'll ask one of the friends he has with him to enter the discussion and name a figure. "Not something I can't afford," he'll say; "remember I have other expenses too, more essential than this. But sufficient for our friend here, of course." His nominee will be some hale old fellow who's practiced the art of flattery all his life. "Now, sir," he says, "you're the luckiest man in town —and don't you tell me you're not! Why, never mind anything else, you've got a chance many a man would go down on his bended knees for and not have your luck—to be admitted to the society and share the hearth and be received into the bosom of the leading family in the Roman Empire! Worth more than all Croesus' treasures or all Midas' millions, if you know when you're well off. I've seen many a gentleman of quality would be only too glad to associate with my lord here, even if he had to pay for it, just for the prestige, just to be seen in his company, as his friend and companion for all to see. But you—I can't find words to express your good fortune— on top of all that you're actually going to be paid for being so confoundedly lucky. In my opinion, unless you're quite shameless such-and-such is quite enough." And the sum he names is minute—especially when your hopes had been so high.

But you have to make the best of it; you're in the net now 21 and couldn't escape anyway. Well, you shut your eyes and let them put you in harness. To start with, you're docile with him; he doesn't pull on the bit or apply the spur too hard, until without noticing it you've become quite used to him. And of course thereafter people outside envy you; they see you living in the establishment and coming and going as you please, quite one of the household. But you can never understand why they think you so lucky. Still, you put a cheerful face on it and fool yourself into thinking things will improve shortly. But things turn out the opposite of what you hoped for; it all turns out like Mandrobulus' sacrifice in the proverb; [17] you

17 According to a scholiast, Mandrobulus dedicated a golden sheep to Hera in thanksgiving for having found a treasure. On the anniversary of

decrease in stature, so to speak, every day; you're on the re-treat.

22   And so, slowly, gradually, as though you were just begin-ning to see in the dim light, you begin to realize that those golden hopes you entertained were nothing more than bub-bles coated with gold, but that the troubles are real enough—and serious, intransigent, unceasing. "What troubles?" you ask: "I don't see what's so troublesome in this sort of situa-tion; I don't understand what it is you're saying is so dis-tressing, so intolerable." All right, my dear fellow, I'll tell you. You see whether you don't think it's all very wearying, and not only wearying but undignified and degrading and, in fact, only fit for slaves—that isn't a minor issue, you know.

23   In the first place, bear in mind that from that day you can't think of yourself as a free man of good family. All those notions—birth, freedom, ancestry—you'll have to leave outside in the street when you sell yourself into servitude like that, make no mistake about it. Freedom won't be prepared to go with you when you enter so disreputable, so ignominious a contract. You're a slave, then, however much you dislike the term; and necessarily the slave of not one but many masters, going about your menial tasks with eyes downcast from morn-ing to night "for sorry wage." [18] And of course, not having been brought up a slave from childhood, you are slow to learn; you are well on in years when you go to school with Servitude, and you will not make a very good impression or be much use to your master. Memories of freedom will creep into your thoughts; they will spoil you for slavery, make you kick against the pricks from time to time and acquit yourself but poorly in your station. Or do you think the claims of freedom are met if you are not the son of a Pyrrhias or a Zopyrion,[19] if you have not been sold like a Bithynian [20] under

---

the event his offering was another sheep, but this time of silver; the next year it was of bronze.

18 An epic phrase, which may be a variation on various Homeric tags.
19 Common slave names.
20 Bithynia was the source of many slaves.

a shouting auctioneer's hammer? My good fellow, you wait till the new moon comes around: [21] you'll rub shoulders with Pyrrhias and Zopyrion; you'll hold out your hand just like the rest of the servants and take whatever it is you get. That's being sold. No need for any auctioneer when a man shouts his own price and for long seeks to espouse a master for himself.

Wretch! I am tempted to call you that—particularly since you have pretensions to being a philosopher. If you had been captured and sold by a pirate or brigand, you'd feel sorry for yourself and think you were miserably unlucky. If somebody had laid hands on you and were hauling you off as his slave, you'd be very indignant: you'd invoke the law, you'd cry out to heaven and earth at the top of your voice, there's nothing you wouldn't do. But you sell yourself for a few obols—at this stage in your life, when even if you'd been born a slave it would be time for you now to be looking for your freedom—you've sold yourself, virtue, wisdom and all! After all those long harangues from your noble Plato and Chrysippus and Aristotle in praise of liberty and depreciation of servility! Are you not ashamed to compete with flatterers and riffraff and vulgar buffoons? To be the only foreigner in all that mob of Romans, shown up by your Greek cloak and your wretched Latin? To eat at rowdy banquets crowded with all kinds of flotsam, and most of the company depraved? You trot out cheap compliments, you drink more than is decent; and the morning after, when the bell rings, you rouse yourself, shrug off the sweetest hours of your sleep, and chase up hill and down dale with your legs still spattered with mud from yesterday. Were you so short of lupines and wild herbs, had even the cold springs stopped running, that your desperation brought you to this? No, it is clear enough. It is not water or lupines you wanted so badly, but cakes, meat, sweet wine; you are caught like the pike—hooked, precisely, through the gullet that gaped so wide for them—and it serves you right. Well, the rewards of your gourmandise are not far to seek. Like a

24

[21] I.e., until payday.

monkey with a collar round its neck, you amuse other people but think yourself in the lap of luxury because you can stuff yourself with dried figs to your heart's content. But liberty and nobility of mind are gone, along with all such sentiments; and with them is gone all memory of them.

25   It would be endurable to exchange your liberty for slavery if shame were all it involved, if you didn't have to work like a veritable servant. But think—are your duties any lighter than Dromo's or Tibius'? [22] Because the studies your employer engaged you for, and in which he professed so passionate an interest, mean nothing to him: you know what the proverb says—"What does an ass want with a lyre?" Manifestly they are consumed with yearning for Homer's wisdom, Demosthenes' eloquence, Plato's lofty idealism! Why, if you took away the gold and silver trimmings from these people's minds, and the worries that gold and silver bring, all you'd be left with would be conceit, effeminacy, self-indulgence, licentiousness, arrogance, ignorance! No, that isn't what he wants you for. He wants you for your long beard and serious manner, for the natural way your Greek cloak sits on your shoulders. Everybody knows you're a scholar or rhetorician or philosopher, and he thinks it's a good idea to have somebody like that too in the crowd that precedes him when he walks abroad. It will suggest that he is a man of culture, an ardent enthusiast for Greek learning. My dear man, it's your beard and cloak you've hired out, it seems, not your wonderful conversation.

So at all times you must be seen with him and never lag behind. Get up early in the morning and make yourself conspicuous in his attendance, and don't desert your post. Now and again he'll put his hand on your shoulder and utter some nonsense or other, so that whoever happens to be near can see that he doesn't neglect the Muses even when he's walking down the street: he makes creditable use of his time when
26   he's out for a stroll. And you, poor fellow, you trot about all

22 More slave names.

over the place, sweating and out of breath, sometimes running beside his litter, sometimes walking, up and down hills most of the time—you know what Rome's like. And when he calls on a friend and goes in to talk to him, you haven't anywhere to sit; you stand there because there's nothing else you can do, reading the book you brought with you. By the time night comes upon you, you're hungry and thirsty; you snatch a miserable bath, and it's all hours before you get to dinner—midnight, in fact, or near enough.

And now your stock has dropped. Nobody there takes any notice of you any more. If some fresh figure appears, you're pushed into the background; and there you lie, in the most obscure corner, merely watching the courses brought in. If they get as far as you, you gnaw at the bones like a dog, so hungry that you're glad to get the tough mallow leaves the rest of the food is wrapped in; they're a treat to you—that is, if they get past the people sitting above you. And that isn't the only insult by any means. You are the only one who doesn't get an egg; you have no call to expect the same treatment as guests and strangers all the time—have some sense! And the bird you get isn't like the others: your neighbor's is plump and juicy, you get half a chicken or a tough pigeon, a downright insult; it shows what they think of you. Then, many a time somebody else turns up unexpectedly, and they run short; the butler will murmur to you that "you're one of the family," remove your plate, and go and put it in front of him. And when the sow's or deer's paunch is brought in for carving, you'd better be in favor with the carver, or else you'll get a Promethean helping—bones wrapped up in fat. And again, how can any free man, even if he have no more gall in him than a hind, endure the way the plate flashes past you so quickly, though it stayed with your neighbor till he was tired of stuffing himself? Then there's the wine; I haven't even mentioned that yet. Everybody else is drinking some delicious vintage, you alone have foul thick stuff; you have to take care to drink from a silver or gold cup so that its color won't reveal your degradation to the company. And if only you could get enough of this! But you can call time and again, and the steward "acts as if he did not notice." [23]

27   In fact, vexations pile up thick and fast. Practically everything annoys you; and worst of all is when some wily knave ousts you in everybody's favor, some dancing master or laddie from Alexandria stringing Ionic songs [24] together. How can you hope to be held in the same regard as those who serve Love's pleasures, who furtively convey billets-doux? So you, at your obscure corner of the table, self-effacing in your shame, lament your lot, and well you may—feeling sorry for yourself, cursing the fate that gave you no touch of these graces. I think you actually wish you could write love songs, or at least sing someone else's prettily; you can see what it calls for to be in favor and have a name. If it fell to you to play the wizard, the clairvoyant, one of those who hold out hopes of rich inheritances and high office and piles of wealth, you'd do that; for they get on with people too, as you can see, they do well. You'd be any of these, and gladly, so that you be not discarded and superfluous. But what a plight you're in—you aren't even convincing at that! All you can do, in fact, is make yourself small, bewailing your neglect to yourself but putting up with it and saying nothing.

28   And if her ladyship's young favorite dances or plays his lyre, and some tell-tale servant whispers that you are the only one who didn't applaud, that'll get you into real trouble. So, thirsty as you are, you must croak like any frog out of its pool; make sure they notice you applauding, lead the chorus; most studiously add, ever and again, some compliment of your own when all else are silent, to underline your base servility. You know, it's really rather amusing: there you are starving with hunger, aye and thirsty too, and yet you anoint yourself with oil, you crown your head with garlands! It makes you look like the gravestone of a long-dead corpse when the

23 *Iliad* XXIII. 430.
24 I.e., love songs.

mourners make their offerings: the stone gets the oil and garlands all over it, the mourners drink up and feast themselves
on the victuals.

And if he's of a jealous disposition and has good-looking   *29*
children or a young wife, and you're not altogether a stranger
to Aphrodite and the Graces, then you'll have a troubled time
of it; don't underestimate your danger. For a king has many
ears, and many eyes; and not only do they see the truth, they
are forever reckoning it something greater than it is, lest they
should seem to slumber. As at a Persian banquet, then, you
had better keep your eyes down at table, in case some eunuch
see you glance at one of the concubines—for another eunuch
has had his bow taut all the time, ready to punish anyone who
lets his gaze wander beyond bounds, with an arrow through
the jaw as he drinks.

Then, after the dinner, you go and sleep for a few hours.   *30*
But at cockcrow you're woken up. "What a life!" you think,
"what a miserable existence! And what a life I left behind
me long ago! I had friends, my days were carefree; my sleep
was determined only by my desires, I came and went as I
wished. And look at the pit I've rushed headfirst into! What
for, in heaven's name? What is this splendid reward? Couldn't
I have done better for myself than this and kept my liberty
and freedom of action as well? I'm dragged here, there, and
everywhere—a lion bound by a thread, as the proverb says.
The most pitiful thing of all is, I don't know how to win
respect and I can't win popularity. I'm a hopeless amateur
at the game—especially when I'm up against professionals,
who've made an art of it. I've no charms to recommend me;
I'm no boon companion; I can't so much as raise a laugh. I'm
well aware my presence is just a nuisance often enough, particularly when he's in his best humor; he thinks I look surly,
and I just can't get in tune with him. If I keep a solemn
countenance, he thinks me disagreeable and can hardly abide
me; if I smile and give my face its happiest shape, his immediate reaction is contempt—he despises me, I remind him

of an actor in a tragic mask playing a comedy. In fact I've wasted my life: I've lived for someone else—what other life shall I have for myself?"

31   You're still communing thus with yourself when the bell rings, and you're back to the same round, running all over the place and standing waiting; better anoint your groin and behind your knees if you want to complete the course.[25] And after that, dinner as before, and going on as long. It's the very reverse of your old way of life. Loss of sleep, perspiration, exhaustion: they're gradually undermining your health: they're giving you consumption or pneumonia or arthritis or gout— that lovely disease! Still, you hold out, and though you ought to be in bed many a time, that's out of the question too; saying you're ill sounds like an excuse to get out of your duties. So, what with one thing and another, you're perpetually pasty, you look as if you were at death's door.

32   Well, that's life in Rome. Now let's suppose you have to go into the country. Leaving other things aside, it'll be raining, as often as not, and you'll be the last to get there—even the horses they give you are no better than that! You hang about until there isn't a room left, and then they pack you in along with the cook or her ladyship's coiffeur—and they don't even put down plenty of brushwood for you to sleep on!

33   And I have no hesitation in telling you Thesmopolis' story —you know Thesmopolis, the Stoic?—of what happened to him when he was in the service of a certain wealthy and luxury-loving great lady in Rome; it's very amusing, and the same thing may very well happen to somebody else. They had to go to the country one day. The first comic trick that was played on him, he said, was the company he was put with: there was he, a philosopher, sitting next to one of those obscene creatures who plaster their legs with depilatories and shave off every hair on their face. She thought the world of him, as you may guess; and she told Thesmopolis the name of this fairy—"Swallowkins"! Just think of it, an old man like Thesmopolis, with his severe face and his gray beard—you

25 Athletes did this before a contest.

know how long it was and how solemn it made him look—
having to sit next to a laddie like that! All rouged, his eyes
made up and darting sly glances, his neck thrust forward—
Swallow? a plucked vulture, more like! And but for the philosopher's earnest request he'd have sat there with his hairnet
on! Thesmopolis had to put up with enough odious behavior
all the way as it was—the creature sang and whistled, and no
doubt he would have danced in the carriage if he hadn't been
restrained!

But anyway, there was more of the same in store for him. *34*
The lady called him to her. "Thesmopolis," she said, "be
an angel and do me a great favor! Don't say no, and don't
wait for me to ask you twice!" Naturally he said he'd do anything she wanted. "I'm asking you," she said, "because I can
see you're a good man and considerate and sympathetic. You
know my dog Myrrhina? Take her into your carriage and look
after her for me—see that she has all she wants. She's in pup,
poor thing, and she's very near her time. These dreadful
servants won't do a thing I tell them: they won't put themselves out for me when we're traveling, let alone for her. I'll
be terribly grateful, believe me, if you'll look after my sweet
little doggie, I'm *so* fond of her."

Well, she begged and begged, she almost wept; and Thesmopolis said he would. It was so funny; the little doggie
peeping out from his cloak under his beard—and piddling on
him all the time, too, though Thesmopolis didn't mention that
detail—and yapping in its shrill voice as Maltese terriers do,
and licking at the philosopher's beard, especially if it had
some of yesterday's soup still clinging to it. Later on, at
dinner, the fairy, his companion, was making fun of the rest
of the company, quite wittily; when he directed his wit at
Thesmopolis, "I've only this to say of Thesmopolis," he said,
"that our Stoic's now turned Cynic!" [26] The little doggie, I
gather, actually littered in his cloak!

Thus do they make fun of their servants, insult them rather, *35*

[26] I.e., become a dog-philosopher; the Greek word κύων, from which
"Cynic" is derived, means "dog."

gradually rendering them tame to their insolence. I know an orator too, a fellow with a sharp tongue, who was told to make a speech at the dinner table; [27] he made an expert one, very incisive and well-constructed. Certainly he received the congratulations of the company, as they drank—for speaking not by the water clock but by the wine jug [28]—which enterprise he undertook, so it is said, for two hundred drachmas. Well, that is perhaps tolerable; but if old moneybags fancies himself as poet or historian and reels off his own works at the dinner table, then you must rupture yourself to think up flattering compliments and new terms of praise. Some of them actually want to be admired for their looks; they have to be told they're Adonises and Hyacinths, though their noses may be as long as your forearm. Anyhow, if you don't cater to their vanity, you're for the quarries of Sicily [29] right away—you're envious, you're treacherous! And philosophers and orators they must be; if they do perpetrate a few solecisms, in this very point must their style be redolent of the Attic, of Hymettus; [30] let it be law hereafter to speak as they speak.

36   And yet, perhaps one could put up with the way the men behave; but oh, the women! For this, you must know, is one more thing women are very keen on—having a few educated people on their payroll, to keep them company and follow their litters. It is one more embellishment to add to their others, they think, if they have the name of being educated ladies, philosophers, poets not much less accomplished than Sappho; wherefore, you see, they too take their hired rhetoricians and scholars and philosophers about with them. And when do they give them audience? This'll amuse you too. While they're making up, or having their hair done, or else at dinner; those are the only times they're free. And many a

27 After-dinner speeches were not usual; this therefore is merely an entertainment of the same kind as the songs mentioned in sec. 18 above.

28 In law courts, a speaker was timed by a water clock.

29 Like political opponents of Sicilian tyrants, or the Athenians captured in the last battle of the Sicilian expedition in 413 B.C.

30 A mountain near Athens where honey was produced.

time, when your philosopher's in the middle of some discourse, her lady's maid will come in and hand her a note from her lover. All discussion of virtue stops—it must wait till she's replied to lover-boy and hastens to give ear again.

Eventually, at long intervals, the Festival of Cronus [31] or the Panathenaea [32] comes around, and you have a sorry cloak sent to you, or a tunic that's falling to pieces [33]—and oh, the amount of fuss that goes into the conveying of it! First somebody gets wind of it while your lord and master is still at the stage of considering the matter; he scurries in and gives you advance notice, and gets a tidy tip for his information. And the next day a dozen of them come to bring it to you, every one of them with his story of how vigorously he approved the idea or how he suggested it or how he had the job of choosing it and chose the best. And they all end up a bit richer; although they hold their noses up at what you give them.

As for your actual salary, it comes in dribbles, two or four obols at a time; and you have to importune and make a nuisance of yourself to get it, too; to flatter his lordship and go down on your knees to him; to pay due observance to the steward as well, a different kind of observance; and then you mustn't neglect the personal friend whose advice he listens to. And when it does come, it's all spoken for: you're in debt to somebody, tailor or doctor or shoemaker. You don't make anything out of what they give you—it's "not a gift at all." [34]

And jealousy mounts: more and more you are traduced to your master, and he is only too glad nowadays to listen to the tales against you. For he can see that by now your unending labors have exhausted you: your service is halting, you are worn out, gout is creeping upon you. The fact is, he's culled your choicest flower; he's taken the best years of your life, you've lost your vigor and bloom in his service. He's

37

38

39

[31] The mid-winter festival corresponding to the Roman Saturnalia.

[32] The "Festival of Athens," one of the great local festivals.

[33] Gifts were given at these festivals, as at our Christmas; cf. sec. 19 above.

[34] A reference to a proverb, used also by Sophocles, *Ajax* 664–65.

made a tattered rag of you, and now he's looking around for some dunghill to throw you out on, and keeping his eyes open for some healthy body who can support the fatigue. So some charge is trumped up against you: you once tried to seduce one of his young lads, or you're corrupting his wife's innocent maid—at your age!—and out you go, thrown out, to wander into the night with your cloak drawn about your neck! You've lost everything, you don't know where to turn, and the companion of your declining years is gout—an excellent friend! After all this time, you've forgotten all you ever knew. Your belly's distended like a sack; it's insatiable, it won't be put off, it's a curse upon you, because your gullet calls and calls for what it's used to, and putting off the habit comes hard.

40 And no one else will take you on now; you're past it, like an old horse whose very hide has lost its value. And then, the scandal of your dismissal is exaggerated in people's imaginations: you are made to appear an adulterer or poisoner or something of the kind. For your accuser's very silence makes for credibility, and you are a Greek, loose-living, an easy prey to all kinds of criminal tendencies. That's what they think we're all like, you know. And no wonder; I think I know why they have the opinion they do of us. Many a Greek enters a household and, because he has no other useful accomplishments, sets up as clairvoyant and sorcerer and deals in love potions and evil spells. And this they do while laying claim to culture, while wearing the philosopher's cloak and sporting great long beards. No wonder people put us all in the same category, when they see models of virtue—so they suppose—acting like that; and particularly when they notice their sycophantic behavior at the dinner table and in society generally, and the servility they will stoop to for money.

41 Having shaken them off, their employers naturally hate them, and try their best to do away with them for good if they can. You can see the way their minds work: they think that since their ex-servants know every little detail about them, have seen them naked, they are going to reveal all the unmentionable side of their character. That's what sticks in their throat. Because they're all exactly the same, you know; they're just like those beautiful books you see—gilt spines and crimson binding, but inside Thyestes banquets on his children's flesh, or Oedipus lies with his mother, or Tereus with two sisters. They're the same: magnificent to look at, admired by everybody—but inside, beneath the crimson, they've a whole tragedy to hide. Leaf through any one of them and you'll find quite a story, worthy of Euripides or Sophocles, though outside they're rich red and backed with gold. And they're well aware of this; and they hate their cast-offs and plot their destruction, lest one of them should come out with the whole tale and let the world know what's so familiar to him.

But still, let me draw you a picture of the life, after Cebes; [35] you can have a look at it and then see whether you want to enter on it. I should gladly have called in an Apelles or Parrhasius or Aëtion or Euphranor to help me with the drawing, but you don't find painters with such lofty conception and such a command of technique these days; so I'll sketch the picture for you as best I can.[36]

Well then, let us have in it lofty, golden gates, not down in the plain, but high on a hill. The way up to them is long and steep and slippery, so that many a time, when a man thinks he is almost at the top, his foot slips and he is thrown head over heels. Suppose Wealth personified to be sitting inside, looking like solid gold, lovely and desirable. The lover climbs the hill with difficulty, approaches the gate, and is struck with astonishment at the sight of the gold. Hope—lovely herself, and clad in splendid raiment—takes him in

42

---

[35] *The Tablet,* a description of an imaginary allegorical painting representing human life, although ascribed to Cebes (here by Lucian, and commonly elsewhere) is certainly not by him. Cebes was a Theban philosopher who figures in Plato's *Phaedo* and *Crito* as a friend of Socrates.

[36] Lucian describes pictures several times in his works; the "description" (this is the literal meaning of *ecphrasis;* see Introduction, p. xi) was a stock feature of the sophistic repertoire. Here, of course, the description is an allegory, which is a rare enough taste in Greek writers other than Plato.

hand and leads him in. He is awestruck on entering. Suppose now that from this point Hope still leads the way, but two other female figures—Deceit and Servitude—take charge of him and hand him over to Toil. Toil wears the poor wretch down with hard work, and when he is ill and grown pale, turns him over to Age. Last comes Contempt, who takes hold of him and hales him off to Despair. From now on, Hope is nowhere to be seen: the bird has flown. And now see him thrown out, not by the golden gate wherein he came, but by some forgotten back door—thrown out naked, pot-bellied, pale, and old, covering his nakedness with his left hand and throttling himself with the right. As he goes, Repentance meets him, uselessly weeping and only adding to his miseries, poor wretch.

And there is my picture complete. My dear Timocles, now take a careful look at it with your own eyes: note all that is in it. Do you fancy stepping into the picture by that gate and being thrown out thus ignominiously by that back alley? Whatever you do, remember the sage's words: "Don't blame God: the fault lies where the choice is." [37]

[37] Plato, *Republic* X. 617e.

A TRUE STORY

Book I

Athletes and people who take an interest in the care of the **1** body do not confine their attentions to physical exercise and attaining a good condition. They take thought also for relaxation at appropriate intervals; indeed, they consider it the most important element in training. Similarly, in my opinion, literary people should after extended reading of serious authors relax mentally, to refresh themselves against subsequent exertions. They will find this interlude agreeable if they **2** choose as company such works as not only afford wit, charm, and distraction pure and simple, but also provoke some degree of cultured reflection.

I trust the present work will be found to inspire such reflection. My readers will be attracted not merely by the novelty of the subject, the appeal of the general design, and the conviction and verisimilitude with which I compound elaborate prevarications, but also by the humorous allusions in every part of my story to various poets, historians, and philosophers of former times who have concocted long, fantastic yarns—writers I should mention by name did I not think their identities would be obvious to you as you read. For instance, **3** Ctesias of Cnidos, the son of Ctesiochus, wrote an account of India and its customs; he had neither himself seen nor heard from any reliable source the things he wrote about. Iambulus, too, wrote a long account of the wonders of the great ocean; anybody can see it is fictitious, but it is quite entertaining none the less, as a theme.[1] And there have been many others

---

[1] *A True Story*, whatever it may now be to us, is thus in intention literary criticism (see Introduction, p. xxiv). This aspect of it, however, we are not in a very good position to judge, since many of the works Lucian is making fun of are not extant—for instance those of Ctesias and Iambulus, mentioned here, and of Antonius Diogenes, who (according to Photius, *Bibliotheca* 111) wrote *On the Wonders Beyond Thule;* this work included

who have written with the same intention, purporting to relate their own travels abroad and writing about great beasts
and savage tribes and strange ways of life. The founder of
this school of literary horseplay is Homer's Odysseus, with his
stories at Alcinous' court [2] of winds enslaved and men with
one eye and cannibals and wild men, of many-headed beasts
and of how his crew were drugged and transformed; he spun
many such fanciful stories to the Phaeacians, who knew no
better.

4   So when I came across all these writers, I did not feel that
their romancing was particularly reprehensible; evidently it
was already traditional, even among professed philosophers; [3]
though what did surprise me was their supposition that nobody would notice they were lying. Now, I too in my vanity
was anxious to bequeath something to posterity; I did not
wish to be the only one to make no use of this liberty in
yarn-spinning—for I had no true story to relate since nothing
worth mentioning had ever happened to me; and consequently I turned to romancing myself. But I am much more
sensible about it than others are, for I will say one thing
that is true, and that is that I am a liar. It seems to me that to
confess voluntarily to untruthfulness acquits me of the charge,
should other people bring it. My subject, then, is things I
have neither seen nor experienced nor heard tell of from anybody else: things, what is more, that do not in fact exist and
could not ever exist at all. So my readers must not believe
a word I say.

5   I set out one day from the Pillars of Hercules and sailed
with a following wind into the western ocean.[4] My voyage

---

a description of a trip to the moon (see secs. 10–27 below), and is Lucian's
main source and target here. In general, *A True Story* is redolent of
earlier literature, and we can certainly recognize for instance frequent
allusion to Herodotus among others.

2 See *Odyssey* IX–XII.

3 An allusion to Plato's penchant for allegory (e.g., *Republic* X).

4 I.e., from the Straits of Gibraltar into the Atlantic; an early version
of tales of sub- and trans-Atlantic civilizations.

was prompted by an active intellect and a passionate interest in anything new; the object I proposed to myself was to discover the limits of the ocean and what men dwelt beyond it. For this reason I took a great deal of food on board, and plenty of water. I got hold of fifty men of my own age and interests, as well as quite a store of arms, hired the best navigator I could find at a considerable salary, and strengthened the ship—a light transport—for a long and trying voyage.

For a day and a night we sailed along gently with a following wind and with land still in sight. At dawn next day the wind began to rise, the sea grew stormy, and the sky was overcast. Soon we could not even take in sail, so we ran before the wind and let ourselves be tossed hither and thither for seventy-nine days.[5] On the eightieth the sun came out suddenly, and we saw a mountainous, thickly-wooded island close by, with the sea murmuring gently around it—for by now the swell had almost subsided. So we put in and went ashore. There we lay on the ground for a long time, after our long ordeal; however, we did get up, and split ourselves into two parties, thirty staying to guard the ship and twenty coming with me to explore the island.

6

Going through the woods, about six hundred yards from the shore we saw a bronze pillar with a faded, worn inscription in Greek which said "Hercules and Dionysus reached this point." Nearby, on a rock, were two footprints, one a hundred feet long, the other smaller. The smaller I supposed to belong to Dionysus, the other to Hercules.[6] We made our obeisances and went on. Before we had gone very far, we found ourselves beside a river running wine very like Chian; it was of some size and depth, even being navigable in some places. We were led to put much more confidence in the inscription on the pillar when we saw this evidence of Dionysus' visit. I decided to find the source of the river. Going upstream I found, not indeed any spring from which it issued, but a

7

5 Lucian is generous with his figures throughout, as all "romancers" are.
6 Herodotus, IV. 82 speaks of a footprint three feet long left by Hercules in Scythia.

great many large vines loaded with grapes. By the root of each of these flowed a trickle of clear wine, and it was from these that the river was formed. We could actually see a lot of fish in it. Their flesh was vinous both in color and taste; anyway, we caught some and got drunk eating them. Of course they were full of wine lees when we cut them open. Later on, though, we hit on the idea of mixing them with water-fish and thus diluting this strong wine-food.

8   Then we crossed the river where there was a ford, and discovered some vines of a marvelous kind; they had firm, thick stems lower down, but the upper parts were female figures, complete in every detail from the flanks up. They looked just like the pictures one sees of Daphne turning into a tree just as Apollo takes hold of her. The vine shoots, loaded with grapes, grew from the tips of their fingers; the hair of their heads also was tendrils and leaves and fruit. They gave us welcome as we approached and greeted us in Lydian, Indian, and—the majority of them—Greek. They also kissed us, and anyone who was kissed became drunk immediately and began to stagger about. But they would not let us pluck the fruit, crying out in pain as we tugged at it. Some of them even evinced sexual passion; two of my comrades embraced them, only to find themselves caught by the genitals and unable to free themselves. They became one with the plants and took root beside them; their fingers at once put forth shoots, tendrils grew all over them, and they too were on the point of bearing fruit.

9   We left them and hastily regained the ship; there we told those who had stayed behind everything that had happened, including our comrades' affair with the vines. Then we took some jars to fill with water and also with river-wine, and camped for the night on the shore near the boat.

In the morning we put to sea with a gentle wind. About midday, when the island was out of sight, a whirlwind suddenly arose, whirling our ship around and raising it some forty miles into the air. But it did not deposit us back on the sea, for when we were hanging in mid-air a wind struck, bil-

lowed our sails, and carried us along. For seven days and as   *10*
many nights we sailed through the air, and on the eighth saw
a large tract of land suspended in the atmosphere like an
island; it was bright and spherical, and bathed in strong light.
We put in to it, anchored, and went ashore. On exploring the
land, we found it to be inhabited and cultivated. We could
see nothing from it during the daytime, but when night fell
many other islands became visible near to it, some larger, some
smaller, the color of fire. There was also another land below
us, with cities, rivers, seas, forests, and mountains; this we
supposed to be our earth.

Deciding to continue the voyage, we fell in with and were   *11*
apprehended by what they call Horse-vultures. These are men
mounted on great vultures, which they manage like horses.
The vultures are very big and most of them have three heads.
You may imagine their size from the fact that every one of
their feathers is longer and thicker than the mast of a big
cargo ship.[7] The job of these Horse-vultures is to patrol the
land and bring any intruder they may come across to the
king—as they did with us.

The king inspected us, and guessing from the look of us
and from our dress that we were Greeks, asked us, when we
said we were, how we had managed to cover all that distance
in the air to get where we were. We told him the whole story;
whereupon he launched into a complete account of himself.
It appeared that he too was a man, called Endymion; he
had been snatched from our earth one day while he was
asleep and conveyed to where he now was, and on his arrival
had become king of the country. The land was, he said, what
appeared as the moon from earth. He told us to be of good
heart and not suspect danger, for we would have everything
we needed. "And if I am successful," he said, "in the campaign   *12*
I am now beginning against the inhabitants of the Sun, you
will have the happiest life imaginable with me."

We asked him who the enemy were and what the quarrel

---

[7] Cf. *Odyssey* IX. 318 ff. for the stake with which Odysseus and his men
put out the eye of the Cyclops.

was about. "Phaëthon," he said, "the king of the Sun-dwellers
—for the Sun is inhabited just as the Moon is—has been conducting a war against us for a long time now. It began when
one day I collected together the poorest people in my realm,
with the intention of sending a colony to the Morning Star,[8]
which is uninhabited and deserted. Phaëthon was jealous of
the idea. He mounted his Horse-ants and encountered us halfway there to prevent the colonization. Well, on that occasion
we were defeated, being unequal in strength, and withdrew.
But now I want to restart the war and send out my colony.
So if you would like to join my expedition, I shall mount you
all on vultures from the royal stables and provide all your
equipment. We start tomorrow." "All right," I said, "if you
want us to."

13   So for the time being we stayed to be entertained at his
court. At dawn we rose and took our positions, the scouts
reporting that the enemy were near. The army numbered
a hundred thousand, not counting baggage trains, engineers,
infantry, or allied forces from elsewhere. Eighty thousand of
these were Horse-vultures, twenty thousand were troops
mounted on Vegetable-wings—another kind of bird, also very
large, with vegetable shoots all over its body in place of
plumage, and quill feathers just like lettuce leaves. Next to
these were the Millet-slingers and Garlic-fighters. Allies came
to his assistance from the Great Bear also—thirty thousand
Flea-archers and fifty thousand Wind-runners. The Flea-archers ride great fleas—hence their name—and each flea is as big
as twelve elephants. The Wind-runners are infantry, but
travel through the air without wings, in the following manner:
they wear tunics that reach to their feet, and by so girding
them as to make the wind belly them out like sails, they are
blown along like ships. They are generally used as light troops
in battle. There were also supposed to be seventy thousand
Sparrow-acorns and five thousand Horse-cranes coming from
the stars above Cappadocia. As they did not arrive I did not

---

8 Cf. Greek expansion in the Aegean and Magna Graecia.

see them; hence I have not presumed to describe them—report made them out wonderful creatures, too wonderful to be credible.[9]

This was Endymion's army. They were all armed the same way: the helmets were made of beans, which grow big and hard there; the breastplates were all of overlapping lupine scales, stitched together, the scales being hard as horn. The shields and swords were Greek in style. When the moment came they were drawn up as follows. On the right were the Horse-vultures and the king, with his best troops around him; we were among these. On the left were the Vegetable-wings, and in the center the allied contingents in no particular formation. The infantry numbered about sixty million, drawn up as follows. On the Moon there grow enormous spiders, each one much bigger than the islands of the Cyclades; these were instructed to spin a web across the sky between the Moon and the Morning Star, and as soon as they had constructed a plain by this means, the infantry was drawn up on it, under the command of Bat, son of Fairweatherlord, and two others.

The enemy left wing was held by Phaëthon with the Horse-ants. These are great beasts with wings, just like our ants except in size,[10] for the biggest of them was two hundred feet long. It was not only their riders who fought; they themselves were very effective with their horns. There were said to be about fifty thousand of them. On their right were drawn up the Sky-gnats, also about fifty thousand in number, all archers riding on great gnats. Next to them came the Sky-dancers, light-armed infantry but useful in battle none the less, for they slung great radishes from long range, and whoever was struck by them could not last even a short time but died from the foul-smelling wounds they caused; they were said to rub mallow juice on their missiles. Close by them were drawn up the Stalk-mushrooms, heavy-armed close fighters, ten thousand of them, so called because they used mushrooms as shields and

14

15

16

----

9 Herodotus often withholds his own belief in what he reports.
10 Cf. Herodotus, III. 102 for ants bigger than foxes, and cf. *Cock* 16.

asparagus stalks as spears. Near them were the Acorn-dogs, sent to Phaëthon by the people of the Dog Star. There were five thousand of them, men with dogs' faces [11] fighting from winged acorns. It was reported that some of the enemy's allies also missed the battle—the slingers he sent for from the Milky Way, and the Cloud-centaurs. The latter did arrive, unfortunately, when the battle was already over; the Slingers did not appear at all, for which reason it was said Phaëthon afterwards vented his anger on them by scorching their land. This was the force with which Phaëthon advanced.

As soon as the standards were raised and the donkeys on each side had brayed—they used donkeys as trumpeters—they began to fight. The Sunite left fled at once without waiting for the Horse-vultures to come to close quarters, and we followed them, slaughtering as we went. Their right wing, however, overcame our left, and the Sky-gnats pressed their pursuit as far as the infantry. Then, when these came to the rescue, they turned and fled, especially when they saw their own left wing beaten. It was a splendid victory, with many prisoners taken and many casualties; a great deal of blood flowed on to the clouds, so that they appeared to be dyed red, as we see them at sunset. A deal of blood also dripped on to the earth, leading me to wonder if it was not some similar event in the heavens long ago that made Homer suppose Zeus had rained blood at the death of Sarpedon.[12]

Returning from the pursuit, we set up two trophies, one in celebration of the infantry battle, on the spiders' webs, the other on the clouds for the fight in mid-air. In the middle of this activity, scouts announced that the Cloud-centaurs, who should have reported to Phaëthon before the battle, were approaching. And indeed we could see them close at hand; they were a very odd sight, a mixture of men and winged horses. The human part, from the middle up, was the size of the Colossus of Rhodes,[13] the horse part as big as a cargo vessel. I

---

[11] Cf. Herodotus, IV. 191 for dog-headed men in Libya.
[12] See *Iliad* XVI. 459–61.
[13] Cf. *Zeus* 11.

do not record the numbers of them, however, lest I be disbelieved, so many were they. Their commander was the Archer of the Zodiac. When they saw that their side had been beaten, they sent a message to Phaëthon to tell him to come back and attack again, and themselves made a formation attack upon the scattered Moonites, who were in disorder all over, in pursuit and in search of plunder. They routed the whole army and pursued the king himself to the city, killing most of his birds. They also tore down the trophies and overran the cobweb plain. I and two of my comrades were taken prisoner. By now Phaëthon was on the scene also, setting up his own trophies. We were taken to the Sun that day, our hands tied behind our backs with a piece of cobweb.

They decided not to besiege the city but turned back and built a wall through the sky between Sun and Moon, so that the Sun's rays no longer reached the Moon. The wall was made of a double thickness of clouds; the Moon was totally eclipsed and plunged into continuous night. Endymion was severely tried by these measures; he sent to beg the Sunites to tear down the wall and not make his people live their lives in darkness, promising to pay tribute, to conclude an alliance and not to make war again, and expressing readiness to give hostages for the observance of these conditions. Phaëthon's people held two assemblies. In the first they would not temper their anger in the slightest degree, but in the second they changed their minds,[14] and peace was concluded on the following terms.[15]

                19

Terms of the peace treaty concluded between the Sunites with their allies and the Moonites with their allies.

                20

1. The Sunites shall demolish the separating wall, not invade the moon again, and restore the prisoners at fixed rates of ransom.

2. The Moonites shall give autonomy to the other stars and not bear arms against the Sunites.

3. Each party shall assist the other in the event of any aggression.

---

[14] Like the Athenians over Mytilene; see Thucydides, III. 36 and 49.

[15] Cf. any Greek treaty, e.g., Thucydides V. 18.

4. The King of the Moonites shall pay to the King of the Sunites a yearly tribute of ten thousand jars of dew, and give hostages of his own subjects to the number of ten thousand.

5. The colonization of the Morning Star shall be undertaken jointly, and anyone of any other nationality who so wishes shall take part.

6. The treaty shall be inscribed on a pillar of amber and set up in mid-air at the border.

Sworn to by Fireman, Hot, and Blazer of the Sunites, and by Nighttime, Moonday, and Flashbright of the Moonites.

21   These were the terms of the peace. The wall was pulled down at once, and we were released from captivity. When we reached the Moon, my comrades and Endymion himself met us, weeping for joy. Endymion wanted me to stay and take part in the colonization; he promised me his own son in marriage (there not being any women on the Moon). I did not want to, however; I asked to be sent down to the sea again. When he saw that we were not to be entreated, he entertained us for a week before sending us off.

22   I should like to describe the novel and unusual things I noticed during my stay on the Moon. First of all, they are born not of woman but of man; their marriages are of male with male, and they do not even know the word "woman" at all. Up to the age of twenty-five they all act as female partners, and thereafter as husbands. Pregnancy occurs not in the womb but in the calf of the leg, for after conception the calf grows fat. After a time they cut it open and bring out a lifeless body, which they lay out with its mouth open facing the wind and bring to life. I imagine that this is the origin of the Greek word "calf," [16] inasmuch as on the Moon it is this part of the body that produces young, and not the belly. But I shall tell you about something more marvelous yet. There is on the Moon a kind of men called Treemen, and the manner of their generation is as follows. They cut off a man's right testicle and plant it in the ground; from it there grows an enormous tree

---

[16] The Greek word for "calf of the leg" is literally "belly of the leg."

of flesh, like a phallus. It has branches and foliage, and its fruit is acorns as long as the forearm. When they are ripe, they harvest them and carve men from them, adding genitals of ivory, or of wood for the poorer ones; these are what they use to consummate their male marriages.

When a man grows old, he does not die, but dissolves into the air like smoke. They all consume the same food; they light a fire and roast frogs on the embers—on the Moon there are a great number of frogs flying in the air—and as they are roasting they sit in circles as if around a table and suck in the vapor that arises; [17] this constitutes their meal. Such, then, is their food; their drink is air compressed into a cup to give off a moisture like dew. They do not, however, perform the functions of evacuation as we do; indeed, they do not have orifices where we have them—in their intercourse with the young they use orifices behind the knee above the calf of the leg.

To be beautiful on the Moon is to be bald and hairless; people with a thick head of hair they abominate. On comets the opposite holds good: it is people with good hair who are thought handsome, as some foreigners told me.[18] They grow beards, though, just above the knee. They do not have toe-nails, and they all have one toe on each foot. Over the buttocks they all have large cabbages growing, like tails; these cabbages are evergreen, and do not break off if the owner falls on his back.

When they blow their noses they get a bitter honey; and after hard work or exercise the whole body sweats milk, to which they add a drop of the honey to make it congeal into cheese. They make from onions a very shiny oil, as fragrant as perfume. They also have a lot of water vines; that is, the grapes are like hail. To my mind, it is a gust of wind shaking these vines that bursts the clusters and makes hail fall on earth. The belly they use as a bag to put necessaries in; it opens and shuts, and appears to contain no intestines, only an

23

24

---

[17] Cf. Herodotus, I. 202.
[18] Because "comet" means "hairy star."

inner lining of thick hair—their young creep inside when it is cold.

25   The clothing of the rich is of soft glass, that of the poor of woven brass;[19] their land is rich in brass, which they moisten with water and work like wool. I hesitate to mention the nature of their eyes; it sounds incredible; still, I will do so. Their eyes are removable. They can take them out at will and put them away until they need to see; then they insert them and their sight returns. They often lose their own and borrow other people's to see with; some of them, the rich, have a large reserve of them. For ears they have plane leaves—except the acorn people, who have wooden ones.

26   And I saw another marvelous thing in the palace. There is a huge mirror there, suspended over a quite shallow well. If you go down the well you can hear everything that is said down here on earth; and if you look in the mirror you can see every city and nation just as if you were standing over them. I actually saw my own people and country when I was there; whether they saw me too I cannot say for sure. Anyone who does not believe this has only to go there himself some day to find out that I am telling the truth.

27   Well, anyway, we took a fond farewell of the kind and his court, embarked, and set out. Endymion actually presented me with two glass tunics, five brass ones, and a complete set of lupine armor, all of which I left behind in the whale. He also sent a thousand Horse-vultures to escort us for the first

28   sixty miles. On our journey we passed various countries, and actually landed on the Morning Star to take on water; it was in process of being colonized. Entering the Zodiac, we passed the Sun on our port bow, almost touching the land as we sailed; many of the crew were very keen to land, but the wind was against us and we did not. We could, however, see

---

[19] Herodotus, VII. 65 speaks of clothing "made from wood"—i.e., of cotton—and Lucian extends the idea. This seems witty enough in itself; the pun Harmon sees on ὑαλίνη, "of glass," and ξυλίνη, "wooden," becomes a little laborious if one notes that Herodotus does not actually use the word ξυλίνη. (*Lucian,* tr. A. M. Harmon, "Loeb Classical Library" [Cambridge: Harvard University Press, 1913], I, 279, n. 1.)

that the land was fertile and rich and well-watered and full of good things of many kinds. The Cloud-centaurs, Phaëthon's mercenaries, saw us and flew at the ship; learning, however, that we were covered by the treaty, they went away again. By now the Horse-vultures had left us too.

29

We sailed all that night and the next day, and by evening had reached Lamptown, as it is called; we were now on the downward voyage. Lamptown lies in the air between the Pleiades and the Hyades, but is much lower than the Zodiac. Going ashore, we did not find any human beings, but saw a lot of lamps running around and hanging about in the marketplace and around the harbor. Some of them were small, as it might be the poorer ones; a few were big and powerful— they were very bright and distinct. Each had his own dwelling or lamphouse; they had names, like human beings, and we heard them talking. They did us no harm; in fact, they offered us entertainment; but we were apprehensive and none of us was prepared either to eat or to go to sleep. They have a Town Hall in the middle of the city, where their archon [20] sits all night long calling each one of them by name. Any of them who does not answer to his name is condemned to death for desertion; death involves being put out. We stood and watched what happened; we heard lamps making their defense and giving their reasons for being late. I also recognized our own lamp there. I spoke to him and asked him how things were at home, and he told me all about it.

That night, then, we stayed there; the next day we set sail and were now traveling near the clouds. At this point we actually saw Cloudcuckooland,[21] to our surprise, but were prevented from landing on it by the wind. I gathered, however, that their king was called Hookbeak, son of Blackbird. I thought of the dramatist Aristophanes, a wise and truthful man, whose works arouse undeserved disbelief. Three days after this we could in fact see the ocean, but no land except the islands in the sky, which now appeared a bright fiery color.

[20] Roughly equivalent to a mayor.
[21] Invented by Aristophanes in *Birds*.

On the fourth day, about noon, the wind gradually slackened and fell, and we were deposited on the sea.

30   When we touched the water we were delighted beyond belief, beside ourselves with joy, and celebrated as gaily as we could in the circumstances. The sea was quiet and the weather calm, so we dived overboard and swam about. But it seems that a change for the better is often the prelude to greater disaster, for after only two days' sailing in calm weather, as the sun rose on the third we suddenly saw a great number of sea beasts and whales. They were of various kinds, and one of them, the biggest of all, was not far short of two hundred miles long. It came at us with its jaws wide open, disturbing the sea far in front of it, and washed about with foam; it was showing its teeth, which were much bigger than our phallic symbols, all as sharp as stakes and white as ivory. We said our last words to each other, embraced, and waited. The beast was now on us. Sucking us in, it swallowed us, ship and all, but before its teeth crushed us, the ship tumbled inside the gaps between them.[22]

31   When we got inside, it was dark at first and we could see nothing; later on, however, when the whale opened its jaws, we saw a great cavern, broad in every direction and high, big enough to hold a large city. It had fish large and small, and fragments of many and various animals were lying in the middle of it, as well as ships' masts, anchors, human bones and merchandise. In the middle also there was land, with hills—formed, I suppose, by the settling of the mud the creature swallowed. There were even woods with trees of all kinds; vegetables were growing, and the whole area appeared to be cultivated. The circumference of the land was thirty miles. Sea birds could be seen also, gulls and kingfishers, nesting in the trees.

32   Well, for a long time we wept, but eventually we roused the

22 The following account has much in common with the story of Jonah and the whale, but they probably both come from a common source. Neither this nor the description of the Heavenly City in *Story* II. 11 is necessarily or even probably mockery of Christianity.

crew and had the ship underpropped. We ourselves lit a fire
by rubbing sticks together and made a meal from what we
could get. There was plenty of fish of all varieties lying about,
and we still had the water from the Morning Star. On getting
up the next day, whenever the whale opened his jaws we
saw sometimes mountains, sometimes nothing but sky, and
often islands. We realized that he was moving swiftly through
the sea in various directions. When eventually we grew ac-
customed to this state of things, I took seven of the crew and
went into the wood to explore it thoroughly. Not quite a
thousand yards away I came upon a shrine—to Poseidon, as
the inscription showed—and shortly afterward upon a large
number of graves, with gravestones, near a spring of clear
water. What is more, we heard a dog bark and saw smoke
in the distance. We concluded that there was some kind of
habitation there. So we hurried on, and found ourselves in   *33*
the presence of an old man and a young one who were very
carefully tending a plot of land and irrigating it with water
from the spring.

We stood there in simultaneous delight and fear. They
seemed to be in the same state, and stood speechless. At last
the old man spoke. "Who are you, strangers?" he said. "Are
you spirits of the sea, or unfortunate human beings like us?
For we are men, brought up on land but turned sea creatures,
swimming about with this beast that envelops us, not even
very sure of our condition. We suppose we are dead, but we
trust we are alive." I replied. "Sir," I said, "we too are men,
newly arrived, swallowed with our ship just the other day.
Now we have come out to see what things are like in the
wood, for it seemed thick and extensive. It looks as if some
spirit has guided us to the sight of you, so that we may realize
we are not the only people enclosed in this beast. But you
tell us what happened to you. Who are you? How did you get
here?" He refused to answer our questions or ask any until
he had offered us what entertainment he could.[23] Taking us

[23] Obeying the ancient code of hospitality, as exemplified in Homer.

with him to his house—which was quite complete, equipped with beds and other furniture—he set vegetables and fruit and fish before us and poured us wine.

When we had had all we wanted, he asked what had befallen us. I told him the whole story: all about the storm, the events on the island, the journey in the air, the war, and *34* everything else up to the descent into the whale. He expressed great surprise and in turn told us his own story. "My friends," he said, "I am from Cyprus. I set out from home to trade, with my son, whom you see here, and many of my servants as well. I was sailing to Italy with an assorted cargo in a large vessel, which you may have seen broken up in the whale's mouth. Well, we had a good voyage as far as Sicily, but on leaving there we were seized by a strong wind and for three days driven out into the ocean. There we came upon the whale. He swallowed us, crew and all. Only we two survived; the rest were killed. We buried them and built a temple to Poseidon, and now we live like this, growing vegetables and living on fish and fruit.

"The wood is very big, as you can see. It has vines in abundance, which produce a very sweet wine. You may have noticed the spring; its water is very good and very cold. We make beds of leaves, we can light a fire whenever we want, and we snare birds that fly in. We can catch living fish by going out into the monster's gills; we also bathe there when we feel like it. And then there is a lake not far off, over two miles around, with all kinds of fish in it; we swim in it and sail a small boat I built myself. It is twenty-seven years since we were swallowed.

35   "One could perhaps put up with the rest, but the neighbors who live near us are unpleasant, offensive, unsociable savages." "Why," I said, "are there others in the whale too?" "A great many," said the old man, "and they are unfriendly and monstrous in shape. The western part of the wood, by the tail, is the land of the Saltfish, a tribe with eels' eyes and lobsters' faces; they are warlike and fierce, and they eat raw flesh. Of the sides, the starboard wall is in the possession of the Sea-satyrs,[24] who are human in their upper parts and like lizards below; they are not so lawless as the rest. The port side is held by the Crabhands and the Tunnyheads, their friends and allies. The land in the center is inhabited by the Shellbacks and the Flatfishfeet, a swift and warlike tribe. The eastern regions near the mouth are mostly desert because they are periodically flooded by the sea; still, I have this patch of ground, which I rent from the Flatfishfeet for five hundred oysters a year.

"Well, that is what the land is like. You must find out the best way of fighting all these tribes, and how we shall live."

I asked him how many there were of them, and how they were armed. They were more than a thousand strong, he said, but their only arms were fish bones. "Well then," I said, "since they are unarmed and we are not, the best thing to do would be to bring them to battle; if we beat them, we shall live hereafter with nothing to fear." This was agreed, and we went off to the ship to get ready. The excuse for the war was to be failure to pay the rent; this was now due, and indeed they sent to collect it. The old man made a rude answer to the collectors and chased them away. The Flatfishfeet and the Shellbacks were incensed with Scintharus (that was the old man's name) and took the offensive against him with a great deal of clamor.

Expecting this attack, we waited in full armor. Ahead of us we had laid an ambush of twenty-five men, with instructions to rise and attack when they saw the enemy had passed them. They did rise in their rear and began to cut them down, while we too, also twenty-five in number—Scin-

36

37

[24] Transliterated from the Greek the name of these creatures is *Tritonomendetes*. According to Herodotus, II. 46, *mendes* was Egyptian both for "goat" and for "the god Pan"; with the latter meaning, the half-man, half-animal creatures here mentioned are "Sea-satyrs." (Harmon—Loeb edn., I, 293, n. 1—considers only the meaning "goat" for *mendes* and not unnaturally is puzzled by the result: "there is nothing goatish in the Tritonomendetes as Lucian describes them." True; but there is something Pan-ish.)

tharus and his son were with us—joined with them from the front, fighting bravely, with spirit and might. Finally we routed them and pursued them to their dens. The enemy lost a hundred and seventy men; we lost one, our navigator, who had a mullet rib driven through his back.

38   For that day, then, and the night following, we made our quarters on the battlefield, and we set up a trophy by driving the dry backbone of a dolphin into the ground. But the other tribes heard what had happened and appeared the next day. The Saltfish, under the command of Tunnyfish, formed their right wing, the Tunnyheads their left, and the Crabhands held the center. The Sea-satyrs kept out of the fighting, preferring to remain neutral. We did not wait for them to attack but joined with them by Poseidon's shrine, raising a great shout that echoed in the hollow space as in a cave. They were unarmed; we routed them and pursued them into the

39   wood, and thereafter were masters of the area. Shortly afterward they sent heralds, took up their dead, and made overtures for peace. We decided, however, not to come to terms, and the next day set out against them and cut them down— all except the Sea-satyrs, who fled when they saw what was happening and threw themselves out into the sea from the gills. We occupied the country, which was now empty of enemies, and thereafter lived in security.

Most of the time we spent in exercise or hunting or dressing the vines or picking fruit from the trees. It was like living in a great prison where we were free to live an easy life but from which we could not escape. This was how we lived for

40   a year and eight months. On the fifth of the next month, about the second opening of the mouth—the whale opened his mouth once an hour, you see, and that was how we told the time—about the second opening, I was saying, we suddenly heard a great shouting and uproar; it sounded like someone giving the stroke to crews rowing. In some alarm, we crept right into the monster's mouth, and from a position behind its teeth looked out on the strangest sight I have ever seen— giants a hundred yards high sailing great islands as one does triremes.[25] I know this is going to sound farfetched, but I shall describe it nevertheless.

The islands were long but not very high, and each was over eleven miles in circumference. Their crews numbered about a hundred and twenty of the men I have mentioned, who, appropriately disposed along the sides of the island, were rowing with great cypresses—branches, foliage and all—for oars. Behind them, in what was evidently the stern, a helmsman stood on a high hill at a bronze steering oar a thousand yards long. For'ard there were some forty armed men, the fighting element. They were just like men except for their hair, which was burning fire—they did not need crests. The wind caught the forest area, which was considerable on every island, as if it were sails, filled it out, and took the ship wherever the helmsman wished. They had a coxswain giving them the stroke, and the islands responded vigorously to the rowing like warships.

At first we saw two or three, but later on some six hundred appeared, formed up, and fought an action. Many of them crashed head-on, many were rammed and sunk. Some grappled, fought stoutly, and were very difficult to shake off, for the troops posted for'ard boarded and slew with great ferocity; no prisoners were taken. They grappled not with irons but with huge captive squids, which entwined themselves in the trees and held the island fast. As missiles—and they inflicted wounds—they used oysters, any one of which would fill a cart, and hundred-foot sponges. Aeolocentaur[26] commanded one side, Seadrinker the other. They were fighting over an act of piracy, it appeared; Seadrinker had driven off a good many herds of dolphins belonging to Aeolocentaur, to judge from the accusations they hurled at each other as they called out their kings' names.

Aeolocentaur's fleet won in the end, sinking some one hundred and fifty of the enemy islands and taking three others with their crews; the rest backed water and got away. After

25 Cf. Herodotus, II. 156 for floating islands in Egypt.
26 Aeolus was the god of the winds.

pursuing them for some way, the victors returned to the wrecked ships when evening came on, took possession of most of them, and recovered their own, of which no fewer than eighty had been sunk. They also set up a trophy for the battle of the islands by pinning one of the enemy islands to the whale's head with a stake. That night they spent in the vicinity of the monster, attaching their hawsers to him and riding at anchor hard by; they had anchors, big, strong ones made of glass. The next day they made sacrifice on top of the beast, buried their own dead on him, and sailed off in high spirits, singing a kind of victory paean. That was what happened in the battle of the islands.[27]

Book II

1   Latterly I grew tired of being stuck there and could not bear to live in the whale any longer. So I looked around for some way of getting out. My first idea was to cut a tunnel in the starboard wall and get away that way. We began to hack away, but after going a thousand yards without any success we gave up digging and decided to set fire to the wood. We thought that this would kill the whale and then we would have no difficulty getting out. We did set fire to it, then, beginning from the tail region. For a whole week he did not feel it, but on the eighth and ninth days we could see that he was not well; his jaws opened more slowly and shut again quickly every time. On the tenth and eleventh days, mortification finally set in and he began to stink. We realized on the twelfth day, only just in time, that unless we wedged his molars apart when he opened his jaws, to stop them from closing again, we should probably be imprisoned in his dead body and die there. So we propped his mouth open with great

27 Lucian uses a Thucydidean turn of phrase here; cf. the famous last sentence of Book VII, concluding the account of the Sicilian expedition.

beams and got the ship ready, taking on board as much water as we could and other supplies. Scintharus was to navigate. Next day the whale at last died.

2

We dragged the ship up, swung it from the teeth, guided it through the gaps between them, and let it down gently on to the sea. Then we climbed on to the whale's back, sacrificed to Poseidon, and, since there was no wind, camped there for three days by the trophy. Getting away on the fourth day, we came across and went aground on many of the dead bodies from the sea fight; it was a startling experience to measure them. For some days we had a mild wind behind us; then there was a fierce gale from the north, which brought a very cold spell. The whole sea froze, not just at the surface but to a depth of six fathoms; we could actually get out and run on the ice. The wind continued unbearably, so we hit on the idea (it was Scintharus who suggested it) of digging an enormous cave in the water. There we stayed for thirty days, lighting fires and living on fish, which we got by digging them out of the ice. But eventually supplies began to fail, and we left the cave. The ship was frozen in; we extracted it, spread the sheet, and swept along smoothly and easily, gliding over the ice as if we were sailing. By the fifth day the temperature had risen; the ice melted and all was water again.

We sailed for some thirty-five miles and put in at a small desert island, where we took on water (our supply having now run out) and shot two wild bulls—whose horns were not on their heads but under the eyes, as in Momus' prescription.[28] Shortly after leaving, we entered upon a sea of milk, not water, with a white island, covered in vines, standing out of it. The island was, as we later found out by eating it, a huge, very solid cheese, three miles around. The vines were loaded with grapes, but when we squeezed them to get a drink it was not wine that came but milk. A shrine had been built in the center of the island to the Nereid Galatea,[29] according to the

3

---

[28] So that they could see what they were doing with them; cf. *Hermotimus* 20.

[29] *Gala* means "milk."

inscription. As long as we were there, the earth provided bread and meat, and we drank the milk from the vines. Tyro,[30] the daughter of Salmoneus, was said to be the ruler of these regions; she had been given the office by Poseidon after departing this life.

We stayed five days on the island and set out on the sixth; a breeze took us on our course, and the sea was rippling gently. On the eighth day—we were past the milk by now, and were sailing on blue salt water—we saw a large number of men running on the sea. They were like us in anatomy and size, and in every respect except the feet, for theirs were of cork—which is why they were called Corkfeet, I suppose. We were surprised to see that they walked quite confidently on the waves without going under or getting wet. They actually came up to us and greeted us in Greek; they were in a hurry, they said, to get to their country, Cork. They accompanied us for some way, running alongside, then turned aside and went off, wishing us *bon voyage*. Shortly afterward a number of islands came in sight; not far off on the port bow was Cork, the city they were hurrying to, built on a great round cork. A long way off and slightly to starboard were five enormous ones, rising high out of the water, and burning very fiercely.

Straight ahead there was one flat, low island, nearly sixty miles away. We were soon close to it, and a marvelous air breathed round us, sweetly scented, such as the historian Herodotus says issues from rich Arabia; [31] as it came to us, it was like the scent of roses, narcissuses, hyacinths, lilies, and violets, and of myrrh and laurel and flowering vine too. Reveling in the odor and hoping for comfort after our long labors, we drew gradually closer to the island. Once there, we found many great harbors all around a tideless coast, and rivers of clear water flowing gently into the sea; we saw meadows and woods and melodious birds, some singing by the riverbanks and many in the branches of the trees. Light air breathed gently all over the land, sweet breezes played and

---

30 *Tyros* means "cheese."

31 III. 113.

softly rustled the trees; the branches as they swayed gave forth delicious unending melodies, like the sound of flutes in a deserted place. With them were mingled human sounds, in some numbers; not noisy, but as they might sound at a banquet, some playing the flute, others singing, and some clapping their hands to flute or harp.

We were bewitched by all this and put in to land. Mooring the ship and leaving Scintharus with two of the crew on board, we went ashore. On our way through a flowery meadow, we fell in with the guard on their patrol; they bound us with wreaths of roses (the strongest chains they have) and took us before the governor, informing us as we went that this was what was called the Island of the Blest, and that the Cretan Rhadamanthus [32] was its ruler.

When we reached his precincts, we took our position as fourth in the line of those awaiting judgment. The first case concerned Ajax, the son of Telamon; the question was whether or not he was to be allowed to associate with the heroes. The prosecution argued that he had gone out of his mind and taken his own life.[33] Finally, after a great deal of discussion, Rhadamanthus decided that for the present Ajax was to take a dose of hellebore [34] and put himself under the care of Hippocrates, the doctor from Cos, and be admitted to the banquet later when he regained his senses. The second case called for a decision in a matter of the heart; Theseus and Menelaus were taking issue over which one of them Helen should live with.[35] Rhadamanthus decided in favor of Menelaus, on the grounds that he had gone through a great deal of toil and danger over his marriage; added to which Theseus had other wives in the Queen of the Amazons and the daughters of Minos. Third came judgment on the issue of precedence between Alexander, son of Philip, and Hannibal the

6

7

8

9

---

[32] One of the judges of the dead in Hades.

[33] Cf. Sophocles, *Ajax* and *D. D.* 29.

[34] The traditional cure for insanity; cf. *Sale* 23, *Hermotimus* 86, and sec. 18 below.

[35] Cf. *Cock* 17.

Carthaginian; it was given in favor of Alexander, who was accorded a seat next to Cyrus the Elder of Persia.[36]

10 After these cases, we were taken into the court. The judge asked us why we had set foot on the holy ground while still alive, and we told him the whole story as it had happened. He made us stand aside for a long time while he considered our case in conjunction with his colleagues; the latter were numerous, and included Aristides the Just, of Athens. When he had reached his decision, they announced that on the charges of inquisitiveness and traveling in foreign parts we were to give account of ourselves when we died; for the present, we were to stay on the island for a fixed period of time, as members of the company of heroes, and after that to depart. They also fixed the outside limit of our stay, namely seven months. *11* At this, the wreaths fell off us of their own accord; we were released and taken into the city, to the banquet of the blest.

This city is made of gold throughout and has a wall of emerald around it.[37] There are seven gates, each a single piece of cinnamon wood. The foundation of the city, all the land within the walls, is of ivory. There are temples to all the gods, made of beryl, with great altars inside made of single blocks of amethyst; here they offer hecatombs. Around the city runs a river of fairest perfume, a hundred royal cubits broad and five deep, very convenient for swimming. There are baths also —great glass buildings with cinnamon burning inside, with warm dew instead of water in the actual troughs.

12 Their clothing is fine purple cobweb. The people themselves have no bodies: they are intangible, without flesh; their only attributes are shape and form.[38] Although devoid of body, they have position and movement, they think and speak. It is, in fact, as if it were naked soul moving about, endowed with the semblance of body; without touching them one

36 Cf. *D. D.* 12. Lucian's "history" is ironic.

37 This passage reflects the universal dream of El Dorado; it is not a parody of Christian hope. Cf. *Story* I. 31 ff. and n. 22.

38 This description appears to borrow from Plato's theory of "ideas" or "forms."

would never be convinced that what one saw was incorporeal; they are like shadows, but upright and not dark. No one grows old; each person stays the age he was when he came.

They have neither night nor bright daylight; the light that envelops the land is like the gray dawn in the early morning before the sun is up. They have only one season, moreover— it is always spring with them—and only one wind, the west wind.

All kinds of flowers bloom in the land, and all kinds of plants are cultivated for their shade. The vines bear fruit twelve times a year, once a month. Pomegranates, apples, and other fruit, they said, ripened thirteen times, twice in their month of Minos. Corn puts forth not grain but fully finished loaves at the ends of the stalks; thus the general appearance is that of mushrooms. There are three hundred and sixty-five springs of water around the city, as many again of honey, and five hundred of perfume; these last are smaller. There are seven rivers of milk and eight of wine.   *13*

Their banquets take place outside the city in what is called the Elysian Fields, a beautiful meadow with all kinds of trees thick around it giving shade to the diners; cushions of flowers are strewn on the ground. It is the winds that serve everything: they are the waiters. They do not pour the wine, though; that is not necessary, since around the table are great trees of quite pellucid glass whose fruit is wineglasses of every shape and size; and on arriving at table, the diner plucks one or two of these and sets them at his place, where at once they fill with wine. That is the way they get their drink. As for garlands, nightingales and the other melodious birds pick flowers with their beaks from the meadows round about and fly overhead singing and snowing flowers. The way they scent themselves is as follows: thick clouds draw perfume up from the springs and the river, settle over the banquet, and, as the winds squeeze them gently, rain down a sort of fine dew.   *14*

At dinner they give themselves to music and song, Homer's poetry being very popular; Homer himself is there, and sits next to Odysseus at table. The choirs are of boys and girls,   *15* led and accompanied by Eunomus the Locrian, Arion of Lesbos, Anacreon, and Stesichorus [39]—for I saw him there too; he had managed to make his peace with Helen.[40] When they stop singing another choir, made up of swans, swallows, and nightingales, takes its place; and when they sing, all the woods make music under the direction of the winds.

16 But the greatest inducement to happiness they have is the two springs near their table, that of Laughter and that of Pleasure. At the beginning of the banquet they all drink from both of these, and thereafter spend their hours laughing and enjoying themselves.

17 I should like also to record the famous people I saw there. All the demigods were present, and all those who took part in the expedition against Troy except Ajax the Locrian; he was the only one of them, they said, who was undergoing punishment in the abode of the wicked.[41] Of non-Greeks, I saw the two Cyruses, the Scythian Anacharsis, Zamolxis the Thracian,[42] and Numa of Italy. There were Lycurgus the Spartan, Phocion and Tellus from Athens, and the wise men except Periander.[43] I also saw Socrates, the son of Sophroniscus, chatting with Nestor and Palamedes; [44] around him were Hyacinthus of Sparta, Narcissus of Thespiae, Hylas, and other handsome youths.[45] He seemed to me to be in love with Hyacinthus —at any rate, he was the one he was arguing most with. I was

[39] Famous choric or lyric poets.

[40] One of the few remaining fragments of Stesichorus is a "Palinode" or "Recantation" on Helen, in which the poet appears to deny an earlier malicious statement about Helen in his work (all the "denial" says, in fact, is that she "did not go to Troy"!). Stesichorus was said to have been struck blind for his "malice," and to have had his sight restored upon "recanting."

[41] For raping Cassandra when Troy fell, and for blasphemy on his journey home.

[42] Cf. *Zeus* 42.

[43] The tyrant of Corinth is regarded as too cruel for heaven.

[44] See *D. D.* 20. 4 and n. 62.

[45] Cf. *Sale* 15 and n. 21, and *D. D.* 20. 6.

told that Rhadamanthus was displeased with him and had often threatened to expel him from the island for his nonsense if he didn't drop his self-deprecation [46] and enjoy himself. Plato was the only one missing. They said he was living in the republic he constructed himself, under the constitution and laws of his own devising.[47] The people best spoken of there were Aristippus and Epicurus; they were pleasant and obliging, and convivial company.[48] Aesop the Phrygian was there too; he acts as their jester. Diogenes of Sinope had so changed that he had married Lais the courtesan, frequently got up and danced when in his cups, and acted like any drunkard. There were no Stoics in the company—apparently they were still climbing the steep hill of virtue; [49] and about Chrysippus, we heard that he was not permitted to land on the island until he had taken the hellebore treatment a fourth time.[50] The Academics, it was said, were ready to come but were holding back and considering the matter, since they did not yet accept the possibility of there being such an island.[51] And then I suppose they were apprehensive about the judgment of Rhadamanthus too, seeing that they themselves had denied the possibility of proper judgment. Many of them had set out, I gathered, in the tracks of people on their way to the island, but had fallen behind through laziness, without grasping their object, and turned back halfway.

18

Well, these were the most notable of the company; the most respected members of it are Achilles and, next, Theseus. Their sexual practice is as follows. They make love openly, in the sight of all, with both women and men; this is not considered in any way shameful. Only Socrates had sworn formally that his associations with the young were pure; but everybody thought he was guilty of perjury—Hyacinthus and Narcissus

19

[46] Cf. *D. D.* 20. 5 and n. 65 for Socrates' "irony."
[47] Cf. *Sale* 17.
[48] Cf. *Sale* 12 and 19.
[49] Cf. *Hermotimus* 2 ff.
[50] Cf. *Sale* 23 and n. 29.
[51] Cf. *Sale* 27 and n. 34.

kept saying so, anyway, though he himself denied it. Women are common property, and no one is jealous of his neighbor; they are very Platonic in this respect.[52] Boys submit to anyone who wants them, without any resistance.

20   Before two or three days had gone by I approached Homer the poet, neither of us being occupied, and asked him various questions. I said his birthplace was a bone of contention on earth to this day. He replied that he was well aware that some people said he came from Chios, some from Smyrna, and many from Colophon; but the truth was, he was a Babylonian, and his name in his own country was not Homer but Tigranes— he had changed his name when he was held as a hostage [53] by Greeks. I asked him also whether the obelized lines were of his composition; he said they were, all of them. My regard for Zenodotus and Aristarchus and scholars of that sort, with all their pedantry, dropped.[54] Having got satisfactory answers to these questions, I then asked him why on earth he had started with the wrath. He said that was how it had come to him; he had no definite purpose in it. I was also very anxious to know whether he had written the *Odyssey* before the *Iliad* as most people thought; he said he hadn't. Another thing they say about him is that he was blind, but I knew at once that he wasn't; I could see that, so there was no need for me to ask him. As a matter of fact, I used to do this often afterwards, go up and ask him questions, whenever I saw he was not busy. He was very ready to answer, especially after his acquittal in court—Thersites brought a libel action against him on the grounds of having been subjected to ridicule in his poetry; [55] Odysseus spoke in Homer's defense and won the case.

21   It was at this time that Pythagoras of Samos [56] arrived; he

[52] Cf. *Sale* 17.
[53] The Greek word *homeros* means "hostage."
[54] These Alexandrian critics obelized certain lines as spurious, in the earliest editions of Homer.
[55] In *Iliad* II. 211 ff.
[56] Cf. *Cock* and *Sale* 2–6.

had been through seven transmigrations and inhabited as many animals and completed his psychic peregrinations. All his right side was gold. He was admitted to the community, but there was still some doubt as to whether he should be called Pythagoras or Euphorbus. Empedocles [57] turned up too, well cooked and with his whole body roasted; but he was not admitted, despite much entreaty.

In the course of time their athletic contest, the Games of the Dead, took place. The judges were Achilles, who was holding the office for the fifth time, and Theseus, holding it for the seventh. I shall summarize the events; a full report would take a long time. The wrestling was won by Caranus the Heraclid, who beat Odysseus for the title. The boxing was a draw between Areius the Egyptian, who is buried in Corinth, and Epeius. They have no pancratium, and I cannot now recall who won the race. In poetry, Homer was really much the best; Hesiod won, though. The prize for every winner was a garland of peacock feathers plaited.[58]

Just after the games were finished, news was brought that those who were being punished in the abode of the wicked had broken their chains and overpowered their guard and were advancing upon the island, under Phalaris of Acragas, Busiris the Egyptian, Diomede the Thracian, and Sciron and Pityocamptes and their followers. On hearing this, Rhadamanthus marshaled the heroes on the beach, giving the command to Theseus, Achilles, and Ajax the son of Telamon (now restored to sanity). They joined battle and the heroes won, Achilles being particularly successful. Socrates also fought bravely on the right wing—much more bravely than he did at Delium,[59] when alive; he did not run away when four of the enemy advanced toward him, and his countenance showed no emotion. He actually received a special prize afterward for his conduct—a large and very lovely park in the suburbs, to which

22

23

---

[57] Cf. *D. D.* 20. 4 and nn. 57 and 58 there.
[58] The prize at the Olympic Games was a laurel wreath.
[59] Cf. Plato, *Symposium* 220–21.

he used to invite his friends for conversation; he called it the Academy of the Dead.[60]

24 Seizing the vanquished, then, they bound them and sent them back for yet more punishment. Homer wrote an account of this battle; when I left, he gave me the text to bring to men on earth, but we lost it afterward along with everything else. The poem began:

Now tell, my Muse, of the fight of the dead heroes.

Then they boiled beans,[61] as is their habit after a successful war, and held a great celebration at which they ate the victory meal. Pythagoras alone took no part in it; he would not eat, because he disapproves of bean-eating,[62] and sat well away.

25 Six months had gone by, and we were about halfway through the seventh, when an incident took place. Scintharus' son Cinyras, an upstanding, handsome lad, had already long been in love with Helen, and she was evidently passionately fond of the youth; at any rate, they used to exchange glances at table and drink each other's health and get up and go off for walks in the wood by themselves. Eventually Cinyras, in love and not knowing what to do about it, conceived the notion of abducting Helen and making his escape. She was willing; the plan was to go off to one of the nearby islands, Cork or Cheeseland. They had long ago taken into their confidence three of the boldest of my crew, but Cinyras did not tell his father, knowing that he would put a stop to it. They carried out the plan as intended. When night came—I was not there; as it happened, I had fallen asleep at table—they picked up Helen without attracting attention and put out to sea, going as fast as they could. About midnight Menelaus woke up and realized that his wife was not in the bed. Raising a cry and getting hold of his brother, he went to King Rhadamanthus. When day dawned the lookouts reported that they could see the ship a long way off, so Rhadamanthus put fifty of the

26

---

60 Plato, Socrates' disciple, founded the Academy.
61 An allusion to the Pyanepsia, a festival at which beans were eaten.
62 Cf. *Cock* 18.

heroes on board a ship made from a single asphodel log, with instructions to give chase. They rowed hard and caught them about noon, just as they were entering the sea of milk near Cheeseland—they were as near as that to effecting their escape. They sailed back, towing the other ship by means of a chain of roses. Helen was weeping; she was embarrassed and kept her face covered. Rhadamanthus examined Cinyras and his associates, to see if there were any others privy to the plot. They said there were not, and he had them whipped with mallow, bound by the genitals, and taken off to the abode of the wicked.

They decreed also that we were to leave the island before 27 the appointed time, with only one day's grace. At this I besought their pity, weeping at the thought of all the comfort I was leaving to set out once more on my travels. They gave me some consolation, however, by saying that it would not be many years before I returned to them; they showed me in advance the chair and the couch I was to have at table—in excellent company. I approached Rhadamanthus with the earnest request that he foretell the future for me and point out my route.[63] He said I should reach my own country after much wandering and danger, but refused to add when I was to return. He did, however, point out to me the neighboring islands—there were five of them visible, and a sixth a long way off; these, he said, were the islands of the wicked, the nearby ones, "from which," he said, "you can see great flames rising, even at this distance. The sixth one there is the city of dreams. Beyond that—you cannot see it from here—is Calypso's island. After passing these, you will come to the great continent opposite the one where you people live. There you will have many adventures, pass among various tribes, and live among inhospitable men; then at last you will reach the mainland opposite." That was all he said. And he pulled up a mallow 28 root [64] and handed it to me, bidding me invoke it at times

[63] It is standard for heroes in ancient literature to visit the afterworld and learn of the future; cf. *Odyssey* XI and Virgil, *Aeneid* VI.

[64] Cf. *moly*, *Odyssey* X. 281–306.

of greatest danger. He also enjoined me, if ever I reached this world, not to poke fires with a sword, not to eat lupines, and not to associate with boys over eighteen; [65] if I kept these things in mind, he said, I could have hopes of returning to the island.

So then I prepared for the voyage, and at dinnertime joined them at table. The next day I went to Homer the poet and asked him to compose a couplet for me to use as an inscription. He did so, and I inscribed it on a pillar of beryl, which I set up near the harbor. It ran as follows:

> Lucian, befriended by the blessed gods,
> Saw this land and returned to his own country.

29   I stayed that day and set out the next; the heroes came to see me off. Odysseus took the opportunity to give Penelope the slip and hand me a letter for Calypso on the Island of Ogygia. Rhadamanthus sent the ferryman Nauplius with us, to save us from being seized if we were driven on to the islands and vouch for our having other destination.

As soon as we had passed beyond the scented air in our progress, a dreadful smell assailed us in its turn, a smell as of asphalt and brimstone and pitch all burning at once, and an intolerable, foul odor, as of human flesh roasting. The air was dark and murky and precipitated a dew like pitch, and we could hear the crack of whips and a multitude howling.

30   We put in at only one of these islands, and found it precipitous and sheer in every direction; it was rough with rocks and stones, had no trees, and was without water. Still, we clambered up by the cliffs and went ahead through ugly country, by a thorny path covered with sharp stakes. The first thing that struck us when we reached the punishment compound was the general character of the area; blades and sharp stakes thrust out of the ground itself like massed flowers, and there were rivers running around it, one of slime, another of blood, and a third of fire. This last was very broad—impassable, in fact. It flowed like water, heaved like the sea, and

65 Mock-Pythagorean precepts; the first may be genuine.

contained many fish, some like burning brands, others, small ones, like blazing pieces of coal; these were called lampkins. One narrow way led across all three, with Timon of Athens [66] guarding the entrance to it. Nauplius took us across it, however, and we witnessed the punishment of many kings and many private citizens too, some of whom in fact we recognized; we even saw Cinyras there, wreathed in smoke and suspended by the testicles. Our guides described for us the life of each of the victims and the reason for his punishment. The people who suffered the greatest torment were those who had told lies when they were alive and written mendacious histories; among them were Ctesias of Cnidos, Herodotus, and many others. You may guess that, seeing them, I had high hopes for the next world—I knew very well I had never told a lie.

I soon turned back to the ship—the sight was more than I could stand—said good-bye to Nauplius, and sailed off. Soon there came into sight nearby the Island of Dreams, but it was faint and hard to make out. The island itself was like the dreams in a way, in that as we approached, it receded before us, retreated, retired farther off. At last we caught up with it and sailed into Sleep Harbor, as it is called, and landed in the late afternoon near the Ivory Gates and the Temple of the Cock. Then we went into the town and saw many dreams of various kinds. I am going to talk about the town first, because no one has ever written about it except Homer,[67] and what he says is not very accurate.

It is encircled by a wood of tall poppies and mandragoras, among which live a great many bats—the only winged things on the island. Near it there is a river, which they call Somnambule; beside the gates there are two springs, called Deepsleep and Allnight. Around the town runs a high wall all the colors of the rainbow. There are, however, four gates, not two as Homer says: two facing Dozy Moor, one of iron and one of

---

[66] A misanthrope of the fifth century B.C., the subject of a work by Lucian (see Introduction, p. xxii); cf. Shakespeare's *Timon of Athens*.
[67] In *Odyssey* XIX. 559 ff.

earthenware—these were the gates through which frightening and murderous and grim dreams were said to leave; and two facing the harbor and the sea, one of horn and the other, the one we had come through, of ivory. To the right as you enter the town is the Temple of Night, and the Temple of the Cock is near the harbor; these are the principal cults of the island. On the left is the Palace of Sleep; Sleep is their ruler and has under him two satraps or governors—Nightmare, the son of Pointless, and Richman, the son of Daydream. In the middle of the market square is a spring called Idlewater, and nearby are the temples of Truth and Untruth; there too is the town shrine and oracle, whose superintendent and mouth-piece is the dream-interpreter Antiphon, appointed to the office by Sleep.

34   The dreams themselves varied in character and appearance. Some were tall and handsome and well-proportioned, others short and misshapen; some appeared to be made of gold, others were poor and shabby. There were winged dreams among them and monster-dreams and dreams in carnival costume—some dressed up as kings, some as gods, and so on. Many of them in fact we recognized, having seen them before, at home; they came up and greeted us like old friends, took us in charge, put us to sleep, and showed us most excellent and ingenious entertainment. Their hospitality was splendid; among other things, they promised to make us kings and satraps. Some of them actually took us home and showed us our families and brought us back the same day.

35   Well, we stayed thirty days and nights there, and enjoyed ourselves immensely sleeping. Then suddenly there came a great clap of thunder; we woke up, jumped out of bed, took on some supplies, and set sail again. After three days we put in at Ogygia and landed, but first I opened Odysseus' letter. It read as follows:

> Dear Calypso:
>   This is to let you know what happened to me. As soon as I sailed away from you in the raft I built, I was ship-

wrecked. Thanks to Leucothea, I just managed to get ashore in Phaeacia. The Phaeacians sent me home, and I caught a lot of men trying to win my wife and having the time of their lives in my house; but I killed them all. Later, I was murdered by Telegonus, my son by Circe; now I am on the Island of the Blest, and very sorry that I left my life with you and the immortality you offered me. So if I get a chance, I'll slip away and come to you.

Odysseus

In addition to this, the letter said that we were to be entertained. I went inland a little from the sea and found the cave, just as Homer described it. Calypso was at home knitting. She took the letter and read it and wept a great deal. Then she asked us in and gave us a very good meal. She asked about Odysseus, and about Penelope—what she looked like, and whether she was as faithful as Odysseus used to boast she was. We made such answer as we thought would please her. Then we went off to our ship and slept near it on the shore, and at daybreak we put to sea in a freshening breeze.

After riding a storm for two days, on the third we fell in with the Pumpkin-pirates. These are savages from the islands nearby who raid passing ships in vessels made out of great pumpkins ninety feet long; they dry them and remove the pulp, thus hollowing them, and equip them with masts made of cane, with pumpkin leaves for sails. Well, they attacked with two vessels, and during the fight inflicted many casualties with the pumpkin seeds that they used for stones. The fight went on for a long time, and the issue was doubtful; then about midday we saw the Nut-sailors coming up astern of the Pumpkin-pirates. They were their enemies, it appeared, for as soon as the Pumpkin-pirates saw them approaching they forgot about us, turned around, and engaged with them. Meanwhile we hoisted sail and took to flight, leaving them to fight it out. The Nut-sailors were clearly going to win; they were superior in numbers, being five ships strong, and their vessels were stronger. These vessels were nutshells split in half and emptied; each half was ninety feet long. When we had lost

sight of them we attended to our casualties, and thereafter we were in armor almost all the time, and constantly on the lookout for attacks.

39   It was just as well, for before sunset some twenty men mounted on dolphins assailed us from a desert island. They were pirates too; the dolphins carried them safely, and as they leapt they whinnied like horses. When they were within range, they split into two groups and attacked us from both sides, firing dried cuttlefish and crabs' eyes at us. But we were using arrows and javelins; they could not stand up to it, and most of them were wounded when they fled back to the island.

40   About midnight, in a calm sea, we accidentally ran aground on an enormous halcyon's nest, a good seven miles in circumference. The halcyon was riding on it, hatching her eggs; she was almost as big as the nest. She rose into the air and very nearly capsized us with the wind her wings made; she went off, though, uttering a mournful cry. We climbed on to the nest when day began to dawn and saw that it was like a great raft, being made of large trees laid together. There were five hundred eggs in it, each bigger than a jar of Chian wine. The chicks could already be seen inside, and they were making a croaking noise, so we hacked open one of the eggs with axes and dug out an unfledged chick fatter than twenty vultures.

41   We sailed off, and were about twenty-five miles from the nest when some very startling phenomena occurred. The goose that formed our figurehead suddenly flapped its wings and cackled; our navigator Scintharus, who was bald, grew hair; and, oddest of all, the ship's mast began to sprout, putting forth shoots and, at the top, fruit—figs and black grapes, not yet ripe.[68] We were understandably very perturbed at this sight, and prayed to the gods because of the strange nature of the apparition.

42   Before we had gone sixty miles we saw a great forest, dense with pine and cypress. We supposed it was the mainland, but in fact the sea was bottomless there, and on it there were trees growing—they had no roots but stayed upright without mov-

[68] Cf. *Homeric Hymns* VII. 38.

ing, as if they were sailing on the sea. We approached, and when we saw the whole situation we had no idea what to do. It was impossible to sail through the wood—it was dense and continuous—and turning back presented difficulties. I climbed the highest tree to see what it was like farther on, and saw that the forest extended about six miles; beyond it was the beginning of another ocean. We decided to raise the ship on to the foliage, which was thick, and take it across if possible to the other sea. And that is what we did. We put a thick hawser around the ship, climbed the trees, and just managed to haul it up; then we got it on to the foliage, spread the sails, and sailed as on the sea, with the wind carrying us forward. At this point that line of Antimachus [69] came to my mind; he says somewhere,

> And as they journeyed, sailing through the wood.

Still, we made our way through the wood, with an effort, 43 reached the water, and let the ship down again the same way.

Then we sailed through clear, transparent water until we came to the edge of a great chasm in the sea, which was split, just as you often see great gaps in the earth, caused by earthquakes. We struck sail and just managed to bring the ship to a stop in time; she was very near plunging over. We looked over the edge and saw a drop of well over a hundred miles. It was very strange and very frightening: the water stood there as if cut in half. We looked around and saw, not far off to starboard, a bridge of water joining the seas at surface level, going from one side across to the other; so we struck out with our oars and went across by it. With a lot of effort we managed to get across; we never expected to.

On the other side we entered upon a calm sea and came 44 upon a fairly small island, easy of access and inhabited. Living in it were savages, Ox-heads, with horns like the Minotaur in our myth. We landed and went inland to get water and food if possible—we had none left. The water we found close by,

---

[69] A fifth-century B.C. elegiac poet of whose work only some fragments have survived.

but nothing else was to be seen. We did, however, hear a loud lowing not far off. Thinking it was a herd of cattle, we went forward a little and came upon the men. As soon as they saw us they gave chase; three of my crew were caught, but the rest of us made our escape to the sea. There we all put on our armor, not wanting to leave our friends unavenged, and fell upon the Ox-heads as they were dividing up the flesh of their captives. They all panicked. We pursued them, killed about fifty, and took two alive. Then we returned with our captives. But still we had no food; so when everybody else was clamoring for the death of the prisoners, I refused to sanction this course but bound them instead and kept them until a deputation arrived from the Ox-heads to ransom them—that was how we interpreted their head-nodding and mournful, supplicatory lowing. The ransom was a great number of cheeses, dried fish, onions, and four deer; these last had three feet each—two behind, and the front feet joined into one. In return for this we gave back the prisoners; then, after staying there one day, we put to sea.

45   By now we could see fish, and birds flying, and various other indications of the proximity of land; and before very long we saw men sailing in a novel manner, for they were both crew and ship as well, as I shall explain. They floated on their backs in the water, erected their penises, which were very big, stretched sails from them, and then took the sheets in their hands and sailed along when the wind struck. After them appeared others sitting on corks and driving pairs of dolphins by means of reins; the dolphins pulled the corks along behind them. These people did not commit any aggression on us, nor did they avoid us; they rode past without fear or hostility and examined our ship from every side, expressing wonder at the shape of it.

46   That evening we put in at a small island, inhabited by women, as we thought, speaking Greek. They approached us and received us with open arms. They were decked out like courtesans; all of them were young and lovely, and they wore

garments that trailed around their ankles. The island was called Witchcraft and the city Watertown. Well, the women paired off with us and entertained us; but I had a presentiment of something sinister, and remained apart for a time.[70] On looking around more carefully, I saw the bones and skulls of a great many people lying about; but I did not want to raise the alarm, gather my men, and take to arms. I took the mallow in my hand and prayed fervently to it for escape from our present troubles. Shortly afterward, as my hostess was looking after me, I saw that her legs were not those of a women, but a donkey's, with hooves.

At this I drew my sword, seized the lady, tied her up, and questioned her about the whole business. She was very loath to answer but did so, saying that they were women of the sea, called Donkey-legs, and lived on strangers who came to the island; they made them drunk, she said, went to bed with them, and fell upon them as they were sleeping. On hearing this, I left her there tied up, climbed up on to the roof, and shouted to call my crew together. When they gathered, I told them the whole story, showed them the bones, and took them in to the woman I had tied up. At once she vanished, turning into water; still, to see what would happen, I thrust my sword into the water, and it turned into blood. So we quickly returned to the ship and sailed off.   *47*

As dawn began to break we descried a continent which we supposed to be the one opposite to ours, so we saluted it with respect, prayed, and began to debate what to do next. Some thought we should merely land and turn back again right away; others wanted to leave the ship there, penetrate the interior, and see what the inhabitants were like. In the middle of this debate a fierce storm arose, caught the ship, and dashed it on the shore in wreckage. We just managed to swim to safety, each man snatching up his arms and anything else he could.

Such were my experiences as far as the other continent: on

70 Cf. *Odyssey* X, the Circe episode, with this passage.

the sea, during the journey among the islands and in the sky, then in the whale; and after we left the whale, among the heroes and the dreams, and finally with the Ox-heads and the Donkey-legs. What happened on the continent I shall relate in the books to follow.[71]

[71] Lucian never wrote them; this sentence, says a scholiast, is the biggest lie of all!

GLOSSARY

ACADEMY: a school of philosophy founded by Plato.

ACARNANIA: a district in northwest Greece.

ACHAEANS: Homer's usual term for the Greeks in general. Strictly, Achaea was a small area in the north of the Peloponnese.

ACHERON: one of the rivers of Hades; the name appears to mean "woeful."

ACHILLES: the son of Peleus and Thetis; the principal character in the *Iliad*, where he is represented as the greatest of the Greek heroes in the Trojan War.

ACRISIUS: a legendary king of Argos; the father of Danaë.

ADONIS: a youth of great beauty who was beloved by Aphrodite.

AEACUS: one of the judges of the dead in Hades.

AËDON: a woman who killed her own son in mistake for another boy; in her grief she prayed to be changed from human form, and became a nightingale.

AESOP: a writer of the sixth century B.C. who composed "fables," or popular stories about animals, illustrative of moral lessons.

AËTION: a painter of the fourth century B.C.

AGAMEMNON: the son of Atreus, brother of Menelaus, and King of Mycenae. He commanded the Greek forces in the Trojan War.

AJAX: one of the Greek heroes at Troy. After Achilles' death, his mother, Thetis, said his armor should go to the man who had done the Trojans most harm, and the Trojan prisoners nominated Odysseus. Ajax then went mad with anger, slew a flock of sheep thinking they were Greeks, and committed suicide in shame. See Sophocles, *Ajax*.

AJAX THE LOCRIAN: one of the Greeks at Troy. He raped Cassandra at the altar of Athena when Troy fell. On his journey home his ship was wrecked by Poseidon, but he scrambled ashore and boasted of having defied the gods; whereupon Poseidon made the rocks crumble and drowned him. He is represented in the *Iliad* as violent and crude.

ALCAMENES: a Greek sculptor of the fifth century B.C.

ALCESTIS: a descendant of Aeolus, the god of the winds, and hence related to Protesilaus. She agreed to die as a substitute for her husband, Admetus, and was brought back from Hades by Hercules. See Euripides, *Alcestis*.

ALCIBIADES: the son of Clinias, and a companion of Socrates. He was an extremely capable Athenian politician during the Peloponnesian War, and his efforts prompted the Sicilian expedition. Indicted for sacrilege, he went over to the side of Sparta but later returned to Athens.

ALCMENA: the mother of Hercules, whom she bore to Zeus after he visited her. She was the wife of Amphitryon.

ALEXANDER: 356–323 B.C., the king of Macedon known as Alexander the Great. He was the son of Philip of Macedon and Olympias, but for political reasons he claimed descent from Ammon and divinity for himself. He regarded himself as another Achilles; he overthrew the Persian

Empire and spread Greek civilization far to the East, founding many cities bearing his name. Personally very courageous, and a brilliant strategist and tactician, he was also a statesman whose ambition was to weld the Persian and Greek worlds; in this he himself largely succeeded, but his conquests were split up under his successors, who came from the "Companions," or royal squadron, and included Perdiccas, Antigonus, and Ptolemy. He had a violent disposition and killed some of his best friends, such as Clitus. He was tutored by Aristotle.

AMALTHEA: a she-goat who fed the infant Zeus. Her horn, broken off, became the Horn of Plenty, being filled with the fruits of the earth; the legend exists in several versions.

AMMON: the Libyan equivalent of the Greek god Zeus. Alexander visited his shrine in the desert and claimed to be his son.

AMPHILOCHUS: a seer and the brother of Alcmaeon. He was half-divine, and prophesied from a shrine in Mallus.

AMPHITRYON: the husband of Alcmena and thus the putative father of Hercules.

AMYNTAS: the father of Philip of Macedon.

ANACHARSIS: a Scythian philosopher of ca. 600 B.C., sometimes included among the "Seven Wise Men" of antiquity. He visited Greece and is variously represented as admiring and criticizing Greek civilization. Lucian's Anacharsis shows him as interested in the Greek passion for physical culture.

ANACREON: a lyric poet of the sixth century B.C. who wrote hymns and love poems.

ANTILOCHUS: a Greek warrior in the Iliad; the son of Nestor.

ANTIOPE: the mother by Zeus of twins, Amphion and Zethus.

ANTISTHENES: founder of the Cynic school of philosophy. He was born ca. 455 B.C., lived in Athens, and was a follower of Socrates.

ANUBIS: a dog-faced Egyptian deity.

AORNOS: a stronghold in Afghanistan, thought to be impregnable, which Alexander captured by an astonishing feat of arms after crossing the Hindu Kush range. According to tradition, legendary heroes—Hercules and Dionysus—had failed to capture it.

APELLES: a Greek painter of the fourth century B.C.

APHRODITE: the goddess of love, beauty, and fertility.

APOLLO: the son of Zeus and Leto; the god of the arts, especially music, and of medicine and prophecy. He was represented as young and handsome. His most famous prophecies, often ambiguous, were given from his oracle at Delphi and were well known in antiquity.

ARBELA: the name of a town near which Alexander defeated the Persians in 331 B.C.

ARES: the Greek god of war; the lover of Aphrodite.

ARGO: the ship in which Jason went in search of the Golden Fleece. One of its planks was made from the talking oaks of Dodona, and thus the ship issued prophecies.

ARIADNE: the daughter of Minos, a legendary king of Crete. She gave Theseus a ball of thread to guide him out of the labyrinth when he came to kill the Minotaur; on leaving for Athens he took her with him, but deserted her on the journey.

ARION: a dithyrambic poet of the late seventh century B.C.

ARISTARCHUS: an Alexandrian scholar of the second century B.C. He edited Homer, "obelizing," or putting marks against, lines he considered spurious.

ARISTIDES: an Athenian statesman, the rival of Themistocles. He was known as "The Just" because of his unusual uprightness.

ARISTIPPUS: the founder of the Cyrenaic school of philosophy, which held that pleasure is the end of action. Lucian and later writers confused him with his grandfather, who was a companion of Socrates, a courtier of Dionysius of Syracuse, and a man of luxurious tastes.

ARISTODEMUS: an actor of the fourth century B.C.

ARISTOPHANES: a Greek comic writer of the late fifth century B.C. One of his works, *The Birds*, is a kind of Shangri-La fantasy. In *The Clouds* he makes fun of Socrates.

ARISTOTLE: a philosopher of the fourth century B.C., Plato's successor. He founded the Lyceum, the school of Peripatetic philosophy, and applied a mind of universal curiosity to the study of logic, moral philosophy, natural sciences, politics, and literature. For a time he was tutor to the young Alexander of Macedon.

ARTAXERXES: the name of several kings of Persia, the most famous living in the fifth and fourth centuries B.C.

ARTEMIS: the daughter of Zeus, and twin sister of Apollo. A virgin goddess, she was the patroness of wild beasts and of childbirth. A cult involving human sacrifice was dedicated to her in Tauris; see Euripides, *Iphigeneia in Tauris*.

ARTEMISIA: the name of two queens of Caria in Asia Minor. The first fought with Xerxes' expedition against Greece; the second was Mausolus' wife and sister and completed his tomb, the Mausoleum.

ASCLEPIUS: the son of Apollo, but a mortal. He restored the dead to life, for which he was slain by Zeus; later he was raised to divinity as the god of healing.

ATHENA: the daughter of Zeus, from whose head she sprang fully armed; the patron goddess of Athens, goddess of arts and wisdom and of civilization in general.

ATROPOS: one of the three Fates. She severed the thread of life.

ATTIS: a vegetation god of Asia Minor. He was little worshiped in Greece during classical times but later became increasingly popular throughout the Roman Empire.

BABYLON: the capital of the Persian Empire, captured by Alexander.

BENDIS: a Thracian goddess who had some similarity to Artemis. Her worship was introduced into Athens late in the fifth century B.C.

BITHYNIA: a district in Asia Minor.

BRIAREUS: a hundred-handed monster who helped Zeus evade the plot of Hera, Poseidon, and Athena.

BUSIRIS: a legendary king of Egypt who was killed by Hercules.

CAENEUS: the son of Elatus; originally a woman, Caenis, who was turned into a man at her own request after being seduced by Poseidon.

CALLIAS: a rich Athenian nobleman, *fl.* 400 B.C.

CALLISTHENES: a historian, the nephew of Aristotle. He accompanied Alexander as publicist for Panhellenism, quarreled with his policy, and was executed.

CALLISTO: a nymph, the daughter of Lycaon. She was changed into a bear for offending Artemis, and subsequently, by Zeus, into the Great Bear constellation.

CALYPSO: a nymph who detains Odysseus on the island of Ogygia in the fifth book of the Odyssey. She promises him immortality, but he leaves her.

CAPPADOCIA: a district of Asia Minor.

CAPUA: a town in southern Italy

where Hannibal lingered during his Italian campaign.

CASTALIA: the fountain on Mount Parnassus where Apollo's priestess bathed before prophesying.

CASTOR: see "Pollux."

CECROPS: the mythical first king of Athens, born of the soil.

CELTIBERIANS: a powerful race in northern Spain.

CENTAURS: monsters, half man and half horse, who were said to live in Thessaly. They represent animal desire; but Chiron educated Achilles and other heroes.

CERBERUS: a three-headed dog who guarded the gates of Hades.

CERCYON: a malefactor killed by Theseus near Athens.

CHALDAEA: strictly, a district in Babylonia; but the name was applied to the whole of Babylonia. The Babylonians were famous for their prophetic skill.

CHARMIDES: one of Socrates' companions in Plato's dialogues.

CHARON: the ferryman of Hades who rowed the souls of the dead across the Styx.

CHIMAERA: a fire-breathing monster, part lion, part serpent, and part goat; it was killed by Bellerophon.

CHIRON: the Centaur medicine man.

CHRYSIPPUS: a Stoic philosopher and one of the leading exponents of that doctrine in the third century B.C. Nothing is known of his having taken the "hellebore treatment" for madness which Lucian mentions.

CITHAERON: a mountain between Athens and Thebes.

CLEARCHUS: a Spartan general who commanded the Greek mercenary army of ten thousand men which fought for Cyrus the Younger against his brother, the King of Persia. See Xenophon, *Anabasis.*

CLINIAS: the father of Alcibiades.

CLITUS: a close friend of Alexander whom Alexander killed.

CLOTHO: one of the three Fates. She spun the thread of life.

COCYTUS: a river in Hades; the name means "lamentation."

CODRUS: an early king of Athens whose heroism saved his country.

COLOPHON: a town in Asia Minor, the seat of one of Apollo's oracles.

COLOSSUS: an enormous statue of Helius, the god of the sun, at the entrance to the harbor of Rhodes. It stood astride the harbor entrance until it fell in an earthquake toward the end of the third century B.C., some fifty years after its erection.

COMPANIONS: Alexander's royal squadron.

CRANEUM: a park outside Corinth.

CRATES: a wandering Cynic philosopher of the fourth century B.C.

CROESUS: a king of Lydia in Asia Minor during the sixth century B.C. He was famous for his fabulous wealth and also for the sudden change in his fortunes when he misinterpreted an ambiguous oracle and his empire was overthrown by Cyrus the Elder of Persia. Condemned to be burned alive, he was miraculously saved when on the pyre and became thereafter a sadder and wiser man. See Herodotus, I.

CRONUS: a pre-Hellenic king of Heaven; the father of Zeus, by whom he was deposed. His age was the Golden Age.

CTESIAS: a writer who lived in the fifth and fourth centuries B.C. and wrote a history of Persia as well as a fanciful account of India.

CYNEGIRUS: the brother of Aeschylus. He fought at Marathon and died heroically there, his bravery being commemorated by a picture in the Stoa Poecile.

CYNICS: a philosophical sect, not formally organized, founded by Antisthenes and Diogenes in the fourth century B.C.; Menippus, from whom Lucian borrows extensively, was one of its principal exponents in the third century B.C. The Cynic doctrine called for simple living, independence, frankness, and fearlessness; however, many ot its exponents were nothing more than abusive ruffians, aggressive and repulsive rather than independent and unconventional. Cynic asceticism seems to have appealed to Lucian to some degree; he is, however, always ready to castigate excesses in its practice, and Cynic "street-corner preachers" appear often in his works.

CYNISCUS: a diminutive form of "Cynic," meaning "little Cynic."

CYRENAICS: a philosophical school founded by Aristippus in the fourth century B.C.; its doctrine taught that sensual pleasure was the purpose of life. From it sprang Epicureanism.

CYRUS THE ELDER: the king of Persia from 559 to 529 B.C.; he defeated Croesus.

CYRUS THE YOUNGER: the second son of Darius II of Persia. When his brother Artaxerxes succeeded to the throne he attempted to displace him, raising an army that included Greek mercenaries. He met the royal forces at Cunaxa in 401 B.C. and was killed. The story is told in Xenophon's Anabasis.

DAEDALUS: a legendary craftsman, creator of the labyrinth of Minos. He invented wings and flew in the air with his son, Icarus; he himself flew low and survived the journey, but Icarus flew higher and fell into the sea when the sun melted the wax that attached his wings to his body.

DANAË: the daughter of Acrisius, who confined her in a bronze room to prevent her from having children when he learned that he was fated to be killed by her son. Zeus passed into her room in the form of a shower of gold, and she eventually bore Perseus, who in fact killed Acrisius.

DANAIDS: the fifty daughters of Danaus in mythology. Their father gave them in marriage to the fifty sons of Aegyptus, but ordered each to kill her husband on her wedding night; all except one did so, and they were punished in the underworld by having to pour water perpetually into a leaky jar.

DAPHNE: a nymph who was pursued by Apollo and was turned into a laurel tree when she prayed for assistance. The name means "laurel."

DARIUS: the name of three kings of Persia. The first of these (521–486 B.C.) was defeated by the Greeks at Marathon; the second (424–405 B.C.) reigned during the Peloponnesian War, when Persia's support was of consequence to Greek states; the third (died 330 B.C.) was defeated by Alexander at Issus and Arbela and was killed by his own side.

DELPHI: the site of Apollo's most famous oracle in ancient Greece.

DEMETER: the corn goddess (the Roman Ceres) and "Earth Mother." Her daughter, Persephone, was Hades' consort.

DEMOCRITUS: a philosopher, ca. 460–370 B.C., who propounded the "atomist" theory of matter, which was adopted and elaborated by Epicurus and his followers; according to this theory matter consisted ultimately of infinitesimally small particles, whose motion determined the nature of phenomena. He was famous for his many-sided learning and nicknamed "the laughing philosopher."

DEMOSTHENES: an Athenian statesman of the fourth century B.C. He taught himself the art of oratory and applied his skill to the attempt to rouse Athens against the menace of Philip of Macedon, against whom his most famous speeches, the Philippics, were directed.

DIOGENES: a philosopher from Sinope, born ca. 400 B.C.; one of the founders of the Cynic school of philosophy. He is said to have been so ascetic that he lived in a jar. Many pithy sayings are attributed to him.

DIOMEDE: a Greek hero in the *Iliad*.

DION: a citizen of Syracuse who was much influenced by Plato during Plato's visit to Sicily. He later became tyrant of Syracuse.

DIONYSIUS: the name of two tyrants of Syracuse, father and son, during the fourth century B.C. The son was deposed in 345 and thereafter lived in Corinth.

DIONYSUS: the son of Zeus; the god of ecstasy, and especially of religious emotion and wine. He was also the patron of various festivals, including dramatic festivals at Athens. His cult originated either in Phrygia or in Thrace and became very popular throughout Greece, although it was not officially accepted until later than those of Zeus, Apollo, etc. Women known as Bacchae or Bacchants performed his frenzied rites; see Euripides, *Bacchae*. His triumphal progress to Greece from the East was a common theme in art and mythology.

ELECTRA: the sister of Orestes, and daughter of Agamemnon and Clytemnestra. She helped Orestes murder their mother after Clytemnestra had killed her husband.

ELEUSIS: a town near Athens where the Mysteries of the Great Mother were celebrated.

ELYSIUM: in early Greek religion, a region remote from the known world to which went the greatest heroes, who were exempted from death, after their earthly lives. Later it was imagined as forming part of Hades.

EMPEDOCLES: a philosopher of the fifth century B.C. who had some connection with Pythagoreanism. He formulated the earliest "pluralist" philosophy, according to which "Love" and "Strife" caused the four elements of the universe to unite and separate in turn, thus creating change in matter. He had some medical knowledge and a reputation as a miracle-worker. He was said to have died by leaping into the crater of Mount Etna, which later threw out one of his brass shoes.

ENDYMION: a beautiful youth with whom the moon fell in love.

EPEIUS: a figure who is mentioned in the *Iliad* as a boxer and in the *Odyssey* as having made the wooden horse in which the Greeks entered Troy.

EPICURUS: a Greek philosopher who lived from 342 to 270 B.C. The main lines of his physical theory are inherited from Democritus' "atomist" theory; upon this is built an ethical theory in which the greatest good is the pursuit of pleasure. To Epicurus pleasure consisted in peace of mind and freedom from fear, especially from fear of death; he held that the gods either do not exist or, if they do, are not concerned with human life. Epicureans were however generally thought of as sensualists pursuing material pleasures. The Epicurean school was very important in Hellenistic times and later; in Rome its doctrine was expounded by Lucretius.

EROS: the god of love (the Greek Cupid); the word connotes passionate physical desire. According to one tradition, he was the son of Aphrodite.

EUNOMUS: an early poet of whom little is known.

EUPHORBUS: a Trojan warrior in the *Iliad*. He was killed by Menelaus.

EUPHRANOR: a sculptor who worked in Athens during the fourth century B.C.

EUROPA: the daughter of Agenor, King of Tyre. Zeus wooed her, assuming the form of a bull, and Minos and Rhadamanthus were their children.

EURYDICE: the wife of Orpheus, a legendary singer. When she died, Orpheus descended to Hades and so charmed Pluto with his music that he was granted permission to take her back to earth, on condition that he should not look back to see if she was following; he failed to observe the condition and finally lost her. See Virgil, *Georgics* IV. 453–527.

EURYSTHEUS: a king of Tiryns for whom Hercules performed his labors.

FATES: three sister goddesses who controlled human destiny and life. Their names were Atropos, Clotho, and Lachesis.

FURIES: three avenging spirits in mythology who pursued evildoers and inflicted madness. Their names were Alecto, Megaera, and Tisiphone.

GADES: the modern Cadiz.

GALATEA: a sea nymph beloved by the Cyclops Polyphemus.

GANYMEDE: a handsome young Trojan who was carried to Olympus to be the favorite of Zeus and cupbearer of the gods.

GELA: a town in southern Sicily.

GELO: a tyrant of Syracuse early in the fifth century B.C.

GOLDEN FLEECE: a legendary fleece owned by Aeetes, king of Colchis on the shores of the Black Sea. It was hung in a grove and guarded by a dragon. Jason, assisted by Aeetes' daughter Medea, gained possession of it.

GORGON: a name applied to three sisters in mythology, the most famous being Medusa. Medusa had snakes for hair and a generally monstrous appearance, and her eyes turned those who looked on them to stone; Perseus killed her and gave her head to Athena to adorn her aegis.

GRACES: Euphrosyne, Aglaea, and Thalia, daughters of Zeus; they personify grace and beauty. They were said to live with the Muses on Olympus.

GRANICUS: a river by which Alexander won one of his earliest victories over the King of Persia.

HADES: strictly, the ruler of the underworld in Greek mythology, also called "Pluto"; the name is, however, generally used in English to denote that underworld itself. Although wrongdoers were punished there, it does not correspond to the Christian Hell; for the Greeks conceived of the afterlife as a shadowy, insubstantial, futile existence.

HANNIBAL: 247–182 B.C., a Carthaginian general and commander in the Second Punic War against Rome. He invaded Italy and won great victories at Trasimene and Cannae but failed to take Rome. After protracted fighting in the south of Italy, he returned with his army to Carthage on the orders of his government and was beaten at Zama in 202 B.C. by Scipio Africanus. A few years later he was accused by his rivals of plotting against the victorious Romans. Ultimately he fled from Carthage and committed suicide to avoid capture by the Romans.

HEBE: a goddess, the daughter of Zeus and Hera and the wife of Hercules. She typifies beauty and domesticity in a young wife.

HECATE: a minor goddess who was associated with the supernatural, with ghosts, and particularly with the crossroads that ghosts were commonly supposed to haunt. Purificatory offerings were put out for her at crossroads monthly.

HECTOR: the greatest of the Trojan heroes in the *Iliad*. During Achilles' absence from the fight he routs the Greek army; but he is eventually killed by Achilles. He was the husband of Andromache.

HECUBA: the wife of Priam of Troy, to whom she bore Hector, Paris, and other sons. She figures frequently in Greek tragedy.

HELEN: the daughter of Zeus and Leda, and hence the sister of Clytemnestra; a legendary beauty who was immortalized in the *Iliad*. She was married to Menelaus, Agamemnon's brother, and caused the Trojan War when Paris carried her off to Troy. She is most commonly represented as reconciled to her husband after the war, but later legend, and tragedy, use various stories. Theseus abducted her when she was a child, but did not harm her.

HELICON: a mountain in Boeotia, the home of the Muses.

HELIUS: the god of the sun. He was worshiped particularly in Rhodes, where an enormous statue of him, the Colossus of Rhodes, stood astride the harbor entrance.

HEPHAESTION: a companion of Alexander. When he died in 325 B.C., Alexander mourned for him extravagantly.

HEPHAESTUS: the god of fire, metalwork, and craftsmanship, sometimes credited with having invented man. He was lame, and was the husband of Aphrodite.

HERA: the wife and sister of Zeus; the goddess of marriage and women. She was constantly hostile to Troy.

HERACLITUS: an early philosopher, *fl.* 500 B.C. He conceived of the universe as a strife between opposites, and his favorite symbol for the world-process was that of Fire. He was the first philosopher to examine knowledge and the soul. The obscurity of his remarks was famous, and he was called "the weeping philosopher."

HERCULES: the son of Alcmena; his mother was visited by Zeus and bore twin sons, one—Hercules—by the god, and the other—Iphicles—by her mortal husband Amphitryon. From childhood he was of enormous strength. In a fit of madness he killed his own children, for which he was condemned to perform twelve labors at the bidding of Eurystheus, king of Tiryns; these included slaying the Hydra and the Nemean lion and cleansing the Augean stables. Many other adventures are attributed to him; he was a member of the crew of the Argo, he descended to Hades to restore Alcestis to life, and he attacked and captured Troy before the Trojan War. He was killed by a poisoned garment given to him by his jealous wife Deianira; when dying, he commanded that his body be burned on Mount Oeta, and after this purification he was translated to Olympus. He is a symbol of benefaction to mankind.

HERMES: the son of Zeus; the god of commerce, thievery, and speech. He was best known as the messenger of the gods and escort of the dead on the road to Hades.

HESIOD: a Greek poet who wrote probably slightly later than Homer. His principal works are the hexameter poems *Works and Days*—a treatise on farming—and the *Theogony*, a genealogy and account of the gods, starting with Uranus and Cronus.

HIPPOCRATES: the most famous Greek physician; the founder of scientific medicine. A native of Cos, he lived during the fifth century B.C.

HOMER: the supposed author of the *Iliad* and the *Odyssey*. Considerable argument has arisen over his identity and very existence, some scholars believing that no such single author ever existed, that the poems were written by a number of authors who worked with traditional material, and that the final form of the works may have been established by an "editorial committee" of bards. Perhaps the most widely held modern view is that one bard composed the *Iliad* orally in more or less its present form during the eighth century B.C., but that the *Odyssey* was probably written later by someone else. The ancient world, at least in Lucian's time, was no better informed than modern scholars on the details of Homer's life and work; it did, however, generally assume one poet. The poems formed the basis of Greek education and were quoted constantly in Greek literature to support opinion on a very wide variety of subjects; they provided a standard authority for life and conduct. The *Iliad* tells the story of Achilles' anger and Hector's death toward the end of the Trojan War, and the *Odyssey* describes the homecoming of Odysseus and the various adventures that befell him on his journey from Troy to Ithaca.

HORUS: an Egyptian god, identified variously with Hercules, Apollo, and Eros. His cult became popular in the later Greek world.

HYACINTHUS: a beautiful youth beloved by Apollo, who accidentally killed him with a discus; the flower known as the hyacinth sprang from his blood when he died.

HYDRA: a hundred-headed beast which Hercules killed as one of his labors. As Hercules cut off each head, two more grew in its place until Iolaus assisted him by cauterizing the stumps.

HYLAS: a youth of great beauty, either the beloved or the son of Hercules. He sailed with the Argonauts and, when they landed at Cios, went to fetch water from a spring; there, however, he was pulled in by water nymphs enamored of his beauty, and Hercules stayed behind to look for him.

ICARUS: the son of Daedalus. He flew too high with the wings his father made for him, and the wax that attached the wings to his body melted in the sun's heat; as a result he fell into the sea thereafter called "Icarian," and drowned.

IDOMENEUS: the leader of the Cretan contingent at Troy, and one of the foremost of the Greek warriors.

IOLAUS: a companion of Hercules who was miraculously rejuvenated. He helped Hercules to slay the Hydra.

IONIA: the western coast of Asia Minor. It was colonized by settlers from the Greek mainland, as were many of the Aegean islands, perhaps at the initiative of Athens. It was an important part of the Greek world, and speculation about the physical universe first arose there, giving rise to the Greek philosophical tradition. A brilliant civilization flourished in Ionia, but the region was too close to the Persian Empire for comfort.

ISIS: an Egyptian goddess, the wife of Osiris and the mother of Horus. Her cult came to Athens in the fourth century B.C.

ISLANDS OF THE BLEST: the location of the afterlife of the most exalted humans; an alternative concept for "Elysium."

ISSUS: the site of one of Alexander's early victories over the Persians in 333 B.C.

IXION: a legendary figure who tried to seduce Hera, and was punished by being bound to a burning wheel which revolved perpetually.

JASON: a legendary hero, the leader of the Argonauts in the search for the Golden Fleece. After the expedition he took Medea back to Greece as his wife but later deserted her. See Euripides, *Medea*.

LACHESIS: one of the three sister Fates. She assigned the lot of life.

LAERTES: a king of Ithaca; the father of Odysseus.

LEDA: the wife of Tyndareus and the mother of Helen, Clytemnestra, Castor, and Pollux. In one version of the myth, Zeus visited her in the form of a swan; in another, she herself was also thus transformed, and Helen was hatched from an egg.

LETHE: the river of forgetfulness in Hades. Newcomers to the underworld drank of its waters to obliterate memory of their lives on earth.

LETO: the mother of Apollo, whom she bore in Delos.

LIBYA: the Greek name for the continent of Africa.

LYCEUM: the precincts near Athens where Aristotle established his school of philosophy in 335 B.C.

LYCURGUS: a controversial figure of antiquity. He was once thought—by the Greeks and later writers—to be a historical person responsible for Sparta's peculiar constitutional and military system in about the eighth century B.C., but is now more commonly considered to be a local god to whom was attributed responsibility for changes which took place there some two centuries later. In any event, he was venerated as the architect of Spartan custom and legislation.

LYDIA: a region in the west of Asia Minor, powerful in the seventh and sixth centuries B.C., notably under Croesus. It was overcome by Persia when Croesus misinterpreted an oracle given at Delphi.

LYNCEUS: one of the Argonauts; he had extremely sharp eyesight.

LYSIPPUS: a famous Greek sculptor of the fourth century B.C.

MARATHON: the site of the battle fought in 490 B.C. in which the Athenians and Plataeans defeated the first Persian attempt to invade Greece. The battle was celebrated ever afterward as a high-water mark of patriotic courage, and became a stock theme for orators and artists of all kinds.

MARGITES: a stock figure of fun, noted for his stupidity.

MAUSOLUS: a Persian satrap of great power in the fourth century B.C.; king of Caria in Asia Minor. After he died, Artemisia, his wife and sister, erected an enormous tomb to him at Halicarnassus; it was known as the Mausoleum.

MEDEA: the daughter of Aeetes, king of Colchis; a legendary sorceress. When Jason and the Argonauts came in search of the Golden Fleece, she fell in love with Jason and assisted him with her magic powers; he took her back to Greece with him but later deserted her, and she took revenge by killing their children. See Euripides, *Medea*.

MELEAGER: a legendary hero, the son of Oeneus. His father neglected to sacrifice to Artemis, who sent a wild boar to ravage his country; Meleager, at the head of a band, killed the beast. His mother was responsible for his death.

MEN: a Phrygian god who was worshipped in Attica from about the third century B.C.

MENELAUS: king of Sparta, the brother of Agamemnon and husband of Helen. The Trojan War was fought to avenge his wife's abduction by Paris. The *Iliad* represents him as a brave warrior.

MENIPPUS: a Cynic philosopher from Gadara (he was also a slave at Sinope) of the third century B.C. He originated the "serious-comic" style, in which philosophy was compounded with humor; Lucian borrowed the style and sometimes used Menippus' compositions (e.g., *The Sale of Diogenes*) as the basis of his own work. His prose was interspersed with verse. He was said to have hanged himself.

MIDAS: a legendary king of Phrygia about whom various tales were told, the most famous being that of the "golden touch." At his own request, Dionysus granted him the power of changing anything he touched to gold; he soon found, however, that even his food turned to gold, prayed to lose the gift, and did so by bathing in the Pactolus, which thereafter had golden sands.

MIDIAS: a very wealthy Athenian; an enemy of Demosthenes.

MILTIADES: Athenian commander at Marathon. After the battle, he was alleged to have misused the influence he gained by his victory.

MINOS: the son of Zeus and Europa; a legendary king of Crete. He was a legislator and, when he died, became a judge in Hades, like his brother Rhadamanthus. His wife, Pasiphaë, gave birth to the famous Minotaur, which was sired by a bull that Poseidon sent to her; Minos kept the creature, half man and half bull, in a labyrinth built by Daedalus.

MITHRAS: a Persian god, often identified with the sun, whose worship was known about in classical Greece and was very important in Asia. His cult was very popular among soldiers and merchants in the early Roman Empire, although it was never really accepted in Greece itself.

MNESARCHUS: the father of Pythagoras.

MOMUS: the "god" of criticism, rather a literary figure than an object of cult. He is the son of Night in Hesiod's *Theogony*.

MUSES: nine goddesses, the daughters of Zeus, who presided over the arts and intellectual activities.

MYRON: a famous Greek sculptor of the fifth century B.C., one of whose works is the "Discobolus."

MYSTERIES: secret religious rites to which none but duly initiated worshipers were admitted. The most famous were the Eleusinian Mysteries.

NARCISSUS: a beautiful youth who fell in love with his own image in a pool, pined away, and died. He was loved by the nymph Echo, who also pined away until only her voice was left.

NAUPLIUS: a fine sailor, one of the Argonauts. In revenge for the murder by the Greeks of his son Palamedes, he lit false lights on the coast of Euboea to wreck the returning Greek fleet after the fall of Troy.

NESTOR: the father of Antilochus; the oldest Greek leader at Troy in the *Iliad*, where he is represented as garrulous. He owned a cup of great weight, which few but he could lift.

NIOBE: the daughter of Tantalus. She boasted of her large family, claiming superiority over Leto because of it, whereupon Leto's children—Apollo and Artemis—killed them all, and Niobe wept until she turned to stone.

NIREUS: a minor Greek commander at Troy in the *Iliad;* the son of Aglaea and Charops. He was famous for his beauty but unmanly.

NUMA: the second king of Rome; a lawgiver. Important religious reforms are attributed to him.

OCEAN: the name refers sometimes to the Atlantic and other great oceans, and sometimes to the river thought in earliest times to surround the earth. It is the name also of the god of this river.

ODYSSEUS: the son of Laertes and King of Ithaca; one of the principal Greek leaders at Troy, and the hero of Homer's *Odyssey*. He attempted to avoid going to Troy by simulating madness, but his ruse was detected by Palamedes. He later proved one of the cleverest and bravest of the Greeks, and he won the armor of the dead Achilles as a prize for the damage he caused to the Trojans. His resourcefulness and courage are celebrated in the *Odyssey;* the poem describes his journey home, which lasted ten years and was beset by numerous hazards, and his eventual homecoming, which entailed slaying the nobles who had been wooing his wife Penelope during his absence.

OEDIPUS: the son of Laius, King of Thebes, and Jocasta. His parents had been warned that their son would kill his father, so the boy was given to a servant to be exposed on a mountain. He survived, however, and grew up in Corinth, unaware of his true parentage. On a journey to Thebes, he unknowingly killed his father and also freed the city from the Sphinx by answering its riddle, whereupon he was made king and married his own mother. He had children by Jocasta—Eteocles, Polynices, Antigone, and Ismene—and eventually their relationship became known; Jocasta hanged herself and Oedipus blinded himself and went into exile. The legend is a favorite one with tragedians.

ONEUS: the father of Meleager. He angered Artemis by failing to invite her to a feast, and she sent a wild boar to plague his country.

OETA: the mountain on which Hercules' funeral pyre was built.

OGYGIA: Calypso's island in the *Odyssey*.

OLYMPIA: a district in the northwest Peloponnesus where the Olympic games were held.

OLYMPIAD: the interval of four years which separated celebrations of the Olympic games. After 776 B.C. chronology was reckoned in Olympiads.

OLYMPIAS: the wife of Philip and mother of Alexander. She was said to have dreamed, before the birth of Alexander, that she had lain with a snake.

OLYMPIC GAMES: the national games of Greece, held at Olympia. During times of war truce was declared for the period of the games so that all states could compete. The Games were of great antiquity and were celebrated every four years.

OLYMPUS: a mountain in the north of Greece, where the gods were said to live.

ORESTES: the son of Agamemnon and Clytemnestra. When he grew to manhood, he killed his mother for having murdered his father.

ORPHEUS: the husband of Eurydice; a legendary singer of fabulous powers, able to draw beasts and trees after him with his music. When Eurydice died he made an unsuccessful attempt to recover her from Hades, and thereafter shunned the company of women; for this he was torn to pieces by Maenads, female votaries of Dionysus, and his severed head floated, singing, to Lesbos.

OSIRIS: one of the principal Egyptian deities; the husband of Isis. His cult spread throughout the Roman Empire.

OXYDRACAE: a tribe in northwest India which offered fierce resistance to Alexander. Alexander was almost killed while storming one of their towns.

PALAMEDES: one of the Greeks at Troy; the son of Nauplius. He was famous for his great intelligence, and is credited with the invention of the alphabet. He detected Odysseus' ruse to avoid going to Troy and was put to death when, in revenge, Odysseus forged evidence to prove him a traitor.

PANATHENAEA: an Athenian festival that was celebrated annually on Athena's supposed birthday. Every fourth year the Great Panathenaea took place, with greater ceremony. A principal event was a procession represented on the frieze of the Parthenon.

PARIS: one of the sons of Priam of Troy. He was appointed by Hermes to judge a beauty contest in which the competitors were Hera, Athena, and Aphrodite, and he declared Aphrodite the winner when she bribed him by offering to give him Helen; he then went to Sparta and abducted Helen during the absence of her husband Menelaus. In the Trojan War, he killed Achilles by hitting him in his vulnerable heel with an arrow.

PARMENIO: one of Alexander's principal lieutenants.

PARRHASIUS: an Athenian painter of the fifth century B.C.

PATROCLUS: the companion of Achilles in the *Iliad*. Hector killed him when he entered the fighting; this stirred Achilles' wrath and led him to kill Hector.

PELEUS: the father of Achilles.

PERDICCAS: the name of two famous Macedonians. The first was a king of Macedon in the fifth century B.C. The second was one of Alexander's lieutenants; Alexander gave him his ring as he died, thereby appointing him his successor, but Ptolemy and others opposed his claim to the throne, and he was killed by his own troops.

PERIANDER: tyrant of Corinth at the end of the seventh century B.C. He was a patron of the arts and was often on the varying list of the "Seven Wise Men" of antiquity.

PERICLES: a statesman who virtually ruled Athens from 460 to 429 B.C., when he died, and gave his name to the period as the great age of Athens. He brought Athens to greatness, beautified the city, and was the friend of great artists and philosophers.

PERIPATETICS: the members of Aristotle's philosophical school. The name is derived from the *peripatos*, or covered walking place in the Lyceum where the school was founded.

PERSEPHONE: the daughter of Demeter, the corn goddess. She was abducted by Hades to the underworld, and her mother forbade the earth to bear grain until she was returned. At last Hades relented, but because Persephone had eaten some pomegranate seeds in the underworld she had to spend part of each year with him; she returned to earth during the summer months, and her mother smiled again.

PERSEUS: a legendary hero, the son of Danaë. It was prophesied that he would kill his grandfather, Acrisius, who consequently gave him the dangerous mission of killing the Gorgon Medusa. This he did, with divine help; he then employed Medusa's severed head, which had the power of petrifying all who looked on it, against his enemies. He rescued Andromeda from the monster to whom she had been delivered and accidentally killed his grandfather with a discus.

PHAEDRUS: a philosopher and a friend of Socrates. He appears in two of Plato's dialogues besides the one that bears his name.

PHAËTHON: the son of Helius the Sun-god. One day he drove his father's chariot; the horses were too powerful for him and rushed out of control near to the earth, scorching it.

PHALARIS: a tyrant of Acragas in the sixth century B.C. who was famous for his cruelty. He roasted his victims alive in a brazen bull.

PHAON: a legendary ferryman in Lesbos. Aphrodite made him handsome in return for assistance he gave her, and, according to one story, Sappho fell so deeply in love with him that she jumped off a steep cliff for his sake.

PHIDIAS: one of the most famous of Athenian sculptors. He lived during the fifth century B.C. and designed the marble sculptures for the Parthenon.

PHILIP: a king of Macedonia in the fourth century B.C.; the father of Alexander. He was a brilliant soldier and diplomat who subdued Greece, made Macedon a first-rate power, and laid the basis for his son's achievements—particularly by creating a highly efficient army. He was assassinated as he was about to invade Asia.

PHINEUS: a king who was blinded, in one version of the story, for abusing his prophetic powers and, in another, for blinding his children.

PHOCION: an Athenian general and statesman of the fourth century B.C. who was renowned for his virtuous character and military ability. He was an opponent of Demosthenes.

PHOENIX: one of Achilles' tutors. He figures in the *Iliad*.

PHRYGIA: a district in Asia Minor in which Troy was situated.

PHRYNE: an Athenian courtesan of the fourth century B.C. who was famous for her beauty.

PHTHIA: a district in Thessaly, the realm of Achilles.

PIRAEUS: the port of Athens, a few miles from the city. During most of the fifth century B.C. it was joined to Athens by long walls.

PITTACUS: a Mytilenaean political reformer, *fl.* 600 B.C. He was sometimes listed among the "Seven Wise Men" of antiquity.

PITYOCAMPTES: a legendary brigand whose name means "pine-bender." He killed his victims by bending pine trees, tying victims between two of them, and releasing the trees; Theseus killed him similarly.

PLATO: an Athenian philosopher, 428–347 B.C.; Socrates' principal pupil and interpreter. He founded the Academy, the school where he and his followers taught his philosophy. He visited Sicily in an attempt to put into practice his theory that the rule of states should be in the hands of philosophers, but was disappointed in Dionysius II of Syracuse. His theory of forms, or "Ideas," involves a nonmaterial "ideal" world comprehensible only by the intellect and only partially manifested in sensible objects; knowledge, to Plato, is the understanding of these forms, whereas what is commonly called knowledge is uncertain, being derived from sense perception. His ideal state, described in his *Republic*, is founded on his theory of knowledge, and involves a form of communism in which the leaders, or "guardians," will be those fitted by nature and strenuous training for philosophy. The soul, according to Plato, is immortal, and "learning" is really "remembering" what the soul has previously known.

PLUTO: the god of the underworld, also called "Hades."

POLLUX: Pollux and Castor were the twin sons of Leda, one by Zeus and the other by her mortal husband; hence one was immortal and the other was not. When Castor was killed, the two brothers shared Pollux's immortality and returned to earth on alternate days. Known as the Dioscuri, they were the special guardians of sailors and appeared at mastheads to protect them during storms. Pollux was famous as a boxer.

POLUS: a famous tragic actor of the fourth century B.C.

POLYCLITUS: a Greek sculptor of the fifth century B.C.

PORUS: an Indian king who was defeated by Alexander and subsequently became his ally.

POSEIDON: the god of the sea; the brother of Zeus and Pluto. He helped Apollo to build the walls of Troy and was cheated of his pay by Laomedon. He is credited with creating, variously, the horse and the bull.

PRAXITELES: a celebrated Athenian sculptor in marble of the fourth century B.C.

PROMETHEUS: a Titan; a cunning craftsman who created man from clay and gave him fire, which he stole from heaven. When man first sacrificed to the gods, Prometheus divided the sacrifice into portions and persuaded Zeus to choose the one that looked most attractive; in fact it was bones wrapped up in fat, and Prometheus thereby secured the best of sacrificial meat for man himself. As a punishment for his misdemeanors, Zeus pinned him to a mountain in the Caucasus, where his liver was devoured by an eagle each day and grew back again at night; eventually Hercules delivered him from this torture. Aeschylus, in his handling of the myth, gives moral dignity to Prometheus as the champion of man and the civilizing arts.

PROTESILAUS: a Thessalian; the first Greek to land at Troy in the *Iliad*. As had been prophesied, he was killed as soon as he landed. In later versions of the story, he had left behind him a newly-wedded wife, Laodamia, and persuaded Pluto to allow him to revisit her in mortal form for a few hours—after which she killed herself. He was a descendant of Aeolus, the god of the winds, and thus related to Alcestis.

PRUSIAS: the king of Bithynia at whose court Hannibal found refuge after fleeing from Carthage.

PTOLEMY: one of Alexander's lieutenants. He acquired Egypt after Alexander died (the region had been part of Alexander's empire), and all the kings of Egypt who were descended from him bore his name.

PYRIPHLEGETHON: the "river of burning fire" in Hades.

PYRRHO: a philosopher, *ca.* 360–270 B.C., who founded the Skeptic school of philosophy.

PYTHAGORAS: a philosopher of the sixth century B.C., born in Samos, who emigrated to Croton in southern Italy and established a school of followers there. The principal features of his doctrine were his belief in the transmigration of souls and reincarnation of the dead, and his theory of number as the primal element in the "cosmos," or world order. He was influenced by study in Egypt. He left no writings, and consequently his views were often misrepresented after his death, numerous strange "rules" being promulgated

as his. Various stories grew up around him—for instance, that he had a golden thigh. His "brotherhood" in Italy was notable for its religious discipline, the mystic character of its teachings, and its mathematical interests. He had a profound influence on Plato.

RHADAMANTHUS: the son of Zeus and Europa, and the brother of Minos; a judge in Hades, known for his justness.

RHEA: the sister and wife of Cronus, to whom she bore Zeus, Poseidon, Pluto, Hera, Demeter, and Hestia.

SALMONEUS: the father of Tyro. He was slain by Zeus for imitating him.

SAPPHO: a poetess of the sixth century B.C. from Lesbos; a leading figure in a band of female devotees of Aphrodite and the Muses.

SARDANAPALUS: another name for Assurbanipal, the last king of the Assyrian Empire of Nineveh. Lucian uses him as a type of luxury and effeminacy.

SARDIS: the capital of Lydia, the prosperous and cultured center of a rich province. It was burned by the Ionians in their revolt of 499 B.C.

SARPEDON: an ally of the Trojans who was slain by Patroclus.

SCIPIO: the Roman general, known as Scipio Africanus, who defeated Hannibal at Zama in 202 B.C. He was one of the most celebrated military leaders of antiquity, and also a champion of Greek ideas in Rome.

SCIRON: a legendary brigand slain by Theseus. He made his victims wash his feet at the edge of a precipice and kicked them over as they did so.

SCYTHIA: southern Russia; used to represent barbarous regions by many Greek writers.

SELEUCUS: a member of Alexander's army. After Alexander's death, he acquired the region of Syria and founded the Seleucid line.

SEMELE: the daughter of Cadmus of Thebes. Beloved by Zeus, she was persuaded by the jealous Hera to ask him to appear to her in his full might; he did so, in the form of a thunderbolt, which killed her but immortalized Dionysus, their unborn son, whom Zeus saved and concealed in his thigh until he was born.

SISYPHUS: the type of the trickster in mythology. He was punished for his character in Hades by having to roll up a hill a stone that slid down again each time he reached the top.

SKEPTICS: a school of philosophy founded by Pyrrho in the fourth century B.C. and revived in the first century B.C. It held that reality was unknowable, and that therefore one should suspend one's judgment and confine oneself to criticizing the views of others.

SOCRATES: an Athenian philosopher of the fifth century B.C.; the founder of moral philosophy and the "teacher" of Plato. His turning of philosophical inquiry to ethical lines was revolutionary, and his method of "dialectic," or question and answer in argument, lent itself to the pursuit of accurate definition. His view of himself was that he knew nothing but was wiser than other men in that he knew he knew nothing. His constant disclaimers gave rise to the charge of "irony," or the dissimulation of knowledge for the purpose of scoring over opponents by confusing them with logical argument. When prosecuted in 399 B.C. for impiety and corruption of youth—and some of his circle *had* done disservice to the democracy—he refused to change his ways, considering himself a dedicated missionary to Athens; he was condemned to die by drinking hemlock and, according to Plato, he accepted the sentence with courage and indifference. He is the principal participant in Plato's dialogues; since he himself left no writings, it is impossible to determine how much of the philosophy that Plato attributes to him is really his and not Plato's.

SOLON: an Athenian poet and legislator who reformed the constitution of Athens and ended serfdom in 594 B.C. He was regarded as one of the "Seven Wise Men" of antiquity and was said to have visited Croesus during his travels.

STESICHORUS: a lyric poet who died about the middle of the sixth century B.C. and wrote on Helen of Troy, among other subjects.

STOA POECILE: the Painted Porch in Athens, the home of the Stoic school of philosophy, from which the school derived its name.

STOICS: a philosophical school in Athens, founded by Zeno about 300 B.C.; among its later heads were Cleanthes and Chrysippus. It was very influential, especially among Romans, inculcating a doctrine of some nobility which accorded well with the Roman temperament. Its principal tenets were that only the wise man—that is, the Stoic—could be truly virtuous; that the philosopher should aim to live in harmony with nature, which was synonymous with reason and divine providence; and that only such a virtuous life could be called "the Good," everything else being "indifferent." Much of Stoic theory was concerned with logic and linguistic philosophy. One of the most famous Stoics was the emperor Marcus Aurelius.

STYMPHALIAN BIRDS: mythical birds of prey which Hercules killed as one of his labors.

STYX: the river in Hades across which Charon ferried the dead. The name means "hating."

TANAIS: the river Don in southern Russia, reached by Alexander during one of his campaigns.

TANTALUS: an ancestor of Agamemnon and Menelaus. He stole the food of the gods and was punished in Hades by being made thirsty and compelled to stand up to his chin in water that always receded when he tried to drink. There are several versions of the legend; in one of them, Tantalus stands at the edge of the water.

TELEPHUS: a legendary Greek warrior. On the way to Troy he was wounded by Achilles, who cured him with rust from his spear; he then guided the Greeks to Troy.

TELLUS: the Athenian whom Solon, in a conversation with Croesus, chose as the world's most blessed man because he lived an upright life, had children, and died fighting for his country. See Herodotus, I.30.

TEREUS: a king of Thrace in legend. He married Procne, but seduced her sister Philomela and then cut out her tongue to prevent her from telling what had happened. She embroidered the story on cloth, however, and showed it to her sister, whereupon Procne killed her own son, Itys, and served his flesh as food to Tereus. When he found this out, Tereus tried to kill both sisters; but he was turned into a hoopoe and the sisters into a nightingale (Procne in the Greek version, Philomela in the Latin) and a swallow.

THALES: an early Ionian philosopher, or, as we should say, scientist; he predicted an eclipse of the sun, and considered water the original substance of the world. He was one of the "Seven Wise Men" of antiquity.

THERSITES: an ugly and abusive demagogue in the Greek army who railed at Agamemnon and was silenced by a blow from Odysseus. See *Iliad* II.

THESEUS: a legendary national hero of Athens, with some affinity to Hercules as a benefactor and warrior. The son of Aegeus, he was revered as an early king who unified Attica with Athens as its capi-

tal. He slew various local brigands, such as Sciron, and then went to Crete and killed the Minotaur, which annually took the lives of seven youths and seven maidens sent by Athens as tribute to Minos, her Cretan overlord. He was assisted in this task by Minos' daughter Ariadne; as he entered the labyrinth, she gave him a ball of thread with which to guide himself out again; and he took her with him on leaving Crete but abandoned her. He fought against the Amazons and married their queen Hippolyta; Hippolytus, their son, was passionately desired by his later wife Phaedra. He abducted Helen when she was very young, and is associated also with the legends of the Argonauts, the Seven against Thebes, and Oedipus.

THETIS: the goddess mother of Achilles.

THRACIAN HORSES: mythical horses which ate human flesh. One of Hercules' labors was taming them, which he did by killing their master Diomede and feeding him to them.

THYESTES: the brother of Atreus, who was the father of Agamemnon and Menelaus. Atreus murdered Thyestes' children and served him their flesh at a banquet, and the curse put upon the house of Agamemnon resulted in the murder of Agamemnon and his wife Clytemnestra.

TIMON: a famous Athenian misanthrope who lived at Athens at the end of the fifth century B.C.

TIRESIAS: a legendary prophet and adviser to the royal house of Thebes. In punishment for striking a pair of mating serpents with his stick, Zeus changed him into a woman; later he was changed back into a man. After this wealth of experience, Zeus and Hera asked him whether man or woman enjoyed sexual pleasure more; he replied that woman did, whereupon Hera struck him blind and Zeus bestowed on him the gift of prophecy in compensation.

TISIPHONE: one of the Furies. The name means "avenger of murder."

TITANS: primeval deities, the children of Heaven and Earth. Their dynasty preceded the Olympians, and they were overthrown when Zeus deposed Cronus, their leader and his father.

TITHONUS: the brother of Priam of Troy; the husband of Eos, goddess of the dawn, who begged Zeus to make him immortal. The favor was granted but he was not made eternally youthful; as a result he became withered and was kept shut up in a chamber.

TITYUS: a giant who assaulted Leto and was punished in Hades by having his liver perpetually torn by two vultures.

TRITOGENEIA: an epithet of Athena. Apparently it refers to her connection with water; she was not, however, a sea deity.

TROPHONIUS: a Boeotian hero who was worshiped at a shrine in Lebadea. The shrine gave oracular responses and was said to spirit the questioner to Hades, where it gave direct revelations.

TYRE: a Phoenician port which offered considerable resistance to Alexander during his Persian campaign and required a great feat of arms to capture.

TYRO: a famous mythical beauty. She was the daughter of Salmoneus and was beloved by Poseidon.

XERXES: a king of Persia, 485–465 B.C. He mounted the second invasion of Greece, which was defeated at Salamis and Plataea; his preparations included building a bridge over the Hellespont and cutting a canal past Mount Athos. He flogged the sea when it refused him passage.

ZAMOLXIS: a Thracian deity, better spelled "Zalmoxis."

ZENO: a philosopher who founded the Stoic school in about 300 B.C.

ZENODOTUS: an Alexandrian scholar of the third century B.C. He edited Homer, "obelizing," or putting marks against, lines he considered spurious.

ZEUS: the supreme god of the Greeks, identified by the Romans with Jupiter. He was the son of Cronus and Rhea, the brother of Poseidon and Hades, and the husband of his own sister Hera. When Cronus was overthrown Poseidon became ruler of the sea, Hades of the underworld, and Zeus of the heavens. He is represented in mythology as living on Mount Olympus and wielding thunder and lightning. There are a great many legends concerning his birth and amours. He was father of Athena, Apollo and Dionysus among others.

The Library of Liberal Arts

The American Heritage Series

The Library of Literature

. . . .